MIRANDA DICKINSON

'Funny, charming and heart-warming'

ROSIE WALSH

'Claire's warm-hearted and touching debut sends us the message not to let life pass us by trying to seem too perfect and waiting for the "likes"'

ALICE PETERSON, author of *If You Were Here*

'Fresh, funny and heart-warming, with themes of friendship and the importance of being true to yourself. I loved it!'

SARAH J. HARRIS

'A fresh, funny take on Insta-life, full of warmth, wit and the kind of characters you miss when you reach the end'

KATIE MARSH, bestselling author of *My Everything*

'Such a gorgeous book, full of heart, friendship and the importance of keeping it real'

LAURA KEMP, author of *The Year of Surprising Acts of Kindness*

'What a book! . . . Touching, joyful and smart'

ALEX BROWN

living my best li^fe

Claire Frost grew up in Manchester, the middle of three sisters. She always wanted to do a job that involved writing, so after studying Classics at Bristol University she started working in magazines. For the last ten years she's been at the *Sun on Sunday*'s *Fabulous* magazine, where she is Assistant Editor and also responsible for the title's book reviews. She can mostly be found at her desk buried under a teetering TBR pile. You can follow her on Twitter: @FabFrosty, and Instagram: @therealfabfrosty.

CLAIRE FROST

living my best lie

SIMON & SCHUSTER

London · New York · Sydney · Toronto · New Delhi

A CBS COMPANY

First published in Great Britain by Simon & Schuster UK Ltd, 2019
A CBS COMPANY

1 3 5 7 9 10 8 6 4 2

Simon & Schuster UK Ltd
1st Floor
222 Gray's Inn Road
London WC1X 8HB

Simon & Schuster Australia, Sydney
Simon & Schuster India, New Delhi

www.simonandschuster.co.uk
www.simonandschuster.com.au
www.simonandschuster.co.in

A CIP catalogue record for this book is available from the British Library

Paperback ISBN: 978-1-4711-8151-1
eBook ISBN: 978-1-4711-8078-1

Typeset in Bembo by M Rules
Printed and bound by CPI Group (UK) Ltd, Croydon, CR0 4YY

For my dad, who I hope would have been proud ♥

Chapter One

Bell

Bell's eyes snapped open as she tried to work out whether the persistent hammering she could hear was in her head or in her *house*. She'd dropped off on the sofa while watching an early evening wildlife documentary about endangered species in the Andes, and the noise she could hear sounded more like someone banging on a window than the call of the yellow-tailed woolly monkey on the TV screen. Suddenly the cushion her head was nestled comfortably against began to shake alarmingly, and it took her another few seconds to realise her phone was vibrating beneath it. Still half-asleep, she jabbed at the green icon.

'Finally! I'm outside; come and let me in.'

Bell managed to get her brain into gear enough to process the good news, which was that the constant knocking noise had, *at last*, stopped. The bad news, however, was that it appeared her best friend was on the other side of her front door.

She shook herself fully awake, levered herself off the sofa and traipsed down the hall.

'What? What's going on?' she stuttered, as she opened the door.

'Duh! It's me, Suze? You know, your best friend who you've been refusing to go for Saturday night drinks with for the past six weeks? Now, are you going to let me in or what?'

Before Bell could open her mouth, Suze stepped inside, closed the door firmly behind her, turned to face Bell and beamed. 'Hi, Bellster! Tonight I'm your fairy godmother and you *shall* go to the ball! Well, into town to a bar full of lovely people, anyway. And I brought wine so I can drink it while you get ready. I might even let you have some if you go and get in the shower right now. I'm sure I can find the glasses.'

As Bell's brain caught up with everything Suze was saying, she finally managed to do more than just gawp at her. 'How did you know I was in? I might have been really busy this evening, for all you knew.'

Suze laughed gently. 'Bell, darling, you haven't been busy on a Saturday night since Colin broke up with you back in January. And despite the many excuses you've been giving me over the past few weeks, I took a wild guess that I'd find you ensconced on the sofa.'

Bell watched Suze take in her fleecy pyjamas and messy top-knot and saw how her friend's expression transformed into the determined look she'd seen so many times before. She knew there was no point arguing, but she really didn't think she could face a night out. Not yet. Seemingly reading her thoughts, Suze scooped her up into a hug.

'I know you've been through a really tough time, but you can't hide away in here for ever, Bellster. And it's going to be a very chilled night, just me and Ellie and a load of mates, none of whom know anything about Colin so you don't even have to mention him if you don't want to.' Suze pulled away and gave a delicate sniff. 'Have you been wearing those PJs all day? Go on, jump in the shower. I'll pour the wine and have a rummage through your wardrobe so you don't even have to decide what to wear. That's how much of a fairy godmother I am!'

Bell meekly allowed herself to be steered into the bathroom, and after standing under the jets of water for a few minutes, she already felt a bit better. She opened her bedroom door to find Suze rifling through hangers.

'Right, moisturiser and hairdryer and then I'll do your make-up for you,' Suze ordered. 'Oh, and get this down you. Cheers!'

She clinked her glass against Bell's and Bell took a grateful gulp. She and Tesco's £4.99 Cab Sauv had been inseparable for almost a month after Colin had dumped her, so she'd spent the last couple of weeks trying to cut down. But tonight definitely called for all the wine. She allowed her friend to primp and preen her, but drew the line at the strappy dress and sky-high heels Suze had picked out.

'I haven't worn this dress since I was at uni – which was many years ago as you well know – and I'm not about to start now,' she said firmly. She pulled on her favourite skinny jeans and finally agreed to a lacy vest top that bordered on the underwear-as-outerwear trend she was sure nearly-forty-year-old women shouldn't really attempt to wear.

'Right, let me give you a refill and then sit down and I'll do that flicky eyeliner I'm so good at.' Suze grinned. 'Don't look at me like that, you know what happened last time you tried to do it yourself. The other evening I watched this ace YouTube video on how to do it properly every time. In fact, I sent you the link on Facebook. Didn't you see my message?'

'No, I didn't.' Bell took a large sip of her wine and then an even bigger breath in. 'I don't have Facebook anymore.'

Suze stared at her friend, her mouth agape. 'Yes, you do, don't be silly. This is you we're talking about, Bell. You who can go barely ten minutes without checking social media.'

'Well, I've deleted it. And Instagram and Twitter,' Bell announced defiantly. How dare Suze say that! Bell hardly ever checked her feeds. Only a couple of times after waking up and on the journey to work, and then a few times in the morning, then not till lunchtime and maybe a few times later on when she hit her mid-afternoon slump, and possibly she did a quick check before she left at the end of the day, too, and if she was at home during the evening she'd have a sneaky look, but – anyway, she wasn't as bad as some people.

She noticed Suze had stopped blending blusher across her cheeks. 'What? It's not that big a deal.'

Suze fixed Bell with a penetrating gaze and said, 'So,

you've deleted all your social media accounts. Do you want to tell me why?'

'I just don't think it's healthy for me at the moment,' Bell said quietly. Then, realising Suze's arched eyebrow meant she wasn't going to let her off that easily, she added, 'And yesterday evening I saw Colin had been tagged in a picture.'

'And? What was the picture of?'

'It was a photo taken the other night of him and some people from his accountancy firm with the caption "Thursday night LOLs". I recognised a few of his colleagues, like Matt and James, and then I saw he had his arm round someone else I recognised. Her name's Tina and she's one of the juniors.'

'They could have just been cosying up for the photo, though,' Suze reasoned.

'Except that one arm was round her shoulders and the other was round her waist. And his lips were stuck to her face.'

'Hmm, really quite cosy, then,' Suze said, grimacing.

'Yep. Christ, could he be more of a cliché? She might not be his secretary, but she's as near as, dammit. It's just so ... *annoying.* Here am I at home every evening lying on the sofa cradling a bottle of wine and grieving for our ten-year relationship, and there's him out on the town fondling some twenty-year-old. He promised, Suze, he *promised* there wasn't anyone else. And now it appears not even two months later there is. God, he's pathetic. Though not as pathetic as me. You'd have thought that in the last thirty-nine years I might have learned how to deal with heartbreak. But no, I'm still the sucker replaying every conversation we ever had, wondering if he ever thought about us getting married and staying together forever, and trying to work out what he really thought about me. About us.'

Tears pricked her eyes and her throat itched with sadness and frustration. She reached for her wine. She was too old to be crying over a man, plus she didn't want her eye make-up to run.

'What a knob.' Suze said.

'I know, but he was *my* knob. Anyway, I thought you liked him. You always said how nice he was.'

'That was until he upset you, Bellster. No one gets to upset you and stay in my good books. And, yeah, he was always nice to me, and you guys seemed nice together. But maybe it was all a bit too, well, *nice*? Where was the passion? Where were the spontaneous romantic nights away? The uncontrollable laughter?'

'I guess after ten years you can't really expect that, though,' Bell said defensively.

'Why not? Of course you've got to be realistic and the honeymoon period can't go on for ever, but there's got to be a spark; you've got to keep the romance alive. Ellie and I are definitely not the perfect couple, but having a long-distance relationship keeps things interesting if nothing else.'

'Maybe men are where I've been going wrong all this time,' Bell sighed.

'You're welcome to join the club any time, sweetie! But

I don't think this is a man/woman thing, I think it's a you/ Colin thing. I know you're upset – it would be weird if you weren't after ten years – but I do think in the long run it's the best thing that could have happened to you.'

'But maybe I was happy in a relationship that wasn't interesting or spontaneous or passionate, or any of the other things you think it should have been.'

'Were you, though? Were you really, Bell?' Suze asked gently.

'I really thought I was. Although the last few weeks have made me think . . . But why do it after ten years? Why didn't Col say something last year or the year before, or however long ago he started to feel unhappy?'

'For the same reason you didn't, I expect. Because what you had felt safe, it felt nice. So why rock the boat? But then maybe he realised that all the things that were missing were all the things he missed.'

'And all the things that dear Tina could provide!' Bell spat. 'I don't even really blame her, though she's not going to be top of my Christmas card list. And I also know that I can't even blame Col one hundred per cent either. See, Suze, I haven't wasted the last six weeks. But, still, what a dick.'

Suze giggled. 'Yep. And cheers to that! And to you leaving social media. And to you not getting slapped with an ASBO for stalking your ex now you don't have Facebook.' They clinked glasses and Bell even managed a smile. She could see that a lot of what Suze had said was true and that she and Col had just got lazy, staying together because it seemed easier than arguing and having a full-on heart-to-heart.

She was shaken out of her reverie by Suze saying, 'Lips together and blot. Excellent, now what do you think?'

She stood in front of the mirror and barely recognised herself. 'Could be worse, I s'pose,' she smiled.

'That's the spirit! Right, come on, my friend, now you look the part let's go party!'

As Bell followed her out of the front door and into the waiting taxi that Suze had magicked up from one of her phone's many apps, she couldn't help but be impressed by Suze's ability to bulldoze her out of her pyjamas and into a bar. She was all too aware of how intimidating she had found Suze when she had first met her. On Bell's first day at work, she had walked into the Style It Out office in her trying-too-hard culottes and had wilted when she'd been introduced to her gorgeous desk mate. But within minutes, Suze had offered her a large coffee and a whole load of office gossip and Bell had decided it was all going to be okay. She realised too that she was never going to pull off a jumpsuit in the same way her stylish colleague could, with her chicly bobbed hair complete with fringe that was exactly the right level of shortness.

The taxi pulled up at the bar and they headed inside just as Suze's girlfriend Ellie was opening a bottle of prosecco.

'Perfect timing,' grinned Suze happily. 'Here you go, Bell. Cheers, everyone! Now you know Els, obviously, and you've met Clara, Jules and Lara before, but I don't think I've introduced you to Lily and Al, have I? Guys, this is Bell, and you are going to love her!'

Bell surprised herself by having a fun night chatting to most of the twenty-strong group of Suze's friends who'd gathered for their regular knees-up.

'It's so hard to get everyone together in one place, but we always put four dates in the diary every year and pretty much everyone manages to make it, unless they're abroad for work or on holiday or whatever,' explained Lily, who Bell learned was a garden designer hoping to make it to the Chelsea Flower Show the following year. Her husband Al was a muscly builder and spent much of the time touching Lily's arm, kissing the side of her head and telling Bell how proud he was of his wife.

Bell tried not to compare their relationship to her and Col's, but inevitably her mind kept wandering to parties they had gone to. He'd never been the touchy-feely type, but she struggled to remember a time when they'd been surrounded by friends and he'd said how much he admired Bell for her career, or in fact, for anything. He'd never been nasty or rude about her, thank god – Col just wasn't that kind of person – he just hadn't said anything about her at all. And, yes, he'd always made sure she had a drink and wasn't stuck talking to Gary, the one friend of his he knew she really didn't like (there had been an incident at a BBQ years earlier involving a football, Bell's glass of red wine and her very pale summer dress, under which she wasn't wearing a bra), but he'd never even have thought of complimenting her in front of other people. Bell, on the other hand, would often find herself telling stories about Col rescuing spiders from the bath and how he was aiming to be made a partner at work within the next few years, in a weird, almost boastful way. She definitely wasn't ready to examine too closely why they'd each acted like this, and pulled herself back into the conversation around her.

'What do you think, Bell, are you up for another drink and a dance?' She looked up to find Ellie grinning at her. 'We're going to relive our youth at Heaven & Hell. Nineties tunes all night – what's not to love!'

'I think that's my cue to leave,' Bell said with a small smile. Seeing her best friend's face start to take on the wheedling expression she knew so well, she continued quickly, 'No, Suze, I'm fine, really, my bed is calling.' She hugged her friend and whispered, 'Thank you for staging an intervention and making me come out tonight. I love you.'

'I was worried you'd hate me!' Suze said, squeezing her tightly. 'Sorry for bullying you into this evening, but I'm so glad you had a good night. See you on Monday, sweetie.'

Bell headed down the road and joined the crowd of people waiting for the bus home. She pulled her phone out of her pocket, checked it for messages, then looked forlornly at her home screen, which seemed strangely empty without its social media apps.

Her attention was caught by a couple arguing across the road. Despite the girl looking upset, no one seemed to be checking she was okay, and Bell dithered about crossing over to talk to her. But at that moment she spied the bus approaching and her need to get home and back into her pyjamas overtook any Good-Samaritan thoughts. Glancing back over to the couple, she realised the girl actually seemed to be having an argument with whoever was at the other end of her phone, while the guy she was with hovered close to her looking awkward and patting her back self-consciously every so often.

The girl gave one last shout of annoyance, screaming, 'And stop calling me Amanda – my name's Millie, you flipping pompous git!' into her phone before stuffing it back in her bag. Bell laughed to herself as she got on the bus and watched the scene through the window. The girl no longer sounded like a damsel in distress and seemed perfectly capable of looking after herself. Though Bell was still glad to see she had someone with her to make sure she was okay. A sudden pang hit her. If there was one thing Colin was good at it was making her feel better when she started bawling at a tear-jerking film, or on the rare occasions she came home from work upset.

Although it wasn't lost on her what a fat lot of good he'd been when it was *him* making her cry back in January!

Chapter Two

Millie

Millie had periodically flirted with Tinder, more often than not finding it the most depressing place to be of an evening. She'd then moved on to other apps, which while not exactly full of positivity and fun, were slightly less hideous. And it was on one of these apps that she'd come across Tom. They'd matched with each other and then the ball had been in her court as to whether she messaged him or not. She'd swiped right mainly because he had the kindest-looking face of anyone she'd seen on her various dating app forays, so one lonely night when five-year-old Wolf was in bed and there was nothing on the TV, she decided she might as well contact him. Their messages had remained very much on the side of pleasant rather than passionate, but when Tom suggested they meet for a drink, she hadn't immediately said no. Wolf's dad Louis would be coming to pick him up on Friday night for his once-every-four-weeks weekend with his son, so Millie had two days of emptiness stretching ahead of her. With nothing better to do, she asked Tom if he was free on Saturday night. His reply came back alarmingly fast.

> Sounds great! What about 8 o'clock at the Duke of York, and then we can go for a bite to eat later if we fancy it? Looking forward to it! T x

Millie knew she should probably tell someone where and when she was going on a date, in case he turned out to be a serial killer, but she didn't really have any friends locally she wanted to tell, or in fact any friends locally at all. She certainly wasn't going to tell Louis this nugget of information as he was bound to try to use it against her at some point; though how he thought he'd get away with it, when he spent half his life parading twenty-year-old after twenty-year-old on his arm, was anyone's guess. She supposed she'd better let her dad know what she was doing, so she sent a quick, breezy text and promised to call him soon.

By the time Louis rang the doorbell at 5.15pm on Friday night, Wolf had worked himself up into a state of huge excitement.

'Daddy!' he yelled, dropping his Spider-Man figurine, running to the door and impatiently waiting for Millie to open it.

'Wolf Cub!' Louis grinned, scooping him up and holding

the little boy aloft like he was baby Simba in *The Lion King*. 'How are you, mate? Good to see ya!'

As Wolfie went into a big spiel about all the superhero toys he'd packed in his little wheeled case to show him, Millie peered round the door.

'Hi, Louis.'

'Millie,' he nodded. 'Right, little man, say goodbye to Mummy and we'll get you in the car and then the fun can really start!'

'Bye, Mummy. You will look after Snuffles for me and give him a goodnight kiss, won't you?'

'Of course, Wolfie. I promised, didn't I? Now you be good and I'll see you back here on Sunday afternoon, okay?'

She'd barely removed her arms from round his small body before Wolf was out the door and skipping towards Louis' huge Range Rover. She watched them leave, waving even after the car had turned out of the road and driven off into the distance.

However nice it was to have a break from being essentially a single parent, it never got easier watching her son disappear up the motorway to Birmingham with his dad. After all, her whole life had revolved around the little boy for the last five years. She willed herself not to cry and began dropping armfuls of toys into the basket drawers by the fireplace, only pausing to pick up Snuffles, the soft toy guinea pig, and give him a quick kiss on his fluffy head.

As her date approached the following evening, Millie began to wish she'd never bothered sending Tom a message in the first place. She'd spent a pleasant day tidying the house, prepping a few Instagram posts and firing off emails to various copywriting agencies asking if they had any work for her. After luxuriating in a bath filled with the posh bubbles Louis had bought for Wolf to give her for Christmas (whatever his faults, Louis had great taste when it came to the finer things in life), she felt happy and calm. That had all dissolved when she'd started thinking about her date that evening.

Since she and Louis had broken up just under two-and-a-half years ago, there hadn't been much space in Millie's life for men. And it hadn't really bothered her that she didn't have a significant other to turn to as, frankly, she had enough on her plate making sure Wolfie was fed, clothed and as unaffected as possible by his parents' separation. Not to mention trying to carve out some kind of career in the fashion/blogging/social media world. But now that Wolf was at school, she'd felt like she should at least try to get herself out there. The trouble was, things had changed so much in the seven or so years since she'd been that feisty girl who had been a match (in every way) for cocky footballer Louis in a Birmingham nightspot. Not only was she older, wearier and far less sure of herself, but the dating arena was a foreign country now. At thirty she felt both ancient and that she was competing with all the younger, prettier, more confident people looking to find the love of their lives – or at least someone they could shag that evening. So when she'd matched with Tom and he'd seemed happy to chat as friends, she'd gradually stopped using the other apps and contented herself with exchanging nice, no-pressure, getting-to-know-you messages every so often. But meeting him in the flesh was something else entirely.

'I don't even know if I want a relationship,' Millie sighed out loud as she smoothed product through her hair and uncovered the hairdryer that had been gathering dust in the corner of her bedroom. But the voice inside her head wasn't going to let her off that easily.

You don't have to have a relationship, you just need some fun.

'Fun!' she grunted over the whirr of the hairdryer. 'Think I'd rather stay in with a glass of cheap wine in front of the telly.'

But that's what you did last night. And the night before, and the one before that, the voice replied.

'Christ, now I'm talking to myself. I really am going mad!'

She heard her phone ping as she put the hairdryer down and hoped it was Tom also having second thoughts. It wasn't, it was her dad.

> Have an amazing time this evening, Millie, you deserve it! Me and Jean want to hear all about it tomorrow! Dad xx

She smiled and turned back to the sparse offerings in her wardrobe. Then she remembered her eBay triumph. Like at least half of the country, she'd lusted after the latest high street collaboration with this year's hot young designer, but also knew she didn't have a hope in hell of queueing at the crack of dawn outside her local store on the morning of its launch to get her hands on any of the pieces. So, when she'd spied an eBay seller flogging her favourite dress from the collection for just a few quid more than it had cost originally, she was both excited and wary. Ridiculously, it had all seemed to check out, and a few days after she'd clicked the Buy It Now button a package arrived in the post containing the coveted dress and a short note:

I hope you enjoy the dress more than my granddaughter, who complained I'd got her the wrong one and in the wrong size but still wanted me to give it to her so she could sell it at a vast profit and buy some festival tickets instead. I only wish I could get into it myself as it's a lovely dress, but I'm sure it will look better on you! Audrey x

And the dress did actually look great on her, Millie was able to admit as she swished the A-line skirt in front of the mirror, before spending an inordinate amount of time taking the obligatory selfie and saving it so she could add filters later.

She considered texting Tom to cancel throughout her bus journey into town, but as 8 o'clock got closer and closer she knew she had lost her opportunity to pull out, which was why she found herself walking through the doors of the Duke of York trying to spot someone – anyone – who looked like the image of Tom on his dating profile.

'Millie?'

She whipped round and there was Tom, looking exactly like his profile picture, standing in front of her.

'Tom? Hi,' she stuttered, leaning in to kiss him on both cheeks.

'You look gorgeous,' he smiled. 'I'll apologise now that I'm wearing the same shirt as in my profile pic – I do have other shirts, but I thought it would help you recognise me. Now, what would you like to drink?'

Tom proved to be just as pleasant company in person as he had been on his messages, and when he popped to the loo, Millie took a second to register how nice it was to be out on a Saturday night without a five-year-old in tow. So much so that when, some hours later, Tom suggested they go and grab a curry, she readily agreed. She felt her phone vibrating as they made their way out of the pub. Her caller display told her it was Louis.

'I just need to get this, it's my son's dad,' she explained. Tom nodded and stood away from her in the pub doorway to give her a little privacy. 'Louis, is Wolf okay?' she said as soon as the call connected.

'Yes, of course he's fine, he's with me, isn't he? Where are you?'

'Out, not that it's got anything to do with you!' Mille replied before she could stop herself. 'I mean, is everything okay?' she tried again in a more conciliatory tone. She needn't have bothered.

'Well, are you out nearby? I need you to come home. I'm outside your house.'

'What? Why are you outside my house? What's wrong? You're not supposed to be bringing Wolf back till tomorrow afternoon. What aren't you telling me?'

'Calm down, Amanda. Something came up, that's all, and I need to drop him back now. How long will it take you to get here?'

'What came up?' she demanded. Tom looked at her questioningly and she shook her head at him.

'You know, stuff.'

'What stuff?' Her anger was clearly palpable, as Tom walked over, put a hand on her shoulder and mouthed 'Are you okay?' She shrugged him off with an apologetic grimace and turned away.

'Look, you know what it's like, when the manager says he needs me . . .'

'I thought you were injured?'

'I am! Well, luckily, the ankle's recovering well, thanks for asking. It's a squad thing. The manager wants us all together before Monday's game.'

'And you couldn't have driven down in the morning instead?'

'The gaffer's called an early start so I didn't have any choice. Come on, Mills, you remember what it's like.'

'So you're putting football before your son. Again. You're not fit to be called a father.'

'There's no need for that, Amanda. Look, I'll pay for a cab home, if that helps.'

'It doesn't help, but fine, you pay for it. And stop calling me

Amanda – my name's Millie, you flipping pompous git!' She jabbed her phone to end the call and let out a shout of frustration.

'Millie? Are you okay?' Tom asked, once more placing his hand lightly on her shoulder.

'No, not really,' she sighed. 'Sorry, Tom, I have to go. Thank you so much for this evening, it was nice.'

'Don't worry, of course your little boy has to come first. But it *was* nice, wasn't it? Maybe we can do it again sometime?'

Suddenly everything felt too much for Millie. She knew she should have stayed at home with that glass of cheap wine and Saturday night TV. Dating just wasn't something she had the time, or in fact the energy, for anymore. She'd been stupid to think otherwise.

'Look, Tom, I don't think I'm in the right place at the moment. Sorry, it's nothing personal. You're a lovely guy.' She cringed with guilt as she spoke and glanced anywhere around her rather than look at his face. Thankfully, she spotted a black cab approaching and waved it down.

'Sure, okay,' he replied slowly. 'Nice to meet you though, Millie. Take care of yourself.'

'Yep, and you.' She gave Tom a quick, embarrassed hug and got into the taxi. As it drove off, she turned and looked out the back window and saw him raise his hand sadly, then cross the road with his shoulders hunched round his ears.

Louis' sports car stuck out a mile on their ordinary suburban road.

'Millie, you made it!' he said, sidling out of the driver's side.

'The cab needs paying,' she replied, opening the passenger door and shaking her head at Louis' choice of vehicle – he had at least three cars to choose from and an Audi TT hardly seemed the ideal choice when he had Wolf on board. She gently unclipped the sleeping five-year-old from his car seat, thankful that Louis had at least had the sense to put him in his pyjamas so she was able to carry him upstairs and settle him into bed without much bother. She went back downstairs to find Louis standing awkwardly in the hall with Wolf's wheelie suitcase in his hand.

'I brought this in,' he said. 'I'm sorry, Millie, if I'd had any choice . . .' He hung is head penitently.

'Louis, don't forget I know you and can see through your remorse act. You always have a choice, you just made the choice that Wolfie wasn't important in this situation.'

'We had a great day together and he was asleep anyway, so it wouldn't have made a difference if I'd brought him back at the crack of dawn. Stop trying to make me feel guilty.'

'It made a difference to me.'

'Ah, now we're getting to the crux of it. You're just pissed off you couldn't stay out and shag whatever guy it was you were seeing!'

'How dare you!' she shout-whispered, aware of Wolf asleep upstairs. 'What I do in my private life has nothing to do with you.'

'It does when it affects my son! Who knows who you were planning on bringing home, especially if it was someone from that mental group you used to go to.'

'That "mental group" was a support group for people suffering post-natal depression, as you well know,' she hissed. 'And I stopped going when we broke up, because, surprise surprise, I wasn't depressed anymore once I wasn't with you!'

'Whatever, Millie. All I care about is that my son is properly looked after and cared for—'

'Are you questioning my parenting?' she interrupted him, incredulously. 'You, the person who barely sees Wolf from one month to the next and certainly doesn't provide for him, feed him or clothe him, despite being a "professional" footballer?'

From the nervous look on his face, it was clear even Louis knew when he'd gone too far.

'Look, I just want the best for Wolfie, that's all. And I know I need to be better at paying for things. Here, have this,' he said, removing his wallet from the pocket of his designer jeans and taking out a wad of twenties. 'Buy him something nice.'

'He doesn't need something nice, he needs a new school jumper and some football boots!' she shot back, barely able to contain her fury.

'Well, buy him those and then buy him something nice with what's left over,' he said exasperatedly. 'Mills, we can't keep being at each other's throats like this, it's not good for Wolfie.'

There were so many things that Millie wanted to say, but just behind her she heard a sleepy, 'Mummy?'

She turned and pulled her son into a hug and said quietly,

'Wolfie, darling, me and your dad were just saying goodbye. You go back to bed like a good boy and I'll come and kiss you goodnight in a minute, okay?'

'Okay, make sure you do, Mummy. Bye, Daddy.'

Louis smiled and waved. 'Night-night, Wolfie, sleep well. Love you.'

When she was sure Wolf had gone back to his room, Millie took a deep breath. 'You're right, it's not good for him when we fight, and I'm sorry for getting angry. It's just, sometimes it's really hard, that's all.' Tears pricked her eyes.

'It's okay. I just think we need to be careful what we say and how we speak to each other.' Louis jangled his keys. 'I'd better be going. See you in four weeks, yes?'

'Yes, see you then,' Millie replied meekly. She watched him drive off at speed then have to anchor up at the junction at the end of the road. Wearily, she climbed the stairs and stood outside Wolf's room for a second, before plastering on a smile.

Lying in her own bed half an hour later, she replayed the conversation with Louis. She couldn't believe he could stand there and criticise her when he'd been the one in the wrong the whole time. And that she had let him.

Back in the halcyon first year of their relationship, Louis had barely ever levelled even the mildest criticism at Millie, and instead seemed to believe that everything she did was amazing. However, that all changed when she told him about the baby.

Chapter Three

Bell

The smell of diesel and the tinny beat of house music via a set of expensive, though clearly not soundproof, headphones greeted Bell as she made her way past hordes of glazed-eyed Monday-morning commuters to the back of the bus, which began to creep towards the Style It Out building in the town centre. She noticed one older, headphoneless man sitting on an aisle seat, sporting a well-worn leather jacket and baggy, pale-blue jeans, and she knew before he even opened his mouth exactly what he was about to say, and she *really* wasn't in the mood.

'Cheer up, love, it might never happen!' he grinned at her.

If there was one statement guaranteed to make the recipient even less cheery, Bell was yet to hear it.

'Don't worry, it already has,' she shot back at him. She was half tempted to add that she'd just found out her parents had been killed in a car crash, but she couldn't deal with the bad karma that would inevitably follow from pretending her mum and dad had met a grisly, untimely end, so she contented herself with glaring at him and retreating to the back seat.

'All right, love, keep your hair on, I was only saying.'

Bell leaned her head against the window and shivered. It might be the start of March, but she wished she'd brought her huge, cosy scarf with her to keep out the morning chill. Her sister Cosette always took the mick out of her about the length of that scarf, calling her Lenny whenever she saw her wearing it, after Lenny Kravitz and his knitted monstrosity a few years back. Still, it wasn't Bell's fault Cosette refused to even think about a scarf as a fashion statement and merely saw it as a way for her to stay warm. Luckily Cosette didn't do anything so frivolous as work for a fashion website – her job as a primary-school teacher was much more sensible and was able to accommodate her children, eight-year-old Sophie and ten-year-old Oliver, around whom her and her husband Rich's world revolved.

Cosette had borne the brunt of Bell's shock, sadness and anger in the last few weeks, and Bell had to admit she had been brilliant at letting her rant away. Last night on the phone Cosette had tried again to get her to come down to Devon at the weekend, saying she was worried Bell was obsessing over what had led Colin to deliver his death notice to their relationship. To be honest, she'd only told Cosette about a tiny fraction of the social media stalking she'd really done – if she knew the actual number of hours Bell had spent scouring Facebook, Insta and Twitter for clues about Colin's motives, she'd have been on the first train up to Bell to march her off to the south-west coast and imprison her in the spare bedroom that the wi-fi didn't reach. Thankfully, she'd placated her sister by not only telling her that she'd deleted all her apps, but also about her night out that weekend.

'Well, at least Suze is making sure you're not turning into a hermit,' Cosette had sighed. 'But I'm still going to insist you come to see us. I need you to help stop the kids squabbling, if nothing else. And I'll even get Rich to make his special tiramisu.'

'Well, then, how can I resist!' Bell had smiled. 'I promise I'll come down soon.' She figured that 'soon' was a subjective term and she had at least a few months' grace. The sun might even be shining at that point, which was when the Devon cottage came alive and became a countryside idyll.

Her older sister was prone to mothering her whenever possible, which was probably a hangover from their childhood, during which their parents had largely left the two girls to bring themselves up – Janet and John (yes, they did sound like they were straight out of a kids' storybook, though the reality was somewhat different) believed less is more when it came to child-rearing. They'd thought naming their daughters Cosette and Arabella was a good idea (such delusions of grandeur) and had ordered friends and family to call the girls by their full names at all times, but 'Arabella' quickly got shortened when toddler Cosette couldn't pronounce her new sister's name. Cosette had once tried to instigate a shortening of her own name to 'Cos'. But on hearing seven-year-old Bell refer to her sister in that way, Janet had issued the ultimate threat.

'Arabella Makepeace, if I ever hear you shorten your sister's name to the name of a lettuce like that again I shall be forced to enrol you in daily elocution lessons for the rest of your time living in this house.'

From then on Cosette had been Cosette, and had spent much of her life adding 'Yes, like in *Les Misérables*' to every introduction. Bell had half expected her to use meeting Rich as an opportunity to reinvent herself and change her name, but perhaps Janet had threatened her son-in-law-to-be with a fate even worse than endless elocution lessons, or maybe Cosette had finally accepted her unusual name and the way people began humming the first line of 'Castle On The Cloud' immediately after meeting her. Needless to say, Cosette and Rich had chosen 'normal' names for their two children.

When Cosette had helpfully suggested she be the one to inform their parents that Bell and Colin had broken up, Bell had all too readily agreed. There had then followed the inevitable phone call, during which Janet and John had both told her they were sympathetic about what had happened, but Bell had been able to smell their disappointment despite the thousands of miles separating her from them and their home in Portland, Maine.

Her parents had retired to America with almost unseemly haste once they could tick off Cosette's wedding vows and

Bell's supposedly stable and settled status from their list of obligations. Not that Bell was complaining, obviously. In fact, she'd been worried the news of her break-up would see Janet and John vow to give up their charmed expat existence and hotfoot it back to Blighty to console their heartbroken daughter. Thankfully, they were both far too selfish to even contemplate such an act, and merely contented themselves with telling her how worried they were about her before launching into a long and complicated story about their friend Barbara's son – a dentist called Hal – getting divorced and having to pay his ex millions in the settlement. Bell suspected Hal had been showing a little too much interest in his pretty dental nurse's mouth, so felt she had nothing positive to contribute to the topic and invented someone at the door to quickly bring the call to an end. Although not before her mother had wistfully added, 'I suppose we'll just carry on fielding questions from all and sundry about when our youngest daughter is going to finally get married and produce a grandchild for us. You've really not made things easy for us, Arabella, have you?'

To which she knew the only response was, 'No, Mother, and I am truly sorry.'

As the bus trundled along, Bell let out a long, loud sigh (Mr Cheer-Up Man could go to hell). She was so used to being one half of a couple – Bell to his Col – that it felt like she didn't know who she was anymore without her other half to make her whole.

Even her Instagram account had been full of pictures of

two pairs of feet on a gorgeous tiled floor, his 'n' her drinks in front of a sunset and two hearts drawn on the sand as the sea lapped at their edges. And they *had* been happy together, hadn't they? Maybe not the love's young dream her Insta implied, but whose relationship really was all rose petals on the bed and kissing beneath the Eiffel Tower? No one wanted to see photos of Colin changing the duvet cover because he knew Bell hated doing it and got in a real stress about it, or Bell buying Col a supermarket frozen pizza for dinner because she knew he had a secret love for a poor-quality Pepperoni Passion despite professing himself to be a foodie. No filter was ever going to make her shaving his back hair for him sexy, or him fishing out the decaying food from the kitchen sink plughole in a pair of blue rubber gloves look cute. There was nothing wrong with a little enhancing, tweaking, filtering and, well, *boasting* about their relationship, surely? So why did it all feel like a lie now? Probably because, for all his duvet-changing and sink-cleaning, Colin had clearly not felt the way about their relationship that she had. She'd imagined him proposing and them enjoying their old age together, while he'd been planning his escape. She sighed again.

BEEEEP

Bell was woken from her mental Instagram scrolling by the sound of the bus almost colliding with a cyclist in head-to-toe reflective gear. Deciding she'd rather not take her life in her hands by remaining on a bus driven by a gesticulating, swearing madman, Bell got off a stop early and hurried towards the imposing red-brick building on the corner of the main road. Style It Out occupied the second floor, nestled between a payday loans website and a debt collection agency, like an inverse shit sandwich.

Thankfully, stepping into the Style It Out office was like taking a breath of stiletto-filled, coat-hanger-strewn fresh air, and it always felt a million miles away from the grey day on the other side of the large, slightly crumbling windows on the far side of the room. Bell stepped round a huge pile of what she assumed were belts rather than the snakes they resembled and stopped to rifle through a rail of sunshine-yellow dresses, which were all a similar shade but very different styles. Her eyes snagged on an off-the-shoulder Bardot-type sundress and she pulled it off the rail and held it in front of her.

'Yep, that would look amazing on you, with some cork wedges and a tan, obvs,' Suze said as she walked over to her desk and began relieving herself of her outer layers. 'It won't be long till the sun is shining again.'

'The sun? Oh, you mean that yellow thing in the sky that seems to have been missing in action these past six months? Nah, it's gone, never to be seen again, I've heard,' Bell replied. After one last stroke of the material, she replaced the dress on the rail with the others and plonked herself down on her chair with a groan.

'You really are a ray of sunshine today, Bellster, aren't you? But I did mean it about that dress; you should definitely get in there. It will be on the site in a few weeks and you know it will sell out quicker than you can say "Summer stock has dropped"!'

'I'll think about it,' she grunted. While she was waiting for her computer to stutter and splutter through the ten-minute start-up process, she absent-mindedly reached for her phone to scroll through her feeds. Then, remembering her new lack of any social media apps, she placed her phone face down and drummed her fingers on the desk.

'Saturday night was fun, wasn't it?' Suze beamed at her. 'Though you def did the right thing going home when you did. Next time I think it's a good idea to go clubbing till 3am, please can you kindly remind me I am thirty-eight years old and hangovers do not get better with age. Yesterday was a complete write-off and me and Els barely moved from the bed all day. Although there are worse ways to spend a Sunday I s'pose!' she cackled.

Bell rolled her eyes at her friend but couldn't help laughing.

'You know, Bell, I've been thinking,' Suze declared through a mouthful of coffee and croissant.

Bell rolled her eyes again. 'You, thinking? Is that really wise?'

'As it happens I am very wise. I've been thinking about you. I think you need a new focus.'

'Suze, if you even mention that app beginning with T and ending in -inder . . .'

'No, not that kind of focus. Though when you do want to get back on the horse, I'll be only too pleased to help. No, I mean a focus to stop you fixating on Col. A *project*.'

'Urgh, I'm not a jockey. Anyway, I don't really have time for a project.'

'Erm, but now you're not stalking Colin on social media, you do actually have time, Bellster.' Seeing Bell's face drop, Suze hurried on. 'Look, I'm not saying you suddenly have to start going to yoga raves left, right and centre – although that does sound a-mazing and I'd def be up for coming with you – but what about an evening class or a new hobby or something? Or even just more nights out like Saturday. You used to love dancing, didn't you? It will do you so much good just to get out there again, it really will.'

'I'm just not sure I'm ready yet, Suze,' Bell said quietly. 'But I do really appreciate you listening to me go on and on about me and Col; I know I need to get on with my life, and I will, soon, I promise. I just need time.'

'Yep, okay. But, Bell, I am always here for you, you know. I am totally up for listening to you go on and on about Col for as long as you need. But I'm also not going to give up helping you move on and find who the real Bell is – and that's a promise.'

Chapter Four
Millie

Millie sighed for what felt like the millionth time that day. And it was only 9am. Wolf had been a nightmare that morning, refusing to get up when he would normally be jumping on her bed at six-thirty despite her instructions that he wasn't allowed out of his room until the big hand was pointing to 12 and the little hand to 7. When he'd started school the previous September, he'd been so excited to put his uniform on and race into the playground to see his little classmates. But ever since he'd gone back to school after the Christmas holidays, she'd noticed he was less and less enthusiastic about telling her what games they'd played in the classroom and what books the teacher had been reading to them. He still loved explaining in great detail about how he'd scored a goal in football during their PE lessons – like father like son, she grimaced – but he wasn't quite the same overexcited little boy before and after school as he had been at the end of last year. Millie sighed again as she replayed the scene of Wolfie tearfully eating his cereal that morning after she'd shouted at him to put his school clothes on or she'd have to dress him herself like a baby.

'But Daddy said I'm a big boy,' he sobbed, before looking at Millie with a glint in his eye and adding defiantly, 'And Daddy said I could have chocolate cereal every day if I wanted instead of boring Corn Flakes.'

'I'm sure what he meant was you could have chocolate cereal at the weekend if you're very good,' Millie said firmly, though inside she was fuming. She definitely wouldn't put it past Louis to say he could have the sugar-laden cereal whenever he wanted, especially as he wasn't the one who had to parent him day in, day out. 'Now, are you going to show me what a big boy you really are and put your bowl and spoon in the dishwasher nicely?'

As Wolf continued to whine, Millie had craved the post-school-run silence of the empty kitchen, but now he was at school she turned on the radio to fill the deafening nothingness. After clearing up the kitchen, booking dentist appointments for herself and Wolf and sticking another load of washing on (how did a five-year-old boy get through so many clothes?), Millie finally switched on her laptop. Before she tackled her inbox, she clicked on to the spreadsheets she'd set up to keep track of every penny she was spending, as well as what money was coming into her account. Louis' maintenance payment had been due yesterday, but she was pretty damn sure that when she logged into her online banking it was going to show exactly the same figure in her account as two days ago – an amount perilously close to zero. And she had to find some cash for the babysitter this evening.

She allowed herself one last sigh before logging into her social media accounts. Millie knew that she was lucky to do the job she did, and she was well aware that most people wouldn't see posting images on Instagram as work, but she also knew that most people didn't have a clue how stressful it all was. The constant fear one of the brands she worked with would dislike something she posted, the continual worry about the new breed of Insta influencers snapping at her heels every single day, and then there were the trolls. She squeezed her eyes shut in an attempt to keep their nasty voices out of her head. Besides, she had other things to worry about this month. Like making ends meet – a free handbag from a high-street brand in exchange for a post was great in theory, but it didn't pay the water bill. While spring was in the air and #NewYearNewYou, #Detox and #Veganuary were old news, it still felt like most of the time all anyone wanted to see were images of toned stomachs with hashtags like #Fitspo and #PlantBased, even from mummy and fashion influencers like her. She looked down at her oversized sweatshirt and joggers. What she needed – other than a body like Kayla Itsines and a workout range like Kate Hudson – were a few more of those copywriting jobs like the one she'd done last week

She scanned the comments on her last Instagram post, thankful to see it had over six thousand Likes from the hundred thousand followers on her @mi_bestlife account. Beneath a photo of herself wearing a gorgeous wool coat in front of a cool, weatherbeaten wood panel, she'd written the caption:

> I'm in love with my new alpaca-wool coat from @andotherstories. Perfect for keeping out the chill on my way to pick up Wolfie from school. What's your favourite fashion buy this week? #schoolgatechic #streetstyle #ootd #instastyle #fblogger #fashiongram #mummyblogger #motherhood

She'd also had over eight hundred comments, mostly from people saying how much they liked her coat and that they were off to the shops to buy one now. Millie skimmed over these and kept scrolling until she came to the now inevitable comments from the seemingly incredibly persistent users who pursued her across the internet.

> @Jan247638 You might be wearing a nice coat but you still look like trash. You can't sugar coat a turd

> @Stylista_l257 I feel sorry for your son who'd want an ugly bitch like you meeting them at the school gates

Millie swallowed hard and looked away from the screen. No matter how many times she saw comments like this she couldn't help but be affected by them. Because it was all true.

She knew that beneath the Insta polish she was just trash, an ugly bitch. Of course she hadn't actually bought that alpaca coat – it cost two hundred pounds, for god's sake. She'd paid for it on her credit card and then asked a stranger in the street to take a picture against the wall next to a now-empty shop in the high street. Photoshop had done the rest – after she'd returned the coat and had the money put back on her card, obviously.

As she trudged the two miles to the supermarket and filled her trolley with yellow-stickered items reaching their expiry date, she knew she should report the worst of the trolls and get their accounts closed. Except they'd just spring up again under a different username. She glanced at her watch and realised she barely had time to get home, dump the shopping and make it to Wolf's school. Laden with bags, she half-jogged, half-fast-walked her way home, and arrived at the school gates breathing heavily just as the other mums were all hugging their little ones and relieving them of their bookbags and water bottles. She weaved her way in and out of the bunches of children and adults until she spotted Wolf standing on his own next to the open classroom door looking lost while his teacher glared out across the playground.

'Wolfie, there you are!' Millie smiled, trying hard to keep her flushed face hidden from Mrs Boyle who taught the reception class. 'Have you had a good day?'

'Ah, Wolf's mummy, I was beginning to get a bit worried,' the teacher said, raising an eyebrow.

'Sorry, Mrs Boyle, I got a little held up, it won't happen again. See you tomorrow,' Millie murmured, feeling about as small as a five-year-old herself. She steered her son out of the playground and along the pavement, and he slipped his small hand into hers. As they got further away from school and nearer home, Wolf perked up and began chattering away about his favourite football team, Aston Villa, and who they were going to buy before the transfer window shut.

'Mummy, please can I get some more stickers for my Premier League album? I've only got a few more to get and the last pack were all boring ones I already had. And you said last week I could?'

'We haven't got time today, I'm afraid, Wolfie,' Millie replied, then, seeing her son's smile drop, she hastily added: 'But if you're really good then we'll get you some at the weekend.' Wolfie's face lit up and Millie's heart leapt. She knew how expensive the stickers were – Louis had been the one to buy him the album and his first packet of stickers, and she'd been the one who had to fork out a fiver every week since only to find that all the packs seemed to have the same stickers in them and a few players still remained elusive. But she'd do anything to see that grin more often.

'I'll make you some dinner, and remember Bridget is coming over later to look after you while I go to a work event. Don't look like that, Wolf, Bridget is lovely.'

'But she treats me like a baby,' he whined.

'She's just a bit old-school and likes to do things her way.'

'She makes me go to bed at seven o'clock, even though

I tell her you let me stay up until seven thirty. And she smells musty.'

'Wolfie!' Millie said, trying not to laugh. 'She just likes her lavender talcum powder and it can smell quite strong.'

'Isn't talcum powder for babies?'

'Well, yes, but also some grown-ups, especially older ones. Anyway, Bridget isn't coming over until six o'clock, so we'll make sure you've had your bath and are in your pyjamas when she gets here, and when you go to bed you can have your story CD on for one story – and only one story. Okay?'

'Okay, though I might choose a really, really long story!' he said cheekily. 'Where are you going tonight, Mummy?'

'It's just an event for some people who do a job like me. I won't be too late.'

'People who type on their phones and their computers all the time?' he asked, at the same time as Millie's phone lit up with more Instagram notifications. 'Will you come and say night-night when you get home even if it's really late?'

Millie put her phone in her pocket and bent down so her face was level with the small boy's. 'Of course I will, darling.' She ruffled his wavy blond hair that was starting to curl into the corner of his eye again, and made a mental note to bribe him with sweets to sit still for ten minutes at the weekend so she could trim it. 'Even if you're snoring so loudly the whole road can hear you!'

'I don't snore, Mummy!' Wolfie cried indignantly, racing into the flat, discarding his coat and shoes in the hall. 'Not as loud as Bridget anyway.'

When Bridget knocked on the door a few hours later, Wolfie was indeed bathed and in his pyjamas, but both he and Millie were exhausted. It had not been the easiest couple of hours. Not long after they'd arrived home, Wolf had been lying on the sofa when Millie noticed his school sweatshirt was all pulled and frayed at the bottom.

'How did you do that, Wolfie?' she asked with a sigh.

'Don't know,' he mumbled, eyes glued to his sticker book.

'You've got to be more careful, we haven't got the money to buy you new jumpers every two minutes.'

Wolf continued to stare at his stickers.

'Wolf, are you listening to me?' Millie raised her voice and snatched the book away from him. 'Look at me when I'm talking to you, please. There'll be no more money for stickers if you keep going on like this, do you hear me?'

'I did it playing football, I didn't mean to,' he said, his eyes filling with tears for the second time that day. 'You're always telling me off about money. Daddy never does. Why can't I live with him?' And he ran out of the room.

Millie bit back her retort about his daddy never actually giving her the money he was supposed to, which would mean she wouldn't have to go on about it all the time, and instead stared at the open living-room door. She knew how much Wolf idolised his dad and she would never actually say anything derogatory about Louis to him, however much she was tempted. The very thought of him looking after Wolfie for more than a few days made her want to laugh. Except it wasn't actually funny.

Wearily, she climbed the stairs to the little boy's room and found him curled up on his bed. She went over and scooped him into her arms.

'Oh, Wolfie, I'm sorry for shouting. And I know you didn't tear your jumper on purpose. Sometimes being a grown-up is hard and sometimes we really have to watch how much money we're spending on things, but money is never the most important thing in life. The most important thing in my life is you, and it always will be.'

'I'm sorry for getting angry, Mummy. And I'll try really hard not to break my school uniform, I promise.'

'I know you will, darling,' she replied, kissing the top of his head. 'Now, let's get you in the bath, otherwise Bridget will have to wash and dry you and you know how much she likes using talcum powder!'

Wolfie giggled and got undressed, but things were still a little stilted between the two of them. Feeling like the worst parent ever, Millie spent longer than normal making up a story with him and his rubber ducks in the bath and then playing the towel-monster game afterwards. Wolfie had only just pulled his pyjamas on when Bridget arrived, and Millie hadn't even started to get ready herself.

'Hi, lovey, I'm not early am I?' Bridget asked, glancing at Millie as she opened the door. 'What time are you going out?'

'No, not at all, I'm just running a bit late. Come in, Bridget. Thanks so much for babysitting tonight, I know Wolfie has been looking forward to seeing you.' She crossed her fingers behind her back and hoped Wolfie hadn't heard her fibbing. 'Wolfie, come and say hello to Bridget,' she called.

He walked into the living room, clutching his fire engine, and allowed himself to be kissed and fussed over by Bridget with only a small wrinkle of his nose in Millie's direction.

'Always happy to help you out, Amanda, you know that, especially when I get to see this little cherub. Now, has he had his hot milk yet?'

'Erm, Wolfie doesn't have milk before bed anymore. He's a big boy now, aren't you, darling? Anyway, Bridget, I've bought some of those lemon biscuits you like, shall I make you a cup of tea before I go?'

'Ooh that would be nice, lovey, thank you. Then young Wolf here can tell me all about how he's getting on at school, can't you, dear?'

By the time Millie had made Bridget her tea and made sure Wolfie was happily chatting away and not stealing all the biscuits, she had precisely ten minutes before she had to leave. It hadn't been that long ago that she would happily spend the best part of three hours getting ready to go out, with a playlist on in the background, a glass of wine in her hand, and the contents of both her wardrobe and her make-up bag thrown all over the bed. That felt like a lifetime ago now, though, as she hurriedly pulled the straighteners through her hair, applied the thickest layer of foundation she could get away with and dragged on the studded denim skirt and black off-the-shoulder top she'd found at the back of her drawer that morning. The rock-chick look never went out of date, she'd reasoned earlier, but glancing at herself in the mirror Millie realised she looked like she'd raided her 16-year-old self's wardrobe. She didn't have time to change, so she stuffed her lipstick and eyeliner into the front pocket of her handbag and ran down the stairs. As she pulled on her black tasselled ankle boots and reached for her trusty but ancient leather jacket, Wolf and Bridget came into the hall.

'You look nice, Mummy,' Wolf said, winding his arms round her waist. 'A bit like a witch, but much prettier. You can borrow my wizard hat if you want?'

'Yes, you look, erm, lovely, dear,' Bridget said. 'Though don't you think you might be a bit cold in that skirt?'

'Ah, it will be lovely and warm inside, don't you worry. Text or call me if you need anything, won't you? And, Wolfie, I think I'll be okay without that hat, but thank you for the offer. You be good for Bridget, and I'll come up and see you when I'm home. Love you, little wolf cub.'

'Love you more, Mummy.'

Once the train had chugged its way out of the suburbs and eventually reached the bright lights of London, Millie found a bus that would take her into the centre. She sent a text to Bridget reminding her what time she'd be home as well as repeating her plea to text or call her if she needed to. She knew she was lucky to have such a kind neighbour. After her mum's death when she was nineteen, Millie had learned to only rely on herself. However, she had a real soft spot for Bridget, who clearly enjoyed mothering both Wolf and her whenever she could – in fact, she was one of the few people

Millie allowed to call her by her full name of Amanda, as her beloved mum had done – but she still hated having to ask her for favours.

Milie retrieved her eyeliner and lipstick from her bag and proceeded to apply both as the bus drove over what felt like constant speed bumps. She'd barely thought about the evening ahead of her, but now she had less than fifteen minutes before she arrived, she wondered what on earth she was doing. Of course, it had been flattering to be invited to a PR agency's big party in London, plus it would be the perfect networking opportunity. But the idea of walking into a trendy city-centre venue and rubbing shoulders with the cool crowd made her nervous. She was very definitely out of practice, plus she knew that most people there would be barely out of college, let alone have reached the grand old age of thirty like her.

The bus hit Soho and Millie contemplated staying exactly where she was and letting it take her right back to the train station again. Her phone buzzed with a text. She saw it was from Bridget and her heart leapt.

> dont.worry.about.us.the.bairn.is.all.tucked.
> up.in.bed.you.have.a.good.night.lovey

Bridget might not have quite mastered the art of punctuation in her texts, but Millie knew that if she came home now the old lady would worry she'd done something wrong and that Millie didn't trust her. She had no choice. She had to go to the party.

Chapter Five

Millie

Millie gave her name at the door to the two girls importantly holding clipboards as if their 17-year-old lives depended on it, and then she climbed the stairs of the imposing multistoreyed Georgian building until she reached the third floor where she was under instructions to 'turn left and keep going'. However, the clipboard crew's orders were obsolete as she could hear the bass of some track she was probably supposed to know but didn't (apart from the odd tune here and there, Millie had barely heard any new songs in the last five years unless they had the words 'Peppa Pig' or 'superhero' in them) coming from the end of the corridor, plus the door kept opening to deposit pretty young things on the other side as they headed towards the 'washrooms'.

Millie took a deep breath and stepped inside. Immediately, she felt the deep bass of the music course through her body and lodge itself in her chest. She was looking around in the hope of recognising someone – anyone – in the throng of young bodies before her, when she felt two people appear on either side of her.

'Millie, so lovely to meet you,' trilled the girl to her left. 'I'm Franny, and this is Nats. Welcome to Best Dressed PR's birthday party! You look amazing. Let's get you a drink.'

'So lovely, I mean, *cool,* to be here,' Millie shouted above the music as she kissed the air next to first Franny's and then Nats's cheeks and was led over to the bar area.

'So we have a blueberry Moscow non-mule and a mockito made with apple juice, and I can tell you they're both delicious!' Nats beamed. Seeing the confused look on Millie's face, she added quickly, 'Of course, if you wanted alcohol we have red wine, white wine or beer. Although I think that might be alcohol-free lager, actually.'

'White wine would be great, thanks,' Millie said, relief at the impending alcohol relaxing the tension in her face and allowing her to actually smile. 'Although, better make it a spritzer, thank you,' she told the waistcoated man behind the bar who was flipping glasses and bottles with an air of superiority. He grunted in a nondescript way, but slammed a wine glass full of liquid down on the bar, and Millie took a grateful slug. Seeing she now had a drink in her hand, Franny and Nats resumed their pincer movement and each took one of her arms and propelled her into the centre of the room,

'Not sure how many people you know,' Franny said in her sing-song voice. 'So we'll do some introductions. Ooh, look, you've probably never met MaryAnna, Frankie and Sonya before, have you? They are just the coolest.'

Before Millie could even open her mouth, she'd been manoeuvred into the middle of a large group of people whose attention was all focused on three women.

'Guys, say hello to @mi_bestlife, I know she's been dying to meet you all. Millie, this is @MAFlash, @FrankieG and @SonyaStyle. Enjoy!' And with that, Franny and Nats melted away into the crowd.

'Mills, come here, so good to see you, mate, it's been far too long!' Sonya's familiar northern tones cut through the constant beat of the track playing through the speakers above them. 'I can't even remember the last time I saw you on the dance floor at one of these things. How the hell are you?'

'Ah, you know me, Son, never much of a party girl,' Millie grinned as Sonya enveloped her in a bear hug.

'Yeah, right, I'll never forget that night in Birmingham. But what happens in Birmingham, stays in Birmingham, right!' She laughed, tapping the side of her nose. Despite growing up somewhere in the Shires, after spending a weekend in Leeds with her friend who was studying fashion design at uni Sonya had decided she was going to reinvent herself as a northern fashion blogger with an edge, and since then had adopted as northern an accent as possible. Millie had always been impressed and a little envious of Sonya's ability to carry it all off – her accent only ever showed signs of strain when she was really drunk, and then her cut-glass poshness pushed its way out. Millie and Sonya had enjoyed some particularly raucous nights out in Birmingham together a fair few years ago, so Millie knew the truth about her private-school education, but she was pretty sure no one else in the room had a clue that Sonya wasn't quite as gritty as she made out, and there was no way she was going to burst their bubble as Sonya was such good fun. And she just happened to be one of the biggest Insta street style stars in the country.

'Loving the rock-chick look, Mills,' Sonya shouted.

'Not looking too bad yourself. Leopard-print has always been so you.'

'Lucky it's gonna be big next season, ain't it,' her friend grinned as she readjusted her sunglasses on top of her afro and tugged down her gold leopard-print midi dress. 'Hey, MaryAnna, Frankie – Millie and me go way back, she's a good'un.'

'Super to meet you, darling,' drawled MaryAnna, air-kissing her, then immediately turning back to the group of eager girls around her to continue telling what looked to be a fascinating story judging by the expressions on their faces.

'Millie, I think we've met before, no?' Frankie smiled. 'At some launch or fashion party a while back I seem to remember. Although one gets invited to so many of these evenings, doesn't one?'

'Yes, I think you're right, brilliant to see you again.' Millie returned her smiles and kisses, although she couldn't recall ever seeing Frankie before in her life. Still, she seemed pleasant enough, if one of the plummiest-sounding people she'd ever met. 'How are things going with you?'

'Well, just fabulously actually. Obviously this is top secret, but I've just signed a contract to join the cast of *Made In Chelsea*. I've known half the cast since we were tiny, but it's never felt like the right time. But now with my fashion line in the works . . . oops, that's another thing that's top secret, obvs! Anyway, what are you up to, Millie?'

'Well, I won't be joining the cast of a reality show any time soon,' Millie smiled. Sonya honked with laughter beside her.

'I can't think of anyone less likely to appear on *MIC*, *TOWIE* or, god forgive us, *Geordie Shore* than you, Millie. Your private life is far too private for the likes of them. Me on the other hand . . .'

'Oh my god, Son, you'd be amazing on something like that. What about *Love Island*? Or are you loved up with that YouTuber now?'

Sadly, Millie didn't get to find out how Sonya's love life was faring as at that moment Franny and Nats reappeared towing along yet more people to add to their group.

'Everyone, this is Joe and Ciara from Styleitout.co.uk and Cesca and Carly from Styleitlikebeckham.com. I'll leave you to introduce yourselves. Does anyone want another drink? Millie, you were on the alcohol, weren't you, and more mockitos for everyone else, yes?'

'I'll have whatever Millie's having,' Sonya shouted over in reply, nudging Millie as she spoke. 'She knows how to party after all! Ciara and Joe, wasn't it?' she asked, sticking out her hand to the newcomers. 'Great to meet you.'

'It's so amazing to meet you, Sonya, I've loved your Insta feed for, like, years,' gushed Ciara, an excitable-looking twenty-something sporting ombre hair and three-quarter-length trousers.

'And I've loved yours, Millie,' Joe nodded seriously, his carefully constructed quiff not moving an inch. 'It's so cool to see someone showing mums that they can be stylish, too.'

'I'm surprised Millie's feed is so up your street, Joe,' Sonya laughed.

'Well, of course, I'm not a mum myself . . .' Joe paused and Millie caught Sonya's eye and smothered a giggle. 'But you have such a loyal following and are leading the way when it comes to young mothers. And they're exactly our core customers,' he finished, fixing his intense gaze on Millie.

'Sorry, where did Franny, or was it Nats, say you worked?' Millie asked, feeling she should take pity on poor earnest Joe.

'Style It Out,' Ciara supplied quickly. 'I don't suppose you've heard of it . . .'

'Of course we have,' said Sonya robustly. 'I think it's a great little site, actually. Anyway, let me introduce you to MaryAnna as I'm sure she'd love to meet you.'

Sonya glanced over her shoulder and muttered to Millie to stay where she was as she'd be back soon; however Franny/Nats (they seemed interchangeable to Millie) glided over with another glass of wine and a steering arm towards more people for Millie to meet. While she was well aware that chatting to everyone she could was the right thing to do, as you never knew when you might need that obscure contact you'd made at a party, Millie was annoyed she wasn't able to catch up properly with Sonya. And then before she knew it, it was almost 10pm and time for her to get to the train station as fast as she could so she didn't miss her last train home. Bridget might be a dear, but she wouldn't take kindly to being left with Wolfie overnight.

Millie did a quick sweep of the room to locate her friend and saw she was ensconced in the corner with Frankie G, MaryAnna and co., and while Millie wanted to say goodbye to her, she had absolutely no wish to engage in another round of air kisses with a bunch of people she barely knew, so she decided to sneak away without anyone noticing. She turned round to place her empty glass on the bar and came face to face with Franny/Nats.

'Oh, you're not off already, are you, Millie?' she pouted.

'I'm afraid so. I've left my son with the babysitter and woe betide if I'm late getting home. But thank you er, Franny and Nats, of course, for an amazing evening, it's been great fun.' The PR gave no indication whether she was indeed Franny or if Millie had picked the wrong name, merely making a cooing sound as she put her head on one side and pulled a sympathetic face.

'Oh, yes, it must be really hard being a working mum, I can't imagine how you do it, Millie. Now, don't leave without picking up one of our goody bags, will you?'

There was no way Millie was going to leave without a goody bag, having already spied them by the door earlier.

'Oh, that's so kind, thank you,' she beamed. 'Thanks again and see you soon.' She gave Franny/Nats the obligatory air kisses and headed for the loo on her way out. Not only did she need to go before her long journey home – those glasses of wine were making themselves known – but she had been to enough fashion parties to know that it was prudent to sort through the goody bag and dump the crap stuff as soon as possible rather than lug the whole thing home. Generally, the heavier the item the less appealing it was, unless it was a bottle of alcohol – which seemed unlikely in this case given the lack of adult drinks on offer during the evening. Sure enough, she found a heavy brochure for a cruise company that she immediately put in the bathroom bin. Despite claims that cruises were the new holiday of choice for millennials, she couldn't see her and Wolfie setting sail any time soon. A musty-smelling air spray also found its way into the rubbish, as did a DIY mocktail kit. But a quick rummage confirmed a bar of chocolate, a hand cream, a moisturiser and some vouchers, plus even a scarily neon slogan T-shirt that looked like it just about might fit her – and there was no denying that #livingmybestlife splashed across a top was on brand when it came to her Insta feed.

Satisfied she hadn't weighed herself down with unnecessary stuff, Millie quickly changed out of her heeled boots and into the canvas pumps she'd shoved into her bag at the last minute, then hot-footed it to the tube in the hope that it would get her to the train station faster. As it was, she managed to catch the train with ten minutes to spare and rather wished she'd detoured for a burger – it had been far too long since she'd hoovered up Wolf's leftovers after his tea. Instead, she had to make do with the chocolate from her goody bag while the train chugged its way out of London. She smiled to herself about the white lie she'd told a baby-faced PR she'd chatted to about where she'd bought her outfit. There had been no way she was going to admit she'd had both her trusty denim skirt and her leather jacket for the best part of fifteen years and had absolutely no idea what shop she'd bought them from, other than knowing they probably cost less than a tenner as she'd been as skint as most 16-year-olds at that point. The term 'vintage' was always a great cover-all anyway, she thought as she composed an Instagram caption to accompany the picture she'd asked Franny/Nats to take of her with Sonya and Frankie, which also happened to have MaryAnna posing just behind them.

> Such a stylish evening partying and catching up with these fashionistas *heart eyes emoji* @MAFlash @FrankieG @SonyaStyle. Thanks for the invite @BestDressedPR #instastyle #fblogger #styleblogger #styleinspo #outfitinspo #fashiongram

By the time she let herself into the house an hour later, she was exhausted. As was Bridget, it appeared. Millie gently shook the older lady, but her snoring showed no signs of abating. She tried again, this time omitting the gentleness and adding a determined, 'Bridget, it's Millie, I'm back now so you can go home. Bridget, did you hear me?'

'What? Who? Ah, Millie, you're back, why didn't you say? Did you have a good evening, lovey?'

'Yes, thank you, Bridget, though I'm tired now, as I'm sure you are, so let's get you home. Was Wolfie okay?'

'Oh, yes, sweetheart, he was no trouble, no trouble at all. Though I think we've eaten all of those biscuits between us,' she said, wiping crumbs from her ample chest.

'I'm glad you enjoyed them,' Millie said. 'Now, have you got your embroidery and your book? And here's the money I owe you for tonight. You are so kind to babysit for me,' she added, giving Bridget a soft peck on her cheek.

'Get away, lovey, it's no trouble, as I keep saying. In fact, it gives me an excuse to get away from Philip and his snoring for the evening. As soon as he sits down in front of the telly he's off, I tell you!'

Millie smiled, thanked Bridget again and watched until she'd shuffled back to her own house five doors down and was safely inside. Millie closed the front door and tried to stop the guilt overwhelming her. It really wasn't fair of her to make Bridget, who must be pushing seventy-five despite looking pretty spritely, to stay up till almost midnight waiting for her. But she didn't have anyone else to ask. With her own mum gone ten years now and her dad all the way out in Wales with his second wife and her family, it wasn't as if she had Wolfie's doting grandparents to turn to. She barely knew anyone her own age locally and all the mums at Wolf's school looked too cliquey and intimidating to approach. Though she supposed she should start sorting out some playdates for him and his little friends – another thing to add to her ever-growing mental to-do list. The one person she should be able to turn to when she needed to go to networking events in the evening was the very last person she would even consider contacting to help her out. It just wasn't worth the hassle and disappointment of getting in touch with Louis. He'd only let her – and worst of all, Wolfie – down, after all.

Chapter Six
Bell

Although Bell was able to admit that she'd had a good night with Suze and her friends, she had very much been looking forward to resuming her nightly position at home on the sofa. Annoyingly for her, and much to Suze's delight, a couple of work events she was forced to attend were coming up over the next few weeks, which meant not only making an effort with her hair, make-up and, of course, her outfit, but also to chat to other industry people. It wasn't that long ago that Bell had thrived on this type of evening – a few glasses of not-quite-top-of-the-wine-list red and a whole load of gossip and checking out what competitors were up to made for a fun time. But over the years she'd gradually stopped going to the events she was invited to – and then stopped being invited to them at all – preferring to go home and watch a box set with Col or even just catch up on her overflowing inbox.

But there were some events she really couldn't get out of

and the annual high-street fashion awards by *Styler*, one of the country's biggest-selling magazines, was one of them. Thankfully, she'd have Suze by her side, as this year her friend was coming too. Less thankfully, the other person going with them to the awards was her boss – and the company's CEO – Marian.

It didn't help that Bell had had a nightmare of a day. It had started with her being late for a meeting after getting caught up in a conversation with Ciara and Joe on her team, who were chatting about how tired they were after going out last night with a bunch of PRs and bloggers.

'Feeling a bit delicate, are we?' Bell had smiled, in an attempt to engage with them on a cool-boss level.

'Just tired, as we didn't leave the bar till after 2am,' Joe explained. 'Though we were on mocktails all night, obviously.'

Oh, yes, how could she have forgotten that no one under thirty seemed to drink anymore? She was glad Aftershock and sambuca had been the order of the day when she was young and out partying with fashion-industry folk several nights a week.

A chat message popped up from Suze:

> God, how do they even stay awake that late without alcohol?! Bring on the bright blue alcopops, I say!

Bell typed back viciously:

> They make me want to spike their snowflake-infused mocktails with a large bottle of vodka. And I don't care if that makes me a bad person.

Suze quickly typed back:

> *Reports esteemed colleague to HR for force feeding the young'uns alcohol* *winky face emoji*

Bell snorted. 'Well good for you, Joe, and you, Ciara. Did you meet anyone interesting last night?' she asked, trying to show she was interested in the lives of her junior staff.

'Just some influencers – you know, MaryAnna, Frankie Gable, Sonya, that lot. And Millie came down for a bit early on. They're so lit. And Sonya had heard of Style It Out and I think she seemed super-interested in hooking up in some way.'

'Great. Well, good for you,' Bell repeated lamely. Then quickly clicked her browser to start googling who the hell MaryAnna, Frankie, Sonya and Millie were. But it seemed Suze had beaten her to it as her chat app flashed up on her screen.

> So MaryAnna is apparently @MAFlash and has 1 MILLION Insta followers!! @FrankieG and @SonyaStyle have around 250,000

each, and I know who Millie is *smiley face emoji* – @mi_bestlife is a mummy blogger type who sometimes actually posts some interesting stuff. And isn't 22 years old. Unlike the others. Yay!

Bit of a coup Ciara and Joe rubbing shoulders with such big influencers (that word makes me want to vomit!). I bet they all earn 10 times what we do just for posting some crap about teeth whitening and designer handbags. Christ, I feel ancient.

Suze had flicked an elastic band at her friend, rolled her eyes, and glanced at the clock in the corner of her screen. 'Oi, Granny, isn't it time you were in that really important meeting you were telling me about yesterday?'

By the time Bell had rushed into the meeting room, paper flapping from her notebook and her cheeks flushed, she already knew the next hour was not going to be her finest. Marian had proceeded to point out the holes in her marketing strategy for the company's next three months, and Bell had spent the rest of the day stressing out that all the bright young things in the office were snapping at her heels with their talk of collabs and sponsored posts.

'Bellster, you know Marian always has at least three negative things to say about everything and that's when she's being nice,' Suze reassured her when she cornered her in the loos at 4pm and told her they'd better start getting ready if they weren't going to be horribly late.

'Argh, I've not finished that spreadsheet or sent that email I promised Nigel I'd definitely write today. And now I've got to spend an evening with my boss who thinks I'm crap, plus I look like I haven't slept in a week.' Bell stared into the less-than-flattering mirror in front of her. Even Suze couldn't deny that her friend wasn't exactly looking her best.

'Okay, so you've got a breakout on your chin and those bags are giving you panda eyes, but it's nothing some strong concealer, tons of highlighter and a bit of contouring can't sort.'

By the time Bell returned, laden with her hair straighteners, cosmetics and the jumpsuit she'd cajoled one of the buyers into lending her for the evening, Suze had touched up her own make-up and was changing into a dress that Bell had privately thought looked rather like a sack when she'd seen it on the coat-hanger by her desk. Needless to say, Suze looked all kinds of amazing in it.

'There you are, I thought you'd run off home!' She grinned at Bell. 'Zip me up, will you? Then I'll get started on you.'

By the time her friend had finished with her for the second time in a week, Bell felt she at least resembled someone who worked in the fashion industry. Her navy jumpsuit gave a nod to the seventies with its cute buckled belt, and her trusty black patent heels poshed it up enough without looking too try-hard. She'd pulled her blonde hair back into a messy-but-not-too-messy bun, and under a dim light you could barely notice the bumpy skin around her chin and jawline (who got spots at thirty-nine years old, for god's sake?), and she even had the appearance of some angular cheekbones, thanks to Suze's magic illuminator brush.

They were both loading themselves up with handbags and tote bags containing flat shoes when Marian swept in, fresh from the salon, and probably her stylist and make-up artist. She looked incredible – coiffed, styled and polished to within an inch of her life, but in a 'yes, I'm fifty, and I look great' way, rather than a 'yes, I'm fifty but I'm trying to look like I'm twenty-five' way. Even Helen Mirren would be jealous.

'Excellent, you're ready. Right, ladies, let's go.'

It was an hour's drive into London from the Style It Out office and, as they got into the car Marian had ordered, Bell suddenly panicked that they were going to have to make polite conversation the whole way there. She knew that every second in such close proximity to her boss was a second in which she could shoot herself in the foot by saying something stupid, which was quite likely after the day she'd already had. Both Bell and Suze were very relieved when Marian made it clear that she wouldn't be engaging in idle chit-chat with her employees, as she immediately began tapping at her phone. They glanced at each other and managed to stifle their giggles like nervous schoolgirls, but both realised it was probably safer to follow their boss's lead, even if in Suze's case it was to catch up on all the tabloid websites instead of wade through boring work emails. Finally they reached central London and the jam-packed roads around Leicester Square where the venue for the night's event was located. Marian slipped her phone into her clutch bag and turned to eyeball the two younger women.

'Got your mingling faces on? Good, let's go wow the rest of the fash pack!'

From anyone else, this sentence might have sounded ridiculous, Bell mused. But from Marian it just sounded right, although she could also hear the thinly veiled instruction that this was a working event, not just a chance to down a load of fizz.

There were a small bunch of photographers outside the front of Café de Paris and they raised their cameras and fired off a barrage of shots as Marian climbed gracefully out of the car – she clearly exuded a kind of look-at-me glamour that meant they took her picture without even thinking about it. But they quickly lost interest when Bell and Suze emerged and they realised they weren't anyone famous. Once all three of them were inside the impressive venue, they had their photo taken against a backdrop of the magazine and its sponsors' logos. That done, and with the flashes still smarting their eyes, they were handed a glass of what they were told was a 'ginspiration' cocktail and made their way into the main room. Marian was quickly enfolded into a large group of important-looking people, so Bell and Suze were free to explore on their own.

'Flipping heck, this is swish, isn't it?' Suze whispered as they stared at the sweeping staircases, glittering chandeliers and the ballroom full of people before them. Suze was the first to regain her composure, and after a sweep of the room to see if they could spot anyone they knew – other than a few minor celebs who they recognised but definitely didn't 'know' – she finally exclaimed. 'Look, there's Karina, let's go and say hi to her.'

Although she was very 'fashion', Bell couldn't help but love Karina King. She worked for the country's largest online clothing site and was one of the industry's shining stars, having been made CEO of a business worth millions at just thirty-two. Karina greeted Suze and Bell like they were all best mates who hadn't seen each other for months, despite them being no more than vague friends who only saw each other about once a year at events like this. But still Bell couldn't hate her; she was just too lovely. Plus, she was always the best dressed in the room, even when she was standing in the middle of hundreds of the high street's biggest players.

'Karina, so good to see you. You look amazing,' Bell gushed.

'Thanks, darling, it's vintage Galliano, though I'm passing it off as one of ours for the purposes of this evening – always working, hey! How are you? It's been far too long. We need a proper catch-up – message me and let's sort, yes? And do you guys know MaryAnna? No? Well, let me introduce you. Mar, this is Bell and Suze and they're a total scream, you'll love them!'

Bell and Suze gave each other a secret high-five with their eyes as they air-kissed MaryAnna hello. Sadly, their conversation was hampered by the fact that MaryAnna was so enthusiastic about literally everything anyone said she was in danger of turning into a fashion caricature; she had clearly decided to model herself on Eddie from *AbFab*.

'God, she must have said "super" about a million times in one minute. I didn't even know there was such a thing as "super-on-trend". But that's influencers for you,' Suze murmured to Bell later. 'Even Insta stars like her know not to bite the hands that feed them.'

But at least MaryAnna didn't seem to mind having a picture taken with them both, and Bell thought smugly that they'd been able to go one better than Ciara and Joe. MaryAnna did ask to check the photo on Suze's phone, though. 'I have to be super-careful with my brand and everything,' she explained with a patronising smile, as she deleted a couple of the images she didn't like and handed the phone back to Suze. 'I'll try to regram it, Suzie, so remember to tag me when you post it. Super-lovely to meet you girls and hope you have a super night.' And off she wafted to join a group of pouting, selfie-taking girls who greeted her as if she was the messiah.

'I swear one of those girls just bowed to her,' Bell said, shaking her head.

'When I reach a million followers I'm totally making everyone bow to me,' Suze smirked.

'Riiight. How many have you got now?'

'Eight hundred. But you never know, if @MAFlash regrams my pic, I might have eight hundred *thousand* come the morning.'

'Ha! If you really get to eight hundred thousand by nine o'clock tomorrow, I promise I'll bow down to Suze The Almighty. In the meantime, shall we get another drink?'

As Style It Out wasn't up for any kind of award, the pair made the most of the free booze and canapés and clapped along when each of the winners was announced. They gave Karina a massive whoop when she went up to collect the trophy for best online retailer ('That will be us one day!' Suze laughed tipsily), and even managed a cheer when MaryAnna bagged the Insta star award ('I bet she's *super*-pleased!' Bell grinned at her own joke). By the time Marian swept over to them and declared it was time to leave, they'd both had at least one cocktail too many and were trying desperately not to burst into giggles at every opportunity.

'God, you'd think we were nine, not thirty-nine,' hiccuped Bell, trying to take off her heels and put on her flip-flops discreetly in the corner.

'Speak for yourself, Granny! I'm only thirty-eight as you well know. And I damn well hope I'm going out and getting pissed when I'm as old as someone like Marian.'

'Ready, ladies?' Marian appeared beside them, still perfectly groomed and definitely not wearing flip-flops. Bell and Suze glanced at each other and their shoulders shook with laughter.

When she got into work the next morning a little bleary-eyed but surprisingly headache-free, the first thing Bell did was bring up Suze's Instagram page on her computer. It seemed that MaryAnna had indeed regrammed Suze's pic and her followers had almost doubled to over 1,500.

'I know, it's hardly 800k, but it's not bad,' Suze said, looking over Bell's shoulder. 'God, I'm knackered. I need to get this coffee down me and then hopefully I'll wake up a bit.'

'Suze, Bell, I've just seen your picture,' Ciara cried as she came running over waving her phone. 'That's so awesome. Isn't MaryAnna super-nice? What did she say to you? Did she mention she'd met me the previous night? I can't believe she gets to go to a party every single evening.'

It wasn't long before they'd both been forced to recount last night's events numerous times as word spread round the office, and Bell noticed that many of the junior staff seemed to look at her with new-found respect. As the day wore on, Suze's likes and followers continued to grow and the Style It Out office was a buzz of chatter and glances over to their desks. Marian even came out of her office to find out what all the hubbub was about.

'Good work, ladies,' she nodded at Bell and Suze with the glimmer of a smile. 'Now, where are we with spring/summer first drop? Charlie, I need to see something this afternoon.'

The office continued to have an excited air about it all day and no one seemed much in the mood for work. Bell tried valiantly to complete her spreadsheet despite everyone chatting around her, but Suze was determined to draw her into the conversation.

'Bell, you've seen those superhero movies, haven't you?

Charlie won't believe me that Superman is in the Avengers films. I swear he was in the one I saw.'

'No, he's DC and the Avengers are Marvel. They're different franchises,' Bell replied without thinking.

'Hold on, you're saying Superman isn't in *any* of the Avengers films, not just the one I saw with Els the other week? How come you know so much about it, Ms geekface?'

'Comic-book films were Col's thing, so I guess they became my thing too,' Bell said, looking up from her computer. 'God, that sounds a bit sad when I put it like that.'

'Well, it's not surprising. Don't forget you spent ten years with him, so it's only natural you're going to find it hard when you do "Bell and Col" things without him. And that's okay. But now you have to see these things as "Bell and Suze" things, or "Bell and Cosette" things, or even just "Bell" things, because it is okay to do things on your own, too. In fact, the more you do these things on your own and not with Colin, the more you'll make your own stories and create your own narrative.'

Bell stared at her. 'Er, Suze, have you been reading that life-coaching book again?'

Suze shrugged.

'Ha, I knew it!' Bell laughed. 'You and your make-your-own-narrative rubbish.'

'It's not rubbish! I know it sounds a bit mumbo jumbo, but there is something in it, Bellster. You need to find out who you really are and what *you* enjoy, after being part of Bell and Col for so long. And while we're on the subject, I think what you need is some inspiration. I know you've come off social media, but it's not all evil, I promise. Stop rolling your eyes at me! Instagram is great if you follow the right people.'

'Ha, like you, you mean!'

'Well, I am well on my way to becoming an influencer dontchaknow,' she laughed. 'I mean it, though, there are loads of people on Insta who are just normal people doing normal things, but posting really interesting thoughts and ideas.'

'#NoFilter, of course,' Bell said scathingly. 'Look, I'm really pleased you're now bezzie mates with MaryAnna and co.—'

'I'm not!' Suze protested. 'This is nothing to do with her. Though she does mention some really inspirational people in her posts sometimes, when she's not plugging fitness gear or whatever.'

'I'll take your word for it, Suze, but I just think it's a slippery slope for me. I'm better off without social media at all.'

Chapter Seven

Bell

Bell tapped her fingers on her desk, trying to come up with a password she wouldn't forget three seconds after she'd entered it. Finally, she typed 'SuzeMadeMeDoIt1' and hit 'Enter'.

'Welcome to Instagram,' pinged her email. 'Here are our suggestions for who to follow.'

'What, you've actually done it? Yay, well done, Bellster,' cried Suze. 'I thought I'd at least have to use the thumbscrews.'

'I decided it was the only thing that was going to shut you up, to be honest.' Bell cast a rueful gaze at her friend who was pulling her chair over to Bell's computer. Her comment completely went over Suze's head as she happily commandeered Bell's mouse and started clicking.

'Ooh, @With_Bells_on, I'm loving your work with that new username! Right, I'll follow a load of people I really rate to get you started. But remember this is all about positivity and inspiration. No moaning Marys and whinging Wendys for you!'

Later that evening, Bell lay on the sofa with her laptop on her knees, scrolling through the feed Suze had curated for her. While she liked cat videos as much as the next person, she wasn't so enamoured with images of rainbows overlaid with mindless mantras like 'It will all be okay as long as you believe in unicorns', or a row of gin bottles and the line: 'It's the weekend so beGIN as you mean to go on'. But among the cheesy affirmations and cute animals, there were a few posts that Bell 'Liked'. Some were from fashion-industry accounts that she could never be bothered to follow in the past but now realised could be quite helpful for brainstorming in the office. She could hear Suze's voice inside her head telling her that this account wasn't supposed to be about work — it was about her 'personal development', whatever that meant. (Suze had sanctimoniously told her: 'It means whatever you want it to mean, darling,' when she'd asked, leading Bell to suspect that Suze had no idea either.) She continued scrolling and ended up saving a couple of posts about books she liked the sound of, an interiors pic with a gorgeous armchair in the background and a recipe for banana muffins that looked yummy. She even began following a few new accounts to add to her 'inspo list' (yep, Suze again), including an urban gardener and a very cool-looking potter who made the cutest pieces decorated with recycled materials.

Bell was feeling pretty pleased with herself, especially as she now had something positive to report back to Suze the next day. She was about to put her laptop down and contemplate watering the rather brown-looking plants in her living room when her attention was snagged by an account called @mi_bestlife. The name rang a bell but she couldn't work out why, so she clicked on the profile. Oh, yes, now she remembered: it was Millie, one of the 'influencers' Ciara and Joe had met the other day. Well, if she was anything like MaryAnna, she was hardly going to be someone Bell would find inspiring. And her username didn't even make sense – it would have to be pronounced 'Mih' (as in Millie) for it to work, and 'Me Best Life' would only be clever if she was from Liverpool. As she started clicking through @mi_bestlife's images, there wasn't a single shot of the Mersey and quite a few of the Thames, so she decided Millie/Mylie was probably a bit dim and definitely not inspirational.

But then she paused. She clicked on one of the images and zoomed in. It wasn't just her name that was familiar, it was her face, too – and Bell never forgot a face, in fact she prided herself on the fact. Her brain whizzed through everyone she'd come across in the last few months like facial recognition software sorting through police mugshots. Ding! Finally, she had a match: Millie looked strikingly like the girl she'd seen arguing into her phone opposite the bus stop that night out with Suze's mates. She peered again at the screen, then continued scrolling through Millie's feed in search of a post from that night. She felt like some kind of private detective, and her Sherlock-like efforts were rewarded when she finally found what she was looking for.

'Aha, Millie/Mylie, got you!' Bell crowed, clicking on the image to read the full post. Beneath a bedroom selfie of Millie wearing a gorgeous dress Bell recognised as being part of that cool high-street collection that had sold out immediately were the words:

> Such an amazing night with good food, good wine and of course, good mates. Felt sad leaving the little one at home, but he was as good as gold, so I'm told. ♥ #ootd #goingoutout #babysittersrule.

Glancing at the clock on the top-right of her screen, Bell was taken aback. She stretched out her hunched-up limbs and realised she'd just spent the last half an hour nosing around inside Millie's life – or her life according to Instagram, anyway. She'd checked out various images of an angelic-looking little boy she presumed to be the 'little one' Millie had referred to in her post, learned that his name was Wolf (er, what kind of a name was that?!) and that he and Millie lived in a gorgeous apartment and seemed to have an idyllic life filled with organic food and wooden toys designed to help darling Wolfie's life skills.

Bell shut her laptop with a bang. She and Colin had half-heartedly tried to have children, and when she didn't fall pregnant after a couple of years she suggested they both go to the doctor for tests. Colin wasn't keen and made it clear he didn't want to discuss it anymore. It gradually became obvious the subject was off the agenda and Bell too stopped mentioning it. She knew how stubborn Col could be about these things, and she was fairly ambivalent about the whole kids thing anyway. Sure, she'd coo over a workmate's baby when they brought them into the office, and she loved her niece and nephew with all her heart, but she'd never felt like that was what was missing from her life. In hindsight it was a bit strange that neither of them really pushed the issue. They never made a decision *not* to have children, but that was just how her and Col's relationship had been. It had ticked along nicely with neither of them wanting to rock the boat, least of all Bell.

She could see now that, although it wasn't kids that were missing from her life, something definitely was. Even two months down the line, she still felt like a stranger in her own world without Colin. Maybe their relationship hadn't been as exciting and passionate as Cosette and Suze had lectured her it should have been, but it had been something. Now she was untethered and set adrift without any of the skills she needed to survive on her own island. She felt her eyes fill with tears.

'Right, come on, Bell, sort yourself out,' she shouted into the cold air of her living room. 'Enough moping and more doing. You are an independent woman who is well able to strike out into the world on your own.' She jumped to her feet and whooped, 'You show them, girl!' Then quickly realised how ridiculous she looked (not that there was anyone to see her), felt herself blush and began plumping up the cushions before heading to the bathroom and muttering, 'God, Suze has a lot to answer for,' while she got ready for bed.

*

'So, feeling inspired yet?' Suze asked as she sat down at her computer the next morning. Bell wasn't sure if she was being serious, but she wasn't in the mood for either jokes or life-coaching clap-trap. She'd not been able to get to sleep and had resorted to making herself a hot chocolate liberally laced with the end of a bottle of rum she'd found at the back of the cupboard. Unfortunately, the 'end' of the bottle had turned out to contain more than she'd thought, and after finishing her hot drink, she'd moved on to slugging it back neat, which had definitely had a warming effect. Sadly, it had worn off by the morning, to be replaced with a burning, sloshing feeling that she worried was the start of a stomach ulcer.

'No,' she grunted. 'Today is not a day for feeling inspired.'

Suze side-eyed her friend and chose neither to continue to bait Bell further with her line of questioning nor to indulge her in her apparent foul mood, so she merely raised an eyebrow and proceeded to neatly write out her to-do list for the day.

Annoyed Suze hadn't risen to her comment, Bell made a show of huffing and puffing at her computer before taking herself off to the breakout area, where she spread pages of a report across the table and stared hard at the result in search of the answers that so far had remained irritatingly elusive.

'Ooh, Bell, I love those trousers, you are so styling out the structured sportswear trend,' Charlie said as he walked past the breakout area. Bell paused, unsure whether he was taking the piss out of the only-slightly-posher-than-joggers trousers she'd pulled on this morning, along with her trusty

Adidas zip-up, or if he was actually being serious. But thanks to his thumbs-up and genuine smile, she decided to take it as a compliment and flashed him a grin.

'Thanks, the structured sportswear trend was exactly the look I was going for, glad you noticed.'

Buoyed by his comments, Bell retrained her focus on to the papers in front of her and immediately spotted what it was she'd been missing for the many hours she'd been looking at it through glazed eyes. Of course she needed those extra figures or none of it made any sense!

'Charlie, you're a genius!' she shouted over to him. He looked momentarily confused, but then grinned back at her and said, 'I aim to please,' and walked off.

'Someone's a bit more cheerful now,' commented Suze later as they sat at their desks cradling huge mugs of tea. 'Did I see you flirting with Charlie boy earlier?'

'Hardly,' Bell scoffed. 'Also, I'm not sure I'm exactly his type. Wrong sex for a start.'

'Well, whatever's thrown that black dog off your shoulder, I'm all for it.'

'If only everything was as easy to solve as how to make my marketing spend add up, eh?'

'Maybe you're overthinking things,' Suze said gently.

'Me? Overthinking things? What can you mean?' Bell smiled. 'Anyway, enough of your life-coaching, I've got a fashion shoot to go to.'

'Yeah, well, enjoy, and think of me in the corner all on my own while you're swanning off with the talent, won't you.'

Bell didn't often make it out of the office, but she always made sure she went along to the two big photo shoots of the year – the summer shoot in the first quarter and the autumn/winter one near the end of the summer. As she made her way to the studio nearby, she thought back to the very first photo shoot she'd gone to, back when the thought of the glitz and glamour gave her butterflies. But twenty-five-year-old Bell had quickly learned that shoots were in fact hard work, especially if you were a lowly assistant and had to be on hand to fetch everyone's lunch, as well as console weeping models, hold pins, steam clothes and bulldog-clip material away from the camera. And yet, even now, despite knowing just how unglamorous a shoot could be, Bell still got butterflies about seeing the clothes come to life in beautiful images.

The studio was a hum of activity when she arrived, with the definite undercurrent of a team up against it. Harassed stylists sorted through rails of clothes, a hair and make-up artist fussed over three models who stood quietly waiting to be summoned by the photographer, who was standing by the lights with his assistant. He glanced up as Bell entered the fray.

'Bell, sweetheart, look at you!' he cried, coming over to kiss her on both cheeks. 'You look great and, er, quite sporty?' he said, taking in Bell's one-stripe trousers and Adidas jacket.

'You know me, Ade, Sporty, Scary, Baby, Posh and Ginger all rolled into one spicy girl!' Bell cringed and felt her cheeks colour.

Suze always teased her about what she called her 'schoolgirl crush' on Ade. A former model himself, he was undeniably gorgeous, with sculpted cheekbones, closely cropped fair hair and piercing blue eyes. He was also married to a beautiful, petite woman named Bethan, who three years ago had given birth to twins who were surely bound for the pages of *Vogue* if the photos Ade readily shared were anything to go by. It wasn't even that Bell fancied Ade, it was more that she was a bit overcome by not only his looks, but also what a good photographer he was.

Bell always loved watching Ade at work, seeing how he got the models to give exactly the pose and expression he wanted. And since his camera was attached to a shiny Mac with a huge monitor, she found seeing the results of the shots immediately appear on the screen utterly awe-inspiring. Clicking through the hundreds of frames was like looking at a high-tech version of one of the flipbooks she and Cosette would play with when they were little; the pictures turning into a moving image to tell a story.

Bell knew Style It Out were lucky that Ade still agreed to shoot their campaigns for them, despite him being more in demand than ever and able to command large fees from bigger companies. But he always told her how much he loved going back to basics and making their shoots about the clothes, rather than focusing on a set that had cost thousands of pounds to build. There was certainly no danger of any such set on Style It Out's budget.

'Here, grab a drink,' she said, tossing him a can of Coke

during the break for lunch. 'The shots are looking great, aren't they?'

'Yeah, I'm really pleased. Though it's always weird shooting summer dresses when the weather's so grey outside. Good job we've got all the yellow filters on the lights to warm everything up a bit, otherwise those poor models would look deathly pale, despite their fake tan.'

'Do you mind if I take a few behind-the-scenes shots later, for Insta?' Bell asked self-consciously.

'Course not. How are things going with you, anyway? Ticked anything off that bucket list we talked about last time?'

Oh god. Bell had completely forgotten drunkenly creating a list with Ade during the last post-shoot team drinks. It was meant to be all the things she wanted to do in life but hadn't as yet achieved, and it was quite a list; it had involved activities as diverse as building an igloo and eating at a three-Michelin-star restaurant, though she couldn't for the life of her remember what else was on there.

'Didn't you mention getting more seriously into photography?' he nudged.

Oh, yes, apparently she had confessed her love of his profession and told him how much she wanted to hone her own skills behind the camera. Nothing to do with her being even more overwhelmed by Ade than usual when they were sitting side by side in the pub, obviously.

'That's some memory you have! Most of what I remember from that night involves a magically refilling wine glass,' she grinned at him, then finished lamely, 'But, yeah, when I have more time I'll definitely get on that photography thing.'

'Well, if you need any help, just give me a call,' he said, touching her shoulder lightly as he got up to fill his plate. Bell tried not to jump as his skin burned through her clothing.

She'd never told Col about her secret bucket list (or her crush on Ade, for obvious reasons), and although at the time she hadn't really thought why this was, now she was able to recognise that it was the type of thing Col would have chuckled at then patted her shoulder – in a very different way from Ade – before telling her they should book that weekend in the Lake District they'd been talking about. He just wouldn't have got it.

'Coming to the pub in a bit, Bell?' Ade asked later as she helped pack away his camera and equipment.

'No, I'm going to head home, I'm afraid. Lots to catch up on,' she replied.

'Aww, that's a shame. But I mean it about the photography stuff, do drop me a message if you need any advice or just want a chance to practise your camera skills, won't you.'

Back at home, Bell trawled through the hundreds of emails she'd received while she'd been out of the office that afternoon, hitting delete on any she could before tapping out replies to the most urgent. Her fingers then strayed to Instagram, where she scrolled through the day's posts from her supposed new inspirations. Most of what was on there was fun but hardly motivating. Noticing she hadn't seen a post from @mi_bestlife, she searched for her handle and spotted she'd put up a new pic with a lengthy screed beneath it. The image showed a picture of her adorable son in full football kit with the words:

> Sometimes life doesn't quite turn out how you might want it to and it throws you a curveball, but the universe has always got your back. Whatever happens I know I've always got my little Wolf by my side. I hope he grows up to know just how loved he is and to always remember that the world is his for the taking. But the most important piece of advice for him has to be: when life gives you curveballs, score some goals! #striker #goals #littleangel #thisisfive #mummyblogger

Bell thought she might vomit. As cute as little Wolf undoubtedly was, she found Millie's declaration unbearably twee.

'Urgh, her life is just too perfect for words,' she sighed when she was telling Cosette about it on the phone later.

'Maybe it is, but you know as well as I do that social media is hardly a true reflection of real life. And if he's anything like Oli was when he was five, he'll be a right nightmare!' Cosette laughed. 'Although, did I tell you what the headteacher said when Rich and I went into school the other week?'

'Oh god, no, what awful things had he been up to?' Bell asked, feeling immediately guilty as her sister had told her at the time she was worried about being called in to see the head, and she'd completely forgotten to ask her what had happened.

'Well, she proceeded to tell us what a brilliant pupil he was, so much so that they were thinking about asking him to be head boy in September! There I was questioning him about his wrongdoings when in fact he'd been a model pupil. Christ, I felt so bad we ended up taking both him and Sophie to McDonald's for their dinner.'

'That's amazing news, good for Oli. Tell that nephew of mine that I'll take him to the cinema to see a film of his choice when I next see him.'

'Will do, though you do know what you're letting yourself in for, Bell?' Cosette warned. 'He'll hold you to that promise and you'll have to sit through two tedious hours of the latest Minecraft movie. Rather you than me!'

'Well, I've watched enough sci-fi movies with Col to have an appreciation of these things.' There was a beat of silence.

'How are things on that front?' her sister asked tentatively.

'I'm so busy at work I don't have much time to think about it,' Bell said, omitting any confession that when she was tucked up in bed her ex and their relationship still filled her mind. 'He emailed me today, though.'

'Did he? That's good. What did he want?'

'He suggested we start sorting out our joint assets, although as this amounts to the forty-two-inch TV I hate, because it takes over half the lounge, and the house itself, there isn't that much to sort. He can pick up the rest of his books, CDs and kitchen stuff whenever he wants.'

'And how do you feel about that?' Cosette probed.

'I know a clean break should be the best solution all round, but it's so . . . final.'

'But isn't that a good thing, Bell? It's not like you want to get back with him, is it?'

Bell cursed her sister for being so reasonable. 'Of course not!' She paused. 'Well, not really, anyway.'

'Bell, I know it's horrible, but it is for the best,' Cosette said gently. 'Have you thought what you're going to do with the house? You know, we could lend you a bit of money if you wanted to buy Colin out? No, don't say anything yet,' she added quickly as Bell began to protest. 'Take some time and think it over and then let's have another chat about it. I know how much you love that place and how excited you were when you moved in, and it would be a shame to lose it if you didn't have to. Anyway, have a think.' She took a breath. 'Actually, that reminds me, Rich asked me to ask you if you happen to want some photographic equipment. He bought a pretty expensive SLR camera from his mate a few years back, but it's been taking up room we don't have in the loft for ages so I've threatened him with eBay. But he thought it was worth mentioning as you do, and I quote him, "fashion and photography and all that shit".'

There was silence as she waited for Bell to respond. 'Bell, you still there? Don't feel you have to take it, but I said I'd ask. He won't want much for it.'

'Er, yeah, no, yes I might be interested,' she stuttered in reply. 'You haven't been recruited by MI6 and started secretly listening to my conversations, have you, Sis?'

'What? What are you talking about, you weirdo?' Cosette said, confused.

'Don't worry. But, yes, get Rich to email me some details and I can put the money straight into his account.'

'Really? Amazing! I'll get him to sort it out for you. And just so you know, if I really did work for MI6 I'd be the best spy ever. I've always fancied a bit of James Bond action.'

'Haven't we all, Cosette, haven't we all.'

As she ended the call, Bell thought that, weirdly, maybe @mi_bestlife was right. Sometimes life really did throw you curveballs, and maybe you did have to use them to score some goals. She pulled her laptop on to her knee and began googling photography classes nearby.

Chapter Eight

Millie

It had been a trying few weeks. After the initial excitement of seeing his dad had worn off, Wolf had started asking why he hadn't been allowed to spend longer with him that weekend, and when he was going to see him again. He'd now taken to marking off the days on a calendar till his next weekend with Louis, and it was often the first thing he talked about when he woke up in the morning. Millie wanted to encourage him to have a meaningful relationship with his dad, but it was all becoming a bit much if she was honest.

She'd messaged Louis to warn him how desperate Wolf was to spend an entire weekend with him, and he replied:

> That's my boy! Why don't we change it up and I'll have him this coming weekend? I'm guessing you haven't got plans.

To make things worse, the Sunday evening after her ruined night out with Tom, she'd been idly looking at the gossip news sites when she'd spotted pictures online of Louis with a very young blonde girl on his arm. His 'squad thing' ordered by the manager turned out to be a massive night out. He must have driven home breaking the speed limit at every turn, and then made up for being late to the party by drinking until dawn, at which point he and the girl were pictured stumbling into a taxi together. Still worse was that Millie couldn't even be bothered to confront him about it. It just wasn't worth the inevitable argument, which he was bound to twist around so she ended up in the wrong, not him.

Millie's relationship with Louis was complicated. It always had been, she supposed. In many ways, they'd made the most unlikely couple. They'd first met almost seven years ago in a bar in Birmingham. Twenty-three and determined to work hard at her job as a fashion buyer and to play hard in every spare minute she wasn't at work, the only thing on Millie's mind that Saturday night had been fun, fun, fun. So when a bunch of good-looking guys had offered to buy her and her friends drinks, she wasn't going to refuse. The girls stood by the bar giggling and nudging each other while all five guys competed to be the first to catch the bartender's eye, and eventually came over carrying pints of beer, pitchers of vodka Red Bull and a tray of shots.

'We thought you might be thirsty!' smirked a stocky guy, who had clearly been taking hairstyling lessons from One Direction, when he saw Millie's raised eyebrow.

'Well, never look a gift horse in the mouth and all that!' she replied.

'Cheeky! Though it has been said parts of me – or should I say, a very specific part of me – has the girth of a horse!'

The guys all jeered.

'That's not quite what your last girlfriend said, though, mate – wasn't it more a pony she compared it to?!' one of the others heckled. Cue more laughter and hilarity, obviously. 'Here you go,' the heckler added, handing Millie a drink. 'Cheers to gorgeous boys meeting gorgeous girls and everyone having a good time!'

Millie rolled her eyes, but joined in with the general giggling and whooping.

'I'm Louis,' he said, sticking out his hand. Millie looked up at his athletic build, closely cropped dark hair, chocolate-brown eyes and chiselled cheekbones and immediately thought: player.

'Millie,' she replied warily, shaking his outstretched hand.

'Pleased to meet you, Millie,' Louis said, pulling her shoulder towards him with his other hand and promptly kissing her on the cheek. 'What's a gorgeous girl like you doing in a bar like this without a boyfriend by your side?'

'How do you know he's not waiting for me at home?' she threw back.

'Is he?'

'No, I'm happily single,' she smiled.

'That's because we've only just met. Do you live in Birmingham – you don't have an accent?'

'I grew up down south, but yes I live here now.' Millie decided she wasn't going to make anything easy for him, especially as a quick look round at her friends revealed they hadn't bothered to get any further than first names before giving up on the chat and getting to know the others better, on a physical level at least.

Louis noticed her glance. 'Don't worry, they all look happily engaged! Although poor Martin has been left on the sidelines again.' He nodded at the gangly, awkward-looking lad staring into his pint nearby. 'But what he doesn't have in looks, poor bugger, he makes up for on the pitch – he's our goalie.'

'You're a footballer?' Millie asked. A player in every sense of the word, then.

'Yeah, we've been known to kick a ball around,' he grinned. 'We play for Walsall.'

'Is that good?' She refused to be impressed.

'Well, we're in League One, so we can't be too rubbish, and we won our match today three–two. I may have scored one of those goals,' he laughed. 'And it's every boy's dream to play football professionally, so, you know, mustn't grumble.'

'League One? That's the third division, right?'

'I can't pull the wool over your eyes, can I! Yep, it's not the Premier League or the Championship, but that just means I've got something to aim for. And let's just say me and my agent are feeling pretty excited about the future.'

'Good for you,' she smiled. 'Have you got the typical footballer's mansion and fast car?'

'Why, do you want a ride?' he asked suggestively.

Millie couldn't hide her giggle. 'I bet you spend a lot of time picking up girls in bars like this and then "giving them a ride".'

'Maybe,' Louis smirked. 'Though none of them are as pretty as you.'

'Smooth!' She laughed and clinked her glass against his. 'Though you'll have to try harder than that with your cheesy chat-up lines.'

'Who says I was trying to chat you up? I was just making polite conversation, I'll have you know. Fancy a sambuca?' he asked, grabbing a couple of shots from the tray next to him. 'They're all too busy snogging so we might as well drink theirs too.'

Several sambucas later, the bartenders made it clear it was chucking-out time. Millie's friends were all saying goodbye to their chosen guys in time-honoured fashion, and even Martin seemed to have managed to pull, judging by the mass of writhing limbs in the corner.

'If you give me your number, maybe I can show you my sports car collection and house – sorry, *mansion* – one night?' Louis said, leaning against the bar as they both surveyed the carnage around them.

Millie was loath to admit, even to herself, how much she'd enjoyed their flirty banter – and how attractive she found Louis, despite knowing he was trouble with a capital T.

'Maybe. Depends if you have a swimming pool, home cinema and games room complete with full-size snooker table. Anything less and I would be hugely disappointed and couldn't possibly refer to it as a footballer's mansion.'

'Well, you'll have to come round and find out. Though don't forget your bikini.'

'I wouldn't dream of missing out on a glass of bubbly in the hot tub – I presume you have a Jacuzzi?'

'I could hardly call myself a footballer without one, could I?'

He grinned, then his eyes seemed to darken even further and he held her gaze as he bent his head to kiss her. Millie surprised herself by not even trying to resist, and instead allowed herself to enjoy the long, delicious moment.

'Aye aye, King Louis is having his wicked way with a lady again!'

'Yeah, thanks, Yatesy.' Louis grinned at his mates as they all jumped on him and descended into general rowdiness.

Millie was fairly sure that despite allowing him to type her number into his phone, the only way she was going to hear from Louis again was some kind of booty call. However, whereas his mates quickly moved on to fresh blood (their phrase), Louis kept up a constant barrage of messages until Millie reluctantly agreed to a date as long as it was 'anywhere but that flashy mansion of yours'.

Obviously, she googled him extensively beforehand and found that while he appeared to live in a fairly nondescript new-build three-bed house in an ordinary suburb of town, it was true that he seemed to be tipped for soccer stardom by those in the know. She also found out he was twenty-two years old, his parents lived in Staffordshire and his pre-match routine involved wearing the same pair of underpants for every game, among other things.

'The internet can be most illuminating,' she remarked as they shared spring rolls and spicy prawns in an upmarket Chinese restaurant a few weeks later.

'Except when it comes to you,' Louis replied, licking chilli sauce from the ends of his fingers. 'You barely seem to exist!'

'That's the way I like it.' She shrugged. 'Anyway, you can ask me anything you want to know face to face. Isn't that what going on a date is all about?'

'But you have the upper hand as you already know stuff about me!'

'As I said, that's the way I like it.'

'You're not like anyone I've ever met before,' he said later as they walked towards New Street station together. Millie had even allowed him to hold her hand.

'You mean, I haven't immediately agreed to shag you and you can't work out why?' she smiled.

'No, yes, well maybe,' he replied, laughing. 'But you're different. You look so cool and seem so sorted. And, well, you know things . . .'

'Yes, well, I might only work in fashion, but I'm also a twenty-three-year-old well-educated woman who makes it her business to, as you put it, *know things*. Though so do most women, actually. Who have you been going out with, for god's sake!'

'Erm, well, they've mostly been young and blonde and, er, enthusiastic,' he said, his cheeks flushing.

'So you have a type.' Millie raised her eyebrow. 'And I appear to be the antithesis of that type, being older than you, brunette and not quite as enthusiastic. Interesting . . .'

'As I said, I've never met anyone like you before. I've clearly been missing out.'

Although Millie refused Louis' invitation to go back to his place ('*Well, you can't fault a guy for trying!*'), she did agree to another date. And another. And by date six, she did agree to go home with him ('*Although I haven't brought my bikini so I hope that doesn't mean the hot tub is out of bounds.*').

In some ways she felt older and more mature than Louis in his football-team bubble; in others she realised he was winning at being a grown-up: he had his own home, a car and a career he loved that was only going to get bigger. She was sharing a rented terraced house that could do with some TLC from the landlord, had nowhere to park a car let alone the money to buy one, and although she enjoyed working for a high-street chain as a fashion buyer, she wished she had a more creative outlet for her passion. Her friends were all excited she was dating a footballer – and indeed many of them tried out a few of Louis' teammates for size themselves, though other than a few one-night stands here and there, nothing much came of it. However, they were also worried she was going to get hurt.

'They're all good craic, but hardly marriage material, are they, Mills,' her friend Bronagh declared over copious amounts of cheap white wine one night. 'And I know you're not planning on marrying him, but it's been six months now, so it has. Are you serious about this thing?'

'I know what you're saying, Bron, but what does serious even mean at our age?' Millie slurred. 'Look, he's hot, funny, and pretty damn good in bed, so I'm not complaining!' The girls all shrieked with laughter, though Millie refused to give them any more details. 'Let's just say he knows how to stay fit!' she cackled.

And then a few months later, Louis got his big break and was signed to Championship side Wolverhampton Wanderers. Within weeks his life changed completely – suddenly he was attending press conferences and official photo shoots and being offered sponsorship deals. And the money poured in. He quickly sold the three-bed semi and bought a five-bedroom detached house in a nicer part of town, as well as a flashy boy-racer car. Weirdly, Millie's life didn't really change at all. Sure, she occasionally got her picture taken by the *Birmingham Mail* when she attended some event or other with Louis, but she still worked nine to five in her job – there had been vague promises about a potential promotion at some point – and she still lived with her housemates in their slightly run-down terrace. Although she did now spend quite a bit of time at Louis' place.

'You know, you should just move in,' he said, one night when they were lying on the sofa watching some terrible action film on his massive HD TV.

'Nah, I couldn't deal with you leaving all your stinky socks on the floor,' she replied, wriggling around to get comfy on the huge sofa.

'I'm being serious, Mills. I'm asking you to move in with me.'

'I'm being serious too.' Millie picked up the remote from the coffee table and paused the DVD. 'We've not even been together a year yet. It's too soon.'

'Well, it will be a year next week, won't it? And who says it's too soon? Plus, it's not like I don't have the room. You could have your own space and everything.'

'*I* say it's too soon. You're still young, Louis, you don't want to be shacking up with someone at twenty-three.'

'You don't know what I want. And twenty-three is hardly that young,' he replied, petulantly kicking the side of the sofa.

'I know that moving in together is a big step no matter what your age. Look, maybe we should just enjoy what we've got for a while and then see.'

'I just hate to think of you in that place.' Louis shuddered. He rarely came over to her house. He'd never been the biggest fan of her compact room and now he had so many bedrooms he didn't know what to do with them he reasoned there was no point them both 'suffering' when they spent the night together. Millie wasn't complaining, but she definitely drew the line at giving up her room and moving wholesale into his pad. Seeing she wasn't to be moved, Louis went to grab the remote again.

'Not so fast, Mr Price. I was thinking that if, as you rightly point out, next week it's a year since that fateful night of sambuca shots and cheesy chat-up lines, we should do something to celebrate.'

Louis was immediately back to overexcited man-child. 'Yes! Right, I'm thinking . . . no, actually I'm not going to tell you what I'm thinking. You leave this with me, I'm going to surprise you.'

Surprises weren't really Millie's bag. 'Well, okay, I'll leave the plans to you, but on the condition it's not a surprise. You have to tell me the exact plans at least twenty-four hours beforehand, deal?'

'Ooh, I like you when you get bossy. Although, I guess that means I like you all the time, then, doesn't it!'

Millie threw a cushion at him, hard.

In the end, Louis told her most, if not all, of what he'd planned, and Millie couldn't help but be impressed. He arranged a day off training for himself and booked a day's holiday with Millie's boss, who had been only too happy to help when he'd told her who he was. 'She would have agreed to practically anything I asked!' he crowed when he relayed the conversation to Millie.

'I wish you'd asked her for that promotion she's been promising me, then,' she grumbled.

Then he'd booked them a suite at a luxury spa hotel an hour's drive into the countryside. Not only did he treat them both to two hours of treatments that left Millie gently snoring into her fluffy dressing gown, but he'd also arranged champagne followed by one of the yummiest dinners she'd ever had, all in a private dining room with their own waiter.

'You really have pulled out all the stops, LouLou, thank you,' she sighed when they finally fell on to the massive bed laden with scatter cushions later that night.

'Anything for you, Amanda. And, yes, if you keep calling me LouLou, then I'll be forced to use your full name.'

'When you say anything . . .?' She raised her eyebrows suggestively.

'At your service, Amanda.'

Eight weeks later, Millie sat in one of the tiny cubicles in the Ladies at work, her eyes squeezed tightly shut. Taking a deep breath, she pinged them open and stared down at the plastic stick in her hand. In that moment she knew her life would never be the same again.

Now, staring at her phone reading the reports about Louis' night out with his teammates and various beautiful young women again, Millie grimaced. She loved Wolf with all her heart and couldn't imagine a life without him, but given the chance to live her life again, she knew she would make different choices. And maybe Louis would, too.

Desperate to do something positive, Millie fired off a quick Instagram post using a photo she'd taken the day before of Wolfie's toys all over the floor. Obviously, she'd spent a good thirty minutes perfecting exactly the right set-up. She'd hidden the huge Batman lair that took up half the lounge (Louis' birthday present to Wolfie. Predictably, he had loved it, though Millie couldn't help but think the eighty quid Louis had spent on a massive piece of black plastic could have been better used on food and clothes for his son.). Then she'd laid out the good rug and scattered on top of it the educational games and wooden train set her dad (on her instruction) had sent Wolf as gifts, along with a beautifully illustrated book about children around the world that she'd never quite managed to read to him, and the old-fashioned abacus she'd bought from a local charity shop. She added a few filters to the image, before writing:

> Oh to be young again! Wolfie is forever making up little stories and acting them out with his little friends, and it's so lovely to see him playing so happily every day, lost in his imagination. Although tidying up afterwards can be a nightmare! #playdates #growingupfast #myboy #thisisfive

She pressed Share and almost immediately Likes began to roll in, as did the comments. She tried not to read any of them for fear they were negative, but she couldn't help but see two flash up from familiar usernames.

> @Jan247638 Poor kid, I bet in all his games he's imagining he has a mummy who actually does something proper for a living and doesn't just leave him to get 'lost in his imagination'. Someone should call the Social

> @Stylista_I257 Ha! You'll never be young again, love, you're just a dried up old wannabe whose tits are down to your arse

Millie clicked out of the app before she could read any more. She felt like throwing her phone at the wall and watching it shatter into tiny pieces. Except then something was bound to happen at the school and they wouldn't be able to get hold of her and would probably call Social Services, knowing her luck. She knew there was no point replying to the trolls, but she just couldn't fathom what made someone sit there every day firing off such horrible comments. She should probably feel sorry for them: their lives were clearly so boring that they had to anonymously hate on people. But today, at least, she just felt furious.

Chapter Nine

Bell

'Bell, that's amazing,' screeched Suze looking over her shoulder at the confirmation email in Bell's inbox. 'You are such a dark horse. Who knew you had such David Bailey tendencies. Though I always knew my Insta inspo idea would work. Are there any other courses at the community centre as well as photography? My iPhone is enough for me when it comes to taking pics, but I'd be up for doing a pottery class or maybe a painting course. I've always wanted to do a bit of life-drawing,' she guffawed, nudging her friend.

'All right, calm down, you perv!' Bell laughed, pleased at her workmate's reaction to her taking the bull by the horns and signing up to an evening class. 'The community centre also has a leisure centre and outdoor pool, you know, so maybe you could take up synchronised swimming.'

'Erm, I know it's March, but it's hardly tropical outside, is it?' Suze exclaimed.

'Well, hopefully summer is on its way. Anyway, I can't believe I didn't know the community centre existed and, even better, it's only fifteen minutes' walk from my house. If I'd known, I'd have been swimming all last summer and taking evening classes left, right and centre.'

'Would you, though?' Suze said, cocking her head to one side and looking at her. 'I can't really see Colin spinning pots and doing yoga classes.' Sensing Bell's mood start to shift, she hurried on, 'Anyway, what made you go for photography? It's nothing to do with handsome Ade, is it?' She grinned slyly.

'No, of course not!' said Bell robustly. 'Although he's offered to help if I need some practice.'

'Of course he has!' spluttered Suze. 'Although I know what kind of help he's thinking of . . .'

'I'm not even going to dignify that comment with a reply. Except to say that, of course Ade is ridiculously good-looking, but he is also a ridiculously good photographer – who also happens to have a wife and two small children. And anyway, I've always been interested in photography, I'll have you know. Just because you have a one-track mind.'

'Els wasn't complaining about my one-track mind last night.'

'TMI, Suze, TMI.'

The only problem with the Wednesday evening photography classes Bell had signed up for was that she'd need to leave work an hour early each week. Which meant asking Marian's permission. She became more and more anxious about the conversation as the day wore on, until Suze got so sick of her friend procrastinating that she cried, 'Just tell her the truth, Bell. It's not as if you don't work through most of your lunch hours and answer emails at home every night. Marian's hardly going to call you a slacker, is she? Just go and get it over with now.'

'I know, I know,' Bell mumbled, rooted to her seat.

'Her office door's open so she hasn't got anyone in there with her at the moment,' observed Suze, leaning back in her chair to eyeball the glass office in the corner of the room. 'What's got into you? You're Style It Out's marketing ace, so go market yourself to Marian.'

'All right, I'll go now if it makes you happy!' she replied, still not moving. Suze raised her eyebrows at her and eventually Bell slunk off across the floor.

'Hi, Marian, have you got a sec?' she said brightly, after first knocking on her boss's door.

'Of course, Bell. Shut the door,' Marian replied, looking up from her computer but continuing to type, until finally clicking her mouse and resting her hands on her desk. 'What can I do for you? Is anything wrong?'

'No, no, everything's fine,' Bell hastened to reassure her. 'I just wanted to talk to you about a new, er, project I'm thinking about doing in my spare time.'

'Oh, great, sounds interesting.' Marian looked at her quizzically.

'Well, hopefully. Er, you probably know that I've recently split up with my partner, so, erm, I've decided to start an evening class. In photography. Which is exciting. But I'll need to leave work an hour early every Wednesday. I'll make up the hours, of course, and I won't let it interfere with my work here, Style It Out is always top of my priorities and—'

Marian held up her hand and smiled. 'Bell, that's fine. Of course you can leave early, you didn't even need to ask. You know how much I value your work here and I trust you to manage your workload how you see fit. Let me know how your photography class goes, won't you?'

'Thank you, and yes, of course. Right, well, thanks again, Marian.' She turned to go.

'Oh, and Bell?' Marian said. 'I hope you're doing okay after your break-up. I know you're a tough cookie, but the end of a long relationship is never easy, so look after yourself.'

'I'm okay,' Bell replied without missing a beat. Then she paused and rethought her response. 'Well, I'm getting there, anyway. But thanks for asking, Marian.' Then she turned and fled back to her desk.

Bell was on such a high after talking to Marian she high-fived Suze and resolved to work harder than ever so that her boss's belief in her would never be put to the test.

'Today is the start of a new me!' she declared.

'But I quite liked the old you,' grinned Suze. 'Don't go getting all goody-two-shoes on me, will you?'

'Of course not, I just want to keep Marian happy as she's been so nice to me.'

'And you will. Especially if you stay this happy yourself – that's the most important thing. What? What's wrong?' she asked, suddenly seeing her friend's smile fall as she stared at her computer screen.

'Colin. He wants us to sell the house.'

'Sell your house? But that's your *home*. Let me look.'

Suze nudged Bell out of the way so she could read the email that Colin had sent to Bell's work account, knowing she wouldn't be able to claim not to have seen it, as she might on her personal email.

'"Dear Bell, I hope you are okay and haven't had too much of a delay getting to work thanks to the recent road works on the main road into town. I wanted to email you as I thought it was time we discussed what we're going to do with the house we jointly own,"' Suze read aloud. 'God, it's like he's emailing the council or something, it's all so formal. Has he forgotten that up until a few weeks ago you two were in a relationship?'

'Col was never one for big displays of affection,' Bell replied drily.

'Indeed. "I know I said in my email two weeks ago that we didn't need to make any decisions immediately, but as I haven't heard from you with any firm plans, I thought I'd send a follow-up message so we can start to move things forward." Oh my god, is he for real? Do people even speak – well, email – like this? It's like he's discussing a business transaction.'

'Maybe that's all he ever saw our relationship as: another deal, a transaction, devoid of emotion.' Bell shrugged. All the previous excitement and happiness she'd felt had dissipated in the seconds it had taken her to see the message and scan-read it, like a balloon that had lost all its air.

'I'm sure that's not true.' Suze lightly touched Bell's shoulder and wished she'd kept her thoughts to herself for once. 'It's probably just because he wrote the email when he was in work mode in the office. Anyway, what else does he say? Blah blah . . . "I think it would be prudent to ask three estate agents to take a look at the property and give us some quotations for a quick sale and then we can decide which one we should engage. I am happy to oversee this process if that is easier for you. Rest assured, Bell, I would never want to see you put in a difficult position home-wise, so if you would prefer to remain living in the property, I would be open to you buying me out of the house, subject to the estate agents' valuations and your financial situation, of course." Well, of course! Urgh,' Suze said, shaking her head and puffing her cheeks out. 'Bell, darling, I don't know what to say. Are you okay?'

Bell was staring straight ahead at the screen in front of her, her mouth a perfect straight line.

'Bellster?'

'Don't worry, I'm fine.' She turned to look at Suze. 'I was just wondering whether Tina knows what a pompous git Col can be.'

'Oh my god, so pompous!' Suze cried. 'Although, to be honest, I didn't know old Col had it in him. He always seemed a bit, well, spineless, I suppose.'

'Really? That's another thing you never told me. I think

he's always been confident that he knows how to get his own way with me, which has made him arrogant and, yes, pompous. And maybe some of that is my fault because I'd often go along with whatever he wanted as it was just easier. You know how much I hate arguments.'

'Ha, you're the least argumentative person I have ever met in my entire life, Bellster! But that isn't a bad thing, darling. It just shows what a lovely person you are. And if someone else takes advantage of that, then it just shows what a nasty person they are. Colin's behaviour is not a reflection on you.'

Bell shook her head. 'I don't agree, Suze, but I'm not going to argue with you about it, obviously!' She managed a smile. 'Anyway, I suppose I'd better decide where I'm going to live in a few months' time.' She felt tears threatening again and gulped hard.

'Right, coat on, computer off, you and me have a date with the bottle of sauvignon blanc that's currently taking up space in the door of my fridge. And it just so happens that I was going to cook spag bol this evening, so now you can save me from giving myself a carb coma from all the leftovers that I always promise I'll put in the freezer but never do.' She put her hand up as Bell was about to protest. 'I know it's only five, and I also know how much you want to keep Marian happy, but we can both come in half an hour early tomorrow if you so wish. Some situations call for an early finish and a large glass of wine, and this is one of them.'

Bell didn't dare disagree.

As they sat in Suze's tiny kitchen and talked over giant

bowls of pasta and goldfish bowls of wine, Bell was surprised how practical her happy-go-lucky friend could be when necessary.

'Right, we need to look at all the options,' she said, pointing her fork in a way Bell found rather menacing. 'First, I assume you jointly own your home and are jointly responsible for the mortgage?' Bell nodded. 'Okay, you need to find the paperwork, discover exactly how much you still owe and then find out what the house itself is worth. Then you'll need to do the maths about whether you can afford to buy Colin out and keep the house yourself – which I presume is your preferred option?'

'Yep. The house has its, er, quirks, but as you say it's my home. Though how I'm going to make the money side work, I have no idea. Maybe we should sell it and I could buy a tiny flat or apartment. At least that way I won't have to stress about things.'

'But is that really what you want? No, I didn't think so,' Suze said when Bell shook her head sadly. 'What about your parents, would they lend you some money, do you think?'

'Janet and John are happily frittering away my inheritance in the US,' she said with a hollow laugh. 'Not that I disagree with them doing so, but it would definitely never cross their minds to help out their grown-up daughters, financially or otherwise. I can hear my dad saying, "If you're old enough and wise enough to leave full-time education, you're old enough and wise enough to stand on your own two feet, girls!"'

'Hmm, is there anyone else who might be able to help out? I absolutely would if I could, but as you know, Style It Out hardly pays us a massive salary and sadly I never came into the fortunes some of my trust-fund friends did in their early twenties.'

'Ha, imagine. Anyway, you'd have spent it all on amazing vintage clothes, knowing you, Suze! But even if you were sitting on a small fortune, I wouldn't let you give any of it to me, you know that.' She paused, then said slowly, 'I was talking to Cosette the other week and she did say something about them maybe lending me money if I needed it for the house. But she and Rich have the kids to worry about as well as their own home down in Devon, which has definitely seen better days, so it's not something I really want to take her up on.'

'Your problem is you never put yourself first, Bellster. If Cosette is offering this chance, then you should take it. She and Rich are smart people and aren't going to put themselves in financial jeopardy in order to help, much as they love you.' Seeing Bell look less than convinced, she tried a different tack. 'At least there's one positive thing to come out of all this.'

'What's that then?' asked Bell, closing the calculator app she'd been tapping away on.

'Well, you can make Colin take away that awful faux-leather sofa he insisted on you having in your living room. The number of times you've told me how much you hate that sofa!'

'Oh my god, you're right!' cried Bell, more animated than she'd been all evening. 'It's been there so long now that I barely even see it when I'm in the living room, but it is totally hideous. Think of all the gorgeous sofas I could buy to put in its place. Well, that's if I had any money, obviously.'

'I'm going to say this one more time,' Suze said firmly. 'Call Cosette and talk to her about her offer. You can have legal documents drawn up and everything if you're worried about paying her interest and doing it all properly.'

Bell sighed. Suze's phone lit up on the table and showed Ellie was trying to FaceTime her.

'Look, I'll get on home and leave you to it. Thanks so much for dinner, Suze, and all your life-coaching. Again. Say hi to Ellie from me. See you tomorrow.'

Bell was out the door before Suze could even open her mouth. She loved her friend and she knew Suze loved her, but she also knew that she'd asked a lot of her these last few months, taking her away from Ellie, and she needed to make sure she invested enough time in her own relationship.

When Bell arrived home, she walked into the living room, threw her coat and bag on the floor and stretched her arms above her head. In her peripheral vision, she caught a glimpse of brown faux leather and shuddered. She picked up her phone, wandered into the kitchen and pressed 'call'.

'Hi, Cosette, it's me.'

Chapter Ten

Millie

'Mummy, Mummy, me and Daddy went to this place and there was a massive pool and Daddy put some blow-up things on my arms and I floated around and it was brilliant!' Wolf cried as Millie opened the front door to him and Louis early one Sunday evening after he'd spent the weekend with his dad.

'That sounds amazing, Wolf. Did you like being in the water? Because I know how you can sometimes feel about bathtime.'

'It's different from a bath, silly!' he replied scornfully. 'It's a big pool and there were loads of flamingos and unicorns in the water and Daddy lifted me up to sit on them and I flew around. It was ace!'

Louis grinned. 'I think he'd really love swimming lessons. Maybe you could take him to the local leisure centre to learn? In fact, I'll give you the money now,' he said, thrusting some notes at her.

'Yes, I don't see why not, I'm sure there must be a council pool round here. I'm just surprised – he can be a bit scared of water sometimes,' Millie half-whispered over their son's head.

'No, you weren't scared, were you, Wolfie! That's my boy! Right, I'd better be getting back, but let me know when you manage to book those lessons. Come and say goodbye to your old man, Wolf Cub.'

When Millie was putting a still overexcited Wolf to bed a few hours later she asked, as casually as she could, 'So you enjoyed playing in the pool with the blow-up flamingos yesterday? You weren't a bit worried about the water? Because you know it's totally okay to be a bit scared of things sometimes.'

Wolf looked at her for a few moments and then lowered his eyes. 'I was maybe a *little* bit scared at first but then Daddy said that it's not a good idea to show you're frightened and you have to pretend you're not. And then he put me on the unicorn and I liked splashing the water with my feet.'

'Well, I know Daddy said that,' Millie began, choosing her words carefully. 'But it doesn't mean you can't tell Mummy, or your teacher if you're at school, that you're scared about something, all right? We all get frightened sometimes, even me, even Daddy!'

'I don't think Daddy gets scared!' Wolf laughed. 'He's never scared when he's on the pitch and scoring goals, and I want to be like him when I grow up.'

'You're right, Wolfie, he isn't scared on the pitch anymore, but when he was younger, I think he was definitely a bit scared. And that's okay. Listen, I want you to promise to tell me whenever you're feeling scared and I will take the scariness away, okay? Pinky promise?'

'Pinky promise, Mummy.' Wolfie linked his little finger with hers and she gave him a hug.

The next morning, before he'd even tried his luck asking for chocolate cereal, Wolf announced, 'I think I really want to have swimming lessons, please, Mummy. And then I can go to Daddy's pool in his friend's house and go on the unicorn again.'

'Okay, let me see what I can do, Wolfie.' Millie smiled at her son.

After searching online she found the community centre twenty minutes' walk away had a pool, so she wasted no time in calling up that morning to enquire about lessons.

'You're in luck!' the jolly man on the other end of the phone said. 'We've just had a cancellation for the new term's beginners' class. Bloody cheek cancelling at this point, let me say, but in this case it all works out well. The classes are at five pm every Wednesday and term starts the day after tomorrow. Is that okay?'

'Brilliant, thanks so much!' she replied, feeling very pleased with herself that she'd be able to message Louis so soon to tell him she'd sorted the lessons.

Wolf was fizzing with excitement on Wednesday after leaving school and having 'swimming tea'. This was much like any other dinner except Millie had decided she didn't have time to cook and get him to his lesson on time without the threat of him being sick in the pool, so the meal consisted of pitta bread, ham, houmous and a selection of Wolf's favourite veggies, cut into strips, all of which she'd prepared before pick-up.

'I like swimming tea,' Wolf informed her through a mouthful of raw carrot.

'Good, and I like little boys who sit properly at the table and don't speak with their mouth full,' she said, sounding almost exactly like her own mother had nearly thirty years before.

They arrived at the community centre with time to spare, which gave Millie a chance to have a quick look round. 'I can't believe we live less than twenty minutes down the road and have never been here before!' She beamed at the lady at reception. 'We're here for my son's swimming lesson.'

'Great, let me tick his name off the list,' the woman said pleasantly. 'Right, you can get to the changing rooms by going down this corridor and out of the door at the end and you'll find them in the building just on your right. Then if you go back outside and wait on the poolside, Wolf's teacher will be there to take a register.'

'Okay, great,' Millie said. 'Though, how do you get to the pool from the changing rooms once you're back outside?'

'Sorry? You can't miss it. The pool is literally right there.'

'But inside another building?' Millie asked, confused.

'Well, no, it's an outdoor pool! Sorry, didn't you know?'

The woman looked worried. Although not as worried as Millie.

'Erm, no, I didn't, but great, thank you,' she said brightly. 'Come on, Wolf, let's get you changed.'

Unfortunately, Millie had dressed for the sweltering air of the leisure centres she remembered from her youth and not the actual outdoors, and the moment she stepped outside, the outdoors began to make itself known. The heavens had well and truly opened and she and Wolf made a run for it to the changing rooms. Once inside, things weren't much better, as the floor was a mass of puddles and broken tiles and the building smelled of a mixture of chlorine, urine and harried parents.

'Here you go, Wolf,' she said, handing him his Peppa Pig bag. 'I'll blow up your armbands while you get your trunks on.'

Once he was ready she led him gingerly across the tiles towards the door.

'Ready, darling?'

'I think so,' Wolf gulped.

Thankfully, the rain had eased off to a miserable drizzle, and she was able to hand Wolf over to the teacher without looking like she'd taken a dip in the pool herself.

'Excellent. Welcome, Wolf, I'm Miss Jones,' the teacher said bracingly. 'Mum, you can watch from under that shelter there.'

Millie breathed a sigh of relief and sidled off to the little covered seating area the teacher had pointed out. Wolfie looked so small and vulnerable standing on the side of the pool next to the other kids. There were a few boys who were at least a head taller than him, but she noticed there were also a handful of little girls and one other boy who looked even younger – and more scared – than Wolf. It was clear the teachers knew what they were doing, though, as by the end of the half-hour lesson, even that scared little boy was splashing around happily in the shallow end with his armbands on.

'Okay, class, everyone out up the steps, please,' Miss Jones called. 'Well done, what a brilliant lesson! I think we'll have you all swimming like fishes in double-quick time. Right, off you go and I'll see you next week.'

'That was ace, Mummy!' Wolfie said, giving her a wet, chloriney hug. 'Did you see me be a fish? Miss Jones said I did really well kicking my legs; did you see?'

'I did, Wolfie, and you were brilliant! Now, let's get you dressed before the rain really starts up again and we both have to swim home!'

'Ooh, do you think we might have to swim home? I'd be able to practise my kicking then, wouldn't I?'

'No, darling, I'm sure it will be fine.'

'But, Mummy, you said—'

'I know, Wolfie, but let's concentrate on getting you dressed for now, okay?'

Ten minutes later, they were both rather damp but all their clothing was in the right place. 'Just let me fish my keys out of my bag and then we can go,' Millie said.

'Fish? Mummy, have you got fishes in your bag?'

'Hold on, Wolf, I need to just—'

'Fishes in the water, fishes in the sea, we all jump up with a one, two, THREE!'

'Wolf, shush a minute, I can't hear myself think.'

'I never hear myself think. Mummy, do you always hear yourself think? Am I doing it wrong?' replied Wolf, puzzled.

'WOLF! Just be quiet a minute. I can't find my keys.'

'Did you have them when you left the house, Mummy?'

'Wolf!'

'But that's what you always say to me when I've lost something. You always ask me when I last had it and where I put it.'

'I don't know, Wolf, I thought I'd picked them up on the way out, but they're not in my bag. Damn! And I can't remember if it was this week or next that Bridget said she was away.'

'What's Bridget got to do with it? She smells of talcum powder.' Wolf began kicking the tiles with his wet shoes.

'Stop that. Bridget has the spare key and if she's away I'm not quite sure what we'll do. But don't worry,' she added, seeing the five-year-old's smile begin to waver. 'Let's go back home now and see if Bridget is in. But we need to make sure we don't do any dawdling, Wolf, okay?'

'Yes, Mummy.' Wolf skipped to the door, almost tripping over a broken tile.

'Let's go round this way,' Millie instructed. She walked behind the pool and towards the main road, with Wolf trotting along to keep up with her. As they turned the corner, they walked straight into a woman carrying a large camera bag on one shoulder and rootling around in the handbag she had on her other arm.

'Oh, god, sorry,' she said. 'I was just looking for my umbrella and didn't see you there. Let me help you pick up those bags. Is this yours?' she asked Wolf with a smile. 'My niece used to love Peppa Pig, too.'

'Yes, thank you. Peppa's on my swimming bag,' Wolf said, displaying his damp bag for her to see. Meanwhile, the rain had ramped up again and Millie, who hadn't remembered to pick up her umbrella – or it seemed her keys – was getting wet.

'Come on, Wolfie, we're late and we're getting soaked,' she said taking his wrist and walking towards the road. 'We need to visit Bridget, remember.'

'The lady liked my Peppa bag,' Wolf said proudly.

'She did, yes, now you'll need to walk a bit faster than that, come on.'

By the time they arrived at Bridget's they were well and truly wet through, but at least Millie could hear footsteps when she rang the doorbell.

'Bridget! Thank god you're in. Would I be able to get the spare key, please, I seem to have left mine at home.'

'Oh, lovey, look at you both, you're wringing wet. Come in, come in and dry off a bit while I find that key for you. Philip, look who's here, it's Amanda and the wee bairn.'

Thankfully, Bridget located the key pretty quickly, so Millie and an uncharacteristically quiet Wolf were able to go home.

'Thanks, Bridget, you're a lifesaver. Again! I'd better get Wolfie here home as he looks dead on his feet.'

'I'm not dead!' Wolf protested.

Bridget chuckled. 'Off you go, lovey, and make sure the wee boy has some hot milk to warm him up before bed, won't you.'

Millie shot her son a warning look. 'I will, Bridget, don't worry. See you soon, bye.'

'But, Mummy, I'm a big boy now and I don't have hot milk – or cold milk – before bed,' Wolf said to her as they reached their own front door.

'I know, darling, but Bridget was just being kind. Now, let's get you into your pyjamas. You can watch an episode of *Dino Hunt* before bed as a special treat if you promise to sit quietly.'

Millie breathed a long sigh of relief once Wolf was asleep, she'd located her missing keys and had stood under a hot shower to warm up her numb feet. Tonight was definitely a large glass of wine kind of night, she decided. Armed with a tumbler of Merlot (she couldn't even be bothered to reach into the top cupboard for a wine glass and settled for one of the non-breakable Wolfie-proof melamine beakers she always kept close at hand), she picked up her phone and opened her Photos app. In a gap between the raindrops, she'd somehow managed to snap an image of Wolf kicking his legs in glee while holding on to the side of the pool. And while the sky was almost charcoal in colour and the water a dull grey, once she'd got to work with Photoshop, she was able to create a decent-looking image for Instagram. She sat back to admire her handiwork and took a long sip of wine, then posted the picture and a short caption on to her feed. If Louis was looking, he was definitely going to be impressed with her ability to sort out swimming lessons for Wolf in such a beautiful environment! It wasn't just professional footballers who could live the luxury life, she mused. Well, the appearance of a luxury life, at least.

Chapter Eleven

Bell

Bell walked round the outside of the community centre, clutching her umbrella once she'd managed to find it at the bottom of her bag, her stomach a washing machine of anxiety as her new camera Rich had couriered over banged against her hip in its bag. A few hours earlier she'd confessed to Suze how nervous she was.

'It feels like that first day of uni all over again,' she'd said. 'I've got weird butterflies about whether any of the other people in the class will like me and whether I'll like any of them. I've no idea what to expect. All the bumpf the community centre gave me just says they welcome all ages and backgrounds, so they could all be eighty years old and trying to use the 35mm cameras they were given for their birthdays in 1992.'

'They could all be eighty years old and trying to use the iPads and top-of-the-range photo lenses they bought with their own money last week,' Suze had pointed out. 'Or, they could be people just like you who want to understand the basics of how to take a good picture. You need to relax, Bellster. Plus, you never know, you might meet the man of your dreams and swan off into the sunset together – though not until you've taken a picture of it, obvs.'

'Suze, I'm going to say this one more time: I split up with the man I'd been with for ten years less than three months ago. I'm much more interested in making some new friends than *boy*friends.'

'Am I not enough for you?' Suze had asked, all mock hurt.

'You're enough for anyone, frankly! But I'm being serious. I don't have many other people in my life I can truly call a friend. Plus, you have Ellie – and, no, of course that doesn't stop us being brilliant mates, but you need to make sure you're spending enough time with her and not just trying to look after me and my broken heart.' She'd smiled sadly, then rocked her shoulders back and sat up straighter. 'How often as grown-ups do we get the opportunity to make a whole new group of friends who live in the same area? The only comparison I can think of is an NCT group like Cosette joined. And for obvious reasons, I wouldn't have much in common with a group of pregnant women and their partners talking about water births and epidurals, so it's important I make a good impression on my classmates tonight.'

'And you will, sweetie. How could anyone not want to be friends with you? And, no, I'm not being sarcastic. For once I am being serious, too. Bell Makepeace, you're a smart, funny and super-strong woman who's going to have people queuing up to be your friend. Plus, you're going to take some properly good pictures, I just know it.'

Bell still wasn't convinced, but took a deep breath and headed for the large door on the other side of the building she'd somehow managed to miss the first time. The building itself was a fairly unappealing 1970s box with peeling white paint on the outside, and there were further buildings that had been added on at various points over the years, but as she shook out her dripping umbrella and peered inside, Bell was cheered by the bright lights and warmth coming from the reception area.

'Don't suppose you know where the evening classes are held, do you?' asked a Scottish voice behind her. Bell looked back and saw a tall, willowy woman wearing a crochet dress accessorised with a boho belt, knee-high boots and a beret worn at a jaunty angle; it didn't look like it was doing much to shelter her hair from the rain.

'Are you here for the photography class too? I think it's just through here. I'm Bell, by the way.'

'Laura,' she replied. 'Thank god the photography class is inside. I can't believe all those people swimming out there. You won't catch me in my cossie in the fresh air unless I'm in the south of France.'

Bell giggled. 'I'm excited to try it out when the weather gets a bit warmer. Maybe we'll have another heatwave this summer.'

'Hmm, we'll see. Right, in here, I imagine,' Laura said,

pointing to the notice on the door of the room they'd come to at the end of the corridor.

The two of them walked into a room that instantly reminded Bell of a primary-school classroom, except the tables and chairs were made for adults. It smelled vaguely of disinfectant and biscuits, and several tables had been pushed together to form one big bank in the centre. There was a large desk at the back of the room, which Bell assumed was where their teacher would stand, and which was currently covered in equipment and sheets of paper.

'Aha, more keen photographers, I presume! I'm Sheila.' A short, round lady in her fifties or sixties came over to Bell and Laura and offered her hand. 'Hi there, welcome to our first class.'

When they'd both introduced themselves and Sheila had ticked them off her list, she took them over to the three other people in the room. 'This is Rita, Tony and, erm, forgive me, yes, Ben, that's it.'

'Me and Rita have been married thirty years,' beamed Tony, shaking their hands.

'Yes, and it's felt like three hundred,' deadpanned Rita. 'We were just telling young Ben here that these classes are a Christmas present from our son Steven. I think he was so sick of all the photos we took of him when he was little with only half a head or a thumb over the flash that, now our first grandchild is due, he doesn't want the little blighter to go through the same, eh, Tone? Ah, look, here are some more arrivals.'

As Rita and Tony went over to nosy at who else had come in the door, Bell decided she already loved them. Laura marched forward to stand intimidatingly close to Ben, who'd been lounging quietly against the wall.

'So, you're Ben are you? And what's your story?'

'W-what do you mean?' he stammered.

'Well, everyone has a reason for signing up for these classes, don't they? Me, I'm convinced my husband is playing away but I need evidence, so I need to gen up on how to use this thing so I can catch them on film *in flagrante*, if you know what I mean!'

Both Ben and Bell stared at her open-mouthed.

'Ach, get away, only joshing! Sure, my shite ex did do the dirty on me, but I didn't need no photos in order to kick him out. But that's another story. Anyway, I'm a single mum and don't get much chance to get out and do something for myself, so thought I'd sign up for some new life skills as I managed to guilt-trip my mum into offering to babysit. It was either photography tonight or pottery tomorrow evening, so here I am. What about you?' she asked, turning back to Ben, who looked slightly more relaxed now he knew Laura wasn't really planning on becoming an undercover paparazzo.

'Erm, well, I moved to the area for work a few months ago and don't really know anyone locally, so thought this would be a good way to meet people and maybe make some friends,' he said, gazing at the floor in embarrassment. Bell decided to step in and save him from whatever scary remark

Laura was about to make next. She was baring her teeth at him in what must have been a smile, but she rather looked like she might eat him!

'Oh good, me too,' Bell smiled at him. 'Although I'm not new to the area, I've actually lived here for ages, but, er, I didn't realise this place was here, so I thought I'd try it out.'

Sheila clapped her hands and everyone turned towards her. 'Right, I think everyone's here, so if you all want to get a cup of coffee from the urn over there, and there might even be some chocolate digestives as I managed not to eat them all. And then grab a seat in the middle and let's have a chat.'

As they went about pouring drinks, Bell could see that everyone was checking each other out with varying degrees of subtlety. Laura was staring beadily at people as they added milk to their mugs, Rita and Tony were jollying things along and making sure everyone had a drink, Ben was standing slightly apart, stirring his drink continually, and then there were the others, who Bell hadn't been introduced to yet. She counted eight of them, six of whom all looked in their late teens and were dressed almost identically in a uniform of skinny ripped jeans, T-shirts and Converse; the three girls wore scarves tied at the front of their heads, while the boys all sported tortoiseshell glasses. The final two members of the class were a bit older, a man and woman in their mid-twenties who had clearly come together as they barely left each other's side, even when they were making their drinks. Unsurprisingly, they chose two chairs next to each other.

'So I thought we'd start by going round the table,

introducing ourselves and telling the group one thing we'd each like to get out of these classes,' Sheila announced, joyfully clapping her hands together. Bell's heart sank. She hated 'ice-breaker games' at the best of times, and especially when it felt like they were about to begin some kind of therapy session rather than a run-through of Photoshop and aperture sizes. She caught Ben's eye and gave him an 'I know!' look.

'Right, I'll go first,' instructed Sheila, still beaming at them all. 'So my name's Sheila and I've been teaching photography for twenty years now. It may surprise you to know that before I started teaching I worked with models such as Twiggy and bands like The Beautiful South and Lisa Stansfield.' A ripple of admiration went round the group as they digested the information that their tutor had actually photographed some famous people and so was probably half-way decent, though Bell could hear one of the uniformed girls next to her ask the boy beside her who Lisa Stansfield was. 'And the one thing I want to get out of these classes is to find some new talent!' Sheila finished with a flourish. 'You never know, any of you in this room might turn out to be a David Bailey or Bryan Adams.'

'Isn't he a singer?' whispered the girl to her neighbour.

'Right, who's next?' Sheila asked. 'Let's go this way, so, Bell, isn't it?'

For a second Bell froze, the nerves she'd felt earlier taking a stranglehold round her throat like tendrils. 'Hi, I'm Bell.' She cleared her throat, shaking off the invisible constrictions. 'I work for a fashion website and love going to photo shoots and seeing professional photographers do their thing, so what I'd like to get out of these classes is understanding what pros do and maybe have a bit of a go myself,' she added shyly.

Bell could feel the girl next to her sit up a little straighter in her chair when she heard her mention what she did for her job, and she smiled to herself, rather pleased she hadn't come across as a complete loser.

Next up were the uniform brigade, and she learned they were all students at the local sixth-form college and wanted to do something they could add to their UCAS form when they were applying for university later in the year, and photography sounded 'cool'. The young couple turned out to be Lynne and Marcus who professed themselves to be 'just best friends who want to do a hobby together'. Bell glanced at Laura when they said this and she raised an eyebrow and smirked back. Rita and Tony explained about their lack of even rudimentary photography prowess and Laura repeated her desire to learn a new life skill, 'and maybe posh up my Insta account'.

'Lovely!' Sheila smiled. 'And finally, our thirteenth member. Ben, do you want to introduce yourself?'

'Yes, well, I'm Ben …' Bell gave him an encouraging smile across the table. 'And I used to love messing about with my dad's old camera when I was younger but never took it any further, so I'd like to know how to use one properly. And, um, maybe make some new friends in the process.'

'Hurray!' declared Sheila happily. 'Let's give ourselves a round of applause, well done, everyone!' The group clapped half-heartedly. 'Call that a round of applause?' cried Sheila aghast. 'Come on now!' With lots of good-natured eye-rolling at each other, everyone clapped a bit harder and Rita even managed a whoop. 'Excellent, I knew you could do it. Right, has everyone brought the most important thing with them – other than themselves – this evening? Good, so if you could all unpack your cameras and place them in front of you on the desk; don't worry about lenses and add-ons, let's just see what we're dealing with and then I can examine your equipment properly.'

The group broke into a collective snicker, but half an hour later they'd all had their equipment intimately examined by Sheila and she called them back together.

'Right, it seems we have quite an array of different cameras among us,' she said. 'So I think the best way forward is for us to split into a few smaller groups. Let's say Rita and Tony as you're sharing a camera, and then Lou and Mel, why don't you join them. And Lynne and Marcus, you could form a group with Ian, Paul, Matt and Lisa, yes? And then that leaves Laura, Bell and Ben. Excellent. Does each group want to take a corner of the room and why don't you tell each other what you already know about the cameras you're holding and then we'll come back together and one person from each sub-group can report back to us all about what you've learned. Brilliant, this is going to be great fun!' Sheila clapped her hands together again and the class slowly began to split into three huddles.

'Pff, I'm glad I'm not stuck with those teenagers,' Laura

grinned at Bell and Ben. 'I imagine their idea of a camera is an iPhone Ten.'

'Well, smartphones are not to be sniffed at,' Ben said quietly. 'Especially when they cost the best part of a grand.'

'Christ, I paid a couple of hundred for my camera and I thought I was splashing out,' Laura shrugged. 'Ach well, I'm sure it will do the job, but I know next to nothing about what any of the bits do. What about you, Bell, do you have any idea about yours – that looks like the real deal?'

'Well, I bought it off my brother-in-law for a steal as he was going to eBay it,' she confessed. 'So who knows. But I've had a bit of a play around with it at home and it seems pretty techy. I know it's got sixteen megapixels and I've got some extra lenses I can attach to it, but other than that, I'm not really sure.'

'Shit, I hope you know a bit more than us, Ben, or we're going to look like right numpties,' Laura cackled.

'Well, I'm no expert, but I think mine is basically a newer model of yours, Bell, so it's got a few more megapixels and a three-inch touchscreen, and can take video in 4k rather than just HD,' he explained. Bell nodded along, but Laura just shook her head.

'I hope Sheila remembers this is a beginners' class – I barely understand megapixels let alone anything else. Right, well, Ben, you best be our speaker. Now we've got that out of the way, what do you think about the rest of the group?'

'They seem nice?' Ben said non-committally.

'Although I don't know which of the uniform brigade is

Lou and which is Ian, to be honest,' Bell said as Laura cackled again. 'Rita and Tony are great, aren't they? And who knows about Lynne and Marcus, they seem to have quite a close "friendship".'

'Ha, you're hilarious, Bell! Well, I think us three should stick together. We're all around the same age, aren't we? I'm forty-one. Ben, you must be about that? Forty-two? Well, you look good on it! And Bell, I'm guessing you're late thirties.'

'Yep, I'm forty later this year.' Bell blanched.

'See, thought so. Anyway, looks like Sheila wants us back in the group now. Come on, let's see if the others know anything at all about the great big hunks of black plastic in their hands.'

An hour later, everyone was packing their stuff away, their minds awash with new information.

'Don't forget your homework is to take a photograph that sums up who you are and then we'll discuss them all next week. If you could email me your pics by next Monday evening, I can put them all on to a memory stick and we can use the centre's big TV to display them. Right, it's been a joy, class dismissed!' Sheila cried, clapping her hands together. Everyone followed her lead and started clapping and Laura joined in with Rita and Tony's whooping.

'Aww, that was fun, don't you think?' Laura asked Bell and Ben as the three of them said their goodbyes and walked outside to the puddle-filled car park, though the rain seemed to have stopped for now at least. 'Shall we swap numbers? I'm going to need someone to WhatsApp later in the week when I'm failing to take a good picture that "sums up who I am", whatever that means!'

Armed with her new friends' details, Bell strolled towards her house, occasionally grinning as she relived some of the evening's more hilarious moments. The uniform brigade had taken the show-and-tell about their cameras pretty seriously, but Rita had been the spokesperson for her group and it seemed she and Tony knew even less than Laura when it came to technical specs. The whole class had been in hysterics when she'd attempted to explain how her camera worked: 'Well, there's an On button and a screen, and then I think you just press the big red photo button and you're done!' Sheila had assured them she would explain all the basics like focal length and aperture as the classes went on, and Ben had nodded beside her, clearly knowing more about what this all meant than the rest of them. Bell thought that he was a bit of an enigma. Good-looking, pretty fit – yes, Bell had noticed his biceps! – pleasant and friendly if a bit quiet; she was surprised he had struggled to make any friends locally.

'You could say the same about yourself – except for the muscles!' she heard Suze's voice say in her head. God, now she was hearing voices. It had been a long day and it was only when she was scrabbling around in her bag for her keys that Bell remembered that she'd bumped into a lady with her son before she'd gone inside for the class. At the time, she'd been ninety per cent certain it had been Millie/@mi_bestlife and her son Wolf, but now, hours later, she wasn't so sure. Although, how many kids were called Wolfie, for god's sake? And the woman did seem to have the same dark hair as the girl she'd seen arguing on her phone a few weeks ago, though today she hadn't noticed it was gorgeous and glossy like last time. But it had to have been her, surely? Bell grabbed her phone, clicked the Instagram app and scrolled through her feed in search of a post from @mi_bestlife.

'Aha, here we go.'

> Such a lovely afternoon seeing my water baby swim a whole length of the pool today – watch out for him at the 2020 Olympics! #waterbaby #MiniOlympian #thisisfive #myboy

The picture that accompanied it was of a tranquil pool, softly lit by rays of yellow light, and a cute little boy grinning out from the water. Bell zoomed into the picture and could see his fingers were white from clinging on so tightly to the side of the pool, and his thin little arms were spotted with goose-bumps. 'Poor kid!' she exclaimed out loud. The image had clearly used all of Photoshop's many enhancements, as well as several Instagram filters. If Bell didn't know better, she would have sworn that Wolfie was smiling out from a gorgeous private pool somewhere in the Med – and it seemed Mille's followers were just as convinced, from the many comments hashtagged with #enjoyyourholibobs and #bringonthesun-shine. She shook her head, amazed at the apparent difference between Millie's Insta life and her actual life.

Chapter Twelve

Bell

Despite now knowing the exact route she needed to take, Bell hadn't been able to stop herself racing across town from work to her photography class every Wednesday, so more often than not she found she had time to kill outside the community centre while she waited for Laura, Ben and the rest of the group to arrive. She'd kept her eyes peeled for another glimpse of Millie and Wolf, but their paths hadn't crossed since that first week of class. However, by the end of March the weather was starting to brighten up, so instead of skulking undercover in the hallway, Bell took the opportunity to stroll over to the pool. With the early evening sun just peeping through the meringue-filled clouds, the water looked most inviting – until she realised that she could see the pale, goosebumped flesh of the kids being taught to swim. She'd promised herself she would start going swimming after Easter, which was only a couple of weeks away, and she tried not to shiver as she watched the children splashing around. She glanced at her watch and realised she needed to get a move on if she wasn't going to be late.

'Where have you been?' Laura said when she saw Bell sidle in just as the rest of the group were pouring their coffee and making their way over to the table and chairs in the centre of the room. 'I was worried you weren't going to turn up – it's not like you to miss out on snaffling a choccy digestive. There are only boring custard creams left now.'

Bell grinned at her new friend's all-too accurate knowledge of her love of the best biscuits. 'I got held up,' she said. 'How are you, Lau, had a good week? Where's Ben?'

'Don't worry, loverboy is just getting you a coffee and some kind of inferior biscuit,' Laura smirked. She liked to tease Bell that Ben had a thing for her, and while Ben was both handsome and attentive, holding the door for her and showing her the right setting on her camera, Bell had no idea how he – or in fact she – felt, so she usually laughed off Laura's nudge-nudge-wink-wink comments.

'Bell!' Ben's face broke into a smile as he came over with two mugs and placed one in front of her. 'You made it!'

'Was there was ever any doubt?' she smiled back. 'Thanks for this. How did you two get on with your shadow pictures, I know you said on the WhatsApp group you were struggling, Laura?'

Last week's homework had been to take an image that demonstrated their ability to use shadows to create an interesting photo, although Bell wasn't too sure she – or any of the rest of the group – had much ability to do anything quite so technical when it came to taking pictures. Nevertheless, she continued to enjoy the class every Wednesday and knew she was learning loads, despite not necessarily being able to put it all into practice.

'It was *so* hard,' groaned Laura. 'In the end I took a picture of the stairwell in my block of flats, emailed it over to Sheila and hoped for the best. You said you'd got yours in early, Ben, didn't you? You're such a suck-up!'

'Well, I was happy with the image I'd taken so thought I'd submit it there and then as I knew I'd be busy the rest of the week.'

'Why were you so busy? Ooh, did you have a date?' Laura probed.

Seeing him start to look uncomfortable, Bell stepped in. 'Laura, leave Ben alone for god's sake! I tried to take my shot of some peonies I bought from M&S the other day, but it was just a bit *meh*. Oh well, I'm sure Sheila will tell us what she thinks in a minute.'

They were starting to get used to Sheila's critiques. For a woman who was generally so jolly, when it came to their pictures she was proving brutal. However, for all the criticisms she gave, she always found something positive to comment on, and it did feel that as the weeks went on every member of the class was getting a bit better, even Rita.

'Okay, class,' Sheila called, clapping her hands together. 'Welcome, everybody. Let's start this evening's proceedings by reviewing our homework images. We'll begin with this one, which is yours, Laura. What does everyone think?' A few people mumbled a comment, but no one wanted to be the first to speak up. 'Well, I think the pattern of the carved staircase is a brilliant subject for a photo, although I'm not sure the lighting is quite right to create the most effective shadow. I think you needed a ray of sunlight shining into the hallway rather than just the artificial light of a bulb, maybe, but it's a good try.'

Bell nudged her friend and smiled, and she noticed Laura let out a breath – it was clear she'd been more invested in the shot than her laid-back demeanour had shown. Sheila continued to go through the group's images, highlighting what they all needed to work on, although thankfully Bell got off fairly lightly: 'I love the pop of colour the pink flowers bring, but because the background is so busy you lose some of the effects of the shadows. Less is more next time.'

Then she brought up an image that made everyone sit up a bit straighter.

'This is Ben's photo, and I think you'll agree it's brilliant.'

The whole class started talking at once, exclaiming over Ben's use of an early evening sunset in the park to make a tableau of children and dog shadows. It had created a joyful, fun image using just the subjects' shapes against the fading sunlight. Only Ben was silent, but despite his cheeks reddening, Bell could see he was pleased by the reaction to his picture.

After lecturing them about not only the way Ben's photo looked, but also the technical know-how behind it, which made the rest of the group slightly less pleased with their own efforts in comparison to his, Sheila finally moved on to that week's lesson about focal length. An hour later, however, most of the class were little the wiser.

'I had absolutely no idea what Sheila was saying for the last twenty minutes,' Tony announced loudly as he waited in the corridor for Rita to finish her chat with Lynne and Marcus.

'I took some notes, but who knows if I'll be able to make sense of them back at home,' Bell confessed.

'Oh well, we'll just have to get Ben to explain it to us, won't we,' chimed in Laura with a cackle. 'Though it's a pity we can't copy his homework like I did at school back in the day.'

'You'll be just fine, Laura,' Ben coaxed. 'It's all about the detail this week.'

'We'll see,' she sighed. 'Right, see you next Wednesday, gang, and good luck with your zooms!'

Bell was on a high when she returned home, until she remembered Colin's latest email, which had hit her inbox that morning. Cosette had convinced her she should borrow some money and buy him out, but he was now digging his heels in after one of the three estate agent valuations had come in substantially higher than the other two. He, of course, felt she should pay the top-end price, whereas Bell believed an average of the three figures felt most fair. His email that afternoon had advised her that he had engaged a solicitor and suggested she do the same. Meanwhile, she was being hounded by estate agents left, right and centre about whether she wanted to put the house on the market and buy somewhere else. Just thinking about the whole mess made her feel a bit sick and completely out of her depth.

In the absence of anything in the cupboard that looked immediately dinner-worthy, she rootled around for the emergency Wagon Wheel she knew was hidden behind the muesli for situations where nothing else but a chocolate, marshmallowy, biscuity treat would do.

Worrying about Colin's demands was one of those situations.

She hated that their ten-year relationship had been effectively boiled down to an argument over five thousand pounds. Despite being at odds over the value of the house, Colin had asked to come over and remove the last of his things from his former home, including *that* faux-leather sofa.

Absolutely, of course, as soon as you like. In fact, I'm away until Easter Monday so you could come and get it on Good Friday.

Thank you for your suggestion, Bell. However, that Friday isn't very convenient for me, so it will have to be the Monday afternoon. I think it will be good to speak face to face. And I'll take the TV with me, too, as I paid the whole cost of it myself last year. I trust that's okay?

At least she could now buy a TV the size she wanted – and that would fit in the lounge without swamping it – Bell reasoned, but now she would actually have to see Colin in real life, as she'd be back from Cosette's by then.

Bell arrived in Devon on the Friday of Easter weekend after battling engineering works and replacement bus services on her train journey down. She gratefully took a large gulp of wine from the glass Rich had handed to her as she came through the door, before being joyfully jumped on by her excitable niece and slightly more serious-looking nephew.

'We've got two whole weeks off school now! Are you staying the whole holidays with us, Auntie Belly?' asked Sophie, using the affectionate nickname she had come up with years before and refused to drop despite Cosette's protestations it was rude ('It's funny, Mummy, and Auntie Belly doesn't mind!).

'Sadly, I have to go home on Sunday afternoon, but that still gives us loads of time to have some fun, doesn't it? I was thinking you two could take me down to the beach tomorrow, that's if you're not too embarrassed to be seen with your auntie now you're head boy of the school, Oli?' Bell said with a smile at her nephew.

'Of course not!' he cried. 'Though, maybe I'll call you Auntie Bell if there's anyone around. I can show you where all the crabs have been – there were loads a couple of weeks ago so I hope they're all still there. We saw a massive one and Sophie was scared of it.'

'I wasn't!' she protested loudly to her brother. 'But I didn't like its horrible claws,' she whispered to Bell and shuddered. 'And its eyes were looking at me like it wanted to eat me.'

Once the kids were in bed, Cosette questioned Bell intently about Colin's latest demands.

'I think you should make a stand and give Colin a best and final offer for his half of the house and see what he says,' Rich pronounced.

Bell nodded. 'You're probably right. I was just hoping Col would be a bit, well, *human* about it – he was the one who walked out, after all. But maybe I need to get firm about it.'

'He's not the man I thought he was, that's for sure!' Cosette said heatedly. 'I always thought of him as a mild-mannered gentleman type, but he's proving himself to be anything but by being so difficult with all this house business.'

'I guess we never really know anyone properly except ourselves,' shrugged Bell, the wine making her feel a bit maudlin.

'Well, I'd say I know Rich inside and out! Wouldn't you say the same, dear husband?' Cosette asked, pouring the last of the wine into her glass.

'Ye-es,' Rich replied, glancing at his wife. 'But I do think Bell has a point. You're inside your own head all day, every day, but you're never inside anyone else's so you can never truly know what they're thinking. You just have to make assumptions based on what they've done and said in the past. And I guess people sometimes change, so you can never really "know" someone inside and out.'

'Hmm.' Cosette was clearly not convinced. 'Well, anyway,

I'm glad Colin is showing his true colours as at least you know you did the right thing breaking up with him.'

'I didn't have any choice – he was the one doing the breaking up,' Bell laughed. 'But you're right, it's much easier to see a person's flaws when you're looking at them from a distance. You can just gloss over the bad bits when you see someone day in, day out.'

'Of course, I don't have any bad bits,' Rich grinned. 'As I'm sure you'd agree, Cosette?'

'Yep, you are perfect in every way,' she said sweetly. 'Except when you ask me where your clean shirts for work are, despite not putting the washing machine on all week, or when you forget to buy a birthday card for your own mother and then ask me to go out in my lunch hour to get one for you, or when it's your day to drop the kids off at school and you don't check they've picked up their lunches so when I get home I find two sets of soggy-looking sandwiches sitting on the kitchen side, or—'

'Okay, maybe I do have my bad bits after all,' he butted in. 'But they just make me more lovable, right?'

Cosette and Bell simply stared at him.

'Okay, okay, my bad bits really are bad and I'll go and flagellate myself in the kitchen. While I'm there I might be so good as to get some tiramisu out of the fridge. Would that help you overlook some of the *really* bad bits, maybe?'

'I thought you'd never ask!' Cosette smiled. 'And grab another bottle of wine while you're at it.'

*

When Bell arrived home two days later, she was both tired and revived. Spending forty-eight hours with an eight-year-old and a ten-year-old was exhausting. Even though, as kids went, they were super-well-behaved, she still had no idea how Cosette and Rich coped with being parents and working so hard in their day jobs. But they had also helped her put everything into perspective. Watching the wonder on Oli's face when he'd shown her the crab he'd caught, and the joy Sophie got from finding the shiniest shell on the beach and handing it to her to keep safe, had softened Bell around the edges. She decided that if the sun came out like the weather forecast had promised, she was going to head to the community centre and its outdoor pool the very next morning. If her afternoon was to be filled by an awkward encounter with her ex, she might as well enjoy the hours that were her own.

It was with mixed feelings that Bell set out for the centre the next day. It might not have been raining, but it was only 17 degrees and she wasn't exactly looking forward to stripping off to just her cossie and feeling the icy sting of the water. Nevertheless, she'd promised herself she was going to go swimming, so swimming was what she was going to do. It was bank holiday Monday, but she was still surprised how busy the pool looked when she made her way round the back of the building. The sun was trying to peep out from behind the clouds by the time she shuffled out of the changing rooms with her beach towel wrapped tightly round her white skin. She'd shaved her legs specially for the occasion, but she was still very self-conscious as she hung her towel on a spare peg and made her way gingerly towards the steps.

'I find it's best to just jump in and get it over with!' came a friendly voice from the water. 'I could see you hesitating, but once you're in the water it's not nearly so bad.'

'Really? It looks pretty cold!' Bell smiled, dipping her toe in and quickly removing it.

'Well, it's not exactly tropical, that's true, but if you keep moving you'll be all right. On that note, I'd better do another length! Enjoy your swim.' And the woman swam effortlessly off towards the deep end.

'Come on, Bell,' she said to herself. 'It's now or never!' She wasn't quite brave enough to jump in, but she lowered herself down the steps and gasped as the water hit first her thighs, then her stomach and then the tops of her arms. But she was in and hadn't had a heart attack from the shock so she supposed that was something. And after a few lengths, she found the woman had been right – while it would have been pushing it to say she was in any way warm, she wasn't as shivery as she'd presumed she'd be. By her fifth length she was able to concentrate less on the temperature of the water and more on taking a look around.

Her half of the pool was divided into lanes and three or four people like her were fairly happily swimming up and down. The other half was where all the splashing and shouting was coming from, as children jumped in, shrieked, swam around a bit and did handstands in the shallow end. There were various parents in the water trying to keep their offspring under control, as well as a few on the pool edge, blowing up armbands, fetching the long, thin noodle buoyancy aids as and when they got chucked out of the water, and holding out towels to shivering children. Out of the corner of her eye, Bell noticed some long, dark hair, and when she pushed off the side to begin swimming her next length, she slowed her stroke and turned her head – there was Millie bending down to talk to her son as she pushed bright-orange bands on to his arms. She watched as Wolf slid into the pool at the shallow end and began kicking excitedly as he held on to the side.

Bell was tiring herself by this point as her lack of any kind of recent exercise began to make itself known, but she was pretty pleased with the twenty-four lengths she'd already done and decided she could just about manage another two.

Breathless and weary, she hauled herself out of the water and on to the side, where she turned and briefly surveyed the scene with satisfaction. Then suddenly, out of nowhere, she felt a painful impact on her right knee and within a split second she heard a huge smack as a small body slammed into hers.

Just managing to keep her balance and not tumble back into the pool, Bell made a vain grab for the child, but he'd already hit the floor and ended up in a heap on the side. There was a beat of silence when all sorts of awful thoughts flashed through her mind and then a loud, plaintive wail.

'Muuuuuuuuummy!'

Bell desperately looked around but his mummy was nowhere to be seen.

Chapter Thirteen

Millie

With the permanent drizzle and chocolate-egg-overload tantrums, Easter weekend seemed to have gone on for ever, so when the rain stopped and Wolfie had asked whether they could go swimming before lunch on Monday, Millie had agreed to stand around on the poolside for half an hour far more enthusiastically than she would normally have done.

'Great idea, Wolfie, a bit of fresh air will do us both good, I think,' she'd said, reaching for his Peppa Pig bag and praying she'd remembered to wash his swimming stuff. The idea of finding an uninviting, chloriney plastic bag filled with damp clothes in the bottom didn't bear thinking about. Thankfully, for once, her parenting skills had passed the test and the only thing she found in the corner of his bag were some discarded underpants that Wolf had refused to put back on after his lesson the week before, preferring to go commando under his jeans. Millie hadn't had the strength to argue.

They had set off to the pool in good spirits, Wolfie chatting away about all the things they could do during the school holidays, which seemed to consist mostly of going swimming and playing football in the park, followed by pizza and ice cream.

'You might get bored if we do that every day,' she'd reasoned. 'But I'm sure we can come up with other things we can do. If the weather stays like this, we could pitch the tent in the garden and have a sleepover outside, or maybe we could go to the zoo to see the penguins one day?'

'Won't the penguins cost a lot of money?' he'd asked, looking up at Millie with concern in his big brown eyes.

'I'm sure we could stretch to a few days out,' she'd smiled in return. Well, that's what credit cards were for, right?

'Yay!' Wolf had skipped along beside her. 'I think I'd also like to do the outside sleepover, but only if you're there too, Mummy. I might be a bit scared on my own. Though I'd probably be okay,' he'd added quickly.

'Remember what I said, Wolfie? It's okay to be scared sometimes, especially if you tell me about it and I can make it all better. Of course I'll be there but we'll have to wrap up warm in our sleeping bags as it will be quite cold at night.'

'Big Ted can keep us warm,' Wolf had said solemnly. 'He's very furry and when I hug him in bed he makes all my face go hot after a while. Mummy, can you come in the pool with me today?'

'I haven't brought my swimming things,' Millie had replied with a sad shake of her head (of course she hadn't brought them, she had no intention of swimming in that pool until the summer – and maybe not even then!). 'But maybe when you get really good at swimming, you can teach me how to do it and then I'll come in the pool with you – deal?'

'Deal, Mummy. Aren't you going to put your hand out – we have to spit on our hands and then shake them when it's a deal, remember.'

Damn Louis for teaching Wolfie that, she'd thought. 'Later, darling,' she'd said. 'Look, we're here now so you can get in the pool and show me how well you can kick those legs.'

Wolf hadn't been in the pool long before Millie felt her phone vibrate in her pocket. She pulled it out and saw Louis' name on the display. She contemplated not answering, but decided to get whatever it was he wanted out of the way now. Waving at Wolfie – who was happily playing in the shallow end and seemed to be getting on well with a little girl, the two competing to make the biggest splashes – she stepped away from the noise of the pool and jabbed at her phone. 'Louis?'

'Millie, how are you?!' Louis bellowed down the phone. It sounded like he was in some kind of tunnel that was full of people. 'Is Wolfie there? We just drew one-all with Everton in the cup and I've got Shane Lowe next to me and he wants to say hello to Wolf – he's Wolfie's favourite player, after me, of course.'

'That's a lovely idea,' Millie said calmly. 'But I'm afraid he's swimming at the moment so can't come to the phone.'

'Can't you just go and get him?'

'Not really, no, I'm afraid. He's playing with a friend.'

'What friend?'

'A girl. I'm not sure what her name is.'

'You're letting our little boy play with random children you don't even know in the swimming pool? For god's sake, Millie, next you'll be sending him out to buy sweets from the shop on his own. He's only four. Is he okay?'

Millie turned towards the pool, which she'd wandered quite a way from, and just made out Wolf still splashing away. 'He's five. And of course he is! I can't believe you're questioning my parenting. *Again*,' she hissed into her phone. She walked a few more metres away from the pool in case Wolf's super-powered hearing could detect she was having another argument with his dad. 'You're unbelievable, Louis.'

'*I'm* unbelievable? You're the one putting our kid at risk!'

'How dare you!'

There was a beat of silence.

'Look, Millie,' he replied, his voice lowering, losing its sharpness and taking on a honeyed, syrupy tone. 'Let's rewind, hey? I just want to speak to my son and give him the surprise of talking to his favourite player. Could you possibly see if he can get out of the swimming pool and come to the phone?'

'Okay,' she sighed. 'Hold on and let me see what—'

'Muuuuuuuuummy!'

'Shit, I have to go, Louis, I'll call you back.'

'But—'

Shoving the phone into her pocket, Millie spun round and ran towards the pool area and the direction of the screams. 'Wolfie?' she cried.

'Mummy!'

Wolf was on the poolside, far nearer the deep end than when she'd seen him splashing about in the water just minutes earlier, and wrapped in an unfamiliar towel as an unfamiliar woman inspected several grazes on his knee.

'Wolfie, what on earth has happened? And who are you?' she asked the woman sharply. 'Come here, Wolf.'

'The lady is called Bell and she picked me up when I felled over,' Wolfie announced proudly. 'She says I'm really brave as I hardly cried at all.' He wiped his arm across his eyes and Millie couldn't tell whether they were wet from tears or just from being in the pool. 'Look at my leg, Mummy! There was loads and loads of blood, but it's all gone now.'

'Don't worry, there was hardly any blood really,' smiled the lady. 'Just a few tiny drops. But Wolf was right about my name – I'm Bell. And you're Millie, aren't you?'

'How do you know my name?' All the adrenaline of the last few minutes was draining out of Millie's system and she felt herself sway as she clutched Wolf tightly, but she didn't want the other woman to see any weakness.

'I've, erm, seen you around.' She saw Bell's cheeks flame. 'And I, erm, follow you on Instagram.'

'Mummy, I'm cold! I think I've done enough swimming today. Can we get changed and go inside and get a drink and a treat, pleeeeeease?'

'Yes, yes, of course, Wolfie. Erm, thank you, Bell, for looking after him. What do you say, Wolfie?'

'Thank you, Bell! Do you want to come to the swimming café with us? Mummy might even let us all have hot chocolate with marshmallows in it if we're good.'

'Well, that's very kind, thank you, Wolf, but I'm not sure your mummy . . .' She tailed off, clearly embarrassed.

'Of course, let me buy you a hot chocolate – or any other drink, obviously – to say thank you properly,' Millie said politely. The last thing she wanted right now was to have to be nice to some random woman, but the random woman had looked after Wolfie and he clearly thought they were all best friends, so she couldn't really refuse.

'Well, if you're sure?' Bell said tentatively as Wolf cheered.

Millie nodded. 'We'll see you in the café in the main building when you're ready.'

She decided Wolf could do without a shower for once and he was so excited about his promised hot chocolate that he got dressed without his usual dawdling, which meant Millie could get him settled at a table in the café before Bell made an appearance.

'Ooh, now that hot chocolate does look special!' Bell grinned at Wolf when she came and joined them a little while later.

'It is de-licious!' Wolf declared, smacking his lips together then spooning another huge mound of cream and marshmallows into his mouth.

'Mind you don't make yourself sick,' smiled Millie, stroking his hair, just glad that the little boy seemed largely unaffected by what had happened at the pool. 'Bell, what can I get you to drink?'

'Well, I think it would be rude not to indulge in a hot chocolate when they look like that, wouldn't you say, Wolf?'

Wolf nodded seriously at her and said, 'Yes, maybe it would be rude to the lady behind the counter if you didn't have one, cos she had a big smile on her face when she squirted the cream on top in a big whooshy way like this!' He made a very flamboyant show of spraying cream and waving his arms around to demonstrate.

'Careful, Wolfie. Right, hot chocolate coming up for you, Bell, and maybe I'll even have one too,' Millie said.

'Did you enjoy your swimming today?' Millie could hear Bell asking him while she went to get the drinks.

'Yes, I did, thank you. Me and Martha were seeing who could do the biggest splashing and I kicked my legs really, really, really hard and all the water went all over her. It was funny!' he grinned. 'But then I couldn't see Mummy so I went up the steps to find her and got a bit scared. And then I fell over and you saved me.' He gazed up at Bell with huge chocolate-brown eyes.

'Here you go,' said Millie, placing a steaming mug in front of Bell. 'There's enough sugar in there to keep us all on a high for the next half an hour!'

'Thanks so much, Millie,' Bell smiled across at her. 'Wolf was just telling me how much he likes swimming. Have you been coming to the centre for a while?'

'No, only a few weeks, really. I hadn't realised it was an outdoor pool so it was a bit of a shock at first. Although I'm not as brave as you and Wolfie. I haven't actually managed to get in the water myself yet.'

'Mummy's scared of the cold water,' Wolf confided in Bell.

'I'm not scared, Wolf, I'm just waiting till the weather's a bit warmer.'

'It's okay to say you're scared, Mummy, remember?'

Millie had to laugh. 'You're right, Wolfie, it is okay, and yes, maybe I'm a little bit scared. But when the sun comes out, I'll definitely come in the pool with you. Now, do you want to have a play with the toys in the corner there while Bell and I finish our drinks? I thought I spied a Spider-Man baddie in the toybox.'

'*Yes!*' Wolf shouted, and then lowered his voice a tiny bit when Millie shot him a warning look. 'I hope they have a Batman too.' And then he ran off to find out.

'He's such a sweetie,' Bell said as they both watched him excitedly pick out figurines and cars from the box and plonk himself down on the playmat.

'Well, some of the time,' Millie grimaced. 'Anyway, do you live locally?'

'Yes, I'm not far. I didn't realise this place was here at all until I started doing photography classes here in the evening, and then I saw the pool and couldn't resist – though you're right to wait till it gets a bit sunnier as the water is pretty cold!'

'Oh, I didn't know they did evening classes, too. I'd love to do a dressmaking course or something, although obviously with Wolfie that's impossible. Not that I mind,' she added quickly.

'Does his dad not live nearby then?' Bell asked. 'Sorry, that was really nosy of me – tell me to mind my own business if you want!'

'It's fine, don't worry. No, he lives in Birmingham, which is where Wolfie and I lived too – until I needed to put some distance between Louis and me. We came down here a few years ago as I thought it was near enough to London if I needed to go there for work, but not too close, you know? Louis still sees Wolf for a weekend every month, though he's not the most – how should I put this? – *reliable.* But he does love Wolf and Wolf adores him, so it could be worse, I suppose.'

'It doesn't sound much fun, though.' Bell wrinkled her nose. 'Have you got family close by who can help out with Wolf?'

'My dad lives in Wales with his new wife and they're getting on a bit, so sadly not, and I don't have a great network of friends here either. So, yes, it's not always much fun. But enough of my moaning! Have you lived round here long?'

'Yes, about eight years. I used to live with my boyfriend, but now I, erm, don't.'

Millie glanced at her. 'You can also tell me to mind my

own business if you want, but there's clearly a bit of a story there . . .?'

'Well, same old, same old, I'm afraid: I think boyfriend of ten years is about to propose at long last, instead he's about to tell me it's all over. Then I see him on Facebook cosying up to his junior colleague. Cliché central!'

'God, what is wrong with them?' Millie sighed. 'Although me and Louis were never really going to last after he started playing in the Premiership. There were too many temptations and he was just too young and too weak. And I had to focus on Wolf at that point.'

'You must be so proud of Wolf, though, he's so well-mannered and polite.'

'I'm glad you think so, though if you spent ten minutes with him at home you might change your mind! But I shouldn't be hard on him, he is really well-behaved most of the time and he's had a lot to deal with since me and his dad split up. I wish he was as happy at school as he is at home.'

'Does he not like school then? He seemed happy enough chatting away to other kids in the pool.'

'I don't know, not as much as he did when he started, anyway. He never really talks about his class or his teacher, unless it's to do with football, of course, but he's definitely quieter than he used to be after school.' Millie sighed. 'But you know what kids are like . . . How many have you and your ex got?'

'Oh, well I don't have any children myself, but my niece and nephew keep me on my toes! I've just spent the weekend with them and, much as it's fun, I was quite glad to leave them with my sister and brother-in-law and head back home – I love them but they're exhausting!'

'Sorry, I didn't realise; you were really good with Wolfie, so I could tell you'd clearly been around kids quite a bit.' She stopped, embarrassed that she'd only known Bell two seconds and she'd already put her foot in it.

Bell waved her away, before suddenly frowning. 'Wait, rewind a little. Did you say Wolf's dad's a Premier League player?' Millie nodded a little warily as Bell gawped. 'Ooh, who is he? Who does he play for?'

'*Was* a Premier League player, yes. Nowadays he's a bit too old and his Achilles is a bit too weak for him to be in the top flight. But he does okay. And, yes, he's still often to be found in the gossip pages with his arm round another blonde reality star with plumped-up lips and overly whitened teeth.' Millie half smiled, half grimaced.

'Ha! Glad to see he too is living up to the clichés!' Bell laughed.

'Oh, yes. His mates used to call him King Louis because he "ruled" the pitch, but now I secretly call him that because, like King Louie in *The Jungle Book*, he's the King of the Swingers, always swinging from one girl to the next! God, Wolfie loves that film, but I can barely watch it anymore because all I can think about is him!'

'That's hilarious – King of the Swingers, love it!'

'Yep, or KL for short. What a sad pair we are,' Millie laughed. 'Here I am in my early thirties, a single mum barely making ends meet, with an admittedly lovely five-year-old son, still pissed off that the only man I've ever really loved cheated on me. And you're in your, what, mid-thirties?, still pissed off that the man you gave ten years of your life to is reliving his youth.'

'True, except I'm in my late thirties, well, very late thirties,' Bell smiled. 'And except that you're also a super-successful Instagram star and I'm also a slightly less successful fashion marketeer. We rock!'

'You work in fashion?' Millie asked, leaning forward in her seat.

'Yes, for Style It Out? I'm marketing manager there.'

'Oh, I think I met a few people from there a couple of months ago. Joe and Clara maybe?'

'Ciara, but, yes, I remember them being so excited they'd met you and @MAFlash. You must know all those other vloggers and Insta stars too?'

'Aww, bless them! Yeah, I know all that lot. Well, I don't actually *know* them, obviously, except Sonya, as we go way back. I know them on social media and I bump into them at events and stuff.' She shrugged.

'Do you enjoy being on Instagram?' Bell asked her curiously.

'Well, I guess it's become my job really, so I don't know whether enjoy is the right word. Why do you ask?'

Bell squirmed in her seat and played with the empty cup on the table in front of her. 'It's just . . . I've read your Instagram and, well, you seem like a different person in real life from the one you come across as in your posts.' She glanced at Millie, but then carried on, 'I kind of thought you were this scarily sorted earth mother who had all her shit together and lived this amazing, glamorous life buying the latest must-have dress every day and feeding your perfect son home-made organic food worthy of *MasterChef*. And, well, without meaning to be rude, that's not really true, is it?'

Millie stared at her, then began toying with her own mug, before looking Bell straight in the eye. 'I can't believe you're questioning my integrity like that.'

'I – I didn't mean to cause offence or anything,' Bell stammered, before seeming to catch herself and sitting up a bit straighter. 'But meeting you in real life, well, you're just not like I thought you'd be. You're more fun, for one thing.'

There was a beat of silence, then Mille's face began to twitch and she let out a honk of laughter. 'Me, an earth mother? You're right, nothing could be further from the truth!' she giggled. 'Of course it's all made up – it's Instagram, that's what everyone does!' She could see that Bell was looking confused, so, still laughing, she reached across the table and touched her arm. 'Sorry, I was only messing with you, I *definitely* don't have any integrity left!' More seriously, she added, 'But I have to pay the bills and feed Wolfie, and if that means creating a fantasy life then so be it. I mean, everyone uses filters and Photoshops their pictures, right? Whether it's Insta or Twitter or Facebook or whatever, it's not real, is it?'

'I guess not.' Bell nodded slowly. 'But isn't it exhausting always pretending to be something you're not? Couldn't you just filter real life a little so it's all a version of reality, rather than another dimension entirely?'

'Maybe,' Millie said. 'But I'm not sure that's what my followers actually want to see. And I'm not sure it's what brands want to see – and ultimately, they're the ones paying me to promote their products so I can buy Wolfie new school uniform.'

'Mummy said we have to watch how much money we're spending,' said a voice beside them suddenly. 'But money is not as important as being happy and healthy or as important as me, is it, Mummy?'

'That's right, Wolfie,' replied Millie, ruffling his hair and flashing Bell a wry smile.

'Right, I'd better be going. I've got a date with my ex.' Bell grimaced as she gazed around the now empty café. 'Oops, I bet the poor lady behind the counter has been waiting ages for us to leave so she can have her break, too.'

'God, I can't believe it's that late!' Millie exclaimed. 'We've obviously been yakking for ever, though it only feels like a few minutes.'

'It was fun, wasn't it? We should do it again sometime.' Bell said. 'I'm going to try to come swimming every Saturday afternoon, so if you and Wolf happen to be free to come to the pool around the same time, why don't we grab coffee again afterwards? Only if you want to, obviously,' she added.

Millie was surprised at how much she really did want to. 'Sounds like a plan!' she replied. 'You'll be able to practise your swimming every week between lessons, Wolfie.'

'Yes! Soon I'll be the bestest in the class at kicking water. But, Mummy, aren't I going to Daddy's on Friday and Saturday and Sunday?' Wolf counted the days off on his fingers and explained to Bell, 'We're having three sleepovers. And Daddy said he'd take me to his friend's house again so we can play on the unicorn and flamingo in the water.'

'Sh—sugar! Yes, you're right again, Wolf! Silly Mummy for forgetting that's next weekend. Oh well, we'll just have to come in two weekends' time to see Bell, won't we?'

'Can I have hot chocolate again?'

'We'll see. Coat on now, and say goodbye to Bell, then make sure you haven't left anything over by the play area.'

'Bye bye, Bell Bell,' Wolfie sang, giving her a sticky hug, then ran over to the toys to pick up his bag, all the while singing to himself.

'He is very cute,' Bell smiled. 'And I was going to say, though you may have other plans obviously as you don't have Wolf at the weekend, but if you are around and still fancy going for a drink on Saturday, we could always upgrade our coffee to a glass of wine?'

'Oh, well . . .'

'Don't worry, I really won't be offended if you say no,' the older woman smiled gently.

'No, it's just I was a bit surprised, that's all. I'm sure you don't want to be spending your Saturday night listening to me go on about myself when you could be out on the town with your friends.'

'I feel a bit old to be "out on the town",' Bell laughed.

'These days if I'm not tucked up in bed by midnight I know I'll pay for it the next day. It's definitely true that hangovers get worse with age, you know.'

'You are not that old! And a glass of wine on Saturday would be lovely.'

They exchanged numbers and Millie collected up both Wolfie and their bags.

'See you soon, Wolf,' waved Bell outside the community centre. 'And see you on Saturday, Millie.'

She turned and walked off down the road and Millie allowed herself a second to bask in the warmth of Bell's hug. Despite the two of them being very different people, there was something about Bell that drew Millie to her. And Wolf clearly felt the same.

'Mummy, Bell has a beautiful smile, doesn't she? If she had more yellowy long hair, she would look like a princess as she's always smiling.'

'Princesses can have hair any colour or length, darling. But, yes, Bell does have a lovely smile. I'm glad you like her because I do too. I hope she might become a good friend.'

'Like I'm friends with Eva at school?'

'Yes. I don't think I know Eva – is she a new friend?'

'Yes, she was nice to me when Zach said something mean. And now he's mean about Eva too.'

'Well, Zach doesn't sound like a very nice person to me so you should make sure you tell the teacher if he says anything horrible to you or Eva again, Wolfie,' she said lightly while inside seething that anyone could be nasty to her precious son. 'Anyway, once we get home, we can write that list of things you want to do during the holidays and we'll see how many of them we can tick off. We can even ask Eva's mummy if she wants to come and play one day if you'd like.'

'Yes! I can show her my Batman lair cos she likes superheroes too. Do you think Bell likes superheroes?'

'I'm not sure, darling, but why don't you ask her in a couple of weeks.'

Once Wolf was in bed, still muttering about Bell and superheroes in his sleep, Millie picked up her phone and put up a quick 'outfit of the day' post on her grid. Thankfully, she'd taken a few pictures in different clothes in the changing room of the big department store in town last week, so, with a few quick Photoshop tweaks, she was able to make it look like the sofa she was sitting on was somewhere much more plush than the battered seating area of a badly lit fitting room. She looked down at the pyjama bottoms and baggy top she was currently wearing and giggled to herself. Thankfully, Instagram was a one-way mirror and no one was able to take a peek inside the real world of Millie Morley.

She glanced at her phone as the notifications piled up and then her heart sank. She quickly blocked the trolls and deleted their comments, but almost immediately another couple appeared.

@WhatAFake You can't get rid of us that easily, you silly bitch. How's that son of yours tonight. Hope your not giving him nightmares with that shit scary face of yours.

@MillieIsAFake What do you know about style? Sweet FA, that's what, ha!

@abigail__stylista Don't listen to the trolls @mi_bestlife! We all love your #ootd – keep 'em coming!

@ClaireBeary You look LIT Millie – love that skirt on you. Love seeing you on my feed #gorge

She 'Liked' some of the positive comments and tried to feel good about what they were saying. But as she lay in bed it was the trolls' words that crept inside her head and spread their poison, smothering every good thought from the day.

Chapter Fourteen

Bell

Swimming always made Bell ravenous. As she shovelled cheese on toast into her mouth, she surveyed her little house from behind the kitchen counter. Once Colin arrived and removed the sofa and TV, the lounge would look much bigger, and she couldn't wait to get stuck in to making the room exactly how she wanted it. She realised she'd been living in a kind of limbo for the past few months, surrounded by Colin's things, but not by Colin himself.

She'd first met Colin at her friend Anne's wedding (she was another mate she barely spoke to anymore, though for the life of her Bell couldn't say why, other than her own laziness at keeping in touch). They'd been set up by Anne, who had got swept away in her own little Bridezilla world and decided to matchmake all her single friends at her wedding, joking that she needed to find them a date before they all hit the heady heights of (whisper it) *thirty* and got left on the shelf for ever. It hadn't gone down all that well with her four single friends at first, but once Bell found herself seated between two not only single but also good-looking men, she'd decided to stop complaining about the interfering bride. Plus, there was a free bar.

Joel, the cheeky chappy on her left, kept topping up her glass and won her over with his jokes and hilarious anecdotes about nights out with his rugby team, so it was a total no-brainer when he asked for her number after they'd slipped out for a fag and a snog at the end of the main course. Later that evening, Joel joined the rugby set to do shots followed by pints on repeat until they all threw up, and Bell had the chance to talk to Colin. They'd got happily tipsy and pissed themselves laughing over the truly cringe-worthy first dance the happy couple had specially choreographed for the occasion. Bell had spent much of the night trying to convince him to hit the dance floor with her, but he was content to watch everyone else go at it, so they'd bonded by making full use of the free alcohol and got steadily drunker from the sidelines. Finally, she'd managed to pull Colin on to the dance floor near the end of the evening and he'd proved himself to be a surprisingly good mover once the alcohol had warmed up his hips. But after one song, he was done and drifted back to the table. Bell had joined the throngs for 'Come On Eileen', then, red-faced, sweaty and high on adrenaline, had bounded over to Colin and kissed him squarely on the lips. He hadn't taken much persuading to respond, and they'd spent the next half an hour snogging like teenagers.

The bride had of course been delighted that her match-making had paid off and made Bell promise that whichever guy called and eventually asked her to be his wife, she would be chief bridesmaid.

As she ate her way through her hangover the next day, Bell had decided Joel seemed the most fun of the two guys, if she had to choose between them, especially since she'd never been out with such a muscle man before and she quite fancied checking out his six-pack. She'd been a little disappointed when it was Colin who had called that evening and asked her to go for a drink. But he was so nice on the phone that, feeling sorry for him, she'd agreed she'd meet him that Friday night, thinking she'd cancel if Joel phoned her too. He didn't.

Five days later Bell had rocked up at the Bull's Head, not really expecting much from her second choice of date. So she'd been pleasantly surprised and then pleasantly happy when they'd re-enacted their wedding kissing a couple of beers later. And the rest was history. Well, it was definitely history now, anyway.

The doorbell rang and Bell stuffed the last of her cheese on toast into her mouth and glanced at her watch. It was so like Colin to be there ten minutes before they'd agreed. She felt very strange opening the door of their house to him.

'Colin, you're here. Early,' she said.

'Bell, nice to see you,' he replied and walked into the hall. Bell had no idea what the etiquette was for greeting an ex, especially one who seemed to have moved on embarrassingly quickly from their ten-year relationship. But thankfully Col didn't lean in for either a perfunctory kiss or matey hug and instead strode through to the lounge and pulled out a tape measure like he owned the place. Which he did. Although only half of it and not for much longer, Bell sincerely hoped.

'How's Tina?' Bell blurted out before her brain could tell her mouth to act cool.

Colin looked at her warily. 'So you heard, then?'

It took all Bell's determination not to spit 'I could hardly miss the news thanks to *that* photo!', and instead merely raise her eyebrows at him.

'Yeah, we're going out now,' Colin said with a self-satisfied smile. She willed her face to remain expressionless as he smugly added, 'I mean, we're boyfriend and girlfriend.'

'Congratulations,' Bell deadpanned. 'Sounds like you've been busy.'

'Yeah, work's been crazy with the start of the new tax year. We're pulling all-nighters at the moment. Hopefully the bonus at the end of it will make it all worthwhile, though,' he laughed.

Bell suddenly wondered why she had never noticed the weird hee-haw sound Colin made when he found something funny, and she shuddered as he continued to bray to himself.

He looked up from typing the measurements of the sofa into his phone and said, 'It looks bigger in here than I remember, even before I move the sofa. Thankfully it will fit in the van I've got outside, so that's a relief. You won't know what to do with all the space once that's gone, though, will you?'

'I'm sure I can find something to fill it,' Bell smiled

through gritted teeth. Despite the swirl of rage and – if she was honest – *disgust* building inside her, she resolved to take charge and be the grown-up in the situation. 'You mentioned you wanted to talk face to face, but I think the money side is best left to our lawyers, don't you agree?'

'I just want us both to get a fair deal, Bell,' Colin said, tilting his head to one side and looking concerned. He quickly straightened up again and began playing with one of the cushions on the sofa. 'But that's not what I wanted to talk about, actually. It's about me and Tina.'

Bell stared at him. 'I'm not sure I need to know the details of "you and Tina", to be honest.'

'I just thought you should know. We're not just girlfriend and boyfriend, we're living together.'

'That was quick!' she replied, her eyebrows almost hitting her hairline. 'I guess that's double congratulations for you then. Unless there's something else you want to tell me?'

'What? Oh god, no, Tina's not pregnant, definitely not.' Colin shook his head vigorously. Bell idly mused that his shocked expression was pretty pathetic considering he was the one breaking the news to her.

'Well, good, as long as you're happy,' she said stiffly. 'I'll be in the kitchen if you want to move your things.' She glanced at the large transit van parked outside and suddenly had an awful thought. 'Tina's not out there waiting to help you load the sofa into the van, is she?'

'Of course not! Matt's here to help me, don't worry.'

Bell didn't reply but sidled off into the kitchen and spent

the next half an hour moving stuff around in one of the kitchen cupboards, pretending to tidy things up.

A little while later, Colin stuck his head round the kitchen door. 'Bell? I think we're done.'

'Great, well, hope you've got everything?'

He came into the room so they were separated by only the kitchen island. 'Look, Bell, I'm really sorry things turned out the way they did. I never wanted to hurt you,' he added in his most heartfelt voice. 'But it was the right thing to do. For both of us.'

Bell summoned the last of her strength and raised her head to meet his eyes. 'You're right, it was.'

They stood in silence for what seemed an interminable length of time but was probably just a few seconds, before Colin said, 'I'll see myself out, then. Take care, Bell.'

As the front door closed behind him, Bell felt all the emotion she'd been pushing down inside for the past half an hour rise up into her throat, and suddenly she was sobbing. She cried for the two twenty-somethings kissing like teenagers in the pub on their first date. She cried for the two thirty-somethings sitting on the faux-leather sofa watching a box set and barely speaking or touching each other but not knowing how to fix it. She cried for their past and for what might have been their future. But most of all she cried for her thirty-nine-year-old, single self.

'Did you have a good Easter?' Suze asked when she strode into the office the following day.

'If you mean did I spend Sunday gorging on more chocolate than both my niece and nephew put together – a hell of a feat I can tell you – then, yes, I did, thank you!' Bell replied with a smile. 'Did you and Els have a nice time at your parents'?' Weirdly, she'd slept really well after yesterday's crying session and felt more refreshed and clear-headed than she had in weeks.

'You look different,' Suze said suspiciously. 'That floral tea-dress looks very pretty on you and there's something about you today. You haven't had a shag, have you?'

'Suze!'

'What? Well, if you've not spent the whole weekend with a hot man why do you look so sparkly?'

'I had a lovely time with Cosette and the kids and then Colin came round for his stuff, which wasn't that pleasant but I'll fill you in on that later. And I went swimming at the community centre and made a new friend.'

'A new male friend?'

'No! Actually it's Millie.'

'Millie? Who's Millie?'

'@mi_bestlife to you.'

'Ooh, well now, tell me everything! Did you confess you'd been stalking her?'

'I absolutely, definitely haven't been stalking her, whatever you say. I've just seen her around a few times. And, no, I didn't mention that to her. She's really nice and we had fun chatting. And her son is *so* cute. We're going for a drink on Saturday, in fact.'

'You're going for a drink with her son?'

'Suze. He is five years old. No, I asked Millie if she wanted to go for a glass of wine together as Wolf is with his dad at the weekend.'

'Hasn't she got loads of friends her own age to go out with? No offence, obv.'

'She's not that much younger than me – only about eight or nine years. And, no, I think she's a bit lonely. She doesn't have any friends or family nearby.'

'Oh. I always get the feeling on social media that she's got loads of mates and hangs out with all the cool people.'

'The wonders of Instagram, eh? You can literally live whatever life you want. Or pretend to, anyway.'

'I don't do any pretending on Insta. Although I did nearly kill my mum in real life over the weekend.'

'Oh god, was she being a nightmare again?'

'She just kept doing The Face whenever me and Els held hands in public or even looked at each other. It wasn't as if we were snogging in the street or anything – I know that if we did, Mum would feel she could never show her face in the neighbourhood again!'

'I thought she'd got a bit better about things?'

'She has. To a point. It's fine when we're inside and she doesn't have to keep up the pretence to the neighbours that her daughter has brought her "friend" home for the weekend. But whenever we were out and met anyone she knew, she couldn't possibly refer to Els as my "girlfriend". Can you imagine the scandal! Seriously, it's all getting a bit boring now. Anyway, I *didn't* murder my mother and we all had a nice weekend, so, you know, it could have been worse. Are you going to tell Ciara and Joe about your new BFF? Your stock is about to go up in this office, let me tell you!'

'No, definitely not. And Millie is not my BFF. Although, if you keep going on about her, you might find yourself relegated to the bottom of the friendship league. Is it time for one of those coffees you make so expertly yet?'

'Flattery will get you everywhere, Bellster. Two cups of Suzie Special coming up. Although, hold on, did you say Colin came round for his stuff? As in, you were there too? And? How did it go?'

'Make me that coffee and I'll give you all the gory details.'

That afternoon, in between emails and meetings, Bell found a few minutes to message Ben. She'd been struggling with their current photography project, mainly, she had to admit, because she hadn't given it as much thought as she would normally, what with going to Cosette's over Easter and dealing with Colin. But also because she just couldn't get her head round the technicalities. And she was already late sending her 'blurry but in a good way' picture (what did that even mean?) to Sheila.

> Hi Ben, hope you had a lovely Easter. This is a bit of an SOS I'm afraid – I need help! With my photography, I mean *smiley face emoji* Don't suppose you have a handy cheat sheet that will explain blur (not the

band, obv, I know everything there is to know about Damon and Alex from years of staring at posters of them on my wall) and make this week's homework less painful? Yours, in hope, Bell x

Within a few minutes, her phone notified her Ben had WhatsApped her back.

Lovely to hear from you, Bell. I had a fairly quiet Easter as I was in the office most of the time trying to get this deal sewn up (I won't bore you with the long and tedious details, but by tomorrow night hopefully both our client and my boss will be happy and I can have a nice lie-down). Of course I'm always happy to help with an SOS situation. Annoyingly, I can't get away from the office this evening, otherwise I'd suggest me popping over to yours (I could check out those Blur posters while I'm there) or for you to bring your camera to the pub (god knows I could do with a drink to get through this deal), but I can talk you through a few pointers over email maybe if you think that would help? Just let me know. Yours, at your service, Ben x

Hmm, your work sounds like quite a big deal (see what I did there?!) at the moment, so if you can't spare the time to talk me through non-Britpop-related blur, do not worry. I will take my mauling from Sheila with good grace. But if you did have a minute to send me a step-by-step guide to perfecting it (a bit like when you let your mate at school copy your homework, but not quite as bad?), then I would be sure to return the favour in the future. In fact, I've just had a thought. My photographer friend Ade invited me to help him at a fashion shoot on Friday afternoon next week to learn about camera stuff – do you think you could sneak off work and come too? He's brilliant and properly knows his stuff, and you could totally geek out with him about aperture or whatever. What do you think? Yours, in excited anticipation, B x

I prefer my friends non-mauled, so I am going to write you that email right now. And I can't think of a better way to spend a Friday afternoon than learning about camera stuff with you, so I'm in – as long as Ade doesn't mind me tagging along? Although I'm going to be at a serious disadvantage as I don't know the first thing about fashion shoots. I'm going to have to think very hard about what to wear. Do I go for I'm-so-cool-I-just-rolled-out-of-bed-like-this nonchalance or I'm-so-fashion-forward-I'm-totally-setting-a-new-trend-in-this-shell-suit-I wore-as-a-teenager-in-the-nineties casualness? Decisions, decisions . . .

'What's so funny?' Bell looked up to see Suze staring at her curiously. 'You've been glued to your phone for the last fifteen minutes giggling to yourself. Come on, share the joke.'

'It's just Cosette telling me about what the kids got up to today,' Bell covered quickly. Her friend gave her a look that said 'I don't believe you but I'm not quite sure why' so Bell smiled angelically back at her and opened a spreadsheet.

She kept her promise to herself and braved the pool again on Saturday afternoon. She wasn't sure she'd ever get used to the shock of the icy water as she lowered herself into the water, but once she was in and moving, she found she relished stretching her limbs out and kicking her way up and down. And even when it began drizzling, she didn't care – somehow swimming in the outdoors in the rain felt liberating. She'd arranged to meet Millie in town so she made sure she had enough time to go home first as she didn't fancy getting ready for her night out in the changing room with its peeling mirrors and old-school hairdryers that looked like a 'have you had an accident that wasn't your fault?' injury waiting to happen.

Back home, she debated what to wear for a drink with a fashionista. Jeans and a black top felt too boring even dressed up with heels, but a going-out dress felt too, well, dressy. Her phone pinged with a message from Suze.

> Send me a picture of what you're wearing.

> I'm currently not wearing anything except my underwear, so no.

> I hope it's matching!

> Suze. Just tell me what to wear.

> I like that dress you wore the other day. But lose the clompy black boots. What about those embroidered flats you bought – try them and send me a pic.

Bell did as her friend suggested and Suze sent a message full of thumbs-up emojis.

> Now do that smoky eye I taught you and go all out with your lippy. And don't forget to have fun! Lots of love x

She'd attached an image of her and Els blowing her a kiss. Bell grinned and did as she was told, then grabbed her bag and pulled the front door closed behind her.

She got to the bus stop just as a double-decker was pulling in, and as she sat looking out of the window at the setting sun, Bell suddenly realised she'd barely thought about Colin all day. Instead her head had been filled with swimming, looking forward to seeing her new friend that evening, and all the things she'd learned that week about photography. Thanks to Ben's bullet-pointed email, she'd been able to produce a passable photo for that week's class and Sheila had barely mauled her at all. She'd even managed to get a decent shot for this week's homework in the bag, plus she had the shoot with Ade to look forward to, so her head was full of shutter speeds and ISO settings.

She got off the bus and snapped the dusky sky as it began to turn from a light fluffy pink to a deep orangey red. Her iPhone was fine, but it was a shame she didn't have her DSLR with her, she thought. It would have made the perfect shot for the theme of 'colour' that the class had been set this week.

She walked into the bar, looked around for Millie and, realising she was first to arrive, decided she might as well order a bottle of wine and two glasses and bagsy the spare booth she'd spotted near the back. She messaged Millie to let her know where to find her and poured two generous glasses of ice-cold Pinot Grigio. She sipped her drink as daintily as she could, but twenty minutes later there was still no sign of Millie or even a message from her.

She messaged Suze, along with a picture of the wine bottle, her empty glass and the remaining full one.

I'm worried I've been stood up . . . *big eyes emoji*

Ha, it's like you're on a date! Although that means more wine for you if she doesn't come! Though I bet she's just running late. Have you done a sweep of the bar for any hot men?

No, I'm mostly staring into my wine like a loser. Actually, I think she's just walked in! Speak later xx

'Bell, I'm so so sorry!' cried Millie, red in the face and flustered. 'I, well, I'd like to say I have a better excuse than falling asleep in the bath, but, erm, I don't. Shit, have you been waiting long?'

'Don't worry, you're here now,' Bell smiled. 'Here you go – cheers!' They clinked glasses and, seeing Millie still looked worried despite gulping down half her wine in one go, Bell topped her up and added, 'I'm not sure there is a better excuse than falling asleep in the bath, to be fair. Lying immersed in warm bubbles surrounded by scented candles is my idea of bliss and guaranteed to make me start snoozing immediately.'

'I'm usually more of a shower girl, but as I had a child-free house for once I decided to treat myself. Obviously I was more tired than I thought. Anyway, glossing over my lateness, did you go swimming today?'

'Yes!' Bell replied proudly. 'I swam forty lengths and only shivered a few times. Fingers crossed we have a nice summer this year and I'll be there every day. Well, maybe not every day, but a lot, anyway.'

'If Wolfie had his way, he'd be there with you! Though I'm still to be convinced about the joys of outdoor swimming.'

'You won't be saying that when it's thirty degrees and you're watching me cooling off in the pool,' Bell grinned. 'That's if I haven't had to move house by then.' She swirled her wine round in the glass. 'My ex is being difficult about me buying him out. Urgh! Sorry, even calling him my "ex" sounds weird to my brain.'

'Hmm, that sounds complicated. Presumably he doesn't want to live in the house himself, so why is he kicking up a fuss? Or is he just being a man?'

'Ha! Though I don't think all men are necessarily obstructive about these things.'

'Just the ones we know, right? Thankfully, Louis owned our house outright, so when Wolf and I moved out we didn't have much to split between us – it was all his to start with. But after ten years you two obviously have a lot to sort out.'

'Yes, I s'pose so, but all the more reason to be human to each other about it, I think. According to Colin, he just wants to make sure it's as fair as possible and he's getting "the best return on his investment". It makes our relationship sound like some kind of financial transaction and not like we spent ten years loving and caring for each other.'

'You must be finding it hard trying to move on after all that time together.'

'Yes,' Bell confessed. 'Though when I'm feeling more practical than emotional, I can see that, actually, it's the best thing that could have happened. Of course, I didn't think that in the beginning and instead drank myself into a miserable stupor. But now I've had a few months to get used to the idea, I can see that Colin was much braver than me and saying he wanted us to split up was actually the kindest thing he ever did for me. Sure, we could have stayed together for another ten years, but it would have been out of laziness on my part. Three months down the line and I'm starting to work out who I am without Colin by my side. Well, some of the time, anyway. The rest of the time, I've been a sobbing mess. But, you know, small steps.'

'Well, you'd never know you'd just been through a huge break-up – you seem so together and sorted, and clearly you know what you want from life,' Millie said.

Bell laughed heartily, though inwardly she was both amazed and pleased that Millie had told her that, even if she didn't really believe her. 'You wouldn't have said that three months ago, I assure you! My friend Suze had to stage an intervention as I didn't leave the house in weeks, except to go to work. But you know what it's like when you just need to hibernate away from everyone. And I was lucky that we didn't have kids – I can't imagine how much harder it is when there are children to think about. How long ago did you break up with Louis?'

'Nearly two and a half years ago now. It was tough at the time, but knowing it was the right decision for me – and Wolf – kept me going.'

'God, it still must have been scary to essentially be a single mum in your twenties having to start again somewhere new, especially after being in a relationship with someone famous.'

'Semi-famous – he's hardly Gareth Bale! But, yes, it was a weird time. Wolf wasn't planned and, despite the fact there was no way I was going to have a termination, neither of us were in any way ready to have a baby. But there we were in our mid-twenties with a newborn and no idea what we were doing. Louis had his football to concentrate on, of course, so he'd either be at training, away playing a match or out "bonding" with the lads, so I kind of had to get on with it on my own. Until one day I woke up and realised I actually couldn't.'

'Why, what happened?'

'A classic case of thinking the way I was feeling was just the baby blues when really I was in the grips of pretty severe post-natal depression. I didn't have much of a support network around me so it wasn't until I took Wolfie to the GP for his jabs when he was about four months old, and the nurse asked me how I was feeling, that suddenly it all came tumbling out. I felt guilty and like a failure, I was barely sleeping and had no energy, and I was still bursting into tears more often than little Wolfie himself. Thankfully, the GP was great and she gave me loads of information about local support groups, which I found massively helpful. I think they gave me an outlet to talk to someone who understood how I was feeling, and things started to get a bit better. My relationship with Louis was really fragile by that point, then I found out he couldn't keep it in his pants and it was kind of the death knell for anything we had left.

'Anyway, I promised myself I wasn't going to go off on one this evening, and we do seem to have been far too serious so far, sorry. Shall I grab us another bottle as we seem to have made short work of this one? And shall I order a few bar snacks to soak some of it up a bit?'

'Ha! I think I may have got a bit carried away – I've never been very good at sipping wine slowly!' Bell laughed. 'So, yes, another bottle and some chips or something would be great. And, Millie, you absolutely were not going on before. I'm glad you're able to talk about what you went through, it must have been awful on your own with a tiny baby feeling like that. But look at you and Wolf now. You're obviously a great mum.'

'Until he has a massive tantrum, and then I'm very much a reach-for-the-wine mum! Speaking of which, I'll be back armed with more vino in a sec.'

When their glasses had been refilled and they were happily stuffing their mouths with triple-cooked chips fried in duck fat and served liberally sprinkled with sea salt, Bell remarked, 'These are yummy, though they should be for seven quid! I do like this bar, but it does slightly have ideas above its station, doesn't it?'

'You should see some of the places I used to go to in Birmingham with Louis. It was hilarious because all the footballers went to these properly posh Michelin-star type restaurants, but most of them, Louis included, were just lads who'd grown up in normal towns with parents who read the *Sun*, worked in Tesco and ate egg and chips for their tea. Suddenly, this whole lifestyle of Veuve Cliquot, truffled eggs and sous-vide potatoes was handed to them on a plate and they didn't know what to do with it. Once we went to this gorgeous restaurant that had got amazing reviews and everyone was talking about, but when they served the escabeche of beetroot with horseradish crumble or whatever it was, Louis just looked scared and hardly ate anything. He was happier having a takeaway from the local Chinese, but he had all this money so he felt he had to spend it on meals out, even if it meant he went hungry.'

'It's a different world.' Bell shook her head. 'And I bet it was a bit of a sea change when you split up and moved down here.'

'It was kind of nice, though,' Millie confessed. 'I was never at home with marble bathrooms and gold taps – again, Louis felt like he had to live up to this footballer lifestyle all his teammates were showing off about, so he did too. It was nice to move into a house I felt comfortable in. And Wolfie was too little to really notice. I missed being able to buy him cute designer outfits, but H&M kids is a thousandth of the price and just as nice really, especially as he seems to grow out of everything the minute I buy it!'

'It's scary how quickly they grow up, isn't it? God, listen to me, I sound nearly eighty not forty!'

'I can't believe you're nearly forty,' Millie smiled.

'I know, sometimes I can't either. But then other times I feel every one of those forty years.' Bell took a sip of her wine. 'I hope you don't mind me asking, but doesn't Louis pay you maintenance for Wolfie? He might not play in the Premiership anymore, but he must be making shitloads still? Sorry, that's the wine talking, you def don't have to answer that,' Bell added, taking another slug from her glass.

'It's lucky that I've drunk just as much as you then, isn't it! Yes, he's supposed to pay me a fair amount each week, but if I get one payment a month I think I'm doing well. I don't think there's anything malicious in it, I actually think he just forgets he has a son sometimes.' She grimaced. 'I can see exactly what you're thinking from your face, and yes, I should probably get some legal advice and put some proper agreements in place at some point.'

'I'd be milking him for everything's he's got if I was you!' burst out Bell, unable to swallow her indignance any longer. 'You should definitely see a lawyer.'

'I know. It's just I don't want to be beholden to him. We're doing okay without his money, it's fine,' Millie replied defiantly.

'That's great if you are, but Wolfie was talking about being careful with money at the pool the other day, wasn't he? And it sounds like you're struggling for cash a bit. Louis must be rolling in it and his money could make all the difference to you.' Aware she definitely wouldn't be saying half of what she'd just come out with if it weren't for the best part of a bottle of wine, Bell softened her tone and reached across to touch Millie's hand. 'Sorry, don't listen to me, I don't know the whole situation, obviously, and who am I to be telling you what to do? The main thing is that Wolf is happy and that you are too.'

'You haven't said anything I don't really know myself, to be honest,' Millie sighed. 'I'm just not sure I have the energy to fight Louis anymore.' There was a pause as she stared into the distance for a few seconds and then continued quietly, 'I guess I'm scared that if I make a fuss about the money, he'll try to take Wolf away from me. And I can't let that happen.'

'Why would he do that? He must know what a good mum you are – just look how happy Wolf is for a start.'

'Well, he wasn't exactly supportive about my PND. He used to joke that I'd had a breakdown or was cracking up. I just can't take the risk that he might use that against me and fight for sole custody.'

'That's so unfair!' Bell cried. 'Christ, you're the one who's almost single-handedly brought Wolf up. Seriously, Millie, you need to get some legal advice and make sure the bastard can't do that.' She took a breath. 'But let's save that for another, more sober day, maybe. Have I told you about the hilarious people in my photography class? They're quite an eclectic mix.'

Millie gave her a grateful look and soon Bell had her in hysterics with her descriptions of Sheila, Rita, Tony and co.

'Ben sounds like a nice guy . . .' Millie said a little later.

'Don't you start, too! He is lovely, yes,' Bell nodded,

smiling as she remembered their WhatsApp conversation a few days before. 'But Suze is convinced we're going to be the biggest love story this country has ever seen, not that she's ever met him, of course. You'd love Suze, you know. She's less scary than Laura, though I think you'd get on with her too, once you've got past her frightening exterior, anyway. But Suze is brilliant. I'm not sure what I'd have done without her the past few months.' The wine was making Bell a bit emotional, and she could feel her eyes filling up.

'She sounds like a good friend,' Millie agreed. 'You're lucky to have someone like that looking out for you.'

Bell pulled herself together. 'I really am. Though you must have made loads of friends through Instagram?'

'It depends on how you define "friends", I guess. Sure, I *know* a lot of people online, but it's not the same *know* as when you see them in the office every day. And when I left Birmingham and came down here, I lost touch with a lot of the mates I used to hang around with. Although, if I'm honest, many of them started drifting away when I had Wolf. I'd gone from party-loving fashion-buyer Millie to a husk of a new mum who wanted to talk about sore boobs and sleep deprivation, and it felt like I didn't have anything in common with my friends anymore.'

'That's sad, you'd have thought they'd have made more of an effort,' Bell said, shaking her head.

'I think a few of them probably did, but by that point I was firmly in the grip of PND and refused to see anyone,' Millie replied.

'Well, now you have me to look out for you so we're all good,' Bell smiled, trying to lighten the rather melancholy atmosphere that had descended. 'I think this calls for another drink! Sambuca?'

'I think I'd better pass, I'm afraid,' Millie laughed. 'I'm definitely going to feel like I've drunk a bottle of wine in the morning and I'm not sure I can cope with feeling like I've drunk a bottle of wine *and* several shots of sambuca, to be honest!'

'You're probably right. Christ, what was I thinking! I'm glad I've got someone a bit more sensible with me. Suze would have been at the bar shouting "shots, shots!" by now. Which would have wiped out tomorrow completely rather than just the morning – I'll still need to stay in bed. I've had a fab time, though. Thank you for coming out, Millie.'

'Thank *you* for inviting me. I haven't had this much fun in ages. Which is a bit sad, really, but I might as well admit the truth.'

'Ha! Well, let's definitely do it again when you next have a child-free weekend. And we're on for coffee next Saturday after swimming, yes?'

'Wolfie would never forgive me if I said no! He's been asking all week when we're going to see you again.'

'Aww, bless him, little does he know what a bad influence I am,' Bell cackled. 'Now, shall we share a taxi home rather than brave the night bus? We saved a few quid on those sambucas, after all.'

Chapter Fifteen

Millie

Millie had suffered through a dull, wine-induced headache all day, and it hadn't been helped by Louis dropping Wolf back full of sugar and overexcitement about his trip to the cinema via the pick'n'mix bar, followed by a stop-off at McDonald's complete with milkshake *and* ice cream. Within an hour of arriving home, Wolf had gone from tearing-round-the-house crazy to moody-and-slumped-on-the-sofa rude. Then he'd topped it off by being sick and coating himself from head to toe in lurid pink vomit that had more than a tinge of strawberry milkshake about it.

Millie wasn't ashamed to admit that she couldn't have been happier when she was finally able to close the door of Wolf's room and head downstairs that evening. Despite him only being home a few hours, it felt like days, especially as he'd worked himself up into such a volcano of tears after the first sickness episode that he'd inevitably vomited again, all over his clean pyjamas and fresh bedclothes. A vomcano, Millie thought to herself wryly.

Once she was in her pyjamas herself and safely ensconced on the sofa with the baby monitor she hadn't used in years, in case Wolfie had any strawberry-flavoured foods left in his tummy to bring up, Millie reached for her phone. She'd posted a Story on her Insta that morning tagging Bell and was pleased to see it had since got thousands of views.

After all the stress of arriving late, she'd had a really fun night, even if they had drunk too much wine. It had been strangely therapeutic to talk to her about her depression after having Wolf. She hadn't spoken about it to anyone for the last few years, mainly because, if she was honest, she still felt embarrassed and guilty about the way she'd felt back then. She'd even taken to apeing Louis and calling it her 'breakdown' in her head whenever she thought about it.

From the moment she'd found out about her pregnancy in the loo cubicle at work, Millie had known she wouldn't be able to get rid of the tiny seed growing inside her. She had absolutely no problem with other people choosing to terminate their pregnancies if that's what they wanted – in fact, she'd even held a friend's hand as she took the pills at the clinic – but instinctively she had known it wasn't what *she* wanted. She hadn't been sure what Louis would say when she told him, but neither had she been prepared for his reaction.

'Sorry, what?' he'd blinked at her over the table in his kitchen where they were eating dinner. 'I don't understand.'

'Well, you're a bit old for me to be explaining about the

birds and the bees, but you know what happens when two people love each other? Sometimes they create a baby,' she grinned, reaching for his hand. 'And for you and me, that "sometime" happened a couple of months ago.'

'But how?' he asked, seemingly completely baffled. 'You're on the Pill.'

'I am, but you know how rubbish I am at remembering to take it sometimes.'

'Have you done this on purpose?' he asked, his eyes huge and round.

'Louis, don't be stupid! But it has happened and we've just got to deal with it.'

'But it happened because of you. Because you forgot to take the Pill?' The confident, muscly footballer sitting opposite Millie seemed to dissolve before her eyes and she'd never seen him look younger – or more scared.

'Because of us both, Louis. My egg, your sperm, you know how it works. Look, I know it will take some getting used to and it's certainly not something I was planning, but we're going to be parents.'

'But I'm only twenty-three.' He looked at her through frightened eyes.

'You'll be twenty-four when the baby's born. And I know, this was hardly how I planned to be spending my mid-twenties either, but there we go.'

'But what about my career? We're on track to get promoted, which will mean we're in the Premiership next season. The actual Premiership, Millie!'

'I know, and here's the thing, it's me this baby is growing inside, me who will have to carry it round for the next seven months, and me who will have to push it out of my lady parts.'

'So I'll still be able to play football?'

'Louis! Have you taken a stupid pill or something? Yes, you'll still be able to play football, in fact, you'll need to play football in order to help me provide for this little thing growing inside me – this little thing that you helped make.'

'But what will my mum and dad say?'

Millie sighed deeply. 'I don't know, Louis. Maybe they'll say, "Congratulations, Louis and Millie, we can't wait to meet our grandchild." Or maybe they won't. But what I can tell you is that I am having this baby whether you like it or not.'

'I never said I didn't want it, Millie!' Louis turned shocked eyes on her. 'I'm not going to make you have an abortion if that's what you're worried about.'

'Nobody can make me have an abortion,' Millie said firmly. 'As I said, I'm having this baby and while I'd very much like you to be part of their – and my – life, I can't and won't make you.'

In response, Louis had burst out crying, and Millie had spent the rest of the evening comforting him. When she woke up the next morning, Louis was on his side smiling expectantly at her.

'I was thinking that now we're going to have a baby, you definitely have to move in!' he'd grinned at her.

Feeling both relieved that she wasn't going to have to bring up their son or daughter on her own, and pretty nauseous thanks to that same unborn son or daughter, Millie would probably have agreed to anything at that point.

Louis quickly seemed to get used to the idea of impending fatherhood, especially as he found he could use it as a display of his general virility when showing off to his teammates. For him, little changed over the next few months. For Millie, everything changed.

She was still loath to give up her house-share, but both Louis' parents and her dad kept saying how silly it was that she had her own place, and that she would have to move in when the baby was born anyway. She knew her dad was anxious about her having a child after only a year with Louis, and the last thing she wanted was for him to worry about her coping with her pregnancy on her own, so a month later she moved the rest of her stuff into Louis' house.

Once they'd got over their initial shock, his parents had been so excited about the prospect of a grandson or granddaughter they'd texted at least twice a day with suggestions about cots or travel systems or breast pumps, none of which Millie had much of a clue about or was that bothered about, if she was honest.

Six months into her pregnancy, she and Louis were over at his parents' house in Staffordshire, a huge modern pile that Louis had paid for and was excessively proud to give to his parents. They were eating Sunday lunch and talking about the previous day's match, in which Louis had scored the only goal of the game, taking his newly promoted side into the top half of the Premiership table.

'We were so proud when we saw you hit that goal on *Match of the Day*,' simpered his mum. 'Such a shame we couldn't come to the game, but we're free for the next few matches, thankfully. It must have been amazing being there and seeing it for real, Millie.'

'It was,' she said, smiling at Louis. 'The crowd went crazy. He was quite the hero.' What she didn't say was that she'd been left to make her own way home from the ground and Louis hadn't reappeared until 4am that morning, when he'd disturbed her already fitful sleep by fondling her breasts and pressing his erection against her thigh. She had murmured something about not hurting the baby and hoped he had drunk enough beer to pass out. Thankfully, he had begun snoring seconds later.

'You know, I was thinking, Mills,' he said now, pointing his knife at her in a way she found quite irritating. 'You don't really need to be doing that job anymore, do you? I mean fashion buying is great and everything, but it's not as if you really enjoy it, do you? Why don't you take your maternity leave early and do something you really want to do, like designing your own clothes or whatever?'

'That's a brilliant idea, Louis! And it's not as if you need the money, is it, Millie?' his mum crooned.

While Millie couldn't think of anything she'd rather do – after all, designing her own fashion range was her dream – she didn't like the way Louis and his mum were ganging up on her and implying that she and the baby were now completely reliant on him.

'Maybe,' she replied. 'Let's see how things go.'

As it happened, a week or so later she was diagnosed with suspected pre-eclampsia and told in no uncertain terms by the specialist at the hospital that she needed to slow right down or she would be admitted to hospital and confined to bed rest for the remainder of her pregnancy. The last three months seemed to drag by. The nursery was all decked out with shiny new baby accoutrements and her hospital bag was packed and waiting by the door. Millie spent hours lying on the sofa watching TV and scrolling through the internet, waiting for Louis to come home from training or another team-bonding night. Most of her friends were at work all day and weren't that sympathetic when she complained about feeling like a beached whale without a cause.

When she eventually went into labour, her overriding emotion was relief, but eighteen hours of pain later, she was unable to feel any emotion at all. By the time she ended up in the operating theatre the following day for an emergency C-section, three short words were playing on repeat in her head: get it out. Thankfully, the doctors did, but Millie was so exhausted by then that as soon as her baby had been shown to her and she'd been stitched back together, all she wanted to do was sleep. However, that was the last thing that was going to happen, as the midwife soon wanted to show her how to get the baby to latch on, and Louis' parents appeared bearing balloons and babygros.

It wasn't until everyone, even Louis, had gone home later that night and she was left with the baby in its cot beside her hospital bed, that Millie's brain was able to process what had happened. She was a mother. And her baby was completely and totally reliant on her.

The first few weeks sped by in a haze of painful breast-feeding, constant nappy-changing and a few snatched hours of sleep. Louis seemed to take to being a father like he had to scoring goals on the football pitch, and he had a knack of jiggling the baby in just the right way to stop him crying. Millie was too exhausted and full of hormones to do more than be thankful he'd actually stopped mewling.

'We really need to decide on a name,' Louis whispered a few days after they'd returned from hospital, when the baby was asleep on his chest and Millie had gingerly sat down on the sofa after putting the washing machine on for seemingly the millionth time.

'I suppose we do,' she replied, mustering a weary smile.

'I was thinking maybe Wolf because I play for Wolves and the baby's our little wolf cub. Then hopefully in a few years we'll have a whole pack!' Louis grinned at her.

Millie screwed up her face. 'What about Jacob or Luke? I've always liked those names.'

'Too Biblical, especially as neither of us is religious. I like Wolf.' Just then, the baby started to wake up, wriggle around and purse his little mouth. 'See, he even knows his own name already!' It was a done deal.

As the months went on, Millie's confidence grew and her

bond with Wolf strengthened as she learned what he needed and when. But her bond with Louis seemed to grow weaker with every month that passed. While he clearly loved being a dad and doted on little Wolfie, he wasn't so interested in the washing and the cleaning and the cooking and the night feeds and the shopping. It frequently caused arguments between them.

'Louis, I'm not asking you to clean the house from top to bottom, just maybe wash your own training kit once in a while so I can concentrate on making sure Wolf has enough clean clothes.'

'But I was out working all day yesterday and I'm tired this morning. Can't you do it?' he whined, sipping a small glass of orange juice.

'Well, when you say working . . . yes, you were playing football yesterday, but you weren't last night, were you?'

'Come on, Millie, you know part of the job involves drinks with the lads after the match, it's hardly anything new.'

'Yes, but you didn't get in till 3am and now you stink of booze and look like you're going to throw up. It's not much fun for me being stuck here all day on my own with Wolf.'

'You wanted the baby, don't forget, Millie,' Louis replied, his anger rising with the strength of his hangover. 'I distinctly remember you saying "I'm going to have this baby whether you like it or not!" and now you have the baby you're moaning you have to look after him. That's not fair on Wolfie,' he added self-righteously. He scooped the snoozing six-month-old out of her arms and began whispering to him. 'Don't listen to Mummy, my little Wolf Cub, Daddy's here now.'

'Louis, that's not fair! For god's sake, I just need you to do some washing, is that really too much to ask?'

'Is Mummy getting angry, Wolf Cub? That's not very nice, is it, especially when Daddy's head is hurting. Maybe Daddy should go for a nice drive and leave you to sleep and Mummy to calm down.'

He handed the baby back to Millie, reached for his car keys and shut the door.

Things had gone downhill from there.

The group therapy had been helpful, but once Millie had moved out of the area with Wolf, she hadn't bothered to find another group nearby, presuming she'd be okay now she was away from the pressure-cooker of her relationship. And she had been, up to a point. She'd never returned to that scary place in her head where she couldn't see how she could possibly be a good mum to Wolfie, but she had experienced definite low moments. Not that she was going to admit to them, though, in case it somehow got back to Louis and he used it against her. As it was, things between them seemed fairly stable at the moment, and that's the way she wanted it to stay.

She had enough problems with random people on social media telling her what a bad mum she was, anyway. Her Story earlier had prompted the trolls to tell her she should be looking after her son and not going out and 'getting shitfaced' as they put it, adding 'wonder what the social will have to say about this'. Millie knew she needed to keep deleting and forgetting about the comments, but sometimes she couldn't stop them adding fuel to the bad-mother fire that was already burning brightly inside her head.

By the time the following weekend came around, Millie was wishing that she and Bell were going for several vats of wine again, rather than merely coffee at the community centre café. The week had gone from bad to worse, with Wolfie acting up at home and apparently misbehaving at school, too. The school secretary had called her mobile on Tuesday with the news that the headteacher had asked her to make an appointment with Wolf's mum and dad at their earliest convenience.

'Why, what's happened, is Wolf okay?' Millie had asked, white-faced in the middle of the Topshop changing room in her bra and pants.

'He's fine, Mrs Price. Mrs Spencer hasn't informed me of her reasons, but I believe there are some concerns over Wolf's behaviour of late. Would Thursday afternoon be convenient for you and Mr Price?'

'My name's Morley, and it's Ms,' Millie said with as much dignity as she could after being told the son she thought she'd brought up okay on her own was causing 'concerns' over his behaviour. 'Thursday afternoon is fine for me, though I'll need to check with Wolf's father.'

'Thank you, Ms Morley,' replied the secretary crisply. 'If

you could let me know if that also suits Mr Price, I'll book a slot in Mrs Spencer's diary. Goodbye now.'

Millie quickly got dressed and dropped back with the staff all the clothes she'd been trying on and photographing. She knew she needed to calm down before calling Louis, so she grabbed a takeaway coffee and walked all the way home to try to get her thoughts in order. Finally, she had enough endorphins from the brisk walk and caffeine from the drink in her system to make the call.

'He'd better bloody pick up,' she muttered to herself. Thankfully he did.

'Mills, how are you?' he asked, all bonhomie and smiles.

'Good, thanks, Louis. You?'

'Excellent, thanks. Guess what? Just had my medical and the doc says I'm match fit again. The gaffer said I might even make the starting line-up on Sunday. Cool or what!'

'That's great, I'm really pleased for you,' Millie said, actually meaning it. She knew from experience how miserable Louis got when he wasn't able to play regularly. 'And Wolf will be excited to see you play again.'

'He's turning into a pretty good player himself, you know. We need to sort him joining a local team – those tinpot games he plays at school aren't enough. No, he needs to be playing proper games against the big boys so he starts to toughen up.'

Millie could tell when Louis was about to go on a rant and so headed it off at the pass immediately. 'It's Wolf I'm actually calling about. Apparently he's misbehaving at school and the head has called us in for a meeting. Can you make Thursday afternoon?'

'My Wolf Cub misbehaving? I don't think so!' he retorted, his voice rising. 'Did you tell them they must have got it wrong?'

'Well, no, I don't know the situation, do I? But I think we should go in to see the head as she's asked and hopefully we can sort it out.'

'You don't know the situation about your own son?! For god's sake, Millie! I can't believe you didn't stand up for poor Wolf. I think we need to look into him moving schools. There are plenty of great private ones round here.'

'Calm down, Louis, the school is a good one, we both agreed on that, didn't we? Let's just see what the head has to say and take it from there. And I'm sorry for not asking for more details, it was just the shock of the phone call, I think.'

'I've a good mind to call them up now and give them a piece of my mind. But I suppose it can wait until Thursday. Fine, I'll see you outside the gates then.' Louis rang off and Millie took a deep, steadying, breath.

As she and Wolf made their way to the community centre on Saturday, he chatted away about how his dad was going to score at least two goals during his comeback match the next day. Millie nodded and agreed in the right places, but inside she was seething with resentment that Louis had been able to muscle in on Thursday, fill his son's head with exciting talk of football and then scarper, while she had to deal with the fallout from the meeting with the head. Still, at least Wolf had a smile on his face for the first time in days.

'Mummy, look, there's Bell in the deep end!' he cried, pulling on her arm as they headed towards the changing room. Millie turned to look and raised her arm to her new friend, thankful to see her beaming face.

Millie still wasn't brave enough to swim herself, but she was happy to watch Wolf splashing around in his armbands. 'Come on, Wolf, show me how many strokes you can do and see if you can beat the eight you did in your lesson this week,' she said from the side of the pool. 'Well done! That's brilliant, keep going!'

At that moment, Bell swam over.

'Look, I'm swimming, Bell Bell!' shouted Wolf, before swallowing a huge mouthful of water and having to be helped to the side by Bell as he began coughing.

'I think it might be time for drinks and some of those delicious cookies they sell in the café,' Bell smiled, once Wolf had stopped spluttering.

'My throat hurts,' he said, rubbing his neck. 'I think I might need hot chocolate,' he added, turning to Millie with his chocolate-brown eyes wide. 'And probably marshmallows too.'

'Don't push your luck, kiddo,' Millie smiled, throwing his towel around his shoulders and giving him a gentle push towards the changing room. 'We'll see you in the café when you're ready, Bell.'

Once Wolf's throat was made better by a hot chocolate

and the grown-ups were on to their second coffee, Millie tried to encourage Wolf to go and play so she could talk to Bell – she was desperate to tell her what had happened at the school that week. But Wolf was far more interested in chatting to Bell about how he was going to be a deep-sea diver when he grew up.

'I think cos I'm really good at swimming I want to do a job in the water with the fishes and I could spend all my days diving down to the bottom of the sea with my friends like in *Finding Nemo*. And maybe even playing with the sharks, cos I'm really brave, aren't I, Mummy? But only if I can't be a footballer like my daddy.'

'I'm sure you can be whatever you want to be because you are a very clever boy.' Bell smiled at him. 'Do you like Lego? I think I saw some in the toybox over there, why don't you see if you can make a submarine for a diver to go down to the bottom of the sea?'

'That's a very good idea, Bell Bell,' he replied seriously. 'I'll make it and then you can play diving with me, okay?'

'Okay, sweetheart, it's a deal.'

'Thank god for that!' Millie said, leaning back in her chair to see Wolf sorting through piles of Lego in the play area behind her. 'Clever thinking, Bell, I thought he'd never leave us in peace!'

'Lego is always a winner for keeping them quiet for a bit – well, it's always worked with my niece and nephew, until they start pushing bits up their noses or arguing about one of them stealing the other's pieces, at any rate.'

'Ha! Thankfully, being an only child, he doesn't have to worry so much about sharing. Only there are lots of other worries.'

'Tough week?'

'You could say that. We were summoned to see the headteacher.'

'Millie, have you been fighting in the playground again?!'

'On this occasion it was Wolfie's behaviour that has been giving the school "cause for concern", so they told us.'

'But he's such a sweet boy, I can't imagine him being naughty in class.'

'I know, but he can also be a little horror like all kids, believe me. Although the way the head spoke to me made me want to start misbehaving, too!'

'Why, what happened?' Bell asked.

'Well, it didn't help that Louis said to meet him outside, so I waited for ten minutes and when he didn't appear I went in to ask for the head myself and it turned out he was already there sipping tea, making himself at home in her office.'

'Grr, so annoying,' Bell sympathised. 'I bet you were already stressed and then being late put you on the back foot.'

'Exactly!' Millie nodded. 'Straight away I looked like a bad parent. And, of course, Louis had managed to charm the head in five minutes flat so she was practically licking his arse by the time I arrived.' Seeing Bell's face screw up, she added, 'I know, I hate that phrase too, sorry, but it was annoying the way he totally had her round his little finger. And then when she talked to us about Wolf cheeking his teacher and lashing out at another boy in his class, it was all directed at me. King Louis just sat there like butter wouldn't melt and let me take all the flak for our son's behaviour. Then right at the end he cut across what I was saying and said, "Don't worry, Mrs Spencer, I'll make sure I talk to Wolfie and I'm sure he won't do it again," and she actually simpered at him and told him the school would do anything they could and she was sure it was just a blip. Seriously, it was like she'd never seen a good-looking footballer before and she was practically salivating all over him at this point. She only remembered I was in the room when I stood up to leave. It was so humiliating.'

'That's awful, Millie, poor you. And poor Wolf, there's obviously something making him unhappy. Did you or Louis manage to find out what it was?'

'Louis' idea of dealing with it was to treat him to pizza and not mention it at all. Then he went home and left me to talk to him, obviously. And Wolf wouldn't really tell me anything. You're right, there's definitely something going on and I have my suspicions it's to do with the boy he punched on the arm. I think Zach's bullying him, not that Wolf would say much, but he's mentioned before that Zach had been nasty to him.'

'Is it worth talking to the school about this Zach? Not to the head maybe, but what about Wolf's teacher?'

'And say what? It's all just me surmising rather than having any proof.'

'True. How's Wolf been since then?'

'Okay. I gave him another talk about telling me or the

teacher if people were mean to him and told him off for being rude to the teacher, but I didn't want to be too hard on him, especially if this Zach is already making him upset. I'm just going to have to keep a close eye on him over the next few weeks. Louis is obsessed with him joining a local football club so he can play against older kids and, in Louis' words, "toughen up a bit". Though I'm not sure him getting the shit kicked out of him every week is the answer.'

'What does getting the shit kicked out of you mean?' Wolf asked, appearing behind her with handfuls of Lego.

'Nothing, Wolf, nothing at all!' Millie said quickly. 'Ooh, your submarine is looking good. Do you need some help finishing it off?'

The next few weeks passed by in a blur of school pick-ups and drop-offs, copywriting jobs from the agency and snatched conversations with Bell over coffee at the community centre. Their Saturday afternoons together had quickly become the highlight of her week; she looked forward to having Bell's measured and calm advice about her problems, and she loved hearing nuggets about Bell's job and all the characters in her photography class. She even found herself giving her friend advice when it came to her relationship with Colin, who was still dragging his feet over the price of their house. She was even more excited about the coming weekend as it was Louis' turn to have Wolf and she and Bell had planned a girlie afternoon of shopping followed by dinner and drinks in town.

'You can give me some selfie tips in the changing rooms,' Bell had laughed.

'It's easy – use the dimmer switch in the changing room, hold your phone up high and then take at least twenty shots. One of them is bound to be okay once you've added some filters and Facetuning!'

And Wolfie was just as excited about the weekend, although he was sad not to be seeing Bell.

'Daddy says I can come on the coach with him and the whole team to the ground on Saturday,' he informed Millie after chatting to Louis the previous weekend. 'And at the end of the match, he's going to get me from the stand with Grandma and Grandad and put me on his shoulders and run round the pitch. It's going to be awesome! I wish you and Bell Bell could see me, Mummy.'

'That sounds very exciting, Wolf. Make sure Grandma takes some photos of you and we can show them to Bell too.'

However, both Wolf's and Millie's excitement was brought to a crushing standstill two days later when Louis texted just as Millie was rushing to get Wolf out of the door in his wellies and raincoat and into the torrential rain that was about to soak them both.

> I need to swap weekends so I'll take
> Wolf next Sat instead. Can you let him
> know? Thks, L

'You have got to be fu—flipping kidding.'

'What's wrong, Mummy? It's very splashy out here, isn't it?'

Millie continued to stare at her phone.

'Mummy, aren't we going to be late?' Wolf asked, a touch of worry creeping into his voice because he'd told Millie he was trying very hard to get one of Mrs Boyle's special stickers that week.

'Sorry, Wolf, yes, let's go.' Millie couldn't bear to burst his excited bubble as he babbled on about diving into deep puddles in his pretend submarine and how he was going to tell his daddy all about wanting to be a diver as well as a footballer. Though she knew she would have to break the news to him after school.

Later, whenever she allowed her mind to wander from the newsletter she was writing for the agency and towards the text Louis had sent, Millie felt anger fizz up inside her. How dare he just drop his son like that, without any explanation or even apology! She still hadn't messaged him back as she was waiting for her rage to die down a little in case she typed something she later regretted. But she couldn't imagine when that might be.

She got up from the table where she'd been working and stretched her crunched-up limbs, then made a cup of coffee and a decision. Sipping the scalding liquid, she pulled her phone from her pocket and fired off a quick text to her dad asking how he and Jean were, before furiously typing a not-nearly-so friendly message to Louis.

> Thank for your message, Louis. I'll call you at 4pm this afternoon so you can explain to Wolf yourself about this weekend. Please make sure you answer when I call. M

Millie knew Louis would be furious she was passing the responsibility back to him, but she also knew that she would have the job of comforting Wolfie later when he'd stopped trying to be brave for his dad and started crying tears of confusion that only his dad could really stem. Louis didn't deign to reply to her message, so Millie just had to hope she wasn't mad for crediting him with a small amount of decency.

'Wolf, can you come into the kitchen for me a minute,' she called to her son that afternoon after school.

'I'm just making a submarine to show Daddy, but I don't have enough Lego,' he complained. 'Can I borrow some from the swimming pool next time?'

'No, I'm afraid not, darling, as otherwise all the other boys and girls won't have any to play with there, will they? Maybe if you're a really good boy we can think about buying you some more for your birthday.' Millie was well aware how much the bricks cost and unless she found a load on eBay there was no way she'd be able to afford more than a small set for his present, but just now she had bigger worries. 'Do you want to speak to Daddy? I'm just FaceTiming him now.'

'But I'll see him tomorrow. Can't I talk to him then? I'm busy.'

'I think he'd like to speak to you now, darling. You

can even press the button. Look, there you go, say hello to Daddy.'

'Hello, Daddy, I'm making a submarine so my diver figure can sit in it and go down to the bottom of the sea and swim with all the whales and fishes and even sharks. You have to be careful that the sharks aren't going to eat you but I'll kick them really hard in the face if they try to bite my legs off cos I'm really good at swimming now and—'

'Wolf Cub! How are you?' Louis cut in. 'Look, son, I've got a bit of bad news. I can't make this weekend now, so we'll have to swap it to next week. Sorry, mate, but you know how it is.'

Millie watched Wolf's expression turn from excited to confused to devastated like a character out of a cartoon. Except this was real.

'But Daddy, you're going to carry me on your shoulders on the pitch! I've told Eva and everyone at school and they're all going to watch the TV and see me be famous. You p-promised.' His eyes began to fill up and Millie longed to go and comfort him, but knew she needed to let Louis see what he'd done.

'Chin up, mate, it can't be helped and we'll do it another time, I promise. And then you can show me the boat you're making.'

'It's a submarine, stupid!' Wolf shouted and ran out of the room.

Millie picked up her phone from where it was leaning against a book on the table.

'I hope you're happy now,' she hissed into the screen.

'That wasn't fair, Millie, you could have told him yourself and not made such a song and dance over it. You're such a bitch sometimes,' Louis snarled.

'Excuse me? I have to go and comfort our son who's crying into his pillow because of you and you're calling *me* a bitch?'

'You're not fit to be a mother, letting him get upset like that,' he spat back and ended the call.

Millie turned her phone face down on the table and trudged upstairs to comfort her distraught son.

Chapter Sixteen

Bell

Bell was both excited and apprehensive about the photo shoot Ade had invited her and Ben to. She might have felt at home popping along to Style It Out's lookbook shoots, but an afternoon helping out on set for a well-known perfume brand was something else entirely.

'You decided to go full-on fashion-forward then,' she joked when she met Ben outside the studio, his jacket open to reveal slim-fit jeans and a plain T-shirt.

'My camo peg-leg trousers are in the wash,' he replied, leaning in to give her a kiss on the cheek as well as a hug. 'Although, don't tell anyone but I have no idea what any of those words actually mean – I speed-read *GQ* on my way here so I would sound more knowledgeable.'

'Well, now you can talk the talk, let's walk the walk, or whatever that stupid phrase is,' Bell laughed nervously.

They both took a deep breath and made their way inside.

Immediately their ears were assaulted by a cacophony of hundreds of voices barking orders at each other. The pair of them cowered in the doorway as bodies pelted in different directions around them, some carrying lighting umbrellas, others heaving massive dark boxes, and all of them in a hurry. Bell had to fight a huge urge to turn round and run away, but then she felt Ben's hand squeeze hers lightly and she gathered herself together. She waited until the youngest and most junior-looking person came past them and quickly stuck her hand out and stepped in front of her.

'Excuse me, do you know where Ade is?' she asked.

'With the creative director over there, I think,' she replied, waving her arm vaguely and barely breaking step.

'Erm, where do you m—. Oh.' Bell broke off as she realised she was talking to thin air. 'Okay, well, I guess we should head over there somewhere,' she said to Ben.

They picked their way gingerly across the vast studio floor, littered with scaffolding from the set and huge pieces of equipment that Bell couldn't even hazard a guess at what they were designed to do, and suddenly she spotted Ade surrounded by people and computers. Thankfully, he looked up just as they were approaching.

'Bell, hi, darling! What do you think? A bit different from our usual shoots, eh? Ah, and you must be Ben from the photography course Bell finally pulled her finger out and joined, great to meet you.' He kissed Bell on both cheeks and shook Ben's hand firmly, clapping him on the shoulder at the same time. 'Right, let's get you both to work. Ben, you can shadow me for the first set of shots and Bell, Eddie's going to show you the ropes with some of the lighting stuff, and then you can swap over, okay?'

Bell nodded mutely and was immediately embarrassed by her lack of ability to form a sentence, which then made it even harder for her to say anything at all, so she continued to perform her goldfish impression until Ben managed to mumble a 'sounds cool'. They dumped their bags, gave each other a scared smile and were borne off by their respective mentors.

For the next couple of hours they were immersed in the shoot's hive of activity, involving lights, cameras and lots of action, while also trying to listen to all the nuggets of information Ade, Eddie and the team were sending their way. While Ben appeared to be lapping up everything he was being told, even asking Ade to explain things in more technical detail, Bell's head was spinning and it was all she could do to nod along and try to follow every second sentence. Finally, a break was called, and Ade steered her over to the catering tables, where they both grabbed a bottle of water.

'Having fun?' he asked, grinning at her.

'It's, er, a lot to take in,' she stammered. 'But, yes, surprisingly I am!'

'Why surprisingly? You're good at this, Bell, and you could be *really* good at it if you weren't so scared of doing the wrong thing all the time. The thing with photography is just to go with what feels right in the moment and then see what you've managed to capture afterwards, you know? Of course, if you're working to a brief like today, then the stakes are a bit higher and you have to get *the* shot, but you still need to go with your instinct and what *feels* right.'

'I'm not sure I trust myself to know that feeling, though,' Bell laughed. 'But this is such a brilliant thing to experience, even just for an afternoon. Seriously, Ade, it's amazing watching you work on something like this. I knew you were a good photographer but those shots you took before were ridiculously cool.' She felt her cheeks flame as she realised what a complete fangirling idiot she sounded and quickly added, 'Ben's really getting stuck into the techy stuff, isn't he? I heard him talking to Eddie and it all sounded like gobbledygook to me!'

'Yeah, he's brilliant at picking it all up very quickly,' Ade nodded. 'He's got that real attention to detail thing going on that you don't see much nowadays. He seems sound. And he looks very into you, Ms Makepeace, you dark horse!'

'No, no, we're not together,' Bell said hurriedly.

'Really? You could have fooled me,' Ade grinned. 'Well, if you're not, then he certainly wants you to be – I saw the way he looked at you earlier. I spend half my life trying to get people to make love to the camera, darling, and I can see in someone's eyes when they really mean it. And he definitely does when he looks at you! The question is, do you like him back . . .?'

Bell was saved from the embarrassment of having to answer as Ade was commandeered by the creative director again, and she barely saw him for the next hour. Just as she was beginning to think her head was going to explode into a thousand tiny pieces, a shout of 'That's a wrap for today' echoed round the studio and immediately crowds of people pooled around her, dismantling equipment and placing it carefully into reinforced boxes.

She tried to help as best she could, but she quickly realised she was more of a hindrance than anything else and slunk off into a corner to check her phone. Suze had been WhatsApping her all afternoon, persistently asking how things were going, despite not getting any reply, and keeping her up to date with Friday-afternoon shenanigans in the office. Bell couldn't help but smile to herself as she read through the messages, especially as she reached the most recent one Suze had sent just a few minutes before.

> I'm going to assume your lack of reply to my ramblings is because you've either shown yourself to be so good behind the camera that you're now responsible for the entire shoot and are about to jet around the world shooting campaigns for D&G, H&M and, er, B&M (sorry, ran out of examples – I'm sure even a bargain-basement store needs photographers though?). Or it's because you're being ravaged by handsome Ade in the wardrobe area as the seamstress continues to thread her needle just metres away. Am I right or am I right? Can you tell I'm a bit bored this afternoon? I know it's almost hometime but tell me how it's going pleeeeeeease xxx

Bell began thumbing out a reply, but was interrupted by Ade's voice behind her and she quickly – and guiltily – hid her phone in her pocket.

'I wondered where you'd got to, Bell! I was just saying to Ben that you guys should get off as it will take us a while to sort all this stuff out and there's no point you wasting your Friday nights too.'

'Are you sure? I feel a bit cheeky swanning in here, faffing around a bit and then leaving you all to do the donkey work,' Bell said.

'Don't be silly, darling, it's fine. This lot are at least getting paid! I hope you've found it helpful this afternoon, anyway. And if you're up for coming along to something again or you just want a chat about stuff give me a bell. Oh god, sorry, I bet you hear that joke all the time!'

'Ah, you know, just a few times,' Bell laughed. 'It's been so cool being here today and though I definitely need to go away and digest it all, I know I've learned loads just by watching you all at work. So, thank you, I can't tell you how much I appreciate it, Ade.'

As she gave him a hug, he replied, 'Any time, darling, I mean it.'

She grabbed her bags and was scanning the room for Ben when Ade added, 'Oh, and Bell, don't forget what I said about just going with your feelings, yes? Ah, here's Ben now, see you both later,' he grinned.

Bell's cheeks turned a fetching shade of red, and she was glad she was able to pull her hair out of its ponytail and round her flaming face as she walked out of the studio beside Ben.

As their planned girlie Saturday together had been stalled thanks to Louis, Bell agreed to Millie's suggestion of an afternoon in the park with Wolf. She was glad of the prospect of some fresh air after the intensity of the previous afternoon, and greeted her friend and a rather subdued Wolf warmly. Thankfully, he perked up considerably when Bell mentioned the possibility of ice cream later, and he happily ran off to play on the slide with the hordes of other kids who had descended on the park as soon as their parents had realised what a lovely sunny day it was. Millie kept one eye on her son as she gave Bell a quick run-down of her and Louis' latest run-in.

'And he didn't give you any reason for having to cancel?' Bell asked, reaching into her bag for her knock-off Ray-Bans as the sun came out from behind the marshmallow cloud that had been hiding it for the past half an hour.

'No, just "work stuff". It's Wolfie I feel sorry for. Whatever Louis says or doesn't say to me, he is Wolf's dad and always will be and he owes it to him to keep his promises.'

'Poor kid,' Bell agreed. 'Have you thought any more about seeing a lawyer?'

'Not really,' Millie said quietly, then before Bell could launch into another speech about why going down the legal route would be a good idea, she quickly added, 'How did your big brainstorm at work go? Was your boss impressed with your ideas?'

'Yeah, it went fine,' Bell sighed.

'Just fine?' She raised an eyebrow. 'I thought you were really excited about your new idea for the site?'

'I was, and my boss was, for a few minutes, anyway. And then some upstart started talking about linking Instagram Story videos to reviews of each product and Marian got all excited about that and forgot all about my idea. So, yeah, it was a bit deflating.'

'That does sound like a cool idea about the Insta Stories though,' Millie nodded, 'I can see that really working.'

'I don't really understand them,' Bell confessed. 'But I'm sure you're right. God, sometimes I just feel so old!'

'I read an article online the other day that said forty is the new twenty, so actually, you're bang on trend!' Her friend nudged her. 'You're stylish, successful and full of ideas, plus you have all that experience behind you that those snowflake millennials just don't. You are #livingyourbestlife!'

'Have you swallowed a motivational-quote GIF by any chance?' Bell laughed. 'Though thanks for the vote of confidence, I definitely need it. I even sucked in photography class this week.'

'I don't believe that for a minute! I thought you said you could really notice the difference in your pics now?

'Well, sometimes, but not this week. Sheila tore my photo of tree blossom to shreds and said it lacked depth of field.'

'I have no idea what that means, but I'm sure it was a one-off. What's this week's theme?'

'Animals. Although unless I take a trip to the zoo, I

have absolutely no idea how I'm going to find a willing subject.'

'Forget the zoo, we're in exactly the right place for animals – and, no, I don't mean the kids running riot in the playground! There are bound to be some cute dogs for you to photograph. Good job you brought your camera. In fact, I can see at least two pampered pooches right now. And one of them even seems to have a rather good-looking human attached to it!'

'Where? Christ, I'm so old I need prescription sunglasses, I can't see anything with these on.'

'The guy with the gorgeous greyhound coming towards us over there.'

'Oh.'

'Oh good, or oh bad? Do you not think a greyhound would make the perfect subject for a paw-fect photo? See what I did there!' Millie nudged Bell. 'What? Why are you looking like that?' Millie had barely finished her sentence when the dog, followed by its owner, jogged over.

'Bell! How are you?'

'Ben, lovely to see you, although obviously you only saw me yesterday,' she stuttered. 'I didn't know you had a dog.'

'I don't, but I take Graham for a walk a couple of days a week for my neighbour as he can't get out as much as he used to. Or rather, you take me for a walk, don't you, Gray?!' He stroked the dog's head affectionately and it responded by licking his hand noisily and wetly. 'Thanks for yesterday, I learned so much from the shoot. It was just amazing to see how something like that works. And Ade is such a talented guy.'

Before Bell could respond, there came a chorus of ear-splintering screams and Millie immediately began to run in the direction of the playground. Thankfully, the shouts quickly turned to shushing and soothing as various parents picked up their children from a heap on the floor and bore them off for head-rubbing and sweet treats. Their sobs faded away until the air was full of shrieks of joy and fear from children spinning on the roundabout again. Her arms full of her son, Millie walked back over to where Bell and Ben had been standing in silence as they watched the scene unfold.

'Is he okay?' asked Bell, full of concern.

'You're fine, aren't you, little man. Just a little bang and a bit of a shock, but he'll be fine.'

'Sorry, Ben, this is Millie and her son Wolf – Wolf goes swimming at the community centre, don't you, sweetheart?'

'I'm going to be a fish when I grow up.' Wolf nodded his head vigorously at Ben. 'Or a submarine man. Or maybe a footballer. Is that your doggy?'

'No, he belongs to a friend. But you can say hello to him if you'd like?'

As Wolf struggled for Millie to put him down, she whispered to him, 'It's okay to be scared of the dog, Wolf. You don't have to pat him if you don't want to.'

'Are you scared of him, Mummy?' he asked loudly. 'Cos I'm not. Hello, doggy, what's your name?'

'This is Graham, or Gray for short,' Ben said solemnly.

'Shake paws, Gray.' The dog lifted up his leg obligingly and Wolf whooped with delight.

'Look, Mummy, we're shaking paws! Hello, Graham, very pleased to meet you,' Wolf said in his politest, most grown-up voice. 'Have you come to play in the park?'

'He loves to run around,' Ben smiled. 'In fact, do you want to throw his ball and see what happens?'

'Yes, yes!' Wolf shouted. 'Please, thank you,' he added, catching his mum's eye. 'Fetch, Graham, fetch!'

Although the little boy only threw the ball a couple of metres, the dog immediately ran to it, picked it up in his mouth, deposited it at Wolf's feet, then looked at him hopefully.

'Again, again!' Wolf said delightedly. 'But I want to fetch it too!'

The three adults took it in turns to throw the ball as far as they were able and both Graham and Wolf ran after it as fast as they could. Unsurprisingly, the dog beat the boy every single time, but it didn't deter little Wolf until finally he lay down, out of breath. The dog, too, was breathing heavily and collapsed next to Wolf, his paw touching Wolf's leg and his wet nose nudging his hand.

'Looks like you've made a friend there, Wolf,' Ben smiled at him. 'And he's a very discerning dog so he doesn't make friends with just anybody.'

'What does dis-disearny mean?' Wolf asked, turning towards the adults.

'It means Graham picked you out of everyone in the park to be friends with,' Bell laughed. 'What a clever dog!'

'He is a clever dog, like a clever clogs, or a clever dog clogs,' Wolf said. 'Mummy, is ice cream good for hurty heads? Cos mine is a bit ouchy still.' He looked winningly up at Millie.

'Ha, you are a clever clogs, too, Wolfie,' she laughed, scooping him up and tickling him as he giggled. 'Yes, I think we all deserve an ice cream after all of that excitement. Although maybe not Graham,' she amended. At the sound of his name, the dog was instantly alert and Ben grabbed his lead before he made a break for it.

'Fancy a 99?' Bell asked Ben.

'Why not?' he grinned, and they followed Millie and Wolf towards the van over by the treeline, pulling Graham back from chasing pigeons as they walked. 'What a beautiful day it is today. It feels like summer is on its way at last. Though can you believe we've only got two weeks of photography classes left until the course is over?'

'Really? God, that's gone so quickly! I took a few shots of Wolfie and Graham together, so I'm hoping I'll have something to send Sheila this week. What about you, have you got a good pic? Although I don't know why I'm asking you as you *always* have a good pic! You are a proper teacher's pet!' she joked.

'I am not!' he protested. 'I'm just a bit scared of Sheila so I don't want to disappoint her. Though I might be a teeny bit more scared of Laura – thank god she doesn't do the critique of our photos!'

'Och, look at that rubbish, it's dark and grainy and totally shite!' Bell said, giving her Laura impression her all.

Ben burst out laughing. 'That is the worst attempt at a Scottish accent I have ever heard – I mean, I'm guessing it was Scottish you were trying to do . . .'

'Hey, shut it, you!' Bell laughed, lightly hitting his arm. 'Or I'll get Rita and Tony to tell you a really long and really convoluted story about that time they went to the Lake District with their son when he was little.'

'Oh god, that was insane. I have absolutely no idea how that story ended – or even started, to be honest – as they went off on about a million tangents and twenty minutes later I had to pretend I needed the loo just to get away. Not that you and Laura came to save me – I thought the three of us were supposed to stick together?'

'We were having too much fun looking at your face when Tony kept talking about the strange man in their hotel room and how he was completely naked except for his socks and sandals.'

'God, don't remind me, it was definitely a case of TMI, especially when Rita started going on about his "dingly-dangly bits". Seriously, I could have done without it!'

Bell cackled with laughter and wiped tears from her eyes. 'The whole thing was amazing.'

Once they'd all finished their ice creams and Graham had helped Wolf clean his hands with his tongue, much to the little boy's delight, Ben patted the dog's head and stood up. 'Right, I'd best get Gray back to his rightful owner, but hopefully we'll see you in the park again soon, Wolf, and it was lovely to meet you, Millie.'

Wolf shook paws again with Graham before Millie produced some wet wipes from her bag and sat Wolf on a bench so she could wash his hands a bit more thoroughly.

'Thanks, Ben, you've really cheered Wolfie up,' Bell smiled.

'Ah, I think that was mostly down to Graham, I just came along for the ride, didn't I, boy?' He scratched the top of the dog's head and Graham instantly stopped pulling at his lead and instead touched his nose against Ben's knee. 'You're such a softie, aren't you! I'm looking forward to seeing if he makes it into this week's homework, too.' He grinned. 'If he does, I'll have to get it framed for him.'

'Now, who's the big softie!' Bell laughed.

When he realised it was time to go, Graham pulled hard towards Bell, put his paws up on her legs and whined.

'Down, boy, don't be so forward!' Ben laughed, pushing him down. 'See you on Wednesday, Bell.' He leaned towards her and gave her a soft peck on the cheek, before striding off across the park in Graham's wake. Bell's stomach fizzed as she watched him walk over the grass and she hugged her arms around herself.

'Well, Ben is even nicer than I imagined!' Millie observed, coming to stand next to her and following her line of sight.

'Yes, he is. And Graham, of course,' Bell said, reaching for her sunnies again despite the clouds that were now starting to litter the sky. Millie merely grinned at her.

Chapter Seventeen

Bell

Bell arrived at the community centre on Wednesday, both eager to start her class and sad that this was the last time she and her classmates would all be together in one room discussing their weekly highs and lows of taking photos. While she'd been on a high after receiving lots of praise from Sheila and the whole class last week for her picture of Wolf and Graham in the park, she had ummed and ahhed about which shot to submit as her favourite of all the pictures she'd taken over the past couple of months. She'd finally decided on an image she'd captured from behind of Millie with her arm around little Wolf, who was wrapped in a towel, as they stood in front of the pool watching people swim up and down the lanes, the sun glinting off the water. When she'd shyly showed it to Suze that morning, her friend had been really impressed and made everyone in the office come over to her computer and see some of her other shots, too.

'I wouldn't be surprised if you left Style It Out and started up your own photography business, Bellster,' she'd said, nodding her head vigorously at Bell. 'Have you shown Ade these?' she'd then asked with a wicked glint in her eye. 'I'm sure he'd be up for showing you his focal length!'

'Suze, you are ridiculous,' Bell laughed. 'Though, actually I have had a few messages from him this week and he's been really encouraging. And, no, not the kind of encouraging you're thinking of! He was asking after Ben as well.'

Bell couldn't wait to see her shot framed and hanging on the wall, along with the rest of the class's favourite photos, and was even looking forward to standing up in front of everyone and explaining why she'd chosen it and what she wanted to do with her photography next.

After class last week, she'd emailed Millie the picture of Wolf and Graham and Millie had messaged back almost immediately telling her how much she adored it and asking if she minded if she put it on her Instagram. Bell had hesitated only to wonder whether Graham's owner would mind, but quickly decided the old man was never likely to see it anyway and even if he was a big Insta user, surely he'd be only too pleased to see his dog immortalised in Millie's feed. Millie duly posted it, along with the caption:

Boy and dog: a portrait. It fills my heart to see the pure, unadulterated joy on Wolfie's face as he plays with Gray the greyhound in the park. Although no one mention the word puppy to him . . . ! Photograph: @With_Bells_on #playtime #parklife #puppylove #thisisfive #myboy #allthelove

Millie's post had got thousands of Likes and Bell herself had been inundated with new followers after her friend had tagged her in the post. Millie had messaged the next day, saying:

> Oh my god, your picture has had 25,000 likes – that's more than any other photo I've ever posted. Clearly I've found the perfect formula: cute child, cute dog and amazing photographer! Please can you take all the photos for my Insta feed from now on (and I'm not even joking!)?

The strong but oddly comforting smell of instant coffee, chlorine and damp greeted Bell as she entered the centre and made her way through the corridors. She smiled and waved at the other early bird members of the class as she crossed the floor and deposited her bottle of Bordeaux on the drinks table – there was no tea or coffee today! Bell was intrigued to see what exactly Rita and Tony brought with them. Laura had bet her a pound it was Advocaat, but Bell was leaning towards Black Tower. ('In the name of the wee man, let's hope not!' Laura had replied. 'No wine should only have five per cent alcohol.') In the event, they were both wrong; Rita and Tony were hot on Bell's heels and plonked a very respectable bottle of prosecco down on the 'bar' before saying hello to the uniform brigade who were the biggest eager beavers of the evening but didn't seem to have brought much to the booze table other than a couple of sad-looking cans of too-cool-for-school IPA. Next, just-good-friends Lynne and Marcus came in, bearing gifts of rosé and white wine, and even Sheila contributed a bottle of Baileys, which elicited 'oohs' from quite a few people. Finally, Laura and Ben walked in together, and while Laura proceeded to produce miniature after miniature of whisky from her bag, Ben drew the biggest cheer by presenting the table with not only a large bottle of gin, but also some posh tonic and a couple of limes.

'I don't think anyone is going to go thirsty this evening,' Sheila declared, clapping her hands in excitement. 'Seeing as we have so much to choose from, let's get stuck in now!' Rita and Laura whooped before Sheila added, 'And then before we all start seeing double, we'll each present our favourite photo and hang it on the wall.' There were a few good-natured groans as the class realised they hadn't got out of that part of the evening.

Bell sipped her G&T and laughed as Laura downed two 'wee drams' that were anything but wee in quick succession, muttering, 'Och, if I've got to stand up in front of everyone I might as well be a bit pished first.'

Sheila tapped her huge glass of Baileys and clapped her hands again. 'Before we start, I wanted to say a huge thank you to everyone for making this one of the best groups I've ever taught.'

'I bet you say that to them all!' Tony heckled.

'Well, maybe, but I actually mean it with you lot,' Sheila smiled. 'We've all learned a lot and I think the photographs we're going to see now really show that. So, without further ado, Tony, why don't you go first!'

'Serves you right for shouting out,' Rita giggled, giving him a push out of his chair. Tony walked towards Sheila who presented him with a large frame turned towards him but hidden from the rest of the class.

'Oh, well now,' he said quietly. 'Is that really my picture?' When Sheila nodded at him and sat back down in her own seat, he stood in front of them all for a few seconds, just gazing at the framed print.

'Are you going to show the class?' Sheila prompted.

'Oh, yes, right, well, this is my photo.' Tony turned it round so the thirteen faces in front of him could see the beautiful head and shoulders image of Rita. Although few people – least of all Rita – would describe her as 'classically beautiful', the photo was striking, and the whole class gave a collective 'wow'.

'Wow indeed,' nodded Sheila, happily, as Tony stood there still too overcome to speak. 'You may not have used all the fancy settings on your camera to get this shot but you have managed to capture the most important thing – the essence of Rita.'

'If that's what capturing my essence is, then he can do that every time!' Rita called out. 'Tone, you're a genius – a photo of me that I actually like!'

'It's bloody brilliant,' Laura said. 'The way you can see every line and wrinkle on her face – sorry, Rita! – makes it seem like the photo's telling the story of her life.'

'Exactly, Laura!' Sheila beamed. 'Well done, Tony, you've nailed it.'

'Well I never,' he muttered, then added louder to the group, 'I'm available for private bookings if anyone else wants their wrinkles photographing,' and everyone laughed and clapped as he hung his photo on the wall and went back to his seat.

Rita had chosen an image of her baby grandson as her favourite ('To show my sons I won't be cutting the kids' heads off in pictures from now on!' she declared), while the uniform brigade had all gone for more abstract images of buses on the move or graffiti in the local skate park. Next it was Lynne and Marcus's turn and they stood up together and showed the black and white shots they'd taken on a beach on a timer of them holding hands and of a heart shape they'd created in the sand with shells.

'It's to signify what we feel about each other,' Lynne said shyly. 'And, um, coming to this class together and working on our homework has made us realise that we want to be together-together properly.'

Laura let out a wolf-whistle and the whole class cheered and whooped happily.

'Ah, young love!' Sheila breathed, clapping her hands in joy. 'Congratulations, you two, now go and hang your photos on the wall – side by side of course!'

Laura grinned at Bell and nudged her. 'I told you they were shagging, didn't I! It warms the cockles of my heart, it does. Shit, it's my turn now – wish me luck.'

Bell gave her a thumbs-up once she was standing at the front with her photo, and thought she'd never seen her feisty friend look so unsure of herself.

'So, this is my photo,' she said, turning it round to face the class. 'I wanted to create something a bit graphic and Warhol-like, more a piece of art than a straight photograph if that doesn't sound too wanky. I took this photo of my friend's lips – she has the most amazing lips you've ever seen and if I wasn't so attracted to the wrong sort of man, I'd be kissing her myself.' She grinned lasciviously as the class tittered. 'And then I played around with the image in Photoshop a bit, blurring the edges and sharpening the fleshy bits, adding some colour and a background, until, well, I made this.'

'That is so cool,' said one of the uniforms, followed by a further five echoes along the same lines.

'It *is* cool,' Sheila agreed, 'but it's not so cool that it's lost the heart at its centre, and that's what makes it so clever. Excellent work, Laura.'

The class clapped hard and Bell took a large swig of her G&T as Sheila invited her to take her place at the front to present her image to the group.

'Okay, this is my favourite image,' Bell said, turning the frame round to show her picture of Millie and Wolf. 'It may not be technically brilliant, and it's definitely not cool like Laura's, but I think it sums up what coming here has done for me over the last few months. I wanted to include the pool in the shot, as swimming outside in the water that's always a few degrees too cold, even though it's almost summer, feels like a big part of my life now. Through it I met not only Millie and her son Wolf who are in this picture, but also all of you, and at the risk of sounding overemotional and twee, I really value the community this centre has created.' She stopped as she could feel a small lump forming in her throat and looked up to see Rita brushing away tears and even Laura looking a bit emotional.

'I think it's a brilliant image that captures all of those sentiments beautifully,' Sheila smiled. 'Congratulations, Bell.' As Bell walked over to hang her frame, the rest of the class composed themselves and clapped hard.

'Well done, Bell,' Ben whispered when she got back to her seat. 'Not sure how I'm going to follow that!'

Sheila nodded at him and Ben slowly got up and stood at the front with his picture.

'Erm, well, I second everything Bell said . . .' The class cheered in agreement. 'But I also wanted to say that coming here every week and talking about light and shadow and how to frame your image has reignited my love for photography. This is my favourite picture, I hope you like it.'

Ben turned round his frame to show a striking image of a girl walking down the street just as dusk was falling. There was something both atmospheric and very personal about it. The class was silent for a beat, and then everyone began talking at once.

'Ben, this is amazing. By using a large aperture, you've

used what light you had in the best possible way to create an atmospheric silhouetted image that draws you in. Well done!' Sheila said.

'And by turning it black and white, you've emphasised the atmosphere and the contrast,' one of the uniform brigade said.

'It's bloody brilliant!' Laura chimed in.

Ben smiled shyly as everyone clapped and cheered and gathered round him to offer their congrats and ask technical questions – or in Rita's case, just, 'Bloody hell, Ben, how on earth did you get your camera to do that!'

Bell stood a little apart from the rest, her eyes fixed on the frame that now hung on the wall.

'Sorry, I should have asked your permission before I submitted the photo to Sheila,' Ben said quietly, appearing by her side. 'But after that shoot with Ade, I was playing around with my camera settings as he suggested, and I realised it was the perfect light just at that point. So I took a few frames of you walking off down the road to the pub to test the settings, then I saw the shots and knew they were a bit special. I really hope you don't mind.'

'Of course not,' she replied. 'I was just a bit surprised, that's all. It's beautiful. Well, I'm not beautiful, obviously, but you know what I mean.'

'You are beautiful. You just don't know it,' Ben said in a voice barely above a whisper.

'Bell, is that you in the photo?' Laura boomed, breaking the moment and making Bell think she'd probably misheard what he'd said. 'I thought so! Ben, you are naughty!'

'It's fine,' Bell protested. 'And it's an amazing picture. The way the evening is closing in and the silhouette is framed is brilliant.'

Sheila clapped her hands and they all returned to their seats. 'Congratulations, everybody. Seriously, some of these images wouldn't look out of place on a professional photographer's website.

'Now, I have a few words to say, but first I think it's time for another drink as there are too many empty glasses in the room!'

Once they were all topped up with their drink of choice, Sheila stood and took her place in front of them.

'As I said earlier, it's been a real privilege to spend the last few months with you all on your photography journeys, and I think everyone will agree that you've all produced some truly exceptional work.' More whoops and cheers from the class. 'It's been lovely to see you all help and support each other. And now I wonder if there's something you could do for me.'

'Ooh, depends what it is, Sheila!' heckled Tony.

'Shut up, idiot!' Rita shout-whispered affectionately then added louder, 'Of course, you name it and we'll do it.' There was a general nodding of heads from the group as they looked at their teacher expectantly. Bell could see Sheila's smile was much stiffer than before and she cast a worried look at Ben, whose face reflected her own, before he spotted her glance and tried to give her a reassuring grin.

Sheila took a deep breath. 'As you'll have noticed over the last few months, the community centre is a little rough around the edges and could definitely do with a lick of paint.' Again, the group all nodded. 'Well, unfortunately, it turns out that the changing rooms could do with a whole load more than a lick of paint, so much so that health and safety have said they need to be completely refurbished.'

'They are a bit of a mess,' Lynne spoke up. 'I tripped over a broken tile when I went in there the other week!'

'Then, it's a good thing they're going to be refurbished, right?' Marcus added.

'Well, it would be if it didn't cost such a lot of money,' Sheila said quietly. 'The problem the council have is that, on the one hand, the changing rooms need thousands of pounds they don't have to get them up to scratch. On the other hand, without the changing rooms they can't keep the pool open, and the pool is the biggest revenue generator in this place, especially now the weather is warmer and the school holidays will be starting in a couple of months. Without the income from the pool, the whole centre is under threat.'

'You mean both the pool and the centre might have to close?' Bell asked, horrified.

'The council haven't made any firm decisions yet,' Sheila said calmly. 'But if they can't find the money for the changing rooms, then, yes, I can't see any alternative.'

Bell sagged in her chair. She felt Ben reach for her hand and give it a gentle, reassuring squeeze, and despite herself, her stomach performed a mini backflip. Shaking herself upright, she frowned.

'Can't we raise some money to help?'

'That would be amazing, of course,' Sheila smiled sadly at her. 'But we're not talking a couple of grand, serious cash is needed. At least twenty-five thousand pounds at the last count.'

Bell slumped back into her seat.

'What does this mean for you, Sheila?' asked a subdued Tony. 'Will you still be able to run these courses?'

'We were due to have a new class start next month, but they've contacted anyone who'd signed up and told them it's on hold for now,' she replied. 'Don't worry about me, though, I'll just have to find somewhere else to hold classes, it will be fine.'

'Somewhere else more expensive, I bet,' Rita harrumphed. 'The reason me and Tone were able to sign up to this course in the first place is because it's affordable and local.'

'Us, too!' chorused the uniform brigade.

'What the fuck is wrong with this country?' Laura sighed, knocking back another large whisky. 'Seriously, it's like the government wants to take all the fun out of life.'

'There must be something we can do, though,' Bell said. 'We can't just give up!'

'Well, no decision has been made by the council for definite yet,' Sheila explained. 'Which is where you all might come in. I know it would make a real difference if everyone wrote to or emailed the council to let them know your thoughts. I can give you the details of who to send to.'

'Good,' Bell nodded. 'Surely if enough people complain, they'll have to listen.'

'Well, they have to listen but they don't have to act,' Laura pointed out.

'But we should at least try,' Ben added quickly. 'Sheila, would you be able to send the details to us all and we'll get the word out as far as we can locally too?'

'Of course,' she smiled. 'Right, sadly it's time for us to pack up and go home, class. Don't forget to take your framed photos, and divide the drinks table up between you, although it looks like we've added a fair few bottles to the recycling box tonight!'

Bell, Laura and Ben said goodbye to everyone and helped Sheila tidy up, then loitered outside chatting.

'I feel a bit flat now,' Bell said. 'Is it weird that I'm craving a cigarette despite not smoking for at least twenty years?'

'Here, have one of mine,' Laura said, rooting in her bag for a battered box. 'And don't look at me like that, Ben, of course I don't smoke. Except when I really need to, and this evening I think we all really need to.'

'I wasn't looking at you like anything,' Ben protested, 'And if you're both having one, then I better had too . . . To be sociable, obviously.'

Laura cackled and handed out the cigarettes like sweeties, and they all huddled round, guarding the flame of her lighter against the evening breeze.

'God, I needed that!' Bell sighed, blowing out a huge plume of smoke. 'Do you think they're really going to close the centre?'

'Well, if you think about it logically, it would probably make more sense for them to knock it down and sell off the land to some rich developer who can build a shiny new block of flats,' Laura puffed.

'I don't want to think about it logically!' Bell cried. 'It's just not fair.' She took another drag and threw the cigarette on the ground. 'Urgh, why do I always think I like smoking when in fact after about ten seconds I realise I really don't?' She stubbed it out with the ball of her foot, then picked up the stub and chucked it in the bin. 'Sorry, I know I sound like a spoilt child, but this place is the best thing that's happened to me in years,'

Ben rubbed her shoulder and stubbed out his own cigarette. 'Let's just see what the council say and take it from there. There's no point thinking about worst-case scenarios until we have to. But we're with you on this, Bell. Aren't we, Laura?' he said, staring hard at her.

'Och, of course. Let me know what you need me to do and I'll do it. Now, I'd better get on my way or my mum will kill me for being late, although first lend me your perfume in case she smells that cancer stick on me.'

A puff of perfume later and Bell and Ben were left staring after her.

'She really is quite scary,' Ben breathed.

'Absolutely, but her heart's in the right place,' Bell smiled. 'Although she can definitely put it away – I was seriously impressed at how she was knocking back that whisky like it was water. God, I can't believe it's work again tomorrow, is it not the weekend yet?'

'We're on the home stretch at least. I thought you enjoyed your job, though?'

'Oh, I do, I'm just being dramatic.'

'Maybe you need a holiday – when did you last have some time off?'

'Well, not for ages, but I'm not sure I feel like going away on my own quite yet and most of my friends are coupled up and not really up for a girlie week in the sun somewhere.'

'I may not be a girl but I'm always up for a week in the sun somewhere,' Ben said, then quickly turned red and started playing with his shirt sleeve. 'Anyway, I'd best be off too. Keep me updated on what the council say and we'll do what we can about the centre, I promise.' He gave her an awkward hug and was off down the road before she had time to reply.

Bell walked home, her mind leaping from one subject to another in a blur of random scenes that skidded into and over each other. She realised the strong G&Ts Ben had mixed were probably even more gin and less tonic than she'd thought. But however dulled her senses may be, nothing could dim the all too shocking reality of the community centre's future. Bell couldn't help but feel that the reason she'd been able to pull herself out of the hole of despair she'd fallen into after her relationship ended was the centre and everything it represented. And if it was allowed to crumble away and close, where did that leave her and the community she now valued so much?

Chapter Eighteen

Millie

'I should only be a few hours, Bridget, and Wolf knows he's allowed to have one story tape once he's gone to bed but then it's lights out. Thanks again for watching him this evening.'

'It's no problem at all, lovey, I just hope you can save that centre and stop the corrupt council trying to close it down. Me and the bridge ladies would be lost without it, I tell you.'

Millie could see Bridget was gearing up for another long monologue and if she wasn't careful she'd miss the meeting at the community centre altogether. So she merely squeezed her arm, reiterated that she didn't think the council were in fact corrupt, merely short of money, and slipped out of the door before the older lady was able to warm to her theme.

Despite the nature of the meeting, Millie was pleased that Bell had invited her along, especially as she'd told her a lot of the other people she knew were going were from her photography class and Millie didn't want to seem like she was gate-crashing. Though it was true that she was just as invested as any of them – seeing the grin on Wolf's face when he doggy-paddled through the water was enough to convince her the pool and the centre needed to remain open to everyone, all the more so as it felt like her little boy was smiling rather less than normal at the moment. She was somewhat apprehensive as she walked into the centre – she only really knew Bell of the people assembled in the large room. But as she scanned the crowd she suddenly recognised Ben from their afternoon in the park, and began to make her way over to where he was leaning against a chair while a formidable-looking woman talked at him, gesticulating heavily.

'Millie! Lovely to see you,' Ben said, waving as he caught sight of her. Looking a little relieved, he added, 'I don't think you know Laura, do you? Laura, this is Bell's friend Millie.'

Millie said hello and tried to smile rather than look like a frightened rabbit as Laura stared at her for a second before launching into an expressive speech, waving her arms in the air at her.

'You're Millie, then, interesting! I know you from those photos Bell took for our homework – you're the one with the wee bairn, yes? Och, you're even more gorgeous in the flesh than you are in those pictures. I'm telling you now I have massive hair envy, I do. When you're blessed only with a bird's nest like mine you know good hair when you see it, and you definitely have good hair. Bell! I was just saying that your woman Millie here has hair to die for.'

'Hi gang, everything okay?' Bell asked, hurrying up to

them. 'Sorry, got caught up at work and then the bus took forever,' she puffed.

'At least you're here now,' Ben smiled. 'Good turnout, isn't it?'

'Yes, it feels pretty full in here.' She turned to Millie and smiled. 'Bridget was all right to babysit tonight, then?'

'Yeah, turns out she and her local blue-rinse friends play bridge here fairly regularly and she even used to come dancing here back in the day. Which meant she was well up for babysitting Wolfie – though he was less pleased. He made me promise not to stay out too long in case she kept coming upstairs to check on him and, I quote, "making him choke on her funny musty talcum powdery smell"!'

'Bless him. How's he been the last few days?'

'I'll tell you later,' Millie whispered. A general move had begun towards the rows of chairs as those at the front had noticed some important-looking people make their way to seats at the table facing them all.

'If everyone could take a seat?' said a middle-aged man with a slight paunch that nudged over his too-short trousers and bags that dragged his eyes down into his cheeks. Millie guessed he was from the council. 'For those of you who don't know me, I'm Peter Hall, council leader, and this is my deputy Michael Brown, plus we also have Sue Stevens, who manages the community centre on behalf of the council.'

Millie smiled at Sue and decided she looked like a decent sort of person, though she was reserving judgement on Peter and Michael. She glanced across at Bell and saw she was listening intently to Peter droning on about the Health and Safety Executive and how the community's health and wellbeing was their biggest priority. She was starting to doze off, until she felt her friend bristle in the seat next to her so she tried to tune back into what was being said.

'We estimate the cost of renovating both the changing rooms, fixing the damp problems in the main building and refurbishing the café to be around fifty thousand pounds.'

There was an audible gasp, though Bell didn't utter a sound and instead gripped the arm of her chair. Millie squeezed her wrist gently.

'As a council, we have a long history of investing in health and leisure facilities and we want to keep this centre open so the local community can continue to enjoy using it, so tonight we pledge half of this money upfront.'

There was a fair amount of cheering, noticeably from an older couple near the front of the room, but Peter held his hand up for quiet.

'However,' he added, and the room collectively held its breath, 'if we can't secure the remaining twenty-five thousand through fundraising or private donations, the council will be left with no alternative but to withdraw its pledge.'

Immediately, a murmur spread through the audience until it became contagious indignation and Millie could hear people saying, 'Well that's that, then, we'll never be able to raise that kind of money,' and, 'Trust the council to make it look like they're doing something when in reality they're actually condemning the building to close right now!'

She watched Bell raise her hand and Peter cleared his throat and said loudly, 'Yes, do you have a question?'

'I have two, actually,' Bell said, her mouth set in a determined line as she stood up and everyone else turned to stare at her. 'First, what is the deadline for this twenty-five thousand to be raised or donated? And secondly, if the centre does close, what are the council's plans for the site?'

'Ooh, good questions, Bell!' cried the lady Millie had heard cheering a few minutes before. 'I told you she was a feisty one, didn't I, Tone?' A chuckle of laughter rippled through the crowd, and Bell half smiled but remained standing and maintained her eye contact with Peter.

'To answer your first question, we've set a deadline of the end of July to raise the money.' He was interrupted by shouts of, 'But that's only two months away!' and 'So soon?', before he continued, 'Should the decision be made to close the centre, it will take effect from September the first. The council will then discuss what to do about the land and whether it could be better used by interested parties.'

'You mean greedy developers!' one person shouted angrily before others joined in with, 'We should have known this was all about selling the land to the posh housing companies!'

Bell raised a hand a second time and Peter wearily nodded at her. 'When you say interested parties, do you mean the land would be taken out of use by the community and sold into private ownership? And if so, would the money raised be used to build a new, modern community centre locally?'

'What she said!' cheered Laura and there were several 'Oohs' from around the room. Millie noticed the council leader's neck redden as he pulled at his collar unhappily.

'No decisions have been made about what will happen going forward should we not reach the target, but we would be negligent if we didn't consider all possibilities on the table,' he managed to get out. 'Now, ladies and gentlemen, unfortunately, my time is up, so I'll leave you in the capable hands of Sue here.' And with that, he walked out of the room, with Michael Brown skulking silently behind him. The assembled locals descended into a cacophony of noise as everyone started talking at once. Bell sat down and Millie turned in her seat to give her a hug.

'You were amazing just then, Bell, actually amazing! He might not have said what we wanted to hear, but at least you got him to admit to the council's plans.'

Ben appeared beside them, his eyes shining. 'Bell, that was brilliant, you've got everyone fired up. Seriously, I think if everyone had a grand to spare, they'd pledge it right here and now thanks to your questions!'

'Thanks, but sadly none of us have that kind of money hanging around,' Bell laughed ruefully. 'But maybe together we can do something. I think we need some kind of a plan, though.'

'We need an action committee,' declared Laura. 'And you're going to lead it, Missy, after that display!' and she began pushing Bell towards the front of the crowd just as Sue attempted to get everyone to settle down, assisted by

Sheila, who whispered, 'Excellent work there, Bell!' then clapped her hands together hard. The room fell silent and Sue smiled at Bell.

'Well, I think we have our leader here,' and everyone cheered as Bell blushed furiously, her previous calm demeanour melting away once the adrenaline left her system. Sue continued, 'Sheila and I wanted to first thank you all for coming this evening and second invite some of you young ones to form a committee to lead the fundraising efforts. We'll both help wherever we can, but it needs some fresh blood, not us old fogies in charge! So if anyone is up for being on the committee, please come and let Bell know. If you don't feel able to be on the committee but still want to be involved in the fundraising – because we *will* raise this money! – then leave your details with me and Sheila. Once we have some firm plans in place, we can let each and every one of you know what you can do to help. Thanks, everyone.'

There was more cheering and lots of discussion as various people ummed and ahhed about whether they could commit to regular ideas meetings or if they were better suited to getting involved once the plans were in place, before forming two lines – one queue in front of Sheila and Sue, and the other around Bell. Millie noticed many of the older contingent veered away from Bell's group and took up safety in numbers around Sue and Sheila. Eventually, everyone had made up their mind, and Millie looked round in satisfaction at the group surrounding her friend. Besides her and Bell, there was Ben and Laura, plus a couple who introduced themselves as Lynne and Marcus (Millie immediately thought 'just good friends – yeah, right!' having heard the whole story from Bell a few weeks before), as well as two boys and a girl who barely looked old enough to be out on their own but said they were in college and had done the photography course with the others. The group was completed by two sporty-looking women in their fifties, who both had their hair pulled back into tight buns and who Millie vaguely remembered admiring as they swam graceful lengths of the pool while Wolf splashed around in the shallow end.

'I'm Di and this is Sarah,' the taller of the two said. 'We're sisters, as you might have guessed!' They smiled at each other and Sarah said, 'I'm the eldest, but Di is still the one with most common sense, even now!'

'Thank you both for joining the committee,' Bell replied. 'I'm sure we'll need both sense and nonsense to help us raise twenty-five thousand pounds! As it's getting a bit late, I wonder whether we should all go away and think about some ideas and then get together again at the weekend, maybe, to chat them through? Anyone who can't make it then can email their ideas over and we'll keep you updated.'

'Sounds like a plan!' Laura agreed. 'Right, fellow committants, see you then.'

The group dispersed as people gathered their bags and drifted out of the building, and Millie hung back in an attempt to wait for Bell and have a chat as they walked to their respective homes. But she could see that her friend was caught up in earnest conversations with various fundraising volunteers and, checking her watch, decided she would have to catch up with Bell another day. She touched her arm gently and said quietly, 'I'd better get back so Bridget can go home. But let's chat on Saturday?'

Bell spun round, her face aghast. 'Oh god, sorry, Millie, give me one minute and I'll come with you now.' She turned back to the old lady she'd been talking to and said smoothly, 'Absolutely, Anna, that sounds like a great idea and I'll put it forward at the committee meeting on Saturday. Make sure you've given Sheila your details and we'll be in touch very soon. Thanks so much for coming this evening.'

She then grabbed her bag from the chair next to her and made for the door, and Millie. 'God, people like to talk!' she said quietly as they slipped out. 'I could have been there for days if you hadn't saved me! Thanks, Mills.'

'It was entirely selfish of me, I assure you, but glad to have been of help!' Millie replied. 'Although I actually did want to, er, talk to you.'

'As long as it's not about damp-course treatments and fairy-cake sales, then I'm all yours,' she grinned. 'Is King Louis being a nightmare again?'

'Actually, no. Well, no more than usual anyway. It's Wolf.'

'Oh no, what's wrong? Is he okay?' Bell turned towards her, her face full of worry.

'Yes and no. We were called into the school again yesterday. Not that KL could come – he's sunning it up in the south of France with that girl from *TOWIE*. So I went on my own, and it wasn't great news. The head said Wolf's behaviour hasn't improved and after several incidents of him getting into fights in the playground, if things don't change they'll be, in her words, "left with no choice but to exclude Wolf from the school".'

'Christ!' Bell exhaled. 'But that doesn't sound like Wolf – fighting in the playground? What's going on? That's not the Wolf I've seen.'

'No, nor me either, although he does have a bit of a temper on him. He's like his dad, quick to get angry or upset, but also quick to forget.'

'What does Wolf say when you talk to him about it?'

Millie looked down at her feet as they walked in time with Bell's on the uneven pavement. 'He just went really quiet. He admitted to fighting in the playground, but wouldn't tell me why.' She looked up and her eyes filled with anxious tears. 'I'm so worried about him, Bell. He's clearly unhappy and as his mummy I should be able to wave my magic wand and make it all better, but I can't. I just don't know how to get him to talk to me.'

'Poor Wolf. And poor you,' Bell replied, slipping her arm through her friend's. 'It sounds like the school isn't doing a whole lot to help either. Maybe he just needs some space to express himself properly away from the classroom. Maybe the community centre has a kids' drama group or something he can join?'

'Maybe, although possibly not for much longer.' Millie

grimaced, immediately wishing she hadn't mentioned the centre's fate after the exhausting evening Bell had already had. 'Louis was talking about getting him into a football academy locally, which would be good, as it means he could make friends with other kids who aren't at his school. Although sorting that out would require King Louis to actually be in the country and thinking about his son, rather than swanning off to Marbella with some pumped-up-lip-pouting bimbo!'

Bell was silent for a couple of seconds. Then she pulled her friend to a stop on the street. 'Are *you* okay, Millie? Because you really don't sound like you are. Why don't you take a step back from the fundraising committee and just help out when you can so you're not under so much pressure?'

'But I want to be involved!' Millie said, stamping her foot in a way she recognised Wolf did when he was frustrated and angry. 'Oh god, listen to me, I sound like such a dickhead!' She started giggling and then found she couldn't stop – and that Bell had started shaking with laughter too. 'Make it stop, my stomach is actually hurting!'

'I know, but "bimbo"? I don't think I've heard anyone say that word since 1995, but it is amazing. Oh god, you're actually hilarious!' Bell tried and failed to control herself and had to grab on to the wall behind her to steady herself she was laughing so hard.

'But it's so apt! I'm totally bringing back the word bimbo,' Millie said, wiping her eyes. 'Thanks, Bell, that was actually just what I needed.'

'What, hysterical laughter? Well, it might not solve any

of our problems and has given me a nasty stomach ache, but, you're right, it's exactly what I needed, too.' Bell tested a smile to see if she could keep the hysterics under control, and thankfully it seemed both of them had managed to get a grip. 'In all seriousness, Mills, come to the meeting on Saturday, but let's go for a coffee in the café first and between us we'll try to get Wolf to open up. Maybe a huge hot chocolate and some sweets will fill him so full of sugar he won't be able to stop talking.'

Millie smiled. 'Well anything's worth a try.' She pulled Bell into a quick hug and kissed her cheek. 'Thanks for being such a good friend. God, I really had better get back and check Bridget is okay. I'll see you on Saturday.'

Bridget was dozing lightly when Millie got home and managed to throw warm tea all over her chest when she abruptly woke up at Millie's hello. Once she was mopped up and packed off with another packet of lemon shortbread biscuits in her bag, Millie watched as she walked down the road, raising a hand goodbye when she reached her front door.

It had been a long day and Millie sighed as she made herself a cup of soothing lavender bedtime tea, sank down into the sofa and opened her laptop, balancing it precariously on her knee. She didn't have much to report on social media, but scrolling through her feed and seeing the amazing days everyone else seemed to have had, she felt she should add her own voice to the crowd. Lacking inspiration as she certainly wasn't going to mention her run-in with Wolf's school and she didn't have anything concrete to post about the fundraising efforts for the centre, she picked up her phone and clicked into her photos app looking for a recent picture that would pull in the lovehearts. Eventually, her thumb landed on an image of Wolfie looking particularly cute as he grinned at the camera with a cheeky glint in his eye. She added a couple of filters and cropped into the shot to get rid of the mess in the living room behind him, then added the caption:

> This little boy tho. My heart bursts with love for him every time he laughs mischievously, giggles as he's telling me one of his jokes, or smiles shyly when he comes home from school with a certificate for being the best-behaved in his class. Please can he stay five years old for ever?! #thisisfive #myangel #love #mumandson #mummyblogger

Millie pressed Share and picked up her tea already feeling lighter and happier.

Chapter Nineteen

Bell

Bell stared at the fifty-seven unread emails that had appeared in her inbox since she'd been in her half-hour meeting with the rest of the marketing team. What with constant brainstorms, catch-ups and presentations, plus her magically refilling inbox, she wasn't quite sure how she was supposed to find time to actually do any work. And even with her whole team at full stretch, there was still a load of that to get through.

'Get your gob around that,' came Suze's dulcet tones from behind her as a large cup of milky coffee landed on her desk. 'Productive meeting?'

'If productive means realising we have even more to do than I'd thought, then yes,' she answered. 'Thanks for this, though, it's the only way I'm going to get through this afternoon.'

'Well, that and the lure of a big glass of red at Smithie's this evening maybe?'

'I would, but I've just got all this to do.' She waved her arm towards her computer and the pile of reports on her desk she hadn't even started to look at.

'Pleeeeeease, Bellster?' Suze implored, and then added a little more quietly, 'I could really do with a chat. Me and Els have been a bit funny lately and I'm not sure why.'

Bell softened almost immediately. 'Okay, Smithie's it is then!'

'Yay, bring on the wine!' Suze whooped. 'I have an off-site at three o'clock so I'll see you there at six, yes?'

'Fine,' Bell replied, turning back to her screen and clicking open email after email and adding more and more items to the to-do list on the pad of paper in front of her.

Bell's day only got busier, to the point that she realised she was absolutely bursting for a wee and hadn't got up from her desk for the last two hours. She hobbled across the office to the loos and only allowed herself a quick glance in the harshly lit mirrors that made her appear pasty on a good day and this afternoon turned her into a vampire with huge bags, before taking a deep breath and returning to the office.

'Ah, Bell, there you are, I was beginning to think you'd run off home!'

Bell took a second to wonder if Emma, Style It Out's head of finance, had been guarding the door of the loos, ready to pounce with her claws fully extended as soon as she emerged.

'Ha! That's funny, Emma, I was just about to come and find you.' Emma raised her eyebrow as if to say 'Hmm, really?!' but Bell knew she had to keep the spiel coming now she'd started. 'I was going to say that I know you're still waiting for those figures and you'll definitely have them by lunchtime tomorrow.' She smiled brightly at her.

'Unfortunately, I need those figures plotted into a graph to add to my presentation for Marian tomorrow morning,' Emma said, her mouth curling upwards. 'If you could send them over this evening, that would be great.' She turned on her two-inch block heel (so last season, Bell thought uncharitably) and marched off back to her domain.

Back at her desk, Bell set to work on her spreadsheet of numbers, crossing her toes that the totals would all end up matching. They didn't. She had no idea why, so had to start from the beginning and try to work out which calculation was wrong. Eventually she located the offending cell and managed to fix it, but not before swearing loudly that whoever had set up the document in the first place had caused the error.

She looked up from her screen to ask which of her team had been half-asleep when they created it, only to find the office was almost completely deserted. She picked up her mobile, which had been lying face down on her desk, and immediately it lit up with a plethora of missed calls and messages from Suze.

'Shit!' Bell cried out loud, before quickly jabbing the call button next to her friend's name. 'Suze, I'm so sorry, I didn't realise the time and I've been stuck here trying to figure out this spreadsheet that some dimwit has fucked up, but Emma needed the figures this evening. Are you okay, are you still at the pub?'

'I had a drink on my own and then gave up on you,' Suze said through a haze of traffic noise that from its volume Bell recognised as the main road out of town. 'Look, don't worry, I know what the Fat Controller can be like.' She sighed. 'I'll see you in the morning, okay.' She ended the call and Bell stared at the phone in her hands, feeling both guilty and pissed off.

She fired off a grovelling text to Suze repeating her apologies, threw her phone on to her desk and pressed Send on her email to Emma. Everything else could wait, she decided; that promised glass of wine was definitely calling, as was her sofa. She'd have to deal with both her emails and Suze's disappointment tomorrow.

Just as she was about to shut down her email, a message popped up at the top of her unread list.

'Could today get any more annoying?' she sighed into the empty office. She clicked on the email's subject line, *Just to keep you up to date*, and began reading.

Dear Bell

I hope you're well and looking after yourself properly.

I wanted to give you a heads-up that my solicitor has emailed your solicitor to reiterate that in order to proceed, you do need to accept the higher valuation we were given on the property or we will have to consider selling the house on the open market instead

> of you buying me out of my share as you have formally requested.
>
> I hope you understand that I'm merely being fair about the situation, and that we can bring it all to a close in a mutually satisfying way.
>
> Regards,
>
> Colin

As she made her way home, Bell wasn't sure which part of Colin's message made her want to punch him in the face most: the part asking if she was looking after herself 'properly', the line about giving her a heads-up (so kind!), or the thinly veiled threat that he would make life really difficult if she didn't cave in and do exactly what he wanted. How could she have spent ten years being in love with a person who was both so patronising and so, well, dickheadish in his messages?

She pulled her phone out of her pocket to look at his email again, and once she'd realised it didn't get any better with a second or third reading, she clicked on WhatsApp and tapped out a message to Cosette.

> Today I've doubled my to-do list, been told off by finance and been patronised by stupid Colin. Oh, and I've still not got any idea how to raise £25k for the community centre and I've managed to piss off Suze. How's your day been?

Less than a minute later, Cosette replied.

> If it's any consolation, the kids have been at each other's throats all evening after Oli told Soph he was going to put her in detention if she annoyed him as he's HEAD BOY, don'tcha know (God, we SO know, thanks, Oli). Rich decided he wasn't going to help referee and left me to calm them both down on my own. I found him half an hour later conked out on the bed. Lucky him, eh? Wanna swap?! I'm sure you and Suze will be fine, and tell finance to fuck off! What's Colin done now?

> Just being a dick about the house – same old! Bleugh, tell the kids Auntie Belly wants them in one piece when she next sees them otherwise she won't be able to shower them both with sweets and presents. And then give the monkeys a kiss from me xx

> Once a dick, always a dick. I've shouted at the kids again and blown them your kisses (they are being so vile I don't want to get too close, to be honest). Chin up, Bell, tomorrow is another day and all that xx

Bell's persistent alarm signalled that tomorrow had turned into today, not that she'd been able to get much sleep what with worrying about Colin's threats, upsetting Suze, Millie's anxieties about Wolf, plus how much work she had to get done, let alone how much money she seemed to be in charge of raising to make sure the local community were able to keep the centre. As lovely as it was that Sue, Sheila and the committee had so much faith in her, she was seriously beginning to wonder whether they had a hope in hell of pulling off the rescue attempt.

She massaged her forehead as she sat up, rolled her shoulders back then tipped her head from side to side. She wouldn't have been surprised if a maelstrom of jumbled-up thoughts had whooshed out of her head and into a puddle on her pillow, but there was no such luck and she was stuck with the whirlwind of disconnected ideas, worries and snippets of information that showed no sign of abating or even turning into more of a breeze.

She'd planned to get into the office early to make a start on her to-do list, though the bus driver seemed to have other ideas as he trundled along at 10mph.

Despite the delays, Bell was still the first person in the office, other than the cleaning staff, who loved to catch up with each other's news at foghorn volume over the noise of their Henry vacuum cleaners. Bell couldn't really blame them – if you had to do the hoovering, you might as well have a good old gossip at the same time, after all – but the din wasn't particularly conducive to productivity.

She peered at the list in front of her, trying to figure out what on earth she'd meant by 'CHP' and 'FSH' in her notes the previous day. When the best she could come up with was that she'd been daydreaming about fish and chips, she realised she should just cut her losses and treat herself to a coffee and croissant at the bookshop café down the road.

'Morning,' she smiled at Suze when she returned half an hour later, and held out a flat white and a paper bag. 'Coffee and pain au chocolat as a peace offering?'

'Don't mind if I do! Thanks, Bellster. Are you okay, you look like you've barely slept?' she asked with her mouth full of flaky pastry.

'Yeah, fine.' She grimaced. 'Other than this place, the small issue of raising twenty-five thousand pounds in six weeks and Colin being annoying again.'

'Oh, well, nothing to worry about then,' her friend deadpanned.

Bell smiled despite herself. 'Last night he told me he was digging his heels in about the price. I've already explained I can't stretch to what he wants so I don't know what he thinks he's going to achieve by doing it. We'll just have to sell the house and I'll buy some rundown two-bedder on the wrong side of town.'

'Er, no you won't,' Suze said to her sternly. 'Right, what's your solicitor said about it? I'll take it from that look that you haven't actually spoken to her about it, yes? Well get on the phone now and make sure it's her top priority. Come on, stop sitting there like a wet weekend and start dialling!'

Thankfully, Bell's solicitor Gloria was in kick-ass mode and told her she would get on to Colin's people immediately and tell them to start managing their client's expectations more efficiently, and assured her she would get the matter sorted for her. Bell already felt lighter by the time she ended the call and didn't even throw her computer mouse at Suze when she gave her an obvious 'I told you so' look.

She whizzed through a load of emails and was feeling quite pleased with herself, until she refreshed her inbox to find another long list of new messages waiting for her. She scanned them, checking for anything that looked urgent, and her eye snagged on one from Marian with the subject line, *Can I see you in my office at 12, please?* Bell glanced at the clock in the corner of her screen, which just at that moment flashed over to 12:00.

'Shit, I've been summoned to see Marian!' she hissed at Suze as she smoothed down her dress and slipped her feet out of her flip-flops and into some wedge slingbacks under her desk.

'I'm sure it's fine, she doesn't bite, remember!' Suze replied, giving her a reassuring smile. 'As long as you didn't nick anything from the new rails when you were home alone here last night then you've got nothing to worry about, right?'

'Right,' Bell answered, sounding unconvincing even to her own ears. She teetered off across the floor, her legs not quite used to the heels after being treated to flats all morning.

'Hi, Marian,' she fake-smiled after knocking and entering her boss's office with as much pretend confidence as she could muster.

'Bell! Thanks for finding the time, I won't keep you long,' Marian said, as she graciously slid her chair away from her desk and gestured for Bell to join her at the low table and two sofas in the opposite corner of the small room. Bell automatically sank down on to the couch and instantly had to inch her way towards the edge so she didn't become consumed by the soft cushions. She was sure Marian always made her prey sit on the squishy seating so she could perch ladylike on the second, harder sofa and have the upper hand before any conversation had even started. She was clever like that.

'Now, Bell, you know that despite some success stories over the past few months, trading conditions are still tough for us and we're having to cut costs wherever we can.'

As Marian started talking and her face lost its smile and became more and more serious, Bell's stomach plummeted. She knew things were tight at Style It Out – and across all fashion retailers – but the figures she'd sent Emma the previous evening hadn't seemed that bad. If she lost her job it would definitely mean losing the house, as without her monthly salary there was no way she could pay even the current fairly modest mortgage on her half of it, let alone on the whole amount. Hopefully, there'd be some kind of redundancy payment, but it would only last a couple of months at the most. She could feel her tummy swirling and her heart was pounding so hard it sounded like it was about to explode out of her ears.

'You know how much I value what you do for the company and how hard you work, but – Bell, are you okay, do you want a glass of water? Don't worry, this isn't about any of your team losing their jobs or anything. I know how invested you are personally as well as professionally in your protegés.'

Bell took a couple of deep breaths of Jo-Malone-filled air and gulped down the butterflies that had fluttered into her throat. 'Yes, I'm very invested in them,' she managed to reply. She just hoped Marian was as invested in Bell herself.

Marian nodded and carried on. 'As I was saying, we have to think very carefully about our spend in certain areas, which is why I don't think we'll be able to pay Ade to do our next shoot, I'm afraid. I know how much you rate his pictures and enjoy working with him, but I wondered, now that you've got some experience behind the camera yourself, whether you'd like to take some test shots for the next look-book for us. I saw a few of your images on social media and they looked great. What do you think?'

Bell stared at her, not comprehending the words that her hearing nerve had transmitted but her brain had failed to translate into sense. 'You want me to take some photos for our campaigns?' she asked slowly, aware she was doing a great impression of a lobotomy patient. Marian nodded and looked encouraging. 'But I've only ever taken pictures for fun, not for proper things like work,' she said. 'I'm not sure I'd be any good at it, to be honest.'

'Well, I like to think I'm a good judge of someone's character, and if anyone can turn their mind and the skills they already possess to something like this, then it's you,' Marian said with a steely gaze. 'You wouldn't be the only photographer involved on the project, as I want to mix it up with different styles so it's quite Instagrammy and feels very real for our customers.'

Bell opened her mouth, and shut it again, still not able to form a proper sentence.

'Of course, you don't have to do it, and you certainly don't have to give me an answer now,' Marian continued with the same intense look at her. 'But if you could let me know either way by the beginning of next week, I can start briefing the teams. Right, well, thank you, Bell.' She stood up and strode back to her desk, leaving Bell to scramble out of the sofa, which of course she'd sunk straight into when she leaned back to try to take in her boss's request.

'I will, I'll have a think,' she stumbled, before adding, 'And thanks, Marian. Thanks for the opportunity and for your belief in me.' She backed out of the room and practically ran back to her desk.

Chapter Twenty

Millie

Wolf was excited to be going to the community centre again.

'Can we go splashing? Will Bell Bell be there? Can we have hot chocolate?' he'd asked Millie when she'd told him that was the plan for Saturday.

'Yes, Bell will be there, but we will have to see about hot chocolate as you can't have it every time you go, you know, and I'm not sure if we'll have time for swimming, but we can always go back on Sunday,' she'd replied, much to Wolf's glee.

They were late leaving the house, thanks to a fraught ten-minute hunt for Wolf's right trainer that had mysteriously ended up in his bedroom instead of in the hallway with the left one. But, thankfully, neither grown-up nor small person had a meltdown and the crisis was averted without too much fuss.

'Wolfie, there's going to be quite a lot of adult talking

today, so you'll have to play a bit quietly sometimes. Is that going to be okay?'

'You mean people are going to say naughty words?' Her son looked up at her, his eyes wide and excited.

'No, darling, I don't think there'll be any swearing,' Millie smiled. 'But you will find some of the talking a bit boring so it's fine for you to go off to the play mat and build Lego. Or I've brought your headphones with us so you can even watch a couple of things on my phone if you get really bored.'

'I fink I might get really bored, Mummy, yes!' he replied, gazing up at her with a serious expression on his face, but a naughty glint in his eyes.

'Funny that, eh, Wolfie!' Millie said. 'But first we're going to have a nice cup of tea and a slice of cake with Bell.'

'Yummy! I like cake. And I do like Bell, Mummy. Though maybe not as much as cake,' he added thoughtfully.

'Don't tell Bell that!' Millie laughed. 'Here we are, can you see Bell through the window at all?'

'There she is, Mummy, look, she's waving at us!'

Wolf ran on into the café ahead of Millie and shouted, 'Bell Bell, we're here! We're having tea and cake with you and Mummy said I shouldn't tell you I said I like cake better than I like you, but I think maybe I like you both the same.'

'Well, cake is lovely, so I'm not surprised it was a close call, Wolf,' Bell grinned at the little boy. He clambered on to her lap, his shoes leaving scuff marks all over her jeans, and she kissed the top of his head. 'You seem a happy chappy today.

Is it because it's nice and sunny outside? Or maybe it's the thought of cake?'

'Mummy said I might be allowed hot chocolate as well as cake. I hope she lets me,' he whispered to her at a volume that Millie was well able to hear as she walked into the busy café area.

'If you promise to play quietly later then I'm sure that can be arranged,' Millie said as she dumped her bags next to the table and bent down to give Bell a hug. 'I'll go and order now, so, Wolfie, why don't you tell Bell what you've been doing at school this week.' She gave her friend a meaningful look and went off to choose between chocolate cake and lemon drizzle, before deciding to get one of each for the three of them to share.

Bell looked down at the five-year-old squirming on her knee. 'Scored any good goals this week, Ronaldo?'

Wolf turned round to face her, kicking her painfully on the kneecap in his haste. 'I did this really cool move where Jordan passed it to me in the middle of the pitch and I passed it back then ran really really fast up to the goal and he passed it again and I put it in the back of the net. Me and Jordan did a high five after we did some cheering and Miss Foster said we were like something out of the Premiership and me and Jordan kept high-fiving each other all day after. So maybe I am a tiny weeny bit like Ronaldo, but as I'm only five now maybe when I grow up I'll be like a superhero Ronaldo and even better than him.'

'That sounds amazing, Wolf! I hope when you become

superhero Ronaldo and play in the Premiership you'll let me and Mummy come to see you play and score goals like that.'

'Of course, Bell Bell. You and Mummy can cheer me on, even when it's all rainy and cold. Daddy says if you can play really well in the rain, which is really hard, then you're a proper footie player. So I have to practise very very hard.' He suddenly looked very serious. 'Although Zach says . . . Ooh, hot chocolate and marshmallows!'

'What do you say, Wolf,' prompted Millie as she placed the tray down on the table, unaware of the tail-end of his conversation.

'Fank you, Mummy, and I'll be very good.'

'What were you saying about Zach, Wolfie?' Bell prompted.

'I can't remember,' the little boy replied as he spooned marshmallows into his mouth.

The adults exchanged a glance, but Millie kept the chat light, focusing on TV shows she and Bell had seen that week and how gorgeous the weather had been recently, before Wolf went off to the play area where Millie could see him, and talk inevitably turned to the centre's fundraising efforts.

'We've had almost three thousand pounds pledged in just a couple of days, which is amazing,' Bell said. 'But I can't see how we're going to get to twenty-five thousand without doing something big. The more I think about it, the more I realise we need to put on a massive event of some kind and get *literally* everyone who lives within a ten-mile radius to come.'

'That sounds, erm, ambitious,' Millie said, raising her eyebrows.

'I know,' Bell groaned. 'But we've got to aim high, haven't we? Otherwise in just a few months we won't be able to come here for hot choc and cake.'

'Don't say that, we're going to make this happen,' Millie reassured her. 'Okay, so we need a big event. What about a summer fair? We can charge people a couple of quid to come in and then have loads of stalls selling cakes and sweets and a bouncy castle for the kids.'

'Yep, it sounds great.' Bell sighed. 'And it will make a couple of grand maybe, but nowhere near what we need.'

'Well it all adds up. But I see what you mean. We need a big draw, though it's not as if the town has any local celebrities to speak of, does it?'

'Well, I'm certainly hoping one of the others has some connection up their sleeve because I definitely don't! Oh well, let's see. How's Wolf been since you were called into the school? Actually, I think he was about to say something before you came over with the drinks. He mentioned Zach – wasn't he the boy he talked about before?'

'Yes! Oh god, that's so annoying that I came back at just the wrong point.'

'I wouldn't worry. At least it sounded like he might want to talk about it, which is the main thing.'

'God, I hope so. He was so much happier today when he woke up because he knew it was Saturday and he didn't have school. I hate the thought of anything making him miserable, let alone something at school that's so much harder for me to fix. Not that Louis is being much help. I finally got hold of him last night, but he barely let me get a word in edgeways as he told me about his amazing holiday with the bimbo – see, I told you I was going to bring that word back!' she laughed as she saw Bell's face crease up. 'But let's not go there now as I can't deal with another stomach ache like the other day!'

The pair both made an effort to pull themselves together, before Bell asked, 'What was wrong with KL then – I'd have thought he'd be all happy and relaxed after his holiday with the b—, I mean in Marbella,' she said, managing not to giggle.

'Oh, he's annoyed at his agent as he'd promised him a transfer to a club in the Championship, but it doesn't look like it's going to happen. Which is hardly a surprise as he's been injured for most of the season – hence why he was able to spend a week sunning himself in Marbella! But he doesn't see it that way and now he's sulking. What, why are you looking at me like that?'

'King Louis! He could work.'

'What do you mean, he could work? Work as what?'

'He could be the big draw we need at the summer fair.'

'Louis? No one's going to pay good money to see Louis at a fair.'

'Don't be so sure.' Bell nodded, warming to her theme. 'We could organise a five-a-side tournament that Louis could be part of. Who wouldn't want the opportunity to play football with a famous Premiership player?'

'Ex-Premiership, now League One. Really? You think people would care that much? God, I can't think of anything worse than playing football with Louis!'

'That's because you're not very good at it, Mummy,' Wolf said matter-of-factly as he presented her with an unidentifiable model of stuck-together Lego. 'When Daddy does dribbling it's like he's on fast-forward cos he's so quick. And if Daddy came and played football in front of everyone then Zach would have to believe me and stop being so horrible.'

Millie glanced at Bell and then hauled her son onto her lap and stroked his hair. 'Darling, is Zach being mean to you at school?'

'A bit,' Wolf mumbled.

'Is he saying horrible things to you or hurting you in the playground?' she probed gently.

'He says that Daddy is a rubbish footballer and that I am too. And then he sometimes trips me up in the playground on purpose and laughs when I fall over.'

'You know the other day when you were told off for fighting, was that to do with Zach?' Millie couldn't help the edge that had crept into her voice; she couldn't bear the thought of some little scrotty kid hurting Wolfie.

'Yes,' Wolf said, fiddling with his Lego. 'He pushed me over and I got angry and said something horrible to him, so he punched me on the arm and pushed me over again and then everyone came and started shouting and then Mrs Boyle came and shouted louder and then I had to see Mrs Spencer. But, Mummy, I never hurted Zach, I swear. I did say nasty things but only cos *he* had and Daddy told me to say nasty things back when someone sayed them to me.'

'It's okay, Wolfie,' Millie said, hugging him to her and feeling the warmth of his little body lean into hers. She swiped her arm across her eyes, her anger building about the way her son had been treated both by Zach and by the school. 'I'll come in and see your teachers on Monday and we'll sort this all out.'

'I don't want Mrs Boyle and Mrs Spencer to be all cross.' Wolf looked at his mum, alarmed.

'They won't be cross with you, Wolfie, I promise. Now that you've told me what's been happening, I can make it all better.' Well, she hoped she could anyway. She hugged Wolf even tighter, until he started protesting.

'Mills, I'd better go and set up the room ready for the action committee. It's absolutely fine if you don't feel up to it and want to take Wolf home now.'

'I want to play with the Lego a bit longer. Pleeeeeease, Mummy.'

Millie looked at Wolf and then Bell and eventually nodded. 'Okay, Wolf, you can bring a small box of the Lego from here into the special room where we're having our meeting. But when we're finished, you have to promise to tidy everything up quickly and quietly. And when we give Daddy a call tomorrow, I need you to tell him exactly what you told me about Zach. Is that okay?'

'Yes, Mummy,' Wolf replied, but Millie could see he was less than happy at telling Louis about Zach bullying him.

Because that's what it was: bullying. Millie felt bubbles of anger rising up inside her chest again, but thankfully Bell placed a reassuring hand on her arm.

'It will be okay, Mills, he's a tough cookie. See you in a few minutes, yeah?'

Everyone arrived promptly for the meeting and the eleven of them sat round in a circle, with Wolf playing happily a little way away. Millie glanced at the five-year-old proudly as he stared intently at the Lego pieces, concentration etched on his face while he decided which ones to add to his creation.

'Thanks for coming, everyone,' Bell began. 'So today is all about coming up with some amazing ideas of how we can raise the full twenty-five thousand pounds and keep this centre open.'

'So no pressure then,' Laura said, and they all laughed nervously.

'I know it sounds like a lot of money – and it absolutely is – but we can do this!' Bell tried to reassure the group, though even she didn't sound entirely convinced. 'We've already had a total of almost three thousand pledged by various people who came to the council meeting on Wednesday, but I was thinking we need one big push rather than loads of little ones to make this happen. What do you all think?'

The group were quiet, until Ben spoke up. 'I think you're right. We shouldn't discount all the little bake sales and coffee mornings people have already promised to do, but they can only raise so much. A big event sounds great – what did you have in mind, Bell?'

Millie glanced at her friend sympathetically, knowing that Bell had rather hoped other people would have some suggestions to share too. But instead she was forced to go straight in with her own idea.

'Erm, well I was thinking a big summer fair, with stalls and fun things for the kids, maybe a bouncy castle and old-school games.'

'We could make it a vintage fair, with a tombola and hoopla and old games like my mum used to tell me about,' piped up Lisa from the uniform brigade.

'Ooh, I like that idea,' nodded Laura. 'We could have a roast pig on a spit and whisky tasting for the adults and things like guess how many sweets in the jar and guess the doll's name for the kids. And hook-a-duck and splat-the-rat and—'

'Sounds like you're volunteering for quite a few stalls right there, Laura!' Bell smiled. 'I also like the vintage idea, as hopefully it will appeal to both the older members of the community and all the kids and their parents. Well done, Lisa.'

'Me and Sarah would be up for having a stall of some of the cross-stitch and knitting we've been doing,' Di added, and everyone began to buzz with chatter and ideas about what stalls they could include.

Ben said, 'What do you think about displaying the photos from our class in the days leading up to the event so people can come and view them when they want and then we'll sell prints of them on the day? I'm sure Sheila can help us sort that.'

'Och, I'm not sure anyone will want mine, but we should definitely give it a go,' Laura replied. 'Well, we seem to have a load of stalls sorted, but what else could we do on the day?'

There was silence while everyone racked their brains for ideas. Millie watched worry lines form on Bell's forehead, so with a glance at Wolf, who was preoccupied with whooshing his Lego creations above his head like spaceships, she said, 'Bell and I were saying we needed a celebrity or someone famous as a big-name draw to get people to come from outside of the town.'

'Definitely,' nodded Lisa, Ian and Matt. 'But there's no one even remotely famous round here.'

'Does anyone know anyone?' Ben asked. Everyone was silent, so Millie eventually cleared her throat.

'I, erm, know Louis Price. He's a footballer that some people might have heard of maybe?'

'He's the one who's seeing that Zoe off of *TOWIE*, isn't he?' Lisa said. 'He's properly fit. God, I'm so jealous you know him, Millie – I'd definitely like to be introduced to him!' Everyone sniggered, though Millie noticed that neither Ian nor Matt was laughing very hard.

'He's a really good player,' Marcus said more seriously. 'Have you seen that goal he scored a couple of seasons ago against Man United? It was awesome.'

'And it definitely doesn't hurt he's easy on the eye,' Lynne grinned.

'Yeah, he'll be a housewife's favourite!' Laura laughed.

'Mummy, what does a housewife's favourite mean?' Wolf suddenly piped up. 'Is Daddy one?'

'Erm, I'll tell you later, Wolfie. Do you want my phone to watch an episode of *Peppa*? Let me put your headphones on for you. Okay, you sit in the middle here.'

'He's so good,' Sarah smiled at Millie. 'He's been sitting there playing with his Lego on his own for ages.'

'He has his moments, but yes, I'm pretty lucky,' Millie agreed.

'Is Louis Price really his dad?' Laura said, asking the question many of them had been thinking but had been too polite to say out loud.

'Laura! It's none of your business,' Ben admonished her.

Millie grimaced but bit the bullet. 'Yes, he is. Though we're not together now, obviously. He lives in Birmingham and I haven't actually asked him if he'll be the guest of honour at the fair, so I'm not sure what he'll say.'

'Maybe Zoe can come with him,' Ian said, but Bell cut in quickly, 'Well, let's see. First, we need to get Louis to agree. We were thinking he could play in a five-a-side tournament and get all the kids and their dads – or their mums obviously – to put teams together ahead of the fair, then everyone would get a chance to play against him.'

'That sounds brilliant, I'd definitely be up for that,' Marcus said immediately. 'Imagine playing on the same team as Louis Price.' Lynne rolled her eyes, but added her support for the idea.

'How are we going to advertise the fair, do you think?' Bell asked.

'On social media, obviously,' said Millie, Lisa, Ian, Matt, Lynne and Marcus at the same time, and they all laughed.

'But we also need to make posters and leaflets as we want everyone to come,' Ben said. 'I know most of us here are on Twitter, Insta or Snapchat, but we need to make sure we get the message out to the older generations, too.'

'True,' Lisa nodded. 'Though loads of people's parents and grandparents are on Facebook, aren't they? The day my mum friend-requested me was the day I deleted my account!'

'Oh god, yes,' Matt agreed.

'We can ask the college to let us print off some posters and things, make them look all professional. And of course we'll put some up round college too. This is going to look great on our UCAS forms!' She grinned at the boys on either side of her.

Di and Sarah, meanwhile, were whispering to each other furiously until they noticed everyone was looking at them. 'Sorry, we were just saying that maybe we could end the day with a big "We Are The Champions" type pool party, with loads of inflatables and balloons and things.'

'Ohmygod, yes!' cried Lisa. 'We could have flamingos and unicorns and those slices of pizza!'

That set the whole group off discussing which lilo they'd prefer, until Bell checked her watch and shouted above the din, 'Okay, I think we've established Di and Sarah's idea for a pool party is a good one and that everyone likes inflatable unicorns. So why don't I type up all our ideas for the day, get a date sorted with Sheila and Sue and then email everything round to people and give everyone a couple of stalls to start working on? Does that sound like a plan? Oh, and Millie is going to talk to Louis and see if he's up for it.'

'He strikes me as a man who's always up for it!' cackled Laura, and even Millie had to smile, though Ben nudged the Scot and frowned at her and looked meaningfully at Wolf, who had taken off his headphones and was starting to look bored.

'Why is everyone laughing, Mummy?' he asked, sliding across the floor on his knees to kneel down next to her. 'Have people been doing swears again?'

'No, it's just grown-up stuff,' she replied. 'Come on, let's get you home, Wolfie.'

'I'll sort the Lego and stuff if you want to get off,' Bell said immediately, and Millie thanked her gratefully. She suddenly felt exhausted, and worried not only about Wolf, but also that now she'd suggested Louis' involvement, the whole action committee was relying on her to persuade him to say yes. What if he flat-out refused and the centre had to close because of her? As she gathered up their things and everyone said goodbye to each other, she noticed Ben hanging back to help Bell tidy up and put the chairs back in place and smiled to herself.

Later on, when Wolf was finally in bed and Millie was able to crash out on the sofa in front of the new BBC drama everyone was talking about, she found she couldn't care less whether the policeman had a drinking problem and was seeing the prostitutes he was supposed to be protecting, and instead let her mind wander to the conversation she knew she was going to have to have with Louis the following day. She would start with asking him to come to the fair, as she knew it would appeal to his ego, and then she would broach the subject of Wolfie being bullied. She sighed.

She'd had her suspicions, as, contrary to her Insta posts, she knew Wolf wasn't perfect, but she also knew he wasn't the kind of child to start a fight or be mean to another kid for no reason. Had she been so caught up in posting pics to her feed about how happy and angelic he was that she'd missed what was really going on beneath the gloss and the filters? Perhaps she was just a bad mum all round.

Chapter Twenty-one

Bell

Bell was in the office early again, but instead of sorting all the million and one things she should be doing, she was hastily typing up her notes from the committee meeting that she still hadn't finished and firing off emails about the proposed summer fair to everyone involved, mentally crossing her fingers Millie would come up trumps and produce Louis as the guest of honour for the day – the whole success of the event depended on it.

Every so often she'd look up from her computer guiltily, as the rest of the Style It Out staff started wandering through the door, raising their hands in greeting and casting her sympathetic grimaces as she hammered away industriously at her keyboard.

Suze still hadn't come in by nine o'clock, and Bell kept glancing at the seat next to her, hoping her friend had magically appeared. It really wasn't like her to be late for work, and Bell opened her WhatsApp to thumb out a quick message asking if she was okay. As she clicked on Suze's name, she suddenly realised that after the apologetic line she'd sent the previous week that Suze hadn't replied to, she'd not thought to ask again how things were between her and Ellie or tried to rearrange the drink she'd failed to go for. She'd been so caught up with the fundraising fair and Millie.

And after the meeting on Saturday, Ben had said he'd like to help her as much as he could with the fair and maybe they should go out for drink at some point. She'd noticed that he blushed a little when he asked her, and after Ade's comments, Bell too had gone a bit red, but had managed to pull herself together enough to agree. Although they hadn't yet managed to settle on a date they were both free, the thought of it made her feel warm and fuzzy somewhere deep inside and had been helping her keep her chin up, as Cosette would say.

What with that and the pressures of work and Marian's proposition – which of course she'd accepted first thing after the weekend, as Marian had clearly known she would – Bell had forgotten all about Suze and what was going on in her world. She quickly messaged her, asking her if she was all right and suggesting a catch-up over lunch. When she hadn't received a reply half an hour later, she sent Suze's deputy Jamie an email casually asking if he knew where she was.

> She's at an appointment this morning but will be in before lunch. Can I help with anything?

When the reply came back, Bell had to reassure him that no, the thing she needed could wait till later. What she really needed was to check her mate was okay face to face.

When she came back to her desk after a rage-inducing meeting in which Emma had pointed out a large financial flaw in her latest budget estimates in front of all the junior members of her team, Bell was not in the best of moods, but when she saw Suze at her desk, she grinned at her and cried, 'You're back! I was all lonely on my own this morning. Did you get my message?'

'Sorry, I haven't had a chance to read it yet. I've got a conference call in five so I'll see you later, yeah?' Suze replied, not meeting her eye and walking purposefully towards one of the small meeting rooms, her arms full of folders.

Bell stared after her open-mouthed. Suze never left her desk early to have conference calls, always preferring to dial in once she knew everyone else would already be on the call so she didn't waste precious minutes of her life making small talk down a phone line with people she was never likely to meet in the flesh. And she certainly had never spoken to Bell in such a dismissive way before. She hadn't even said hello, she realised. Either something awful had happened this morning at her 'appointment' or she was monumentally pissed off with her. Both options were pretty terrifying.

Despite her stomach rumbling loudly around lunchtime, Bell remained in her chair, tapping her foot against the metal base as she waited for Suze to return from her conference call.

'That noise could get quite annoying,' Suze commented

as she swept past, dumped her papers on her desk and went to reach for her jacket.

'I was holding off lunch so we could go and get something together,' Bell said, standing up and shrugging on her cardigan. 'Where do you fancy?' She forced herself to meet her friend's eye, scared she was about to refuse. 'My shout?' she added quickly.

'In that case, what about Patisserie Francine. I fancy something a bit posh, especially if you're paying.'

Bell would have agreed to anything at that moment and she breathed a sigh of relief as she followed Suze out of the building, although she knew she'd need to do a bit more apologising before she was back to best-mate status in Suze's eyes.

Once they were seated at a table in the corner and they'd ordered pots of Earl Grey tea and plates of scrambled eggs and smoked salmon, Bell poured the tea and smiled. 'God, this is the life, maybe we should do this every day.'

'Have you had a pay rise I don't know about?' Suze replied immediately. 'You'd need another mortgage to eat here every day. By the way, have you heard back from your solicitor yet?'

'I'm expecting a call this afternoon, so we'll see,' Bell answered. 'But enough about me and boring money things, how are you? Are you okay after your appointment this morning?' she asked, practically whispering the word 'appointment'.

Suze looked at her, confused. 'I'm fine thanks, it was just a check-up and the dentist complimented me on the state of my teeth, although god knows how when I drink such vats of tea and coffee,' she added, taking a large, less-than-ladylike slurp of Earl Grey.

So Suze really had been pissed off with her then. Bell gulped. She took a deep breath before launching into her heartfelt apology. 'Look, Suze, I know I've been a rubbish friend recently. I've got so much on with work stuff and all the community centre fundraising but none of that matters – I should have made time for you and I'm sorry. Tell me what's going on with you and Els.'

Suze sighed and looked at Bell. 'I totally get you have lots going on at the moment, Bellster, but you can ask for help, you know, you're not Superwoman, no matter what Marian might think. You don't have to do this all on your own. I'm sure there's work things I can take off you or you could delegate to your team – that's what they're there for, after all – and I'll happily come and man a stall or help out behind the scenes at the fair. And if Colin sends you one more dick-headish email, I'll go round to Tina's flat and punch him in the face – okay?'

'Okay,' agreed Bell meekly. There was a beat of silence before she added, 'But I do really want to know about you and Ellie. Is everything all right with you two?'

'Yes. No. I don't know.' Suze looked wretched. 'I think she's having a wobble, to be honest, not that she'll admit it. But she's been all distant and quiet for the past month. It doesn't help that I haven't seen her for over three weeks. I know we've always done the long-distance thing, but sometimes it feels like she's on the other side of the world rather than a couple of hundred miles up north.'

'Have you asked her what's wrong?' Bell said gently.

'I've tried, but she's swerved the question or changed the subject completely. And when you're FaceTiming rather than seeing each other in real life, it's hard to force the issue. She was supposed to be coming down last weekend, but she cancelled, giving me some shit excuse about her mum needing her at home.'

'Maybe her mum's ill or something? She's got no reason to lie to you, and Els just isn't like that, is she?'

'No, I know, that's what's so frustrating about it. Usually if something's wrong she's pretty good at opening up and telling me what's going on in her head, but recently it's as if she's taken a step back from the relationship but won't tell me why.'

'Hmm, it does sound strange and un-Ellie like,' Bell mused. 'All you can do is be as open as possible about how you're feeling and hope that encourages her to talk about what's going on with her, too. When are you next seeing her?'

'She's now supposed to be coming on Friday, but I'm not holding my breath after last weekend,' Suze huffed. 'You're right, though, Bellster, I need to bite the bullet and sit her down and say I can't see a future for us if she can't talk to me.'

Bell put her forkful of scrambled egg down in alarm. 'Be careful, though, Suze. Don't say anything you don't actually mean. You two are great together. Well, most of the time,' she amended as she caught her friend's grimace.

'I know, but what's the point in being in a serious

relationship with someone who can't tell me how she's feeling? We're both grown-ups – well, in age, anyway. Look, Bell, I love Els with all my heart, but I can't be with someone who doesn't feel the same way about me. I'm too old and I've been too burnt in the past.'

'I know, sweetie, and I agree, but I'm just saying don't throw away something amazing, that's all. Or you'll end up sad and alone like me!'

'Er, except you're not sad or alone, Bellster.'

'I know, I was exaggerating for effect, sorry. I may be alone, but actually I don't think I'm sad anymore,' she said thoughtfully. 'Is it weird that I actually feel happier than I have in years?'

'*Yes!*' Suze held up her hand and high-fived her friend. 'Go Bellster, go Bellster, go Bellster—'

'When you've quite finished with the embarrassing Go Jerry hand movements that no one under thirty will have a clue about!' Bell laughed. 'Yes, I may have proved that breaking up with Colin wasn't the worst thing that could ever happen, but you and Els are the real deal, just you remember that. And as Jerry himself would say, "Take care of yourself, and each other."'

'Who's being embarrassing now!' Suze laughed. 'Come on, get your credit card out and pay for this slap-up lunch and then we'd better be getting back to the office before Marian asks where we are.'

Bell did as she was told and then refreshed her inbox on her phone. 'Shit, Gloria's emailed.'

'That's good, isn't it?' Suze asked, peeling her eyes off her own phone.

'Only if it's to tell me that she's scared Colin and his legal team into backing down,' Bell said. 'Otherwise it's really not good.'

'Well open it then!' Suze replied, peering over Bell's shoulder impatiently. 'Come on, stop being ridiculous, I'll read it for you if you can't bear to open it!'

She took Bell's phone out of her hand firmly and clicked on Gloria's name. '"Dear Ms Makepeace,"' she began in her poshed-up 'phone voice'. '"Further to our conversation last week, I am pleased to report that Mr Viner has now agreed to the purchase price we put forward and we will begin the conveyancing process. You may wish to speak to your mortgage provider at your earliest convenience, blah blah."'

'Wow, she actually got him to back down – well done, Gloria!' Bell whooped and clapped her hands, then hugged her friend. 'Oh my god, I can't believe after all the to-ing and fro-ing that he's actually going to let me have the house!'

'Well, let you buy him out, it's hardly him giving it to you,' Suze pointed out. 'But I'm so pleased for you, Bellster, what brilliant news. Oh, you've just had a message from Millie – here's your phone back.'

Bell scanned the message quickly and her smile grew even bigger. 'Yes! Louis says he'll be guest of honour at the fair and might even bring Zoe with him. That should mean we get loads of people signing up to the five-a-side tournament.'

'It sounds like your plan is coming together,' Suze grinned.

'Well, that's two good things that have happened in the last five minutes and these things always happen in threes so maybe Marian will offer us both a pay rise when we get back to the office. That's if she doesn't fire us for taking the longest lunch break known to man! Come on, we're outta here.'

As Bell lay on the sofa that evening, she surveyed the living room from her prostrate position. With the offensive faux-leather sofa and massive TV gone, she'd been able to create a cosy yet airy feel to the room so that it felt like hers, rather than hers and Colin's – without the Colin. The knitted footstool and candy-coloured cushions warmed up the previously neutral palette and there was still room for the piece of furniture Bell had coveted for almost all of the last ten years – a wooden sideboard.

She'd spent many an evening, when Colin was watching some lame TV series, browsing seemingly every single interiors site the internet had to offer – and there were *a lot*. But one evening she'd finally found her dream sideboard and pinned it to her private fantasy-home Pinterest board. The sideboard had then, of course, followed her everywhere she went on the internet for the next month, with ads even appearing on her Insta feed, constantly reminding her of its tantalisingly gorgeous shape, smooth wooden top and cool brushed-metal legs.

Now, months later and with the algorithms long having given up on her, Bell had to hope her dream sideboard was still in stock and that the price tag had remained at an 'oh my god this is really quite expensive but I guess it's an investment' level rather than an 'oh my god this is insanely expensive and I'll have to remortgage the house' level. Thankfully, it was both available to buy and just about in the realms of affordability, so before she could overthink it, Bell put it in her basket and checked out. When the confirmation email appeared in her inbox, she grinned, took a screenshot and sent it to Cosette. Within seconds, her phone started to ring.

'Well, I take it that your new purchase means there's some good news on the house front?' her sister said excitedly.

'Yes, I set kick-ass Gloria on him and Colin finally gave in so we're all go! Well, if you're still okay to lend me the money,' Bell added quickly.

'Of course! You know me, I never go back on a promise. Unless it's to the kids, obviously. Just let me know when you're likely to need it and we'll move our money around so we can transfer it into the relevant account. Oh, Bell, I'm so happy for you!'

'Thanks, sis, I literally don't know where I'd be without you – probably in some depressing flat I'd hate. How are things?'

'Yeah, good. Exhausting, obviously, but fine. Not too long till the summer holidays now, though that's always a double-edged sword of me having some time off but also having the kids twenty-four/seven, too. But on that note, I was thinking we might descend on you for a few days. The kids keep going on about when they're going to see you next, so I sort of promised them we would come to yours at some point, maybe for your birthday? What do you think?'

'You and your promises!' Bell laughed. 'But of course you can, it will be fun. As long as the kids don't mind sharing the spare room and you don't mind bunking up with me.'

'God, I know how much you like to wriggle around in the night. It will be like when the kids were little and they came in with Rich and me to help them settle, but would spend the whole night kicking me in the stomach with their small, but ridiculously powerful, feet.'

'And my feet definitely aren't small! Though I've so got used to having a whole double bed to myself nowadays – it's definitely one of the perks of being single.'

'I'm quite tempted to divorce Rich just so I can have the same,' Cosette giggled.

'Oi, I heard that!' came a voice in the background.

'Don't worry, I need someone to rub my feet while I watch telly and you're the only person I know who'll do it. You can stay, dear husband.'

Bell smiled as she pictured Cosette and Rich in their kitchen in Devon, Cosette sitting at the table with a pile of marking in front of her, and Rich unloading the dishwasher in the background, and she was filled with warmth.

'Erm, you two can never get divorced anyway – it would be far too much effort to decide who got custody of Mr and Mrs Mop.' When they got married more than twelve years before during that downtime between Christmas and New Year, as one of their wedding presents Bell had bought them a Christmas tree decoration of a man and a woman made out of shiny gold foil, with little pearls for their hands and some scraggly wool as their hair. Every year since, they had been guests of honour on Cosette and Rich's Christmas tree and the kids now took it in turns to be the one who placed them in pride of place on the top of the tree instead of a star or an angel.

'True,' Cosette answered. 'Well, it looks as though I'm stuck with him for now, then.'

'It's a hard life, I know. Look, why don't you come down for my birthday in September. You can meet Millie and Suze and everyone.'

'Ooh, I'm still obsessed with Millie's Insta, you know. I want to ask her how she manages to keep her living room that tidy with all her little boy's toys.'

'Erm, she doesn't? She just moves them all out of shot when she's taking one of her set-up images for her feed,' Bell laughed. 'But, yes, you can ask her yourself when you come. Hooray. Now I'll actually have to have that birthday party, won't I?'

Chapter Twenty-two

Millie

Millie breathed a happy sigh as she opened the curtains and saw the sun high in the azure sky, its rays bursting through the trees and bouncing off the window, creating a wall of welcome greenhouse heat. Louis had picked Wolf up the night before and so she was free of parental worry, for today at least. As a reward, she was going to lap up the sunshine and she'd even promised Bell she'd take a dip in the outdoor pool for the first time.

Bell was already waiting for her on the corner as she strolled down the main road, swinging her canvas bag filled with swimsuit, towel and suncream. 'Lovely day for it!' she greeted Bell cheerily.

'Well, if there's one day of the year I'm going to get you in that pool, it's today!' her friend replied, laughing. 'It's going to be gorgeous.'

Lots of other locals appeared to have had the same idea

as the pool was already pretty busy when they arrived. But, thankfully, they managed to bag a spot on the side, a little set back from the water, and they each guarded it while the other went to get changed into her swimsuit.

'I wish I'd thought to dig out my bikini like you, instead of relying on this old thing,' Bell complained, grabbing at her slightly saggy costume. 'Though, to be fair, at least this way I'm covering up my stomach and not subjecting people to too much white flesh. But you look amazing!'

Millie glanced down at her blue and pink block-colour two-piece and waved away Bell's comment. 'I don't get much chance to sunbathe so I might as well bring this out of hiding while I can. Though I think the last time I wore it was when Wolfie was tiny. Anyway, I'll have none of your rubbish – you've got a great figure, especially now you've lost some of that skinniness.'

'Well, I might never have done the pregnancy thing, but I've certainly been eating for two the past few months with all that cake I've been scoffing! I bet you snapped straight back into your skinny jeans like a celebrity after you had Wolf, didn't you?'

'Not exactly, but I definitely had age on my side,' Millie smiled, applying suncream liberally to her arms. 'I can't believe I was only twenty-five when I had Wolfie.'

'God, I was still such a kid at that age,' agreed Bell. 'And at thirty-nine and three quarters, I still am, I guess!'

'Are you going to do anything for your fortieth?' Millie asked.

'I don't know. I can't decide whether I should curl up in a ball and pretend it's not happening or go big with a massive party to show the world age is just a number. Cosette and the kids are going to come to stay around then, so I'll be forced to do something for it.'

'Er, the party option, obviously! It's interesting, I always think of you as being super-confident and not really worrying what other people think,' she said thoughtfully.

'Really?' Bell looked at her incredulously. 'You really think that?'

'Yes. Look at the way you've taken charge of the action committee and got everyone on board with your ideas for the summer fair.'

'Well, they're everyone's ideas, and someone needed to take charge, plus I don't have any kids or dogs to walk or college courses to do, so it makes sense for me to get on with it.'

'But you do have a full-time, full-on job, though.'

'That is true. And it has definitely been full-on of late.'

'But you'd never know it, as you just get on with it, as you say.'

'Well, I care about the centre. Just look at all the people here today enjoying it.' They both drank in the groups of families and friends, lounging in the sunshine and occasionally squirting a thick, white blob of sunscreen on various areas of their bodies, inevitably missing some bits that they would only later realise had turned red and angry without them noticing. Then there were the groups of swimmers in the pool, who ranged from excited parents taking their baby swimming for the first time, to serious swimmers pounding up and down in the marked-out lanes near where Millie and Bell were sitting. The sun glinted off the water, revealing a thin surface film of suncream and a scattering of tiny petals from the trees nearby.

'God, we could be in the South of France,' Millie said, reaching for her phone and snapping a few shots, before lying back and attempting to capture the sun reflecting off her smooth, suncream-shiny, lean legs. 'Got it!' she cried triumphantly, while Bell looked on amused.

'Yes, we could be in the South of France, but we could also be in a small town an hour north of London soaking up every ray the British summer has to offer,' Bell said.

'But the Côte d'Azur sounds so much more . . . aspirational,' reasoned Millie, resisting adding a filter, but making sure she sharpened and brightened the photo just a little, before writing the simple caption,

> La vie en rose! #AndRelax #RnR #splendide #superbe #sunshine #pool

'See, I haven't actually said I'm in France, but if people want to read it that way, then that's up to them,' she said smugly, holding her phone out for Bell to see.

'But it's still a bit misleading,' Bell argued. 'Why not post another pic of the pool now and say you're actually at your local lido and see which post gets the most Likes? Here, I'll write the caption for you.'

'You don't have to do that!' Millie said, grabbing her phone back quickly. 'Fine, if it makes you happy, I'll do a second post. Let me just take another pic, as it would be good to get the edge of my towel and my sunnies in the foreground.'

Millie spent the next five minutes setting up the perfect shot before she was happy, and eventually posted the image with the words,

> It might look like the Cote d'Azur, but it is in fact the lido at my local community centre! Such an unbelievably gorgeous day in the sunshine. Who needs France when good old Blighty is this hot?! #heatwave #lido #swim #sunshine #community #Bestofbritish #Livingmybestlife

'There, happy?' she asked Bell, who refreshed her feed and nodded.

'Look, you've already got loads of Likes and you only posted it about half a second ago!'

'We'll see,' smiled Millie. 'And one of those Likes is yours!'

'Ha, busted! But don't you feel better for being truthful about your picture, like it's more authentic and people are Liking it because they too are out enjoying the sunshine where they live rather than wishing they were in the South of France like you?'

'Maybe. But it's different when Instagram is actually part of your job. I never thought when I moved down here and started blogging and posting on Insta that social media would become my main source of income. At first it was a bit of fun, but as soon as you start making money from it, it's like the rules change. If I post something and only about fifty people Like it, what message is that sending to a brand who were thinking of working with me? It's saying "She can't engage her followers, no one cares what she posts, no one wants to be her". And then the brand will look at the next influencer on their list and DM them with an offer instead of me. And there's the algorithm to think about too. If a follower doesn't Like my post, Instagram may not choose to show them my next one, or the one after that, so then they're being seen by fewer and fewer people and therefore fewer and fewer people will Like them. It's a vicious circle.'

Bell stared at her open-mouthed. 'I had no idea that's how it works. Though if I think about it, that makes sense as sometimes people post things and I never see them unless I specifically click on their profile and check out their grid.'

'Listen to you talking like a pro!' Millie laughed. 'But, yes, you're absolutely right. So you can see why I can't really afford to take a chance and tell the "truth", whatever that really is. No one wants to know that you've had a shitty day, been shouted at by your boss and missed the bus home, plus to top it all off you've got the worst period pain. That's just not what Instagram is all about.'

'But the way you describe it makes it sound like a depressing popularity contest that you'll never win because there'll always be someone who gets more Likes and comments than you, unless you're Victoria Beckham, or whoever.'

'That pretty much sums it up,' Millie sighed. 'Except if you're Selena Gomez and have almost a hundred and fifty million followers. Although even she is out-followed by Instagram itself, so frankly no one can ever win.'

'But does it really have to be about winning?' Bell asked. 'I only follow about two hundred people and I have even fewer people following me, but I still love scrolling through my feed.'

'Your feed that contains pictures that have been filtered at least ten times and probably adjusted in Photoshop, too. None of it's true. Which is why, to keep up with everyone else, you have to add twelve filters and make your post more sparkly and exciting than other people's.'

Millie sat up and took off her sunglasses to look directly at her friend. 'And if you think about it, even when you're talking to people in real life about what you did at the weekend or where you went for dinner, you're always filtering out the bad bits and presenting the side of your life you want your friends and colleagues to see. If someone asks you what you did at the weekend, you don't say, "Well, I sat in front of thirteen episodes of *MasterChef* and inhaled six bags of Wotsits without stopping," even if that's what you really did. You'd say something like, "Well, I caught up on a load of box sets, sorted out my summer wardrobe and cooked a delicious dinner from Jamie's latest book." We're always filtering and brightening and sharpening our lives so we're seen in the way we want to be.'

Bell drew her knees up to her chest and fiddled with the

edge of her towel. 'I suppose I've never thought about it like that,' she said slowly. 'You're right, no one wants to hear that I've spent the whole weekend on my own cleaning the kitchen cupboards and eating chocolate digestives dipped in tea while watching the whole of *Pride and Prejudice* on some obscure cable channel even though I have the DVD on my shelf. Which obviously I've never done. Although that doesn't stop me telling Cosette about those kind of weekends, I suppose. But she's pretty much the only person I'd tell or who would care. But when you're editing pictures into something they're not on social media, that feels much worse, I think.'

'Maybe it feels like that because social media is always there – as you said, you can click on someone's grid and see everything they've posted, whereas a conversation is transitory and can be forgotten in the blink of an eye.'

'True. But I still think there's space on Insta for people to be if not completely real then at least more truthful. Especially when it comes to parenting. I don't even have kids, but I love that account where it's a dad posting pics of what it's really like to be a father.'

'Yeah, he's brilliant and really funny, and is actually doing really well in terms of followers and sponsorship stuff,' Millie conceded. 'Though I do think it's easier for men as they don't have the same ideals to live up to that women have. If you're not all "Oh my god, having a baby is the best thing to ever happen to me" as a mum, then you're somehow judged. Anyway, we've gone a bit serious, haven't we?

I thought today was all about having fun! How are things with you and Ben?'

'That's right, get straight in there!' Bell laughed. 'I don't know what you mean – there is no me and Ben. Here, chuck me the suncream, will you?'

'Yeah, right,' grinned Millie. 'I saw the way he was looking at you at the meeting last week. He definitely fancies you. And you're single and ready to mingle, so what's the problem?' She raised an eyebrow at her friend as the heat rushed to her cheeks.

'Millie! Seriously, between you, Suze and Laura, anyone would think you were trying to marry me off to the poor guy! I am indeed single, but I don't know if I'm ready to mingle. I've just come out of a ten-year relationship with a man who thinks nothing of quibbling over a few grand and a CD collection, so maybe I'm not that bothered about being coupled up just yet. God, it's boiling, isn't it?' she added, fanning her face with her hand. 'I think it might be time to venture into the pool.'

'You could definitely do worse than Ben,' Millie said thoughtfully. 'What? I'm just saying!'

'Well, stop just saying and let's go and swim a few lengths,' Bell replied, pulling her friend to her feet.

As Millie breast-stroked her way up and down the pool, she was glad that she'd chosen the hottest day of the year to take a dip, as although it was pushing thirty degrees in the sunshine, the water itself still had a nasty bite to it. She couldn't begin to imagine what it had been like when Bell first took the plunge back at Easter, let alone how her own tiny, string-like five-year-old son had managed to enjoy splashing around so much weeks before that.

She was dismayed to find she was more out of shape than she'd realised and fairly quickly made for the steps and the safety of her sun-warmed towel. She stood on the side breathing in the unmistakable aroma of chlorine and watching Bell push her way seemingly effortlessly through the water – another thing her friend seemed to excel at, she thought.

Already she could feel the sun beating down on her skin, so she walked back to the spot she and Bell had secured and laid her towel back down before reaching inside her bag for the suncream.

Her fingers automatically closed round the smooth edges of her phone and on autopilot she picked it up and checked her notifications. She was surprised to see her post about being at the lido had received thousands of Likes. While Millie had felt she was more social-media-savvy than Bell and didn't agree with her idea to always post 'the truth', maybe there was something in what she had said, after all.

Later that afternoon, after a toastie and a huge ice cream from the café, the pair were lying lazily on their towels, their bags providing makeshift pillows, and Millie was contemplating whether Bell would notice if she had a short nap, when the older woman said, 'Dare I ask how things are going with Wolf's school? I know Louis has agreed to come to the fair, fingers crossed, but you didn't say how your conversation about the bullying went.'

Millie pulled herself up so she was sitting cross-legged. 'Well, he did his usual "Wolf just needs to stand up to them and punch them back but harder" routine, but when I explained what the school had said about excluding him, he backed down and instead got cross with the school for not protecting his little boy. To give him his due, he managed to get a phone call with the head and by all accounts told her what he thought of the school's lack of support for Wolf and how he was the innocent party in all of this. She seemed to say all the right things like "Wolf's safety is always paramount to us, and he's a valued member of the school", you know the kind of thing. But she never actually promised to do anything about it. Louis was livid when he spoke to me afterwards. I think he's so used to people doing what he says and bowing down before him that he didn't quite know how to handle it. It sounds like he ended up slamming down the phone.'

'That doesn't sound very helpful,' Bell observed. 'Did you go in to see the head, too?'

'Yeah, which was interesting. One of the other mums grabbed me at the gate at morning drop-off and said she'd heard Zach had been accusing Wolf of hitting him and asked if he was okay. I tried to pretend everything was fine, but I could tell she didn't believe me and then she said, "You do know who Zach's dad is, don't you?" I obviously shook my head and then she proceeded to tell me Duncan Dyer is a parent-governor at the school, as well as owner of Dyer's Tyres, who just happen to have donated a large sum of money for the school's proposed new computer suite.'

'No! Bloody hell. Well, that explains a few things, doesn't it,' replied Bell, sticking her shades on top of her head. 'Did you ask the head about it when you had your meeting?'

'Funnily enough, yes! She assured me the school treats all pupils equally, but they had a duty to make sure both Zach and Wolf were happy and healthy and maybe it just wasn't the right school for Wolf.'

'Christ! Could she be any more blatant? Although maybe she's right – if that's going to be their attitude, maybe Wolf is better off in a different school. There must be another one nearby that's got a good Ofsted rating and has a spare place for September?'

'I wouldn't be so sure,' said Millie gloomily. 'The only other one that isn't in special measures or at least doesn't "need improvement" is hugely over-subscribed. I've sent them an email enquiring about spare places for next term, but I'm not holding my breath. And Louis keeps mentioning a private school he's found in Birmingham. Apparently loads of his teammates' kids go there and it's supposed to be brilliant,' she added miserably.

'But Louis would never take Wolf away from you, surely?' Bell reasoned. 'For one, that would mean he'd have to look after him during the week, and from what you've said, I can't see that happening.'

'I know, you're right. But I know his mum is desperate to

be a more hands-on grandma, so I'm sure she'd love to help Louis out with childcare.'

'I'm sure she's great, but Wolf doesn't need his grandmother, he needs his actual mother!' Bell stormed. 'Look, I'm sure that deep down Louis knows that and he wouldn't jeopardise Wolf's happiness. And there's a huge difference between him seeing his son for a fun weekend once a month and looking after him day in, day out, even if his mum is involved. I'm sure it won't come to that, but even if it did, we'd just get you a fuck-off lawyer who would tell Louis to do one!' she added fiercely.

Millie was a bit shocked at the ferocity on Bell's face and found herself trying to placate her, instead of the other way round. 'You're probably right, it's just a bit of bravado from Louis. I'm sure it will all be okay. And at least he said he'd come to the fair.'

'That's the least he can do,' she spat.

'Look, Bell, he's not that bad. He's a good dad when he wants to be and as you said, I'm sure it won't come to that anyway. God, I think I've spent too much time in the sun today, I'm knackered. Do you mind if I head on home?'

'Shit, sorry, Mills, I didn't mean to go off on one at you. I just care about you and Wolf and don't want to see you upset. Look, tell me to butt out if you want to, but if you do get a sniff of an in at that other school, I don't mind coming with you to look round it if Louis can't make it. Or if there's anything else I can do, just let me know.'

'That's so kind, Bell, thank you, I really appreciate it.

And I'm sorry if I went on at you about Ben earlier. I just think he's a lovely guy and could be just what you need right now – someone to take care of you while you're taking care of everyone else.'

Bell had to smile. 'He is a lovely guy, you're right. But, well, we'll see,' she added reluctantly as Millie punched the air with glee.

'Ha, I am so holding you to that "we'll see"! Right, please let me know if there's anything else I can be doing for the committee, won't you. I kind of need a bit of a project to take my mind off all this Louis stuff.'

'Are you sure?' Bell glanced at her shrewdly. 'Okay, well, we need to start handing out leaflets and getting the word out about the fair. Anything you can do on that front would be brilliant.'

'How about I call the local paper and radio stations and see if they'd be up for covering it?'

'Erm, that would clearly be amazing, but do you really think they'd be interested?'

'Definitely. Everyone loves a local story about the community coming together. We should get them to interview some of the oldies and the uniform brigade together and pitch it as an across-the-generations story.'

'You are actually a genius!' Bell sprang up and gave her a hug. 'Although if Rita ever hears you call them "oldies" she'll have something to say to you!'

'I'll definitely watch what I say around her, then. Obviously I can't promise anything with the local media, but why don't I put together a press release and email it over to you and you can let me know your thoughts? Ooh, and I'll have a think about a hashtag we can use, too.' She rubbed her hands together and could feel a bubble of excitement in her tummy.

She needed this, she realised as she sipped a bottle of water on her sweaty walk home. She needed something to make her feel less like a failing mother and more like a capable, successful woman who could make things happen. Because right now, when it came to her family, she seemed to be looking failure full on in the face.

Chapter Twenty-three

Bell

Bell was woozy from the heat when she made it home – via the supermarket to pick up something for dinner. The journey seemed to have sapped her of all her energy and despite the cloying smell of chlorine that meant she should really take another shower and scrub her skin with expensive shower gel to wash it away, she decided to head to bed with a book.

As she turned on the fan and flopped onto the bed, she allowed herself to luxuriate on the soft, cool sheets and think about how much she'd enjoyed her day at the pool with Millie. Except when her friend had pressed her about Ben. She hadn't been ready to confess about the growing closeness she could feel between the two of them, or the fizzing in her belly she got when she thought about him, or even that he'd asked her to go for a drink. For now, she was content for it to be something she kept in a box in her own brain, which she was able to open and peer at when she wanted, but also close and put away when she didn't. And that just wasn't possible if she told Millie or, god save her, Suze, how she really felt.

She knew there were things she should be doing right now, like checking her emails and practising taking amazing pictures on her camera, but it was Saturday evening and she'd lounge around if she wanted to, she thought happily.

She was just drifting off into a blissful doze when her phone began vibrating against her chest where it had fallen from her hand as she entered snoozeville.

'Suze?' she answered groggily. 'You okay?'

'I'm more than okay, as it happens,' her friend replied, her voice sounding like she was on the edge of both laughing and crying. Bell pulled herself up to sitting position, with her pillow resting against her back, as Suze continued. 'Um, Els just asked me to marry her and I said yes!'

'What?! Ohmygod, that's amazing!' The next few minutes was filled with a succession of screams and tearful shrieking as Bell managed to establish that Suze had tried to sit Els down for The Talk as she'd told Bell she was going to, except Ellie had got in there before her and explained that she'd been a bit funny lately because she had something to ask her and she wasn't sure what she would think.

'At that point I had absolutely no idea what she was going to say,' Suze told Bell happily. 'I really thought it was going to be something awful, and then she just came out with it, didn't you Els, and of course I said yes immediately.'

'Well, not quite immediately,' Ellie piped up. 'It was

actually the first time I've seen you lost for words in the whole time I've known you. And then you said yes.'

'I can't imagine you speechless, to be honest, Suze,' Bell grinned. 'Oh, I am *so* happy for you both, you've totally made my day. It's just the best news. Have you set a date yet? Hurry up, I want a massive party!'

'Give us a chance! Though I don't think either of us want to wait too long, so we were thinking maybe January. Everyone's so miserable after Christmas and New Year so we thought we'd give you all something to get excited about.'

'Excellent idea. Dry January can totally do one!'

After a bit more shrieking, Bell ended the call and allowed her ears to adjust to the abrupt return to silence. She swiped her arm across her eyes and tried to examine how she was feeling, before realising that, actually, she wasn't in any way jealous of Suze's engagement, when just seven months before she'd been expecting one of her own. All she felt was joy and relief that Suze was happy and her future with Ellie was more secure.

Finding that she was suddenly wide awake, Bell headed to the kitchen, mixed herself a large G&T and decided a Saturday dinner of prawn cocktail crisps was entirely permissible: another perk of being single.

The next few weeks were a blur of work, worrying she had no idea how to use her camera despite weeks of Sheila's guiding hand and both Ben's and Ade's help, and organising the fair. But somewhere in the midst of it all, she and Ben managed to sort an evening they were both free for a drink, and Bell was able to admit (in her head only, obviously!) that she was looking forward to it.

Despite telling herself it was just a glass of wine in the pub and *definitely not a date*, the morning of the non-date she struggled to decide what to wear. It didn't help that the weather was literally blowing hot and cold one day to the next, so when she looked out the window at 7am and realised the sun was very much shining, she dithered for a good twenty minutes before reaching for the sunshine-yellow sundress she'd admired on the rail in the office many months before. Suze had been right, cork wedges would go really well with it, but they'd also look a bit try-hard for a laid-back non-date, so she went for her trusty Converse instead.

'Someone looks happy today,' Suze commented when she saw her. 'I knew that dress would look amazing on you.' She nodded in satisfaction. 'Doing anything nice this evening?'

Bell was about to finally admit to her non-date, when her phone lit up and she saw she had a message from Ben. 'Hold on, let me just read this,' she replied.

> Hi Bell, I'm so sorry to do this, but I'm going to have to cancel this evening I'm afraid. Sadly, my neighbour who I walk the dog for had a massive heart attack overnight and passed away. His son lives up in Scotland so hasn't been able to get down here yet so I need to look after Graham and sort some

stuff out with the funeral people and social services. Can we rearrange our drink for sometime next week maybe? I'm really sorry to cancel, hope you understand, Ben x

Disappointment streaked through her body, but she tried to keep her face neutral as she glanced up at Suze, who was waiting expectantly for her answer.

'Oh, no, I'm not up to anything this evening, just thought I'd make the most of the sun and wear this dress while I can,' she replied as nonchalantly as she could. As she then thumbed out a reply to poor Ben, she could feel Suze's eyes on her, but she didn't really have the head space to get into a conversation about her non-date-that-had-turned-out-to-be-an-actual-non-date. Plus, she was taking the following morning off work to look round Wolf's possible new school with Millie, so she needed to focus on work stuff as much as she could.

'Whatever you say, Bell.' Suze raised her eyebrows, but let the matter drop for the moment as she too had a mountain of reports and meetings to get through.

Bell was a little early so she loitered outside the school gates waiting for Millie to arrive, hoping she didn't look like some kind of dodgy woman that would be picked up on the school's CCTV before she and Millie had even had a chance to charm the headteacher. She knew Millie was pinning all her hopes on this being the right school for Wolf, and that they would have a spare place for him in Year One come September. So gone were all thoughts of flirty summer dresses, and instead Bell had chosen her most conservative slim-leg trousers and a simple ruched top that had a small cut-away on each shoulder but was otherwise as non-offensive as possible. Now she was worried she looked like she was here for some kind of corporate business meeting.

'Bell, sorry I'm late. Thanks so much for coming with me this morning.'

Bell hugged her friend and kissed her cheek, then gave a little sigh. 'You're not late, I was early. But how do you always manage to wear exactly the right thing and look amazing in it? I work for a fashion website, for god's sake, and still never nail it like you.'

'What, this?' Millie glanced down at her floral maxi-dress that screamed grown-up yet not too mumsy and her bejewelled sandals that glinted in the sunlight.

'Yes! And don't you dare say, "What, this old thing, I found it in the back of my wardrobe."'

'Erm, that is actually what happened!' she laughed. 'Although I have to admit the sandals are new. I couldn't resist them – I'm like a magpie when it comes to shiny, pretty things and they were only a fiver from the supermarket.'

'Do you know, I should really hate you,' Bell said. 'But luckily you're far too nice a person. And I still need all your help with the fair so I can't ditch you until after then, at least! Come on, let's get this over with. You're going to wow them, I promise.'

As soon as she walked through the gates and headed to

the reception area of the school, Bell was instantly transported back to being six years old and trying to tag along with Cosette and her friends in the playground. She'd been roundly laughed at by the ringleader of the group and called nasty names, then been forced to watch forlornly as they all played a game of skipping that she was desperate to be part of, while Cosette kept trying to give her apologetic looks. She'd largely enjoyed her school days, but she'd never forgotten how much she'd wanted to play with the older kids instead of with her own classmates and how upset she'd been when she was told she was too young. Of course, soon she was one of the older kids herself and had probably done the same to the younger ones, but she was painfully aware of how Wolf must feel when Zach and his cronies ganged up on him.

'Ms Morley? I'm Mrs Anderson, pleased to you meet you.' A kind-looking lady with silvery short hair walked over to them and held out her hand.

'Hi, I'm Millie and this is my friend Bell, lovely to meet you.' Millie smiled a little shyly. 'Thanks for finding time to show us round.'

'Not at all, we're always happy to show off our school. Now, shall I give you a quick tour and then we can have a cup of coffee and a chat? Right, well, we have two classes in each year, but we're pretty strict about numbers as we want to make sure we're creating the right learning environment for our children.'

As they walked round the various classrooms, art department, assembly hall and sports facilities, Bell was very taken with the displays of the pupils' work and she could see that Millie was practically salivating at the prospect of seeing Wolfie blossom in the nurturing and creative arms of the school. And once Millie saw the football pitch, she couldn't help but exclaim, 'Wait till Wolfie sees this, he's going to be in heaven, won't he, Bell!'

Mrs Anderson smiled indulgently and led them back to her office. Once they were seated and had hot drinks in front of them, she launched into a speech about the pastoral side of the school and how it supported its pupils.

'Wolf's been having a hard time with some of his peers, I think you said, Millie? Well, our anti-bullying policy is extremely strong and we teach our children about inclusivity and that not all families are the same,' she said, smiling widely at both Millie and Bell, who suddenly realised how her accompanying Millie to this appointment might look.

'I'm sure Wolf's dad will also be pleased to hear that, won't he, Millie?' she said, subtly nudging her friend in the ribs.

'Oh, yes, of course,' Millie agreed quickly. 'Thankfully, Wolf is fairly well adjusted to Louis' and my separation – he's barely known anything else because it happened when he was young. And he understands that he has a mummy and daddy who both love him very much but aren't able to live together and hasn't ever really questioned that.'

'Good stuff,' Mrs Anderson smiled, though Bell still wasn't sure what she thought she was doing there. 'Well, I'm pleased to say that if you do decide Wolf would like to come here in September, we have a place for him in our Year One intake.

Obviously, most of the children will be coming up from the reception class so they do all know each other, but there will be a couple of other new pupils like Wolf, and hopefully he will settle in well. Do you want to discuss it with Wolf's dad and then send my secretary an email next week with your decision? Excellent. Well it was lovely to meet you, Millie, and you, Bell.'

Minutes later they were back outside the gates and Bell was trying not to giggle. 'Do you think she thought we were together?' she chuckled as they headed off down the street.

'No! Well, maybe at one point, but I'm sure she sees all sorts of families in a job like that. Anyway, it looked amazing, didn't it? And Mrs Anderson is so nice. Now all I need to do is convince Louis.'

'Yeah, it does feel like a lovely school,' Bell nodded. 'And I'm sure when you've spoken to Louis and told him all about it, he'll be on board, too. He's got Wolf's best interests at heart, after all.'

'Let's hope so. Anyway, I know you have to get to work so I'll stop gabbing on, but I can't thank you enough for your support today, Bell. Having you with me made everything less nerve-racking. You're such a good friend, thank you. And just so you know, if I was looking for a female partner, then you would *so* be her,' she grinned.

Bell smiled to herself all the way through the bus journey to work. Until she checked her email and was assaulted by a hundred new requests for figures and information and extra meetings. She quickly checked her personal email, too, and saw a load of messages from various members of the committee.

The fair was now only a week and a half away and the organisational questions were piling up, making her feel a bit sick at the thought of everything that still needed sorting. Although it would have to wait until at least this evening as she spotted another five emails land in her work inbox in the time it took her to get off the bus and walk to the front door of the Style It Out building. On her way up the stairs to the office, she quickly fired off a message asking for one final committee meeting at the weekend. After that she'd just have to hope for the best.

Chapter Twenty-four

Bell

On Saturday morning, Bell commandeered a couple of tables in the community centre's café and spread out all the many pieces of paper she'd managed to accumulate over the past few weeks, from a list of stalls and who was going to man them, to a record of the football teams who'd signed up so far. With Louis on board for the tournament, they'd already had twenty teams of five sign up and pay the fee of twenty-five pounds a team, which was five hundred pounds in the bank immediately, but they could definitely do with more people. They still hadn't had the bouncy castle confirmed, as the council's health and safety person had got involved and had to check that everything complied with the rules, but she hoped Lynne and Marcus would bring good news on that front when they arrived.

Bell's phone lit up with a couple of notifications. The previous weekend she had bitten the bullet and reactivated her Facebook account in order to help spread news of the fair and the whole fundraising effort far and wide. She'd been careful to only really use it for this purpose for the last week, but obviously she hadn't been able to resist a quick peek at Colin's page.

It seemed he and Tina were very much still an item and he'd even changed his profile pic to one of the pair of them together. In the whole of the ten years Bell had been with Colin, she was fairly sure his profile image had been him on his own, and his statuses had never been anywhere near as effusive as the 'Colin is feeling lucky to be snuggled up to the kindest, most gorgeous woman tonight' he'd posted the other evening.

At first, she'd felt anger and nausea rise up into her throat when she'd seen his posts, but now, a few days down the line, she was just grateful that his happiness had meant he'd given in on the house price. Bell knew she was happier herself now they'd split up, so why shouldn't he be happier, too? She'd felt very grown-up at that point and had smugly messaged Suze to tell her, who'd quickly replied, saying,

> Well if Tina is happy with someone who ends his emails kind regards, then good luck to them both! x

And Bell had choked on her glass of wine. Thankfully, the notifications she'd just received weren't about Colin cosying up to his sweetheart, but were in fact Facebook friends telling her they were going to try to come to the fair the following weekend, which was cheering.

Once the whole committee had arrived, Bell asked each of them to report back on what they'd managed to get done and what was still outstanding.

'We've finally had sign-off from health and safety for the bouncy castle,' Lynne said, and Bell breathed a sigh of relief. 'And Marcus managed to get them to hire it to us for free after explaining why we're trying to raise so much money. They'll be here to set it up at eight on Saturday morning and we can have it till five o'clock.'

'That's brilliant, you two!' Bell said. 'Laura, how have you got on with the spit-roasted pig?'

'Well, after a fair amount of begging and promising things I won't mention in front of the children,' she said, nodding at Lisa, Ian and Matt as everyone laughed, 'I've managed to wrangle us a pig, a spit and two men to cook it, along with a load of bread rolls, fried onions and apple sauce.' The rest of the group cheered, but Laura put her hand up to silence them. 'I'm not done yet, och no! I've also got a small whisky and gin distillery from Derbyshire to come down and give tastings to anyone over eighteen, and flog their wares, of course. And they've also donated a couple of bottles to the raffle.'

'I'm a bit scared about what you might have promised them, Laura, but well done, excellent work! Now, Di and Sarah, where are you at with the craft stalls?'

'We've got all the local WI ladies to donate blankets and

baby things they've knitted, and me and Di have got enough cross-stitched stuff for a stall,' Sarah replied. 'Plus, the WI is going to do what it does best and provide enough cake to feed the five thousand.'

'Yay, sounds good, thanks, ladies. Ben, you've been looking after the photography display, haven't you?'

'Yep; while we haven't been able to get the prints on a website for people to buy ahead of the fair, we're going to hang all the pictures in the room down the hall on Saturday and I've got a local company to come along to make prints for people and frame them while they wait. I was thinking of charging ten pounds a print and then whatever the company want to charge for the framing service, is that okay?'

'Perfect,' Bell agreed and consulted her list. 'Lisa, Ian and Matt, you've been spreading the word around your college, I know, and you were also looking after the traditional games.'

'Yes, we had to google loads of them to work out what they are, but I think we've sorted hook-a-duck, hoopla and a coconut shy.' Lisa nodded seriously. 'Matt's parents are getting us a load of coconuts from Aldi next week and we're borrowing some balls from the school where my mum works. Plus, she has loads of bunting we can put up around the stalls to make it look more vintage.'

'And my mum's on the PTA at my brother's school and is always running raffles, so she's volunteered to be in charge of that,' Ian added. 'Some of the teachers at college have donated a few things for it, and we've got the whisky Laura's sorted, but do we have much else?'

'Hmm, I'm not sure. Okay, this week, let's contact all the local hotels, businesses and anyone else we can think of and get them to donate a prize. I'm thinking hotel stays, dinners for two, that kind of thing, as we need some bigger prizes,' Bell said. 'Millie, you've obviously got Louis on board for the football tournament, which is brilliant, and Lee, who's a PE teacher at the big secondary school down the road, is going to be in charge of the logistics for it, though hopefully he's recruited some helpers too as we've already got quite a few teams signed up, and fingers crossed more will join up on the day. We're hoping Louis is going to sign autographs and do selfies if people want them, all for a fee, obviously. How did you get on with the local press, Mills?'

'Good, I think,' she said. 'They all seemed interested when I sent them the press release and made noises about coming down to cover it, so we'll just have to see on the day. What I have managed to confirm is that Dream 105 FM are definitely going to set up in the car park for most of the day, so as well as playing tunes and running some giveaways, they were talking about holding some kind of dance-off or DJ-off or something, which will hopefully create a good vibe.'

'Amazing,' Bell replied. 'Oh, and I've spoken to a few people at work and I've managed to get hold of a load of old stock, which they've agreed to donate for us to sell. Just summer dresses, last season's slogan T-shirts and beach bags, nothing fancy – but my friend Suze is going to man the stall and I'm sure she'll find ways to make people buy all kinds of things they never knew they wanted!'

'Bagsy getting a sneak preview before we open!' Lisa laughed. 'That sounds amazing, Bell.'

'Well, hopefully, it will do well. Oh, and I've also contacted someone I follow on Instagram who makes really cool pottery and she's going to come up from London for the day and sell her stuff, too. What else? Oh, yes, inflatables for the pool party in the afternoon. Thoughts, anyone?'

'I might still have the flamingo I brought back from Ibiza last year,' Matt said. 'And we can ask everyone at college to bring any they have as it's all anyone's taking on holiday with them this year.'

'Okay, fingers crossed on that, then,' Bell said, ticking it off her list and deciding it wasn't the end of the world if they only had a couple. 'The centre's lifeguards who would have been on duty on Saturday anyway have both donated their wages for that day to the cause, which is brilliant.'

'I'd better make sure I say thank you properly to them at the weekend!' Laura cackled. 'Have you seen those guys' abs? Seriously.' She started fanning herself with a few pieces of paper from Bell's pile.

'You do that, Lau,' Bell laughed. 'Right, what else have I forgotten? We've got plenty of volunteers to take people's money on the door and Rita and Tony are organising an army of oldies to walk round with collection buckets all day in case people have any spare change. Oh, and we've got face-painting and glitter nails being sorted, too. And Sheila and Sue are going to man a Pimm's stall. They've offered to buy all the drink and fruit themselves as their contribution, which is ridiculously kind of them,' Bell said, a little lump forming in her throat.

'As long as they don't drink it all between them!' Marcus said and they all giggled. 'What happens if it rains, Bell, or do we pretend I never asked that question?' he added quickly.

'Erm, I think we all just pray to the sun gods,' Bell said. 'It's been gorgeous for the past few days and when I checked the forecast it seemed to say temperatures were going to stay in the early twenties for the next couple of weeks, but you never know, obviously.' She wasn't about to admit that she'd been obsessively checking the weather three times a day for the last week. 'I'm not going to worry about it until we have to, as we have the whole centre at our disposal and we'd just have to make it work. Anything else?'

'Is there going to be a master of ceremonies?' Laura asked. 'Someone needs to declare the fair open and introduce Louis, then tell everyone when the various activities are starting and draw the raffle and stuff. You're doing that, yep?' she asked, fixing Bell with a stare that meant there was no way she could refuse.

'I guess . . .' she replied. 'Unless anyone else wants to?' But immediately the rest of the group shouted her down and she was left with no choice. 'Okay, well that seems to be decided. Right, well I think that's it, but text, call or email me if you think of anything else as the week goes on or if you have any questions, and I'll do my best to answer them. I'll be here all evening on Friday and then from seven o'clock on Saturday, ready for opening at eleven. So I'll see you all then – let's get this money raised and save our centre!'

They all cheered and Millie put her arm round her shoulders. Even though Bell was feeling completely overwhelmed by how much she still needed to do and how much she needed to check other people were doing, she cheered along with them until they were all whooped out.

As she sat on the bus home on Friday afternoon, her never-ending checklist looped through her head, snagging on all the things she still had to do, but Bell felt her heart thumping with anxious excitement.

'What if there's suddenly a freak storm, or an accident on the main road so no one can get here, or none of the stallholders turn up, or Louis forgets all about it, or everyone decides to go to the pub instead?' she gabbled at Ben when he met her at the community centre that evening.

'Bell, calm down,' he soothed gently, putting down the takeaway coffee cups he was holding. He placed his hands on her shoulders and forced her to look him in the eye. 'I've checked the forecast and there's not a spot of rain predicted, the stallholders will definitely all come, and I'm sure Louis will too. And even if there is a major accident, which hopefully there won't be, people will find other ways of getting here.'

A moment passed between them as he finished speaking and Bell suddenly registered how close the two of them were standing. Their eyes remained locked for a beat, before he removed his hands and stepped back.

'Now, do you want a flat white or a latte? I couldn't decide which you'd prefer.'

'The flat white, please,' she replied, the corners of her mouth turning up despite herself. 'And then we'd better get started – there's a ridiculous amount of stuff to do.'

'There's always time for a coffee and a chocolate muffin,' Ben declared, producing two delicious-looking cakes from his bag.

'Try as I might, I can't disagree with that statement,' Bell laughed. 'Okay, ten minutes and then we must get on.'

The marriage of caffeine and sugar proved to be the perfect fuel, and for the next few hours the pair put up trestle tables, stacked chairs, and pinned up bunting to a soundtrack of classic nineties hits thanks to Ben's Spotify playlist.

'Do I sound like a complete old person by saying music was *so* much better in our day?' Bell asked as the final notes of No Doubt's 'Don't Speak' played out.

'Well, that would make me a complete old person, too, so I'm saying no,' Ben grinned. 'Right, I think we've probably done pretty much everything we can this evening, and I for one am starving. Do you fancy some celebratory fish and chips?'

Bell looked at the empty wall in front of her and then at the pile of framed photographs she had yet to hang and was about to protest, until her stomach betrayed her with an embarrassingly loud growl that made them both burst out laughing.

'Well, it seems like I have my answer,' Ben grinned.

'Only if I can have mushy peas, too,' Bell agreed. 'Though if you don't mind going to get them, I'll quickly hang these pictures while you're out.'

Half an hour later they were both happily munching vinegary chips, crispy cod and sweet mushy peas while admiring the photography class's pictures on the wall all over again.

'It's a pretty impressive display, considering how rubbish we all were to begin with, isn't it?' Bell observed, taking a swig from one of the bottles of beer Ben had also had the foresight to bring back with him. 'Well, all of us except you,' she amended.

'I was hardly Mario Testino. Not that I am now, obviously,' he clarified quickly. 'I learned so much from Sheila and also from seeing everyone else's photos each week. And, of course, that shoot with Ade was amazing.'

Bell's now full stomach fluttered at the mention of Ade – not, for once, because of his model good looks, but rather at the memory of what he'd said to her about Ben. She glanced at him sitting next to her now and grinned. 'Cheers to that,' she said, raising her bottle and clinking it against his.

'And cheers to you, Bell. Tomorrow is going to be amazing.'

'Well, it's thanks to you too – I'd never have been able to get so much done tonight without all your help.'

They continued to smile at each other and Bell felt the same electricity build between them as it had earlier. Gradually their bodies closed the space between them until their lips were almost touching. Ben moved a fraction towards her and suddenly they were kissing. Bell's brain tried to tell her a hundred reasons why none of what was happening was a good idea, but her heart pushed them all down and she lost herself in the deliciousness of the moment.

She had no more conscious thoughts until some time later when Ben's playlist threw up Rage Against The Machine's 'Killing In The Name Of', and despite them both trying to block the song out, it rather poured cold water on their passion and they found they couldn't stop giggling.

'That's quite an eclectic playlist you have there!' Bell said as she fought back more laughter.

'Erm, yes, got to love the Shuffle button, right?' Ben grinned ruefully as he closed his music app. 'But until that point, I was quite enjoying things.'

'*Quite* enjoying things? Rude!' Bell joked. Their eyes locked again and her body gave an involuntary jolt. She forced herself to look at her watch and her eyes widened. 'Shit, you do know it's gone midnight? God, we need to be back here in less than seven hours.'

'It's fine, we can leave now and clear up this stuff in the morning.' His expression became more serious. 'Bell, I know it's not far, but isn't it a bit late for you to be walking home on your own? Look, why don't you stay at mine and I'll run you back to yours in the car first thing?'

Bell could barely think straight through the fog of hormones swirling around her body, but the one thing she knew was that she didn't want to mess up whatever it was that was going on between her and Ben, even if that meant they were just friends. So she made a great show of laughing off his comment.

'It's not that late, and we live in the Home Counties – it's hardly the Bronx! I'm sure I'll be fine.'

Ben's face fell before he visably shook himself and said in a rush, 'I know. I guess what I'm trying to say is I've really enjoyed this evening and I don't want it to end.'

'Well, heaving those tables around wasn't really that enjoyable, to be honest!' Bell began, before catching his expression. 'Sorry. I don't, I mean . . . I'm not really up for a one-night stand!' she blurted out awkwardly.

'Bell, it's fine,' Ben said, grabbing her hand. 'I didn't mean it to sound like that at all. One-night stands are not my thing, especially with someone like you. Not that I don't want to – y'know . . . I mean . . . Argh!' They both started laughing again. 'Look, I'd love you to come back to mine tonight, but we definitely don't have to do anything. We're both grown-ups and I've got a spare room. . .' He took a deep breath and Bell couldn't stop the corners of her mouth lifting.

'Okay, fine, as long as you promise to wake me up in time so I can pop home first in the morning – I'm not very good at getting up early,' she grinned.

Predictably, Bell didn't end up sleeping in a separate room, but as she used the spare toothbrush Ben had helpfully found her, she did make a promise to herself to take things slowly.

'You know, I haven't even kissed anyone except Colin for over ten years,' she whispered as she and Ben lay facing each other in his bed, both chastely wearing T-shirts. 'Let alone anything else. I guess I'm a bit, well, scared.'

'You don't need to be scared, Bell. But also, let's not rush this. Tonight has been pretty epic—' He broke off to kiss her gently on the lips in case she still hadn't worked out which part of the evening he was referring to. 'But tomorrow is a huge day, for you especially, and we have all the time in the world.'

Relief hit Bell hard in her chest. 'Thank you. For understanding and for being you,' she replied, kissing him.

Ben reciprocated before reluctantly but gently pulling away. 'Come on, we'd best get some sleep before that alarm goes off and I have to drag you kicking and screaming from the bed.'

Chapter Twenty-five

Millie

Despite Louis' assertion he would be at the fair as promised, Millie knew she wouldn't believe it until he was actually physically there, declaring the event officially open. Until then, she constantly felt like her chest was being weighed down by a thousand worries, and she wasn't able to take a proper deep breath in and out.

She had breathlessly extolled the virtues of the local primary she and Bell had visited, to the point where she'd built the place up to be a paragon of early years learning, with teachers coming from across the land to teach there.

'Louis, you should have seen the football field there, Wolf is going to love it. And Mrs Anderson said they're a feeder school into all the local kids' teams, and a couple of the boys and one of the girls in the top class are being considered by the Spurs Academy, no less. And I'm sure they'd love you to come down for an afternoon and talk to the kids about what it's like to actually be a professional footballer, just think how that would help Wolf settle into his new class.' Then as an extra prod in the right direction, she'd added, 'Wolf was really excited when I showed him all the pictures. Although not as excited as he is about seeing you at the fair on Saturday. He is so proud that you're going to be guest of honour, he keeps babbling on to everyone about it!'

'That's my boy!' he had laughed. 'It will be good for him to meet Zoe, too. He'll love her, she's such a sweetie.'

'So Zoe's definitely coming?' Millie had asked. She couldn't decide how she felt about the whole Zoe situation. There wasn't even a tiny part of her that wanted to get back with Louis, but neither was she particularly looking forward to seeing a young, attractive woman on his arm, especially if she was going to be introduced to their son. Not that *her* feelings had even crossed Louis' mind.

'Yeah, she's not filming that weekend so she should be free. And as she said, it'll pull in more punters if she's there, won't it? She's always thinking about other people is Zoe.'

'Great,' Millie replied, stifling an incredulous laugh. 'Okay, well let me know what you think about the school when you've looked through the paperwork, and if there's any problem on Saturday morning, call me as soon as possible, won't you?'

'Millie, I am a grown man and well able to do things for myself. I've said I'll be there on Saturday, so I'll be there.'

She bit back the reply on the tip of her tongue. The last thing she needed was a fight, but she knew from bitter experience that King Louis' promises were not the same as other people's promises.

She wasn't able to join Bell and Ben to start setting up at the centre on Friday evening as Bridget was having some of her bridge ladies round to her house for a glass of sherry. Once she'd put Wolf to bed – which was easier said than done given his state of extreme excitement about the following day and the fact school had finished for the summer and there were six weeks of fun stretching ahead of him – Millie sat on the sofa glued to her phone.

She was still waiting for any kind of word from Louis on what he thought of Wolf's potential school, and every time a notification from the committee WhatsApp group lit up her handset, she felt guilty for hoping it was in fact from Louis. While she knew (fingers crossed) she would see him the next day, she didn't think the fundraising fair was the right time or place at which to discuss their son's schooling, so she was desperate to hear back from him that evening, especially as they had to give the school an answer either way come Monday morning.

Eventually, she gave in, and sent him a bright, friendly message asking if he'd had a chance to read through the material she'd emailed him, then quickly clicked off her messages and opened her Instagram app to distract herself.

Over the last couple of weeks, she'd been posting fewer 'life is perfect' images and made them a bit more 'real'. While she still didn't entirely subscribe to Bell's way of thinking, she could see that many of her followers had reacted positively. Yesterday's picture of Wolf with paint in his hair, across his cheek and all over his hands, holding a decidedly splodgy piece of paper, had gained the most Likes she'd ever had. Her caption had read:

> Apparently this is a picture of a dog playing in the park (no, me neither!). There's more paint on the floor, on the walls and on him than on the paper. Can you use a jet-washer on a child? Asking for a friend, obvs. #artfail #paintmixing #mess #jetwash #parentingfail

Then an influential mummy blogger had reposted her image with a cry-laughing emoji face and suddenly Millie's follower numbers had rocketed and she'd had thousands of comments. She still hadn't escaped her trolls, but this time they'd been shot down by other users almost immediately and hadn't posted again as yet. She was pretty sure they wouldn't be deterred that easily, but Millie was able to smile as she scrolled through the comments for the first time in a long while. She especially loved all the replies from other parents sympathising with her and relaying stories about their own kids' 'creative' activities.

Her scrolling was interrupted by her phone informing her she finally had a message from Louis. Her heart was racing as she opened the app to read it.

> Didn't I email you? Sorry, yeah, that school looks good I think. Let's do it! L

Millie stared at her phone. She didn't know whether to laugh or cry at his off-hand reply. She quickly messaged him back saying she'd email the school right now and would see him and Zoe tomorrow. Obviously, he didn't reply, and all Millie could do was hope that he would actually keep his word for once and turn up at the community centre as planned.

Millie was woken on Saturday morning by Wolf jumping heavily on top of her, yelling, 'Mummy, the fair is starting, we need to get to the pool and bouncy castle now and watch Daddy score some goals!'

Her chest thumped, not just because she was struggling to breathe beneath the clutches of her five-year-old, but also because she was suddenly afraid they'd slept in and were actually already late. She prised her eyes open and stretched out her arm to press her phone: 6.02 AM.

'Wolf, darling, the fair isn't starting for hours yet, don't worry. Now, why don't you get into bed with me and we'll have a little nap until we need to get up.'

'But we need to get up now, Mummy! The sky is all blue and the sun is shining so it means it's time to finish sleeping and have some breakfast. You said it's the most important meal of the day.'

'Yes, Wolfie, but it is quite early still. It's going to be a long day and I don't want you to get tired this afternoon.'

'I like long days,' he declared. 'It means there's more time for eating. Now, can I have chocolate cereal *and* toast pwease?'

Thanks to her wake-up call and Wolf's insistence, they

arrived at the community centre not long after seven o'clock, but found Bell was already there, putting up trestle tables with Ben.

'Did you two go home last night?' she laughed as she gave them both a hug and Wolf hung on to Bell's waist.

'For a bit,' Bell grinned, glancing at Ben, and Millie made a note to interrogate her friend later about what exactly she and Ben had got up to the night before.

'Right, seeing as you're both here nice and early, how do you feel about helping us out?' Bell asked. 'Wolfie, Ben has a *very* important job for you that I think you're going to like.'

'Woof!' came the unmistakable sound of a dog straining on a lead and Wolf immediately started jumping up and down.

'Is Graham here?' he asked, his excitement threatening to explode before the fair had even begun.

'Yes, he is indeed,' Ben said, bending down so he was level with Wolf. 'I was thinking that you could help me take him for a walk over to the football pitches and back and maybe throw his ball to him as you were so good at it last time.'

'Yes! Can I, Mummy, can I?'

'Of course, Wolf, but make sure you do whatever Ben tells you to, okay?'

She grinned as Wolf skipped off with Ben and the dog then turned to Bell. 'What's Ben doing about Graham long-term? Does his neighbour's son not want to take him back up to Scotland with him?'

'No, apparently his wife's got an allergy, so he's asked Ben if he'll adopt him. He's taking him to doggy daycare when he's at work and then picking him up in the evenings at the moment, and it seems to be going okay.'

Before Millie could so much as mention Ben again, Bell said, 'Do you want to dump your stuff inside, and then how do you fancy a bit of bunting hanging?'

When Millie came back out, she found Rita, Tony, Sheila and Sue had all arrived and a car bearing Di, Sarah and Laura was pulling up. The next few hours were spent putting together the stalls, making them look pretty and supervising the bouncy castle and hog roast being delivered and assembled.

'It's starting to look like a proper fair!' Bell said as she and Millie grabbed a drink of water.

It was still only nine o'clock, but the uniform gang were now out in force making the retro games look both cool and fun, while Di and Sarah's craft stalls were crammed with some amazing creations, as well as a few decidedly weird-looking pieces of knitting that Millie couldn't identify. The cake stall was awaiting the arrival of the WI ladies and their wares, while the bouncy castle had already been well tested by Wolf and Daisy, Laura's eight-year-old daughter, who had arrived with Laura's mum half an hour before and had attached herself firmly to Wolf. He didn't appear to be best pleased, but Millie could see he was trying to be polite and let Daisy fuss over him for now, at least.

'It looks amazing,' Millie agreed. 'And the photography exhibition inside is brilliant. I can't believe how professional everyone's photos look.'

'I'm not sure Sheila can either!' Bell laughed.

A few minutes later, Suze arrived, armed with seemingly the whole of Style It Out's stock room.

'Bell, all that bossing people around you've been doing has really paid off, this looks epic!' she cried when she'd managed to extricate herself from the piles of maxi-dresses and playsuits filling her car.

'Ah, glad you approve,' Bell grinned. 'Although, Suze, did Marian definitely say we could have all these clothes? There can't be anything left for the site to sell!'

'Don't worry, I went through the proper channels and didn't just nick them.' Suze rolled her eyes at her friend. 'Anyway, aren't you going to introduce me to everyone? I've heard so much about you all. Not all good I have to say.' She grinned wickedly.

'Suze! Don't listen to her, anyone, especially if she starts telling you anything bad about me.'

'Would I do that? Never! Now, I'm guessing you must be Millie, it's lovely to meet you,' she beamed.

'And you,' Millie smiled warmly. 'That's some wardrobe you've brought with you! I wouldn't mind a rummage myself before everyone else gets here.'

'Then give me a hand setting up the stall and your wish will be my command!'

It didn't take long for Suze to introduce herself to the rest of the gang and enlist various others to help her hang dresses on rails and pile folded T-shirts on to the long trestle tables. Bell jogged over a little while later, waving at Millie.

'What time is Louis getting here, do you know?'

Millie's stomach lurched at the sound of his name. *He better bloody come,* she thought to herself fiercely, though she said brightly to her friend, 'I said any time between ten and half past.'

'Okay, brilliant. God, there's Peter Hall from the council – I'd better go and say hello. Mills, could you check if the radio people need any help setting up their stage, please?'

There was a blur of activity as everyone frantically tried to finish their allotted tasks. So many last-minute deliveries of delicious-looking home-made cakes arrived that an extra table had to be quickly found from the dusty store cupboard to accommodate all the Victoria sponges. The WI ladies also took charge of the Pimm's table as Sheila and Sue were needed elsewhere, and quickly set a team of people to work slicing cucumber and fruit for the huge jugs in front of them. Laura was chatting to the whisky distillery owner, who it seemed was originally from Scotland and had learned everything he knew about single malts up there – and, for once, it looked like Laura wasn't quite as interested in the alcohol as she was in the person talking. Ben was keeping an eye on the uniform brigade as well as the football arrangements, and the whole place was drenched in the mouthwatering scents of roast pork and candyfloss. Millie had already had to remove Wolf several times from the spun-sugar cart, where Bridget and her bridge friends were manning the fort and treating him to swathes of the pink stuff.

'Wolf, why don't we go and have a bit of quiet time inside

before the fair starts as you've been running around a lot outside this morning.'

'But, Mummy . . .' Wolf whined, before seeing Millie looking at him with her 'that wasn't a question, please do what I say right now' stare. She led him inside, grabbed a book from her bag and took Wolf into a corner of the café area that was set up to serve hot drinks and provide some chairs and tables for people who wanted to get away from the crowds for a bit. Thankfully, it was almost empty and Millie was able to spend ten minutes calming Wolf down with the Gruffalo.

They'd just reached the end and Wolf was snuggling woozily into her chest when Bell rushed in.

'There you are, Millie! You haven't seen Louis, have you? It's half past ten and he's not arrived yet.'

'Daddy's here?' Wolf said, raising his head and scrabbling to get off Millie's lap.

'Not yet, I don't think, darling, but why don't we both go outside to look for him. Let me just give Bell something and then we can go.'

She nipped into the small room where they'd put all their belongings and grabbed the coat-hanger she'd hung on the back of the door. 'Don't worry, I'll make sure Louis is delivered into your hands before the opening,' she said to her friend with a hundred times more confidence than she actually felt. 'Now, what were you thinking of wearing for your big moment?'

'You mean the opening? Well, just this, really.' Bell pointed to her denim shorts and light blue vest top embellished with glitter round the neck which, while it had looked pretty first thing this morning, was now covered in dust, dirt and god knows what else.

'Not sure that's going to cut it.' Millie shook her head. 'But this will, so you'd better get changed.' She handed Bell the coat-hanger on which was a cornflower-blue dress with a ruffled V-neck, cap sleeves and a short-but-not-too-short flirty skirt.

Bell's eyes widened with shock. 'It's gorgeous, but—'

'No buts, I'm afraid. It will look perfect on you, I know it will,' she smiled. 'Right, Wolf, let's go and find Daddy.'

As she headed outside with her son clutching her hand, she silently prayed that Louis would be waiting somewhere among the melee outside. He wasn't. There was already a large crowd of people queuing outside the car park and spilling down the pavement. She could even see Ben chatting to a group of three people, holding a camera and microphone, who looked very much like they might work for the local BBC news team, as well as a couple of photographers chatting close by, who she thought were probably from the local newspapers. However, there was no sign of Louis.

'Mummy, look!' shouted Wolf, causing everyone around them to follow his outstretched arm. 'It's Daddy!' The little boy pointed towards the car that had just pulled up on to the pavement opposite the queue and Millie realised she'd never been so pleased to see Louis in all her life. Even if he also had a girl she presumed to be Zoe, from her plumped lips and tiny waist, tottering along beside him.

Millie instantly felt like Cinderella in her cotton playsuit and flip-flops, and wished she'd thought to bring an outfit for herself to change into as well as the one she'd brought for Bell. Then she reminded herself that the day was not about her, or even Louis' new girlfriend, but about raising money to keep the centre open for the community, so it really didn't matter what she was wearing.

She managed to move Louis and Zoe away from the photographers and reporters, who suddenly seemed to have multiplied, and took him inside the centre where news had reached Bell that he'd finally arrived. Her friend appeared, looking just as pretty as Millie had known she would in the blue dress that matched her eyes, with her blonde hair swept back into a messy bun. She'd just had time to add a coat of mascara and a swipe of lipgloss, Millie noted as she grinned at her.

'Bell, this is Louis. Louis, this is Bell, who's the mastermind behind this whole thing.'

'Well, I don't know about that, but anyway, great to meet you, Louis. Wolf's told me so much about you!'

'I have, Daddy, I've told Bell Bell all about that goal you scored at the end of the season from the halfway line and she said you must be really good and I said that you are!' He beamed proudly at his dad and Millie couldn't help but smile as Louis bent down to give his son a high five.

'Well, after that kind of introduction, I'm afraid it's all going to be downhill from here,' he laughed, leaning in to kiss Bell on both cheeks. 'And this is Zoe.'

'Lovely to meet you, Zoe,' Bell said. 'Now, are you ready to get this thing started?'

'Yes!' shouted Wolf. Louis ruffled his hair, then he and Zoe followed Bell through the back of the building, past the pool and back round towards the area where both the radio station stage and the ever-growing crowd of people was located. When everyone saw Louis approaching, they started cheering and inched as close to the stage as they could, although, thankfully, there was precious little pushing and shoving and they allowed Millie and Wolf to slide into the front so he could see what was happening.

The radio DJ faded out the song and boomed into his microphone, 'Please welcome to the stage the head of the community centre fundraising committee, Bell Makepeace!'

Millie watched as her friend walked onto the stage, took a deep breath and smiled at the crowd in front of her. 'Hi, everyone,' she said, her voice shaking a little. As the crowd cheered, Millie saw Bell collect herself and when she spoke again, it was without a hint of wobble. 'Thank you so much for coming along today. As most of you know, several areas of the community centre have seen better days and in order for them to be refurbished and for the pool and the whole centre to remain open, the council needs to spend fifty thousand pounds on the work.' The crowd groaned in sympathy. 'Thankfully, the council have pledged to put up half that money . . .' There were cheers, as well as a few boos from people who clearly thought they should be stumping up the full amount, but Bell continued, 'which is brilliant news.

However, it means we, as a community, have to raise the remaining twenty-five thousand. Thanks to some seriously generous people locally, we've already managed to hit the five-thousand-pound mark, and we hope that, after today, we're going to be much closer to our target, so please dig as deep as you can. All of our stalls and games are well priced, but of course if you would like to pay a little bit more, then that's fine too!' Bell smiled and the crowd cheered again. 'We will also be holding a raffle, where you could win anything from a bottle of whisky to a spa stay for two.' Everyone oohed appreciatively. 'And of course, we also have our five-a-side football competition. If you haven't got your team signed up already and paid your twenty-five pounds, then you'd best be quick as it all kicks off at midday. And on that note, I'd like to introduce you to today's guest of honour. You may have seen him on *Match of the Day* and now he's here to welcome you to our fundraising fair, please give a big round of applause to Louis Price!'

The crowd went nuts, and Millie couldn't help but be swept up in all the cheering. Louis sauntered on to the stage with a ball in his hands, proceeded to send every football fan in front of him into a frenzy by doing a load of keepy-uppies, before kicking the ball into the crowd to huge cheers, and a little bit of scrambling over who got to catch the ball and take it home.

'Good to see ya, everyone!' he called, with his slight Brummie twang. 'I'm so honoured that I was asked to stand in front of you all today and open this amazing event. My own little boy Wolfie comes swimming here and I know how much he loves it.'

'I do, Daddy,' Wolf shouted, and everyone laughed.

'You see! And when Wolf thinks something is great, then I also tend to think it's great, which is why I wanted to come here and meet you all today. So I'll be playing football with you and also signing autographs and doing selfies if anyone's interested?' Everyone cheered again. 'But only if you pay for the privilege!' he grinned, and there was more whooping. But then he held up his hand for quiet and everyone was silent immediately. 'I also wanted to put my money where my mouth is, which is why I'm contributing ten thousand pounds to the save our centre fund today.'

The crowd erupted and Millie's mouth fell open. She caught Bell's eye from the stage, who mouthed 'What the actual f—' at her, but all Millie could do was shrug and cheer along with everyone else.

Bell quickly stepped forward and tried to speak over the noise, which eventually quietened down.

'Louis, I don't know what to say, other than thank you, that is so incredibly generous.' The crowd began whooping again, but Bell continued speaking. 'However, you lot, don't think that means you get out of spending your cash that easily. We need to hit that target, so please get your wallets at the ready. Louis, would you do the honours?'

He stepped forward, and in his most pompous voice he boomed, 'I now declare this fair officially OPEN!'

*

Several hours later, Millie was flagging and in desperate need of a drink. She nabbed two Pimm's from Sheila and Sue, who were back manning their stall and informed her they'd made them extra-strong especially for her, as she looked like she needed it. Then she threaded her way through the streams of families, couples and huge groups of college kids – the uniform brigade had done a sterling job in getting their fellow students along. Finally she spied Bell, who was talking to a group of elderly folk sitting in the shade.

'I'm sorry, would you mind if I borrowed Bell?' She smiled at them, before bearing her friend off round the corner towards the swimming pool, which was currently almost deserted ahead of the pool party later. 'I thought you might need this,' she said, handing her the paper cup full of fruity, alcoholic drink.

'God, thanks, this is exactly what I need,' Bell cried, downing half of it in one go. 'Do you think things are going okay?'

'I think they're going more than okay!' Millie grinned. 'Seriously, this is far more punters than I ever thought would come.'

'Thank god they did, though!' Bell said, tipping the rest of the Pimm's into her mouth. 'Where's Wolf?'

'He's with Ben. There's a group of about twenty kids happily playing with him and Graham over by the football.'

'Aww, bless him.'

'I know, it seems he has an alter ego as the Pied Piper!'

'Ha, he'll love that! I hope the tournament is good, I haven't made it over there yet.'

'Louis seemed to be in his element when I last checked,' Millie laughed. 'Between games he's taking every opportunity to pose for selfies with anyone who'll cough up. Though I don't think Zoe's too pleased with him!'

'Oh, why not?'

'Apparently, he promised her she could come on stage and open the fair with him, but he forgot so she was stuck backstage and barely got any time in front of the camera. I heard her moaning to someone that she might as well go home as there was no point her being here anymore.'

'Oops! Oh well, I'm not sure anyone will miss her,' Bell giggled. 'Though can we just take a moment to talk about Louis' donation? I mean, oh my god, I thought I was going to pass out right there on the stage when he said he was coughing up ten grand for the appeal!'

'I know, I was as surprised as you! Though when I grabbed him earlier to say how grateful we were, he said his agent had mentioned it wouldn't do him any harm to be seen to be so philanthropic, especially with the media there covering it all. He thinks it might be the clincher that gets him the transfer he's been angling after all summer, so it wasn't entirely altruistic!'

'Well, whatever his reasons, it's still £10k so I'm not complaining! God, everyone who's here today seems to be being really generous. I saw Rita and Tony shaking buckets at people, except there were so many notes in there, they weren't making the rattle they should have been!'

'Well, it just shows what we can do when the whole community comes together,' Millie nodded. 'Although, without you at the helm, this wouldn't have happened at all, Bell, you know that.' She nudged her friend. 'Anyway, what's going on with you and Ben then?'

But before Millie could force a reply out of her friend, they heard a shout.

'Bell! Och, there you both are, we wondered where you'd got to,' Laura cried, coming round the corner, followed by Suze and a girl with long, blonde hair whom Millie didn't recognise.

'Are you both downing Pimm's back here without us?' Suze scolded. 'Lucky we brought refills, isn't it,' she added, handing out the cups she'd been precariously holding.

Bell rolled her eyes at her friend and leaned over to hug the blonde woman. 'Oh, Els, you're here too! You've met Laura, I see,' she smiled. 'And this is Millie. Mills, this is Suze's girlfriend, sorry, fiancée, Ellie. Oh, I'm so glad you've all met each other at last!'

'Els, you'll know Millie from Insta – she's @mi_bestlife?' Suze added

'Oh my god, your little boy is so cute!' beamed Ellie. 'That post about him painting was amazing. And I'm sorry to fangirl but I'm so jealous of your wardrobe!'

'Sadly, I have to return most of it to the stores, but a girl can dream,' Millie said, feeling for once that she should be honest about her pictures.

'Well, whether you get to keep it or not, I *so* need to

borrow you as my own personal shopper at some point. as you have the *best* style,' Ellie enthused.

'Any time,' Millie grinned. 'But maybe you can all help me – I've been trying to get out of Bell all day what went on last night with her and Ben, but she's refusing to tell me.'

'What?!' Suze spun round to face Bell. 'You finally got a shag and you haven't told me?'

'Suze! I didn't get a shag, as you so delicately put it,' Bell replied, her cheeks colouring cutely. 'It's early days, but, yeah, Ben is lovely.'

Millie cheered and Suze whooped. 'And last night?' Laura asked, raising an eyebrow. 'And don't give us all that innocent virgin shite.'

'We, erm, kissed and then it was a bit late to go all the way home so I, erm, stayed at Ben's. But I didn't sleep with him!' Bell protested. 'Well, we slept in the same bed, but not in *that* way.'

'I'm sure nothing at all happened while you lay naked under the duvet together,' cackled Suze.

Feeling guilty for having started the conversation in the first place, Millie glanced at her flustered friend and smiled. 'Okay, well, suffice it to say that we're all super-happy for you, Bell. Before you guys came over, I was just saying to Bell that none of today would have happened without her and that she should be so proud of what she's achieved.'

'Seconded!' said Suze immediately.

'Thirded!' Laura instantly replied.

'Fourthed, if that's even a thing?' Ellie laughed.

'Today it is,' Millie grinned. 'Cheers, everyone – to Bell.'

'To Bell!' they all chorused, except Bell herself, who went even redder, but then said, 'Well, I couldn't have done it without this group of amazing women.' and hugged them all hard.

Chapter Twenty-six

Bell

'Did you know you're going to be forty in exactly thirty seconds' time?' Cosette asked, picking up her watch from the table next to Bell's bed where they were both sprawled in their pyjamas.

'Ah, but I've no idea what time I was actually born, and Janet and John sure as hell can't remember, so that means I can stay thirty-nine for pretty much all of the next twenty-four hours, right?'

'Wrong,' Cosette replied happily. 'If I have to be forty-something then you do too, I'm afraid, sister dearest. Okay, three, two, one, happy birthday!' She threw her arms round Bell and kissed her forcefully on the cheek. 'Here's to another forty.'

'Christ, can you imagine what we're going to be like when we're in our eighties? I hope we'll drink as much champagne as I have already these past few weeks, and I'm not even forty yet.'

'I'm sorry to say you are definitely forty now, so you can stop pretending you weren't listening when I said it was after midnight. But I'm sure we'll still be drinking all the champagne by the time we hit our eighties. God, what if I'm still married to Rich then?'

'What?! You're hardly going to divorce Rich when you're seventy-nine and find a toyboy within months and marry them on your eightieth birthday, are you?'

'I might, you don't know. Anyway, we really do need to go to sleep if you're not going to wake up on your fortieth birthday with massive bags under your eyes.'

'Well, according to you, it is already my fortieth birthday and I haven't got bags at the moment. Oh wait . . .'

'Bell! You have not got bags under your eyes at the moment, but you might have a black eye if I have to punch you in the night. So shut up and go to sleep.'

In the two months since the fair, Bell had allowed herself some time off work to recover. At the time, she hadn't quite realised how much organising the entire event had taken out of her. But once the adrenaline of the weekend had disappeared, she'd come down with a summer cold and Suze had given her a lecture about looking after herself ('Don't make me stage another intervention, Bellster!' she'd warned).

Bell had spent a blissful week painting her bedroom, enjoying the new queen-sized bed she'd decided to treat herself to and lounging on the beautiful yet comfortable sofa she'd bought for the living room. It now felt completely like her home, not her and Colin's house, and she couldn't have been happier stacking the dishwasher exactly how she wanted to. She still hated changing the duvet cover, obviously, though as Ben had spent a fair amount of time at her house recently, she'd roped him in to help a few times.

Thanks largely to Louis' generosity, after the fair they'd hit the twenty thousand pounds mark. Although they still had a little way to go to hit their target, the council had agreed to guarantee the community centre's future while they slowly (and somewhat painfully) raised the rest of the money through coffee mornings and other smaller events. In fact, once the local press had run the story, the council had had to publicly say they wouldn't dream of selling the site to developers or risk a huge backlash.

The building work was scheduled to start in the next few weeks, but before then, Bell had the small matter of her birthday party to enjoy there. She'd been intent on organising it all herself, but the combined powers of Cosette, Millie, Suze, Ellie and Laura had finally persuaded her to leave it to them. Individually, they'd all offered to organise it for her, but it wasn't until they'd started a WhatsApp group and bombarded her with messages telling her they were now in control, that she'd actually agreed they could all do it between them.

Now, as she allowed Oli and Sophie loose in her kitchen to make her breakfast with only a small helping hand from their mum, she was actually glad she'd relinquished responsibility for the party.

And it wasn't as if work had calmed down after the fair, either. In fact, it seemed to have ramped up even more in the last few weeks. She'd taken the test shots for Style It Out's new lookbook as Marian had asked, and while she knew they weren't perfect, even Bell herself was pretty pleased with some of the results. Ade had already been a brilliant mentor and she hoped she'd be able to call on him as she continued to hone her skills. She was excited to start working with the professionals the Art Department had booked. Though she knew she'd have to try hard not to let her imposter syndrome get in the way.

'If Marian thinks you can do it, you can do it,' Suze had declared, so Bell was attempting to be grown up and confident about the whole thing.

Suze, too, had exciting times ahead. Her wedding to Ellie was in just over three months, but the pair had somehow managed to pull together an amazing-sounding venue, caterer and band in the space of weeks. Bell was due to go dress-shopping with Suze the following weekend, although her friend had refused to go to the usual bridal boutiques, and instead they were taking a trip down to London to trawl Bond Street and Liberty in search of a chic yet unique dress, according to Suze. Bell was just glad it was her friend's credit card, not her own. Her bridesmaid dress was being made by one of Suze's friends, with the cornflower-blue dress Millie had lent her for the fair as the inspiration. She was in awe of the way Suze seemed to have everything under control, as well as be at the top of her game at work and be house hunting with Els at weekends – it made Bell tired just thinking about it.

'Will Wolf be at your party this evening?' Sophie asked Bell when she'd got bored with whisking the pancake mix and handed it to Cosette to finish. 'I know he's only a kid, but he's really cute and he's brilliant at Lego.'

'You're only a kid yourself, missie!' Bell laughed, tickling her niece then pulling her in for a hug. 'But you're right, he is very good at Lego, and I'm sure you can finish building his spaceship with him later. He might be bringing his friend Alfie with him, too, who also loves playing Lego, so you'll be in good company.'

'Not another boy!' Sophie huffed.

'Well, he is a boy, yes, but you like Wolf, don't you, so you might like Alfie too. And my friend Laura's daughter Daisy will be there as well, so it won't all be boys, don't worry. Ooh, are you going to help Mummy flip a pancake? She's really not that good at it, you know.'

'Ha ha, she's really not, look, Aunty Belly!' yelled Oli, as Cosette inexpertly tossed a pancake onto the floor.

Once they were all munching happily on pancakes topped with fruit, maple syrup and chocolate spread, Cosette turned to Bell. 'So Millie's bringing her new man and his son this evening, then?'

'Well, officially, Wolf is bringing Alfie, and therefore Rob needs to come along, too,' Bell smirked. 'But Mills and Rob have been getting *pretty* close in the last few weeks from what I can gather – not that I've been allowed to meet him as yet!

He's being a sweetie and taking the kids home early this evening so she can let her hair down properly, always supposing this party is a letting-your-hair-down kinda night . . .' She eyed her sister hopefully, but was met with a very clear zipped-lips sign, which her niece and nephew then delighted in copying. She rolled her eyes before continuing, 'Of course, she's taking it really slowly, and she'd never do anything to jeopardise Wolf's happiness and security, especially as he's settled into his new school so well and made such good friends with Alfie. But I have high hopes that "Rillie", as I'm calling them, are the real deal. Not that she has much time to think about a relationship now she's a super-influencer.'

'Her Insta is doing so well. I saw *Cosmo* did a piece on why you should be following @mi_bestlife and she posted about that photo shoot she's done for *Styler* magazine,' Cosette said.

'I know, but that sounded a bit of a nightmare: they wanted to shoot her in her home, but she didn't have time to tidy up properly as she'd been doing some stuff with Karina King – you know my friend who just happens to work for the biggest online fashion site in the country?'

'Isn't that Styleitout.co.uk?!' laughed her sister.

'Sadly not – although then my boss wouldn't be asking me to take some photos for the lookbook, would she, so swings and roundabouts, I s'pose. Anyway Millie was late dropping off Wolf. And then the photographer and his team were waiting outside when she got back after the morning school run and wouldn't let her spruce things up as they wanted to show her "real life". She's mortified that you'll probably be able to see piles of washing-up in the sink and all Wolf's dirty football kit in the background.'

'Well, her posts are all very warts and all now so at least it will be on brand!' Cosette laughed. 'Wolf seemed a very happy chappy when they came round yesterday.'

'His new school is so good for him,' Bell smiled. 'He's almost like a different kid at times, which means Millie couldn't be happier either. Well, except for Louis being a di—, being an idiot, I mean.'

'Aunty Belly, did you just say dick?' asked Oli with big round eyes.

'No, she said idiot, as you well know, Oli. Now be quiet and eat your pancakes, please.'

'Sorry!' Bell mouthed at her sister.

Cosette rolled her eyes and tried not to laugh. 'He can't still be being an idiot about Wolf's school if he can see he's so happy?'

'No, thankfully not. And he seems to be sticking to the financial agreement Millie had drawn up, for the moment at least. I don't think he's best pleased about Rob, though.'

'But every time I open *Heat*, Louis is on the pages with a different model or reality star on his arm!'

'I know, but he's basically a child himself so can't deal with Millie actually being happy.' She checked her phone and saw it was full of notifications and texts. She smiled and decided to read them all later when she had a moment to herself. 'Anyway, enough about him. What are you going to tell me about my party this evening?'

'Nothing!' Cosette, Oli and Sophie all yelled together.

'Not even a tiny, weeny detail?'

'No,' replied her sister. 'Okay,' she relented when she saw her sister's wheedling face. 'I will tell you that Suze is coming over at midday and taking you for a manicure and then you need to be in your glad rags and ready to go at six thirty. Think you can manage that in your old age?'

'Just about!' Bell grinned.

'Remind me again why I thought it was a good idea to let you all organise my party for me?' Bell asked as Suze attempted to blindfold her without messing her hair up.

'Because you trust us with your life and knew we'd do a better job than you anyway?' she replied. 'Ah, let's not bother with the blindfold, but you have to promise to shut your eyes whenever I tell you, okay?'

'Okay, fine. Although not when I'm walking down stairs, Suze. I don't want my Insta post about my amazing fortieth birthday party to be me on crutches in A and E.'

'I know you like social media to be true to life, Bellster, but there definitely is a limit, you know. Let's take a selfie now before either of us fall down the stairs and I'll make sure I filter the hell out of it!'

Once they were in the taxi and Bell was checking through more birthday messages, as well as her notifications, thanks to Suze posting their selfie on all her social media channels and tagging her, Bell casually said, 'Colin Facebooked me earlier to say happy birthday.'

'Good for him. I hope you told him how much you were enjoying your birthday in the house that now belongs *solely* to you!'

'Ha! No, I didn't. In fact, I told him how pleased I was that he and Tina looked so happy together.'

'Bell! I thought you were all about telling the truth on social media.'

'I am. And I am actually pleased he's happy. Otherwise the past year would all have been for nothing.'

'Er, whether he's happy or not has got nothing to do with it. It's about whether *you're* happy. And you are, aren't you?'

'Oh god, yes, I'm absolutely totally ecstatic about turning forty!' Bell laughed.

'Well, it means you get to have a fuck-off party organised by your kick-ass friends, so I'm glad you're ecstatic about it!'

'I actually really am, you know that, Suze. But it's hard not to think about that alternative reality where I'm still with Colin and we're plodding along nicely as I turn forty, with none of the heartbreak, stress and upheaval of the past year.'

'And also none of the joy, love and fun of the past year! If you think back to what you've achieved with the photography class, work and of course the community centre, then it's hardly been a wasted few months, has it? And what about all your new friends? Once you decided I wasn't enough for you, you were off making new mates left, right and centre. And not just female mates . . .' she grinned.

'Colin told me today he and Tina are getting married,'

Bell blurted out. It wasn't quite the way she'd planned on telling Suze, but she was glad she'd managed to say the words out loud and it hadn't felt too awful.

'Oh. And what did you say?' Suze asked curiously.

'I said I truly hoped they'd have a long and happy future together.'

'And do you?'

'Well, I'd be lying if I said I cared *that* much about his happiness, but turning forty has made me more mellow, so I guess I want everyone to be happy.'

'And it's easier to say that when you have lovely Ben and a whole gaggle of your best friends and family waiting to scoff cake and drink champagne in your honour.' Suze smiled. 'Come on, we're here. Don't forget to close your eyes when I tell you.'

They walked slowly through the gates of the community centre and Suze led her through the corridors until they reached the largest room.

'Ready?' she whispered.

'Ready,' Bell replied, a giggle of nerves rising in her throat.

'Then you can open your eyes.'

'*Happy birthday, Bell!*' yelled a hundred voices together as she opened her eyes and looked about her. The room had been strewn with more balloons and fortieth-birthday decorations than a branch of Birthdays R Us, and there were banners hanging from the walls, as well as three huge glitter balls suspended above their heads.

'Now!' someone whispered and the air was suddenly full

of shouts and the sound of party poppers exploding their glitter and paper trails across people's heads and arms.

'Come on, Bell, say hello to your adoring public!' Suze said, pushing her forward.

Bell was completely overwhelmed as everyone in her life she truly cared about was standing – or in many cases, dancing – in one room, in the community centre they'd all helped save.

'Millie, this is just amazing,' she shrieked as her friend bounced over to give her the hardest hug she'd ever had.

'Team effort,' Millie grinned. 'Though Wolf is chomping at the bit to show you the banner he, Sophie and Oli made this afternoon. But first, glass of champagne, madam?'

'Don't mind if I do!' she laughed. 'Now are you going to introduce me to this mysterious man you've been hiding away these past few weeks?' She eyed her friend meaningfully.

'I can hardly refuse when the birthday girl looks at me like that!' laughed Millie. She led Bell over to where assorted children were making each other's hair stand on end with balloons, but before they could reach the tall, friendly looking man playing a game of tickle with a bunch of overexcited children, Wolf spotted Bell and flew towards them.

'Bell Bell! Happy birthday, I hope you don't feel too old. Though Daddy always says you're only as old as you feel and he feels like he's eighteen so that's how old he's decided he is. So hopefully you don't feel like you're forty otherwise that would be ancient!' He beamed at her.

'Thank you, Wolfie,' Bell laughed. 'I think I quite like

being forty if today is anything to go by, anyway, but you never know when I might change my mind. I'm just going to say hello to Alfie's daddy, but you must tell me all about your new football team later on.'

She walked over to Millie, who was now standing next to Rob, and smiled. 'Rob, I'm Bell, thank you so much for coming this evening.'

'Well thank you for inviting Alfie and me,' he replied. 'Have you had a lovely birthday?'

'I've had a day of champagne and cake, with hopefully more of both to come, so yes, I think it's been my favourite kind of day. I'd be quite up for turning forty every day if it was going to be like this. Alfie looks like he's having fun, too.'

The three of them glanced over to the little boy, who was giggling giddily as Laura's daughter Daisy twirled him around.

'Let's hope I don't regret letting him have that glass of cola a few minutes ago!' Rob laughed.

'Oh well, if the worst happens, I'm sure he won't be the only person to end up vomiting down his front tonight if the booze carries on flowing like this!' Bell grinned. She looked up and her grin grew even bigger when she saw Ben walking towards them, a bottle of champagne in his hand.

'I noticed your glasses were empty,' he said as he joined them and topped up their fizz.

'Not anymore!' Millie giggled. 'Oh god, Rob, I think we'd better rescue Wolf and Alfie before Daisy mothers them to death. See you both in a bit,' she winked, leaving Bell and Ben alone.

'Many happy returns, Ms Makepeace,' Ben smiled, clinking his glass against Bell's, before removing it from her grasp and placing it on the table next to them. He leaned towards her and softly kissed her on the mouth. 'Welcome to the forty club.'

'Well, if this is what it's like to join the club, I'm in!' Bell murmured, returning his kiss, gently at first, then gradually with more urgency, until a little voice next to them piped up, 'Bell, are you k-i-s-s-i-n-g Graham's owner?'

The pair sprang apart then burst out laughing as Millie came running over to scold her son.

'Wolf! I told you to leave Bell alone. And don't be rude, use Ben's proper name please. It will be time for you to go home soon if you don't stop misbehaving.'

'Don't worry,' Bell said, still laughing. 'It's probably time we mingled anyhow, it's getting a bit hot in this corner, isn't it, Ben?' She shot him a cheeky grin.

'Yes, I'd best not keep the birthday girl to myself all night,' he replied, raising an eyebrow, just as Oli ran over and said breathlessly, 'Bell, Mum's been trying to get your attention for ages. She says she needs you over there.'

Bell turned to see Cosette waving madly at her and suddenly there was the sound of adults shushing excitable children. Her niece and nephew pulled her to the back of the room where everyone had started to gather, and she was pushed in between Millie, Suze and Cosette, with Laura and Ellie just behind them.

'Ladies and gentlemen,' began Suze, stepping forward. 'First of all, thank you all for coming to this momentous occasion. We invited you because we know how much you care about our friend Bell here and that she would want you to be here to celebrate her reaching the grand old age of forty.' Bell smiled and everyone cheered, before Suze continued, 'Before we all carry on drinking ourselves silly, we wanted to give you your present, Bell. Of course, everyone's brought you a gift – you can't have missed the huge pile of presents over there, after all – but this is a different kind of present, one that hopefully you can keep for the next forty years, if technology allows. Sheila, roll the tape!'

The lights were dimmed and the wall to Bell's right, which had been strangely bare of banners and decorations, suddenly came alive as a large image of Bell when she was a baby was projected on to it. Everyone 'awwed' and the Killers' song 'Human' began playing and the video began. There were messages from everyone in the room that evening, from Lisa, Ian, Matt and the rest of the uniform brigade in the skate park near their college, and Rita and Tony with their son and grandkids, to Di and Sarah, filmed at home cross-stitching. There was even an awkward birthday message from the councillors Peter and Michael, which made everyone laugh, and the WI ladies sang a very tuneful version of 'Happy Birthday', complete with harmonies.

Next up were Laura, Ben and Graham the dog, who was sporting a very dapper neckerchief. Bell caught Ben's eye across the room, and he held her gaze and smiled. Her stomach fluttered appreciatively, before her attention was brought back to the screen, which now featured Cosette, Rich and the kids. At the end of their message, during which Oli and Sophie had referred to her as Aunty Belly, to everyone's hilarity, Cosette said, 'And there's a couple of other people who'd like to send their birthday wishes.'

Then on the screen, sitting on the veranda of their American home, were a very tanned and happy-looking Janet and John.

'Happy birthday, Arabella!' they chorused, before her mum continued, 'I'm so sorry we couldn't be there with you this evening, but your dad and I wanted to tell you how proud we are of how well you've coped this year after you know . . . well, we won't dwell on that. But both you and Cosette have grown up to be the kind of strong, successful women we dreamed of raising, so thank you and congratulations. Finally, as we couldn't be there with you, we wanted to contribute to your party somehow, so we've told Cosette we'll pay for the champagne this evening. Enjoy.'

As her parents disappeared off the screen to be replaced by Suze and Els, Bell glanced at her sister through her welling eyes and saw she too had tears running down her cheeks. 'I hope you got the most expensive champagne you could find!' she whispered. Cosette wiped her eyes, nodded and took another large swig from her glass.

By the time Bell had watched Suze conduct the entire Style It Out office – including Marian – in another rousing rendition of 'Happy Birthday', her tears had turned to laughter. Finally, it was Millie and Wolf's turn and she found she was once again trying to hold back her emotions.

'Bell, it's no exaggeration to say that meeting you this year has changed my life,' Millie began. 'I wasn't in a great place when I first bumped into you in the pouring rain outside this very community centre, but in the space of six months I've gone from harassed mother with no one to turn to, to . . . well, I'm still a harassed mother, but I very definitely have someone to turn to, thanks to you and the local community you led into action. Becoming friends with you has taught me that together we can do anything and no one should have to try to swim through life on their own, especially in a freezing-cold outdoor pool! And that maybe social media doesn't have to be a constant competition. Though you still haven't convinced me that all filters are evil. Your support and kindness has helped me and Wolf through some tough times, and if I'm half the woman you are when I get to forty, then I'll be happy. Now, I think Wolf wanted to say something, didn't you, darling?'

'Yes, I do want to say something, Mummy, but you said I had to be quiet before. Anyway, Bell Bell, do you remember when I told you that I thought I liked you just as much as I like cake? Well now I've knowed you a bit more, I think I might like you even more than cake! Though that doesn't mean I can't have any of your birthday cake, does it? Because if so . . .'

'No, Wolfie, I don't think it means that,' Millie whispered. 'Ready? One, two, three, *Happy birthday, Bell*!'

The lights came back up and all the adults in the room surreptitiously wiped their eyes with the backs of their hands as they cheered. Millie swallowed hard and cleared her throat.

'We wanted to raise two toasts,' she said to the room, her voice a little wobbly. 'The first is, of course, "Happy fortieth birthday, Bell!"' Everyone cheered thunderously and repeated the toast, before whooping madly until Suze shushed them so Millie could continue. 'And the second toast is very simple. It's to friendship.'

Everyone raised their glasses and shouted as loudly as they could, 'TO FRIENDSHIP!'

Acknowledgements

It may have my name on the front (a fact I still can't quite believe, tbh!), but this book, perhaps more than any other, is a proper team effort. Without the creativity and enthusiasm of Sara-Jade Virtue, Jo Dickinson and Emma Capron, Bell and Millie would never have got to live their best lives – and neither would I. The belief and trust they showed in me is humbling. Emma's insightful and encouraging editing has made this book easily a million times better, and special thanks go to Bec Farrell for all her brilliant comments – as well as her superior Lion King knowledge. Thank you to my publicist extraordinaire Becky McCarthy and my magic marketeer Amy Fulwood for all their super hard work in getting people talking about this book. You are both amazing – as are the whole team at Simon & Schuster.

To everyone at *Fabulous* magazine, past and present, for their eternal belief that one day I would definitely get that book I'd been blathering on about for five years into a bookshop. (And, no, it isn't erotic fiction, I promise!) The biggest high-fives go to Team Subs (especially my work wife Kirsty) who have lived and breathed every moment of my book journey with me and haven't once told me to shut up.

Thank you to my talented Super Cool Writing Club pals Stacey Halls, Catriona Innes, Cyan Turan and Sophie Hines – having you all holding my hands and cheering for me has helped me more than you can know.

To every journalist and reviewer who has taken the time to write something nice about this book, thank you from the bottom of my heart. I know all too well how many books you get sent each week and the fact you picked up mine and took the time to write about it is humbling. Thank you to all the bloggers who have championed this book and pushed it into the eager hands of readers thanks to their reviews, posts and tweets. Your enthusiasm and energy never cease to amaze me.

As a journalist and reviewer myself, I've been lucky enough to meet countless amazing authors and bookish people, and it didn't take me long to realise that the book world is one of the nicest, most supportive communities there is. So an absolutely massive thank you to the many, many lovely authors, publicists and editors who have gone out of their way to help me on this journey – and continue to encourage, advise and celebrate new and aspiring writers.

Thank you to my mum for being such a proud mummy (if you know Ellie Frost, you'll know she only gives praise where she really thinks it's due, so I've hopefully done something right with this book!). And to Vicky and Katie for being the best sisters in the world – it is a joy being Frosty Intermediate.

Writing a book takes a good deal of sacrifice, and not just from its author. Thank you Steve for only minding a tiny bit when I have to spend whole days staring at my laptop instead of having adventures with you. And for being the Steve to my Claire for the past twenty years (as well as cooking me tea every night after work!).

She's had one shout-out already, but a final thank you to my fairy bookmother, SJV. You are not only a total hoot, you are also my biggest cheerleader and supporter. I owe you a huge G&T.

Why I'm FINALLY Living My Best Life!

by Claire Frost

Y-E-S: three little letters, one short syllable, but a truly massive word. When it comes to writing a book, getting an agent and finding a publisher, 'yes' isn't a word that's heard very often. For every 'Yes, and have this large amount of money as an advance before seeing your book in the hands of the great and the good,' that's uttered in the course of a year in publishing, there are thousands of 'No, it's not quite right for us,' emails sent to hopeful writers continually refreshing their inboxes.

Too often in life we are told that the answer is no: 'Can I have a pay rise?', 'Will the trains ever run on time?' and 'For the love of god can you put your dirty clothes in the washing basket and not on the floor?'. No, no, and seemingly no.

So when you hear 'yes', that short but powerful word, it can be life-changing – especially when it's followed by the words '. . . we'll publish your book!'

Back in 2014, I took two months of unpaid leave from my job as a journalist and wrote a novel. I make it sound easy and nonchalant, but although I loved writing the story I'd created in my head, I found it ridiculously hard to tear myself away from *Homes Under the Hammer* every morning and sit at my dining room table until I'd typed the 2,000 words I knew I had to write each day if I was to finish it before I went back to work. And I missed my job, or at least I missed having people to talk to. So when I arrived back in the office with 90,000 words under my belt I was eager to chat to my colleagues about what I'd been up to. But after two weeks of, 'So when can I buy it in a bookshop, then?' and me having to explain that, no, I hadn't got an agent yet, and no, I hadn't got a book deal but maybe one day, I quickly shut up.

Over the next year or so, I beavered away at weekends, polished up my manuscript until I felt it was good enough to send to some willing family, friends and a few lovely bookish people I had met through my job, as well as a couple of agents. While I got some invaluable feedback from some super-kind and knowledgeable people, I was also met with the inevitable 'thanks, but no thanks' from the agents I'd approached. I'd very much been expecting this, but rejection is still rejection, and it was impossible not to feel disheartened.

Then my friend Sara-Jade Virtue (henceforth known as my fairy bookmother!), who works for Simon & Schuster, said she'd read the first few chapters that I'd sent her and would I mind if she passed them on to her colleague Emma who was an editor? I replied with a big, fat YES, as you can well imagine!

Months passed, until an email from Emma Capron pinged into my inbox in March 2017. When I finally worked up the courage to open the message, I scanned the type until my eyes rested on the phrase 'this isn't the book' and that familiar feeling of dejection kicked in. Crestfallen, I read the email again – and this time I started to notice phrases such as 'the characters have really stayed with me', 'you've got a fantastic voice' and 'I really think you have something, but I just think this isn't the book to launch your career with'.

After having a coffee with Emma and hearing her explain why she felt my book wasn't right for her to publish, but that she thought I should write a whole new novel that she would work closely with me on, I was totally buzzing – and not just from all the caffeine. Maybe I could be an author after all, I thought as I skipped home. But when I woke up the next morning all I could focus on was the fact that the book I'd written wasn't good enough. My confidence and excitement began to dissolve again.

Over the next year, despite repeated chivvying, prodding and support from Emma, SJ and anyone who'd ever been subjected to my regular rant about my dream of becoming an author, I wrote precisely nothing. 'How's the writing going, have you got anything to send over?" they'd ask. 'No, I'm horribly busy at work/had a terrible cold/hurt my finger/lost the will to live,' I'd bleat pathetically.

If you're reading this thinking, 'What an idiot, I can't believe she had all these opportunities and just kept saying no!' then I am with you all the way! However, if I'm honest, I think I was sub-consciously self-sabotaging and protecting myself from more failure – if I didn't even try then I couldn't possibly fail again, right?

Eventually, the team sat me down and said firmly, 'We still really want to work with you, but to have a book published you do actually have to write some words. So let's talk about what this book is actually about and then you can send us a chapter breakdown in seven days' time.'

Now, being a journalist, I LOVE a deadline, and suddenly my adrenaline kicked in. For the first time in months I felt inspired. I felt confident. I felt like I could actually write a book! So I finally sat down with my laptop and created characters I loved, constructed a plot I was excited about and decided on a structure I thought worked. Thankfully, Emma and the team agreed and they said they would present it at the regular acquisitions meetings attended by all the top bods at Simon & Schuster. And then I heard nothing. The demons began to creep back in and I started to doubt whether my characters were as interesting and believable as I'd thought. Just as I was about to send myself yet another 'test' email to check my inbox was actually working, a notification appeared. I opened the email immediately and scanned the type until my eyes rested on the word 'YES'. I actually had a book deal. That night I drank a vat of wine and stared at that email until my eyes went fuzzy.

However, I'm not sure I still truly believed that Simon & Schuster wanted to publish my book at that point. Or even when I signed the contract that laid it all out in black and white. Or even when I finished writing the manuscript and sent it off to Emma to read. Or even when I first saw a cover with my name on it. Or even writing this now! Being an author has been my dream for so long that I'm not sure it will EVER quite sink in that it's actually happening. But it is – and I really hope you enjoyed meeting Bell and Millie!

I'd love to hear what you think about *Living My Best Li(f)e* and you can contact me @FabFrosty on Twitter and @TheRealFabFrosty on Instagram. And you can read more about my publishing journey at booksandthecity.co.uk/category/features/.

Claire x